Love Beyond Words

by

Emma Scott

Risa,
Lovely to meet you
at #BB19
xoxo
Emma Scott

Cover design by First Edition Design Publishing

Formatting by www.ebooklaunch.com

ACKNOWLEDGEMENTS

A huge thanks to the members of the Clyde critique group for their invaluable input: Susannah Clare Carlson, Andrew MacRae, Scot Friesen, Susan Bickford, Karla Keasey Rogers, Danielle Berggren Wooster, and Vishal Moondrah. Special thanks to Anne Maclachlan for editorial (and moral) support; Elon Kaiserman for police procedural details; and Erin Thomasson Cannon for her invaluable help with navigating the wild world of the romance novel for this newbie, and for the accounting/financial aspects contained herein, though any and all mistakes are mine. Lastly, a very heartfelt thanks to my advance readers for their time and honesty.

This is a work of fiction. Names, characters, events, places and incidents are either the products of the author's imagination or used in a fictitious manner. Any resemblance to actual persons, living or dead, or actual events is purely coincidental.

Suggested listening: "Falling In Love at a Coffee Shop" by Landon Pigg

For my husband, whose help, support, and encouragement made this book possible.

"It's an odd thing, but anyone who disappears is said to be seen in San Francisco."

Oscar Wilde

CHAPTER ONE

"What's your name?" the girl asked.
Javier tossed a pebble into the stream. "Why do you want to
know?"
"Estúpido," she chided. "That's how things start."

—*Above*, by Rafael Melendez Mendón

The café was empty. Silent. Natalie Hewitt sat on her perch behind the register, a book in her hand. She guessed it had been more than an hour since she'd served anyone. The coppery light of dusk streamed in from the front windows to spill over the hardwood floors as it had all afternoon; an uncharacteristically warm day for San Francisco, even in July. Her neighborhood customers were probably at Golden Gate Park, taking advantage. Even the street was empty but for the occasional Muni train screeching past.

Inside Niko's Café the silence was persistent; a silence made for reading if ever one was. Natalie had already arranged the muffins and croissants, swept the floors, and wiped down the wooden tables so that she could read her book, guilt-free.

She wished she'd brought something more enthralling than the dime-a-dozen thriller. It was the sort of book she bided her time with until an author she adored came out with something new. Rafael Melendez Mendón's latest was due in less than three weeks. Just in time, she thought, for her twenty-third birthday.

The thought made her giddy.

She could almost feel the weight of a new Mendón book in her hand; hear the pages turn—rapidly, as she devoured them like a starving woman. And the words… She shivered at the possibilities, wondering what new world, new refuge Mendón would open for her this time. What collection of perfectly chosen words would he drape across the page for her to cry over, and become lost in? She sighed. Three weeks seemed an eternity.

The bell above the door jingled, shattering the quiet, pulling her out of her book. A young man walked in.

She noticed his eyes first. Virtually impossible not to. They were a vibrant crystal blue; the blue of topaz gemstones, or the waters off a Caribbean island. She watched him approach, her breath catching in her throat though she couldn't fathom why. A voice screamed from the back of her mind, *Why? Look at him!*

Natalie did. It was very easy to look at him. Loose curls of black hair fell across his forehead, and came just below his ears. His dusky skin was smattered with the more-than-a-goatee-not-quite-a-beard facial hair that was the popular men's style. He wore a pair of jeans and a cream-colored t-shirt, both elegant despite their simple cut, both obviously tailored; they fit his tall frame to a T. He looked perfectly put together, but for a curl of hair that stuck to his forehead in the heat. In Natalie's mind, that imperfection made his beauty less intimidating. As did his smile that was nothing short of brilliant.

"Hello. A large coffee, please. Iced," he said in a smooth and low voice, tinged with an accent she couldn't place.

She managed a flicker of a smile. Those eyes…ridiculously, brilliantly blue, like… "Windex," she murmured.

"Pardon?"

Natalie blushed to the roots of her hair. "Nothing," she mumbled and hurried to fix his coffee.

While she scooped ice into a glass, the young man glanced about the little café with an interest that, after three years, Natalie had long since lost. Dusk's honeyed light slanted over the simple wooden furniture. Adjacent to the front door, there was an oriel window with a table and two chairs tucked against it, offering close up views of the empty sidewalk on the other side. Natalie thought the young man's gaze lingered there, then he turned back to her, smiling shyly.

Your imagination, she told herself. *There is no way a man that good-looking could be shy. Impossible.*

She set the tall glass of iced coffee on the counter. "Dollar fifty-five, please."

"Oh, I'm terribly sorry, but I need this to-go," the man said. "My apologies. I should have told you."

"No, no, my fault. I should have asked." Natalie rummaged for a clear plastic take-out cup and poured his drink into it.

"I didn't realize anyone served coffee in real mugs or glasses anymore."

"Most places don't. Niko, my boss, thinks it's rude to give to-go cups unless the customer is actually *going.*" Natalie peeked up at him. "He wants people to feel welcome and…um, encourages them to stay."

"I like that." The young man smiled again, wider this time. It lit up his face in a way that made Natalie's heart stutter. He laid two dollars on the counter. "Thank you."

"No problem."

She rang up his change and put it into his hand. Her curled fingers touched his for the briefest of moments as they often did with customers. Unlike with any other customer, Natalie's fingertips tingled from the warmth of his skin long after he'd withdrawn to drop the coins into her tip jar. *You're being ridiculous,* she chided herself. *So he's a handsome man. Get over it.* But 'handsome' didn't begin to cover it, nor explain the strange yearning she felt. A vague desire to…what? Talk to him? *Touch* him? But he was leaving.

"All right." He raised his coffee. "Thanks again."

"Any time," Natalie said. *Stay…*

He turned to go and then stopped. "You know…"

"Yes?" Natalie cringed at how high and tight her voiced sounded.

"Perhaps I'll take something to eat as well. Do you have any recommendations?"

Natalie ducked behind the display case. "The banana muffins are good. Or we have some pumpkin bread left. What…um, what are you in the mood for?" Their eyes met through the glass and Natalie sought refuge in the croissants. "These are nice. Fresh today."

"Yes, that's fine. Thank you."

"Sure thing," Natalie said. It was the third time he'd thanked her. She bagged the pastry and then moved to ring it up.

"I'm Julian, by the way."

She blinked. "I…okay."

"Julian Kovač." He cleared his throat uncertainly.

"Oh. Right, yes." *He's being polite.* She mentally kicked herself. "Natalie Hewitt."

"It's nice to meet you, Natalie."

"You too," she murmured, and her words were drowned by the dinging cash register.

"I'm sorry?"

"I said, you too. It's uh, nice to meet you too." Natalie bit her lip. Customers didn't typically introduce themselves to her; she fought for something to say. "Is it Russian?" she blurted.

"Russian? Oh, you mean…?"

"Your name. I mean, it sounds Russian."

"Croatian, actually."

He didn't look Eastern European and his accent sounded Spanish or maybe Italian. Natalie managed to keep these observations to herself, but struggled to come up with something better to say instead.

"It's all right. I get that all the time. A common mistake," Julian said.

Natalie waved her hands. "No, no, I wouldn't know. I mean…it's a nice name." If the ground opened up and swallowed her she'd consider it a mercy killing.

Julian smiled again. He wasn't just handsome or good-looking, he was beautiful. With reluctance, Natalie handed him the pastry bag.

"Right, well…thank you." He grinned sheepishly. "*Again.*"

"You're welcome."

His gaze found hers, and his smile softened, looked almost wistful. "Okay. Good bye, Natalie."

"Good bye, Julian." She loved the sound of his name on her lips. A smart, sexy name that suited him perfectly.

"Have a nice evening," he said.

"You too."

Natalie battled her shyness, fought for something to say, or the courage to simply call him back and see what happened next. She leaned forward, opened her mouth, and…he was gone. The bell above the door tolled his departure. Natalie watched him cross the street; her gaze stuck on him. A bus trundled past, obscuring him completely, and when it was gone, so was he. Vanished, like a ghost or a mirage.

"He may as well have been," Natalie said, her words swallowed by the café's emptiness, silence descending once again.

The hours dragged after that. Her book couldn't compete with the memory of Julian Kovač's gentle voice, or impossible blue eyes, or that last, wistful smile he'd given her.

At eleven o'clock she shut off the lights and locked the café doors. A night-owl bus rumbled down the empty street, burping and hissing its way toward her. She watched it go past, saw the tired-looking faces of its few riders. She wasn't tired at all. In fact, she felt strangely awake. Her nerves hummed like the electrical lines that harnessed the buses from above and kept them tethered to their routes. She rubbed her fingers on her dress—she imagined she could still feel where they'd touched Julian's hand—and berated herself for feeling so distracted over some strange man she was never going to see again.

From Niko's threshold, it was a two-step walk to her own front door, as she lived directly above the café. She unlocked the white metal gate in front of the stairwell that led to her place and started up the dark, airless passage; her footsteps clapped hollowly on the old stairs.

She opened her front door and flipped on the entry light. Her bedroom—an area only big enough for a bed, a closet, and a nightstand—faced the front door and remained dark, closed off by a curtain. To the right of the entry, the rest of her apartment—a rectangle of living area, kitchen, and a bathroom at the far end—was illuminated faintly by streetlights. She'd decorated sparingly to keep it from being swallowed by furniture, but it was in danger of being overtaken by books instead. The entire wall facing the couch was dominated by bookshelves, and a homeless pile of hardcovers sat stacked at the threshold of the kitchen. Stalagmites of paperbacks ringed her desk by the window, but she couldn't bear the thought of getting rid of any of them, not even those she'd read multiple times. *Especially* not those.

Natalie slipped between her couch and coffee table, past her one ratty chair, and stood at the curved window overlooking the street. She started to close the heavy, thick curtains she had installed upon moving here three years ago but paused, hands clutching the scratchy material as she replayed her conversation with Julian Kovač.

In her mind, she edited it like a script; every awkward moment smoothed out, every cringe-worthy snippet of dialogue reworked. She exuded charm and confidence, her dialogue witty, her demeanor self-possessed. The conversation ended, not with him walking out the door, but with an exchange of phone numbers, and then a date in which a maroon dress swirled around her knees as she and Julian danced swing—her favorite—in the dark of a small club.

She was smiling coyly at him over her cocktail when the phone rang, jarring her from her reverie. The machine picked it up and regaled Natalie with a lecture from Liberty Chastain.

"Nat. It's Lib. You know how I feel about your ancient answering machine. I can just hear my voice bouncing around your place and I hate not being able to see my audience. Anyway, it's possible you got hung up at work, but it's *more* likely that you've got your nose buried in a book and can't be bothered to speak to another living human being. So be it. It's a Tuesday, you're allowed.

"But tomorrow I have a show at the Kyrie and you must come because you haven't been to one of my shows in, like, *an eternity.* And it's possible I miss you, dummy, okay? I know Wednesday's your night off so don't give me any 'I have to work' bullshit. Get dolled up and be there by nine o'clock. Marshall's coming because he understands the true meaning of friendship, and if you don't come I'll have to assume you've forsaken me and I'll cry forever. Okay? *See you there.* Kiss, kiss."

Natalie closed the curtains and sank onto her worn couch. The next day was to be spent finishing up her summer coursework at the university. She'd looked forward to curling up with "yet another book" as reward for completing the summer semester. Only one year to go and she'd have her Accounting degree, a feat that—given the circumstances—she'd never dreamed of accomplishing.

Natalie turned on the lamp next to the couch and opened her old flip phone to call Liberty. She eased a sigh of relief that it went to voicemail.

"Lib? It's Nat. I'll be there. Wouldn't miss it."

She hung up, relieved to have avoided a conversation. Her pride still smarted from her bungling attempts at one with Julian Kovač. Moreover, sometimes she just didn't feel like talking, something an extroverted performer like Liberty never understood. A voice spoke up in Natalie's mind, sounding much like her gregarious friend: *Maybe if you weren't so out of practice you'd have made a better impression on Julian.*

Natalie brushed the thought away and eyed her coffee table where *The Common Thief* by Rafael Melendez Mendón sat, beckoning. She'd read it four times already but had decided to prepare for Mendón's newest by giving his latest another go. She longed to pick it up and become lost in its pages, especially now that she wouldn't be able to do so the next day as planned.

She quelled the resentment; if she missed any more of Liberty's cabaret shows, her phone would stop ringing. *You have to go. Liberty and Marshall are all you have.*

Against her will, her eyes strayed to a photograph on the bookshelf in front of her. A man, woman, and their thirteen-year-old daughter stood in front of a backdrop of jagged mountains, and what looked like a telephone pole but was actually a ski lift. All three wore barely-there smiles.

It had been a rough day, she remembered, full of first-time-skiing frustrations. But Natalie liked this photo better than any of the cheery ones that filled her albums. It was easy to remember her parents as loving and kind. Not so easy—and getting harder every day—was remembering the small details of their brief lives together. The strained moment captured in the ski photo was priceless; her parents were real and human and not perpetually smiling ghosts. And while she appeared as a typical, surly teenager in that photo, she hadn't been. She'd been happy, and every day since she could speak, she'd told her parents she loved them.

She'd told them that day on the ski trip, and she'd told them that morning four years ago when a drunk driver plowed his car into the farmer's market, knocking into people like pins in a bowling alley. Curtis and Tammy Hewitt were killed instantly. A perfect strike. Natalie had stepped away from them to get some green beans from their favorite vendor. She heard a scream, a screech of tires…Her memory of that day had shattered into a million pieces, becoming whole only in her nightmares.

The memory came to her now, broken but trying to put itself together. Panicked, Natalie turned her phone off and picked up *The Common Thief.* She held it for a moment, like a drowning woman might a life preserver, then dove in.

It took a full chapter for the beauty of Mendón's story to work its magic, like a balm, over her pain. The clock read two a.m. by the time she forced herself to close the book. She slipped into her bed, apprehensive for her dreams, but Mendón's writing continued its work: her sleep was dreamless.

CHAPTER TWO

At ten the next morning, Natalie rose sluggishly and with a twinge of guilt for having indulged so late in the Mendón book. But even with eyes burning and her jaw cracking with yawns, she wished she could burrow into her bed and lose herself for a few more hours. She fought off temptation and made coffee instead. She could have all she wanted at Niko's but she wanted to get in and get out before her Greek employers could smother her with their well-intentioned affection.

As the coffeepot burbled, she showered, dried, and then stepped into one of the many vintage dresses from the 1940's and '50's that filled her small closet, each painstakingly unearthed from one second-hand shop or another. She buttoned up the simple blue cotton dress, pinned her hair back from her face, and packed her bag full of accounting textbooks. Three hurried sips of coffee and she was headed for the door. *The Common Thief* sat on her coffee table.

Farewell, my love, Natalie thought. *You were great last night.* An abashed laugh escaped her but faded quickly. She went out, closing the door softly behind her.

***

Niko's Café was a different place in the morning: bustling, loud, full of conversations, burbling milk steamers, laughter, and the constant *ding* of the cash register. Louder than anyone was Niko Barbos. His booming voice filled the café as he talked and laughed with customers and two of the baristas who worked the day shifts. His apron hung from bony shoulders, and his salt and pepper hair looked as if it were trying to fly off his head. He appeared, Natalie thought fondly, more like a mad scientist than a café owner.

"Natalia!" He approached her with open arms and engulfed her in a hug before she could make it halfway across the café. "My little night owl. You've come for your schedule, yes?"

"Yes."

"Petra!" Niko called, as they approached the counter. "Natalia wants her schedule."

The baristas, Sylvie and Margo, waved hello. Sylvie—a light-haired young woman with a warm smile—thanked Natalie profusely for cleaning the grate under the icemaker. "That was on my list of cleanup duties and you know it," she scolded cheerfully.

Natalie tucked a lock of hair behind her ear. "Um, yes, well…I had the time. You guys are so much busier."

"Busier? Yes, let's talk busy." Petra Barbos's voice boomed from within an expansive bosom as she emerged from the back room. The loose folds of skin under her arms jiggled as she flapped a piece of paper at Natalie. "Here's your schedule, glýka. No changes, but you tell me if it's too much for you to do alone. Too busy," she raised an eyebrow, "or too dangerous. No one bothers you, yes?"

"Yes. I mean, no. No one bothers me," Natalie replied. "And no, it's not quite busy enough that I need help." She smiled briefly at Sylvie and Margo. More than once, they'd asked her to join them for a movie or drinks, but Natalie had always declined. In another lifetime, they might've been friends—good friends even—but Natalie kept her distance. She worried that Niko would catch wind of any friendliness and conspire to pair her up with another barista on her shifts, and that was too horrible to contemplate.

Natalie smiled wider. "I don't need any help. It's definitely quieter than mornings, but business is steady."

"I can see that." Niko beamed. "Your registers are perfect, as always! Speaking of such numerical things, how are your classes? Studying hard? Of course you are, my good girl." He patted her cheek. "Next week is month's end. You help me with the books again, yes?"

Natalie glanced with longing at the schedule still clutched in Petra's hand. "Yes. Of course."

"Brilliant! Now, you eat. Come."

"Oh stop, Niko, look at the girl. She's itching to go." Petra handed over the schedule. "Study time?"

"Yes, I'm off to school. Last day of summer courses." Natalie skimmed the schedule, satisfied. It was the same as ever. Five 4pm-to-closing shifts, Wednesdays and Sundays off. She tucked the paper into her bag. "Great, thanks. Um…Bye."

She slipped out of the café, thankfully spared another of Niko's fatherly embraces. But she could feel their affection—his and Petra's—on her back as she left, like a warm wind. She hurried out into the unusual summer heat that was infinitely more bearable.

***

Natalie spent a few hours in the San Francisco State University library, working on tax preparations for imaginary clients. The library was quiet during the summer months; she saw no one from her classes, and no one spoke to her. She worked steadily, satisfied when her numbers added up in orderly rows. On her old laptop, she "filed" the tax documents with the school's simulation program, and rested her chin in her palm, grinning as they were "accepted" with no errors.

Another A grade, another step closer to graduation. Natalie thought her mom and dad would be proud.

***

Club Kyrie was a tiny space under a sprawling bar called De Luxe. It had once been a prohibition-era speakeasy, a reputation its owners took great pride and care to sustain. Natalie, armed with a password from Liberty, approached a sly-looking bouncer in the alley beside De Luxe.

She showed her I.D. and murmured, "Velvetine."

"Much obliged, baby cakes."

He held the door for her that opened on a staircase leading down. Natalie descended carefully in her modest heels into a small, single room painted a conch shell pink and lit by fanciful sconces on the walls. Twenty small tables draped in lacy cloths, each with a little candle cup burning in the center, faced a minuscule stage while two waitresses circulated offering drinks. The atmosphere was secretive and knowing, each patron exuding a sense of privilege for being aware of Kyrie's existence, or for participating in something illicit. As far as Natalie could see, there was nothing illicit about Kyrie except that it allowed smoking long after the state had banned it in public places. She found Marshall Grant front and center—broad-shouldered, ginger-haired, elegantly handsome in his expensive suit—and hurried to join him.

"She lives!" Marshall exclaimed. "And here I thought you'd stand me up."

"Never." Natalie kissed his cheek and eyed her friend up and down. "What's with the suit? Did you just come from work?"

"Oh, honey, did I." Marshall waved his hand. "The bastards have no sense of decency. They kept us late sorting out some tragedy in the Castleman accounts. A kerfuffle that could have been averted had they done like I said and audited the shit out of Lord and Lady Castleman two years ago. You would have loved it. But Liberty would have my balls if I were late, so here I am, in this frog suit." He sipped his drink, his usual gin and tonic, and gave her the once over. "But look at you, Ms. the Riveter! Are we in a time warp, or what? You're 1945 all over! I feel like I'm in danger of being drafted. But seriously, love the hair."

Natalie beamed. She had dug her dress out of a crowded rack at a vintage shop just last week, and it was a trifecta of a great find: it fit her petite size, cost forty dollars, and no one else had found it first. It was classic 1940's style, pale yellow with a purple flower pattern overlay, flowing skirt, buttons from hem to collar. She'd rolled her hair back from her face and pinned it, letting it fall in rich brown coils around her shoulders. Some black eyeliner and red lipstick, and the reflection in her bathroom mirror had smiled at what it saw. Gone was the simple, unadorned accounting student, and in her place was someone from another time. A time where men were gentlemen, and where a woman's silence meant mystery or allure. Natalie looked glamorous and so she let herself feel glamorous. When the waitress breezed past, she ordered a Harvey Wallbanger with a twist.

Marshall cooed. "You're positively radiant, tonight! What gives?"

"Oh, nothing." Natalie's thoughts went to Julian Kovač. "Nothing," she said again, her smile slipping, for nothing *did* happen with Julian the day before, and since she'd let him walk out the door with her customary reticence, nothing ever would.

"Well, if you're this happy now, you're going to burst when I give you your early birthday present." Marshall patted a nondescript bag at his feet.

"What is it?"

"Tut tut, the show is starting." The lights dimmed and the muted conversations around them quieted. "Suffice to say, if I were straight, I'd be getting lucky tonight."

Natalie smirked. "You wish."

Marshall had been two years ahead of her in the accounting department when they'd met. Their paths crossed regularly and they'd shared a class or two before he graduated last year. Natalie assumed they'd go their separate ways, but Marshall had insisted on a friendship. Through him, she'd met Liberty, and it was times like this, sitting in a dim little club, wearing a pretty dress and sipping a cocktail, that Natalie was grateful for her friends. Only through the sheer force of their personalities could she call them such, for had she been left to her own devices they would have abandoned her long ago. They each had loads of friends and it baffled her that they would take a plain, shy girl under their colorful wings.

There were no curtains on the stage, but a small ring of light appeared and then Liberty Chastain stepped into it. She too, was dressed in 1940's era clothing, but it was the uniform of a showgirl in a seedy nightclub: torn fishnets, heels, a flimsy pink camisole over a black leotard. Liberty had spackled her dark hair to her head and blackened one eye for effect. Behind her, three other similarly dressed dancers struck languid, tragic poses. There was no MC, no introduction; the first strains of "Mein Herr" from *Cabaret* filled the tiny room and Liberty began to sing.

Marshall clapped his hands gleefully. "She dedicated this to me! It's mine!"

Natalie smiled thinly. It was no surprise to her that Liberty had tailored her performance to Marshall. No surprise at all.

Liberty filled her performance with more angst and passion than Natalie thought the composers had initially intended. Instead of a sly, cheeky adieu from an inconstant woman to the man who should have known better, her rendition was ironic. Her Sally Bowles was chastising herself for yet another failed affair in which she had been unable to remain faithful. Every line was turned on itself, directed inward, and the result was, to Natalie's imagination, truly spectacular. Too spectacular for the tiny venue and the tiny stage; Liberty should have been famous by now, Natalie asserted. By the time the final chorus came round, Liberty and her back up dancers were stomping their feet and bludgeoning the audience with the lyrics. The small crowd roared its approval.

"*Bravissima!*" Marshall cried between whistles. "I'm telling you, this girl is going to go all the way."

Natalie agreed, dabbing at tears that always surfaced in her eyes when confronted with any ardent emotion.

On the stage, Liberty bowed and thanked the crowd. "You can't get rid of me so easily. Let me wet my whistle and I'll be back."

She and her dancers exited the stage to thunderous applause, then the lights came up, and the crowd got down to business, smoking and drinking. A few minutes later Liberty, wearing a kimono over her Sally Bowles costume and with a cocktail in her hand, appeared. She stopped to chat with other tables full of friends before finally flouncing into the chair next to Marshall.

"Hello, *darlings*!" she laughed, kissing Natalie's cheek. Marshall leaned in for his kiss but Liberty smirked and gave his suit a once-over. "Who died?"

"Disco, and I'm still in mourning."

She patted his cheek and then pinched it.

"What, no kiss?" he wailed.

"You'll get over it. So." Liberty lit a cigarette and blew the smoke up and away from Natalie. "What did you think? I'm so glad you're here!"

"I am too," Natalie said. "I thought it was amazing. You're so gifted, Lib."

Liberty beamed. "Thank you, love." She turned to Marshall. "Well?"

"Pure magic, darling."

"Thank you, my sweet," she replied. "Wait 'til you see my finale."

"Well, don't knock'em dead until I get back from the little boys' room," Marshall said, rising to his feet. "And if you see the waitress, tell her I want another G-and-T, like *yesterday*."

"Yes, dear," Liberty said.

"Sapphire," Marshall said. "None of that well shit."

"Such a diva." Liberty's gaze followed him as he wended his way gracefully between the tables. She exhaled twin plumes of smoke from her nose.

Natalie gave her friend a knowing look. "Liberty…"

"Yes, yes, I'm pathetic, I know."

"But he's so…" Natalie waved her hands, at a loss.

"I know, right? It doesn't make any sense. Every time he opens his mouth and something affected pops out, it's like he's broadcasting how unavailable he is." Liberty dropped her cigarette into Marshall's depleted cocktail glass. It hissed as it struck an ice cube. "But can you blame me? He's tall, gorgeous, smart, funny. He practically lives at the gym and he makes a ton of money." She made a sour face. "I'm not in love with Marshall; I just want a man exactly like him."

Natalie smiled at her friend. "You could probably find someone who fits that criteria if you didn't go out with *Marshall* every night."

Liberty snorted. "This from the woman who hasn't been laid since...I don't even know when. Ever?"

"Yes," Natalie said, her cheeks burning. "Once. I told you about him."

"Oh yeah," Liberty said. "The blond nobody you boned on your trek up here."

What Liberty called her *trek*, Natalie called her *escape*; a migration north from San Diego after her parents' death. The young man she'd met in Santa Barbara smelled of beach sand and suntan lotion, but had been sweet and considerate. Not her romantic ideal, but then who could be? Marshall and Liberty assured her she would meet someone if she just made an effort, but she knew better. She joined them at bars and clubs for the sake of friendship, not to flirt tipsily with strangers, hoping to find a diamond in the rough with a poet's heart. The odds of that happening, she thought, were slim to none. The characters in her books were better company.

Natalie cast her gaze to her drink.

"Oh, honey, I'm teasing you." Liberty drained her own cocktail and contemplated the ice cubes that remained. "You're in love with men who exist only in books, and I'm in love with a man who exists in my mind. We're equally pathetic."

Natalie was inclined to protest but Liberty had practically voiced her own thoughts out loud. And she couldn't chastise Liberty too much over Marshall anyway. Liberty's last boyfriend had been "a little too rough around the edges" and that was all she was willing to say about him—all that she would allow *anyone* to say about him without biting their head off. Marshall was sweet. Kind-hearted. A gentleman.

He's safe, Natalie thought, watching Marshall return. *And that's what Liberty needs right now.* She was careful not to let her concern for her friend show on her face or Liberty would never forgive her.

Another round was ordered, another cigarette lit, and then Marshall turned to Natalie.

"Now, promise you won't freak out. Since I'll be at one of those atrocious conventions in Vegas on your birthday…" He reached under the table and pulled out a rectangular gift impeccably wrapped in red paper and tied with a purple ribbon.

"Oh, Marshall," Natalie breathed. "That's not what I think it is…"

"It's *exactly* what you think it is."

Natalie unwrapped the book. The hardcover was made of rough beige fabric, almost like burlap, with the word *Coronation* etched in black ink. Below that, a crown of straw in the same shaggy black strokes, and then the name Rafael Melendez Mendón.

"What is it?" Liberty peered over and read the cover. "Oh, gawd. Look at you two: a junkie and her dealer."

"Oh my god!" Natalie threw her arms around Marshall's neck, nearly upsetting their table. "How did you get it so early? It's not due for another three weeks!" She sat back, admiring her gift, her fingers itching to open it.

Marshall polished his nails on his lapel. "I have my ways. And a friend who owns a bookstore on Market who gets advance copies. He owed me a favor."

"Oh, Marshall." Natalie laid her hand over her heart. "It's perfect."

Liberty snorted. "You haven't even read it yet. How can it be perfect?"

"Because Rafael Mendón wrote it," Natalie said. "Of course it's going to be perfect."

"Is this the guy who no one knows who he is?" Liberty took the book and flipped to the back page, looking for an author photo. Natalie tensed, watching the proximity of Liberty's cigarette ash to the pristine pages. "He's the recluse that you're so in love with, right?"

"Yes," Natalie said, and snatched the book back. "But I'm not in love with him, for crying out loud. Like you said, no one knows who he is. But I am in love with his writing, I admit. And I'm not alone. His first book, *Above,* was nominated for the Pulitzer and he's won the National Book Award. *Twice.* And every single one of his novels has been an international bestseller."

Marshall dabbed the corner of his eye with his tie and sniffed. "And we're so proud."

Liberty made a face. "If he's won all those awards and whatnot, why is he in hiding? Wouldn't he want to enjoy the fruits of his labor? That doesn't make sense. Is he a weirdo?"

"Nah, he's one of those tortured genius-types like Salinger," Marshall said. "I've read *Above* and I have to admit, it's pretty brilliant."

Natalie beamed.

"Well, I'm glad you're happy, hon," Liberty said to Natalie, giving her hand a squeeze. "But if I see you reading that goddamned book while I'm singing my finale…"

"I would never!"

"Good."

Natalie grinned. "It's too dark in here, anyway."

Marshall and Liberty exchanged shocked glances, and then burst out laughing.

Natalie laughed along with them, but the night began to drag after *Coronation* was hers. Other performers took the stage but she only half-watched. Her eyes kept straying to the book. She ached to go home, curl up on the couch and fall into it, even if it meant another sleepless night. Having Mendón's latest sit a tantalizingly few inches away from her was a pleasant torture.

Finally, Liberty excused herself to get ready for the finale of the evening. The room darkened and a single spotlight made a small moon on the stage. Liberty stepped into the circle of light, and the small club was saturated with her velvety voice.

The desire for her book fell away as Natalie listened to "Maybe This Time." Liberty's Sally Bowles wondered if maybe this time her man would stay, and the song conjured the memory of Julian Kovač walking out of Niko's. Natalie felt each lyric strike her and sink in. She was almost twenty-three years old. Time to stop hiding in the stories of others; to stop taking her joys and triumphs from the characters in Mendón's books and start creating her own. Time to find her own voice before every Julian Kovač who walked into her life walked right back out without her saying a word.

She got home to her tiny apartment that night, determined to get some sleep, to finalize any last course requirements for the summer program the next day, and read *Coronation* when she had the time, like any other person might when they picked up a book. She set it on the coffee table and went to the bathroom to wipe off her makeup.

When she came out, she crossed the kitchen, intending to veer left toward her bedroom alcove. Instead, she found herself sitting on the couch, contemplating her new book. Her hand, of its own accord, flipped it open and trailed over the opening page. She was certain there was no more tantalizing phrase in the English language than Chapter One. *Just the opening sentences*, she thought. No sense in depriving herself.

In Aguilar, the village has one rule: he who withstands the sting of the viper wasp is king. Dead men ringed the nest in final reposes; slaves bowing before their master instead of monarchs bent to receive their crowns. Liliana, her hand swollen and bursting with poison, rose on shaking feet. A weaver. A woman. A queen.

The sunlight was a rosy copper in the east when Natalie turned the final page. She wiped the tears from her eyes, flipped it open to the beginning, and started again.

CHAPTER THREE

The summer slipped away and classes began again in September. Natalie fell into the routine of school and work; reading and pouring coffee, calculating overhead and performing audits for businesses that didn't exist. Business at Niko's picked up in the evening hours. Customers came to warm their faces in fragrant steam and curl their fingers around hot mugs, while the first chill winds of autumn blew leaves in miniature cyclones around the front door of the café.

One night, they blew in Julian Kovač.

It was early evening on a Monday; the café hadn't yet seen its first rush, and Natalie had *almost* forgotten about him, had almost forgotten how stunning he was. This night he wore jeans and a form-fitting black hoodie over a black shirt. The curls of his black hair hung over his forehead and his thin scrap of a beard cut angular lines on his face. His eyes stood out like brilliant blue stars in a night sky, and Natalie stared until he spoke, jarring her from her stupor.

"Hello, Natalie. It's good to see you again."

Natalie's heart fluttered in her chest. His smile warmed her better than the space heater churning under the cash register.

"Likewise." A wave of anxiety grabbed hold of her and squeezed. *Don't screw it up this time.* "How have, uh...how have you been?"

"Quite well, thank you. And you?"

"Fine." Natalie realized this was an exchange one had with an acquaintance, not with a customer. Did he realize that? She couldn't tell; he watched her intently and it seemed as though entire conversations were occurring behind his electric blue eyes. Her own mind had seized up; Natalie could think of nothing to say but for her usual barista spiel: "What can I get for you?"

Julian ordered a regular coffee and a Danish, and the silence continued as Natalie filled his order. She peeked at him from behind the coffee maker and then through the glass of the pastry shelf. He smiled again when she set his order on the counter.

"Keep the change," he said in his quiet voice, and took his coffee and pastry to the table at the oriel window at the front of the café.

She watched him slip a black leather messenger bag off his shoulder and then unzip the hoodie—no ordinary sweatshirt, but the stylish, pricey kind that Marshall cooed over in the fashion magazines. He tossed it carelessly over the back of the opposite chair. The black dress shirt he wore beneath had three-quarter sleeves and Natalie noticed a wide-banded, expensive watch on his wrist, in black and silver. From the leather bag he pulled a pen and a black and white mottled composition book, the kind they sold at the university bookstore in bulk. He sat, opened the notebook to the first page and, after a brief pause, began to write.

Natalie watched all this occur with a mix of shame and relief. Once again, she had failed to dazzle and charm him with her wit or—feeling she was decidedly lacking in both—she had failed to propel the conversation from small talk into something bigger. But he didn't walk out the door again. He stayed and, by all appearances, he had the intention of remaining there for some time. Julian hunched over his composition book, coffee and pastry untouched, and scribbled away. After indulging in watching him—drinking him in—for a solid five minutes, Natalie returned to her book, but with an eye on her customer should he need her.

Hours passed. The café saw a swell of business around seven o'clock, and then it grew quiet again. Close to ten, it was empty but for Julian and Natalie, the former writing almost nonstop, and the latter watching, her own hand aching out of solidarity.

At ten to eleven, Julian set down his pen and rubbed his hand, glancing about as though he were a train passenger who'd fallen asleep only to wake in a strange country. His eyes found Natalie on her perch behind the counter.

"'The sleeper has awakened'," she said with a short laugh.

"Come again?"

"Uh, it's from *Dune*. The book? Sorry, bad joke."

"Not bad," Julian said with a smile. "But I haven't read it."

"It's a good one." She started over to him as he began to clear his plate and mug. "Here, let me…"

"It's no trouble…"

"No, please, it's my job."

She took the dishes from him, but before she could retreat to the counter, he asked, "Do you close soon?"

"In about ten minutes."

"And…you work alone? Every night?"

"Yes. I go to school during the day. At State." She didn't know what prompted her to disclose that. A desire to show she wasn't merely a barista perhaps, though she'd never felt there was anything wrong with that before.

Julian appeared not to have heard anyway. He surveyed the café, his brow furrowed. "Is it safe?"

"The neighborhood is safe. And I live right upstairs, so…"

"Maybe better not to tell anyone that."

Natalie's cheeks burned. "I don't. I mean, not usually."

"I'm sorry." Julian said. "I'm sure I sound like a lowlife myself, asking you those questions. It's none of my business." He hastily pulled on his hoodie and gathered his things.

Natalie bit her lip. She wanted to tell him there was absolutely nothing about him that was creepy. His presence flustered her, that was true, but his strange shyness, so incongruous with his looks, was oddly comforting. But there was no chance she could—or would—articulate any of that, so she stood in the middle of the café, still holding his mug and plate and feeling like a fool.

"You've been working hard. What is it you're writing?" she blurted and her cheeks went scarlet again. "Never mind, sorry. That's none of *my* business."

"It's nothing." He tossed the notebook into his bag and zipped it swiftly. "Not yet. Maybe something. We'll see." He seemed just as at a loss for something more to say and asked, "Do you write?"

"Oh, no, not at all. I study accounting. I read, but I don't have the poetry in me to write.

Julian smiled that wistful smile again. "I doubt that. I doubt that very much." He shouldered his bag. "Good night, Natalie."

"Oh. Good night," she returned, and he was gone, leaving behind the clean, expensive scent of his cologne and that compliment she knew would follow her well into the night.

***

Natalie had thought she let Julian slip away yet again, and her heart sang when he came back the next night. Their initial conversation was almost identical to the one previous: a small exchange of "hellos" and "I'm fines." He ordered another coffee—black—and another pastry that would remain half-eaten. His smile for her was warm but brief. He retreated to the same table he had occupied the night before. The pen and black and white notebook were produced and he immediately set to writing.

By eight o'clock, the café was humming with bits of conversation and the clinking of mugs on saucers. Whenever Natalie had a spare moment, she found Julian either scribbling away in an unbroken stream, or giving his pen a break and tapping it thoughtfully against his chin as he watched the people around him.

Near closing time, it grew quiet again. Natalie tidied up after the rush, wiped down tables, washed mugs and plates, and then picked up her book. She kept her eyes steadfastly on its pages even though the lines of text were rendered incomprehensible gibberish by Julian's distracting presence. At ten minutes before eleven, he stretched and gathered his belongings. Outside, the wind howled to get in.

"Good night, Natalie," he said.

"Good night," she replied, disappointment biting deep. She couldn't even bring herself to say his name.

He walked out for what she thought must be the last time. He'd decided Niko's was too busy to be productive. He wouldn't come back, she was sure of it.

But he returned that next night, and the night after that. Sunday she was off, but Monday he was there. And so Natalie found another routine: hers and Julian's. Every night he came in, every night he ordered a pastry and coffee, and every night he scribbled in his book, neither of them saying much more than cursory hellos and goodbyes. Natalie didn't trust herself to initiate anything, and for whatever his reasons, Julian said nothing, reserving, it seemed, all his copious words for his composition book. Natalie resigned herself to the fact he obviously wasn't there because of her. He was there to work, plain and simple.

The strange ache in her heart wasn't as easy to explain.

CHAPTER FOUR

Toward the middle of October, the black sky was frosty with the promise of winter. The stars glittered coldly and the wind tore at the awning above the door. Inside the café, Julian and Natalie were at their customary places, like actors in a movie. Extras with no lines, just set pieces; the café empty but for the two of them. Julian's hand flew back and forth as his coffee grew cold beside him.

Shortly before ten o'clock the door banged open. Natalie jumped in her seat as two men stomped inside, the odor of stale alcohol billowing around them. They jostled and nudged one another as they caught sight of Natalie behind the counter, and snickered in a way that made her skin shiver. Out of the corner of her eye, she saw that Julian had set down his pen and watched them intently.

"What can I get you?" Natalie asked.

The two men ogled the pastry display, then her.

"What's good?" one asked.

"I'll tell you what's good," muttered the other. They both leered at Natalie, and then chuckled together as if they were being coy and clever and not crude and obvious.

"I'll take a beer," said the first. He had hair the color and texture of straw, and wore a Warriors sweatshirt, stretched taut over his immense bulk. Muscles on top of muscles, and a neck as thick as a tree trunk. The other man had dark hair, and eyes that were bloodshot and hooded. He peered blearily at the menu that was written in lively colored chalk on the wall behind Natalie. His blue windbreaker was stained and rustled when he moved.

Natalie realized with an ugly knot of fear that she was taking inventory of the men in case she was forced to identify them later in some official capacity. There was danger in their loose laughter, an edge to their voices. Her eyes flickered to Julian. The image of a hunting cat came to mind; though still seated, he looked ready to fly off his chair.

"Where the fuck you see beer?" asked the guy in the windbreaker.

"We don't sell beer," Natalie said. "Only coffee."

"See? No beer. Dumbass."

"What else you got?" the blond demanded. His eyes grazed Natalie, up and down, as one would a menu. "Cute," he said, "but small tits."

The windbreaker burst out laughing. "Damn, Garrett."

Natalie's face burned. "I think you had better leave."

"Come on, he's just teasing," said the windbreaker. "Besides, you gotta be friendly to us. Customers are always right." His gaze went to her chest. "And he's right."

He laughed at his joke but his friend, Garrett, only smiled an ugly little smile as he leaned over the counter. "Yeah, be friendly. Be *real* friendly…"

Julian appeared beside the men. He was as tall as they, strong and lean, but they each outweighed him by a good fifty pounds. "I need a refill," he told Natalie, holding up his empty coffee mug. "Can I…?" He inclined his head at the coffee machine. His face revealed nothing but she felt better. The way he looked at her, knowing and calm, reassured her.

Natalie eased a breath. "Go ahead."

The pair of men eyed Julian with churlish expressions and muttered to themselves. She heard only a few words, but it was clear Julian was an annoyance to be waited out. They weren't done yet.

"This place is dead," Garrett told her. "Lock up and come with us."

"Yeah, we're *friendly* guys," said the other. "Let's have a date."

Behind Natalie, Julian steamed milk in a small tin pitcher.

Garrett reached out and ran a finger over Natalie's wrist. "Get rid of him and let's go, eh?"

Natalie snatched her hand away and stepped back. Julian, smooth as silk, slipped into her spot, holding the milk pitcher used for making lattes and cappuccinos. It was throwing off thick plumes of steam for such a small pot; Natalie could hear the milk still bubbling and boiling inside. Julian leaned against the pastry display; his entire attitude casual and relaxed.

"I think it's time the two of you leave. There's nothing for you here."

"Is that a fact?" asked the windbreaker. "Who do you think you are, asshole?"

"He's the milkman," said Garrett. "That supposed to scare us? Get the hell out of here before we break your face. This is none of your business."

Natalie eyed the telephone on the wall by the back door; too far to grab unless she ran. The tension in the air held her fast. If she ran, she might crack it.

If Julian felt any tension at all, it didn't show. "Milk fat acts like grease when heated," he said matter-of-factly.

Garrett blinked stupidly. "What?"

"You can try to *break my face* but not before I scald you. It will burn like hell, you'll be scarred for life, and if I aim well enough, you just might lose an eye." He arched an eyebrow. "But go ahead, if you think it's worth it."

Garrett apparently *did* think it was worth it; he balled his hands into meaty fists and his lower lip protruded like a wet, fleshy shelf. But his friend held him back.

"Fuck this. Let's get that beer."

Garrett let himself be pulled toward the door. "Asshole," he called. "Come outside without your little bucket and we'll see who loses an eye. I'll make hash out of your whole fucking face and you know it, bitch."

The curses and epithets continued, muffled, after the door closed. Garrett banged his fist on the glass, making it rattle, and then they were gone.

Natalie let out a slow breath and took another to calm her racing heart. Julian returned the milk pot to its place on the cappuccino maker. His beauty, up close, made the ugliness of the two men seem far away.

"Thank you," she said. "That was quick-thinking."

"I don't like this," Julian said. "You working alone. At night. Every night." He stared at the window where Garrett and his friend had been, his body rigid with anger.

"Nothing like this has ever happened before," Natalie told him. "Not in three years. I had a couple of run-ins with homeless men before, but they weren't so bad once they had something warm to drink and a bit of kindness. And I have pepper spray. It's in my purse. Usually I have it up front, but I forgot tonight. I forgot..."

Julian looked around at her and some of the tension in him eased, though his eyes were still stormy. "Are you all right?"

When she nodded he said, "I'm sorry, I...what those men said to you..." He appeared to bite back harsh words. "I'll wait with you while you close up."

She nodded and gathered her purse and keys, leaving some duties unfinished for the first time in three years. The milk steamer was crusted over now and needed a cleaning, but could wait. Julian stood at the door.

"Do you take the Muni?" he asked, as she locked up. "I'd like to walk you to the stop and wait with you."

"I live right here," she said, and indicated the locked gate over the door next to Niko's. "Upstairs, remember?"

"Oh, yes. I had forgotten." His gaze swept the street, his blue eyes hard, looking for signs of the two men. He waited for her as she unlocked the gate that led up to the darkened stairway. "Good night, Natalie," he said and closed the gate so that they were separated by the rusted white metal.

"Good night, Julian," she said. "Thank you again."

"I'll see you tomorrow night."

CHAPTER FIVE

The next night, Natalie noticed right away how things were different between her and Julian. He lingered at the counter as he made his order, chatting lightly, and she found the nerve to offer him more coffee later when she saw him pause in his writing. They chatted further before she was pulled away to attend to customers. At quarter past ten the café emptied and then it was just she and Julian. He set down his pen and stretched.

"Is it against the rules for you to have something to eat with me? I'll pay, of course." He pulled out a leather billfold. "I don't want to get you in trouble, but I'd like it if you joined me for a bit. If it's allowed."

"It's allowed," Natalie said, trying not to shout over the sudden pounding of her heart in her ears. She chose a croissant and after Julian paid for it, he carried her plate to his table and pulled out her chair for her.

His blue cashmere sweater was form-fitting enough to reveal he was a regular gym-goer, and made his blue eyes seem backlit for their brilliance. Not wanting to ogle his beautiful physique or become lost in those incredible eyes, Natalie was at a loss for where to look. She concentrated on her pastry and a silence fell between them.

Julian shifted in his chair. "I hate to open the evening with an unpleasant subject, but I've been thinking about last night. Those two men who harassed you."

"I'm sure they won't be back."

"Maybe not but I can't be here every night that you work and I'm not sure I can say anything more without...I don't know, offending your feminist sensibilities perhaps. Or coming across like a creep myself. I just worry."

Natalie blushed and looked away. She was sure Liberty would have spat out some retort about being able to take care of herself thank you very much, but Natalie felt warmed by his concern.

"On that note..." Julian rummaged in his messenger bag and pulled out a small box marked One Touch Security Systems. "This is for you. It's a keychain fob with GPS. Just push the button and it sends the police wherever you are." He cleared his throat. "I'm sorry. A morbid gift, I know, but after last night..."

Natalie examined the box, noting the device was state-of-the-art. "Thank you."

"The least I could do."

She smiled, basking a little in the idea that he cared enough to buy this for her. "It's very thoughtful," she said softly. "Not quite as clever as threatening menacing brigands with steamed milk, however."

"No, I suppose not, but infinitely more practical." He laughed, much more at ease now. "'Menacing brigands.' I suspected you had a sense of humor but wondered if I would ever get to see it."

Natalie turned her plate in little half-circles. "Well, you never spoke to me but to order coffee. There's not much room for comedy between the order-taking and the change-giving."

"You're right," Julian said. "I never did. Speak to you more, I mean. I should have."

"It's all right. I'm quiet. I have exactly two friends and if they saw me sitting here talking to an actual person, they'd wonder if I'd lost a bet."

"I'm glad you're sitting here, talking to me," Julian said, that enigmatic smile whispering over his lips again, and then gone. "It's my fault, though. I've been coming in for over a month. It's just that…"

She leaned forward. "Yes?"

"It's very easy to fall into certain patterns, especially if one is prone to such things."

"Routines of solitude," she said.

"Yes, exactly."

Another silence fell and grew long, threatening to undo their progress. Natalie decided to be bold. Her eyes fell to Julian's closed composition book, two-thirds of its pages now used. She could see where the paper had been written upon and where it was still untouched.

"How is your writing coming along?" Natalie asked and then added as lightly as she could, "Whatever it may be."

"I…yes, it's coming along fine." He smiled thinly and sipped his coffee.

"That's…good," she said. "You know, most writers I see in here tap away on a laptop. Not many still use pen and paper."

"I'm old-fashioned. Or perhaps it's another routine begun when I was a child that I haven't yet been able to break."

"Doesn't seem like it needs breaking. Although your hand might have other opinions."

He laughed. "Yes, my hand complains at times. But after ten years, it's used to the abuse."

"Ten *years*?"

"Longer, actually, now that I think about it. I had a teacher in grade school who bought them for me to…uh, to keep me out of trouble. Anyway, I notice you've always got a book going when it's slow here," he commented. "You're an avid reader, I take it?"

"Oh, gosh yes," she replied. "After bills, food, and school, my money goes to books. Sometimes I feel like I read too much, but I figure it's better than television or poking around online."

"There's no such thing as reading too much."

"My friend Liberty would disagree."

"Liberty?"

"Liberty Chastain. One of my two friends. Massage therapist by day, cabaret performer by night. She's always telling me I need to get out more and not spend so many Friday nights curled around a book." She laughed shortly. "Yikes, that makes me sound like a hermit. Compared to Liberty I guess I am. She's quite…memorable."

"So are you."

Natalie glanced up to find his eyes beholding her intently. She coughed and hoped the light was too dim for him to see her blush. "No, no. I'm just…I like books," she said lamely, and fought the urge to run away and hide.

Julian's smile set her at ease. "Yes, your Friday night company. So, who would that be?"

"Oh, I adore John Irving, Annie Proulx…Octavia Butler is lovely. Oh, but none can hold a candle to Rafael Melendez Mendón. If I had to choose a favorite, it would be him by a mile. Have you read him?"

Julian leaned back in his chair slowly. "I have."

Natalie clapped her hands. "And?"

He sipped his coffee, shrugged.

"Oh, come on! If you've read him, surely you have some opinion of his work? He's too important for indifference."

"I wouldn't say I was indifferent…"

"There are few things in this world I love better than the writing of Rafael Melendez Mendón. To the uninitiated or the *unappreciative*, I feel obliged to at least *try* to convert. I'm reading his latest right now for the third time. *Coronation.* It's just…miraculous."

Julian smiled thinly. "That's a quite a hefty compliment, but there's always room for improvement, don't you think?"

"Not for him." She shook her head. "Sorry, but I adore Mendón and get swept up just talking about him. I have all of his books and have read them ten times over, at least. I've read *Above* twenty times…" She picked at her croissant, realizing how crazy that must sound. "Liberty is right, isn't she? I'm hopeless."

"I'd say you're pretty far from hopeless. There are worse things one could do with their time than read."

Natalie looked to the window where the wind wailed mournfully. Dead leaves swirled outside the door.

"Sometimes I don't feel as though I'm reading Mendón so much as I'm escaping into his stories," she said. "His books are like a refuge from all that is ugly and mean. From pain. They are slices of absolute truth, you know? Truth expressed in the lives of his characters and shining through his prose." She turned her eyes to him. "You really don't have any opinion of him?"

"You're disappointed?"

"No. Well, maybe a little. I don't mean to put you on the spot or anything." Natalie sighed. "Maybe Liberty and Niko—my boss, the eponymous Niko—maybe they're right. That I spend too much time in stories and not enough in the real world." She scoffed. "I hate that term. Mendón's books are set in the real world but tinged with magic. And even when things get dangerous or violent or sad, in the end, you're left with a sense of hope and faith in the goodness of people. That's why I jump when someone says they've read him. I'm hoping they've seen and felt the same things, and that they appreciate him as well as I do." She looked at Julian, a terrible thought occurring to her. "You don't *dislike* his work, do you?"

"I like it fine."

"Okay, I can keep talking to you then," Natalie said with a grin. "I get a little carried away, I know. But you should see the spectacle I make of myself when I catch a customer *reading* him. I just…fly out of myself…out of my *routines of solitude* to talk about the book. Or about Mendón. He's reclusive, but god, I hate the term 'recluse' too. It makes it sound like he's a weirdo. As if there's anything wrong with wanting a little *silence* now and then. He has his own routines of solitude, you know?"

Julian was watching her with an inscrutable expression on his face. She felt her neck grow hot. "Oh jeez, *I'm* the weirdo. Right now. Just going on and on…"

"No." Julian said quietly, almost sadly, "I think your enthusiasm for Mendón illuminates this room better than any light, and I have a new appreciation for him for that reason alone."

A thick silence fell between them. It seemed he wished to say something more but he didn't, and now she wished she had said less. Her father used to tease her that she was like an old engine that needed cranking, but once it got going…

"You have customers and I should go," Julian said, rising.

"I do…?"

Behind Natalie, the bell above the door jangled and a gaggle of elderly women in felt hats and gloves came in. They cooed and gabbled over the pastry display and pondered the difference between a mocha and hot chocolate.

Julian drew on his coat and gathered his belongings. "Good night, Natalie."

She watched him go, rubbing her arms that had broken out in gooseflesh. He'd taken the warmth of the room with him, leaving her cold and with the bizarre sense that he was *disappointed* in her, though she couldn't fathom why.

"Does anyone *work* here?" one woman squawked.

Natalie plastered on a lightless smile. She attended the customers mechanically, her thoughts on the conversation with Julian. By the end of the night, after turning it over and over in her mind a thousand times, she came to one conclusion: she had said too much and made him uncomfortable. *You babbled like a maniac. No wonder he left. He wanted some small talk, not a discourse on Mendón.* She half-wished Niko or Liberty were there so she could say, "See? This is why I don't talk to people. I just mess it up."

After closing, Natalie retreated to her apartment, to her couch, and took up her copy of *Coronation.* She dove deep, not coming up to the surface until she was tired enough to fall immediately and safely into sleep.

* * *

The sedan pulled into the circular drive of a towering condo complex, and Julian Kovač climbed out before the driver could open the door for him.

"Good night, sir," the driver said, his face professionally impassive.

Julian slammed the door shut, and muttered a good night. He strode up to the building, taking the concrete stairs two at a time. Columns of lights—the skyscrapers of the Financial District— rose around him, buffeting the howling wind and breaking it up into manageable gusts.

Bernie, the night doorman, greeted him with a warm, "Good evening, Mr. Kovač," and held open the spotless glass door. Julian muttered another greeting, and yet a third to Hank, the security guard at the front desk. Once inside the confines of the elevator, he spat a curse in Spanish, and jabbed the button marked '15PH'.

The elegant tone of the elevator announced the floor and opened on a small anteroom of rich, maroon carpet. Lights glowed in art deco sconces of pewter and gold. There were no other doors but his. He keyed in a security code on the wall panel, and it swung soundlessly open.

The penthouse was dark, illuminated by the city that glittered through the immense windows that composed one wall. Julian wended between elegant chairs and tables and sofas until he was standing before them.

He looked out over the sparkling constellations of the city and the pool of darkness that was the bay. The Golden Gate Bridge to his far left and the Bay Bridge to his right hung like starry garlands over the blackness, their luminescence converging and blending with Sausalito and Oakland.

"Thousands of writers in the world," Julian murmured. "Astronomical odds. A coincidence of outrageous proportions." He leaned his forehead against the cool glass; his skin still burned when he thought of her, of how her rich dark eyes had shown when she spoke of her favorite author. "So much love…" He sighed. "I couldn't have written anything worse."

CHAPTER SIX

"I met someone," Natalie said when there was a lull—finally—in the good-natured bickering between Liberty and Marshall. They lowered their cocktails with comic sameness, and swiveled their heads toward her.

"What?" Liberty's mouth was agape. "You're joking."

"Ssh!" Marshall hissed, as if silence were possible in his favorite noisy bar on Market Street. "Did you hear that cracking sound? That was hell freezing over."

Natalie gave him a dirty look. "Your support is duly noted. And no, I'm not joking."

"Well?" Liberty rolled her hand. "Who is he? Spill it."

Natalie shrugged. "Not sure I want to, now."

"Don't get in a snit," Marshall said. "Look at it from our perspective: Halley's comet only comes every seventy years…"

Liberty jabbed him with her elbow. "Marshall, zip it." She patted Natalie's hand. "Don't mind him; he's premenstrual. Tell us everything. We'll behave, I promise."

Natalie felt the weight of her friends' attention and wished mightily she had kept her mouth shut. "It's nothing. He's just someone…a customer at the café."

"And? A regular? What's his name? What's he look like? What's he do?"

"Yes, he's a regular. His name is Julian—"

"Julian, Julian…" Marshall mused. "Professional chess player? Debate team captain?"

Natalie ignored him. "Julian Kovač. He's very intelligent, extraordinarily good-looking—"

"*Extraordinarily* good-looking." Liberty nodded knowingly at Marshall. "Not just *ordinary* good-looking."

"*Yes*," Natalie countered. "To be perfectly honest, he's gorgeous. And I'm not sure what he does. Writes, I guess. We haven't gotten that far yet."

"And how far *have* you gotten?"

"Walked right into that one, didn't I?"

"Sure did."

"We've just been…talking."

"That's it?"

"That's it."

Marshall smirked into his martini. "Honey, you aren't a very good story-teller."

Natalie was prepared to let the matter drop. Without juicy details, her friends lost interest. But she eyed the pair, snickering between themselves and sharing confident, knowing looks. Natalie crossed her arms over her chest.

"And he practically saved my life."

This had the desired effect. Again, cocktails were set down with a clatter, and the pair rounded on her again. She told them about the two men who had made advances toward her and how Julian had threatened them until they left.

"Jesus," Liberty breathed. "Nat, those guys could have been bad news. I mean, like the worst."

"I know." Natalie shuddered. "But Julian was so smart about it."

"My hero!" Marshall exclaimed. "You should have banged his brains out in gratitude."

Natalie's face turned scarlet. As a quick diversion, she told them of his nightly writing routine. "And if he hadn't been there that night, I don't want to think what might have happened."

Liberty twirled a swizzle stick around her glass thoughtfully. "So, let me get this straight: he comes in every night for, like, months, writes in some little book, and you guys have chatted and whatnot...and that's it. Have you gone out with him? Outside the café, I mean?"

"No," Natalie said. "We..."

"He's weird," Liberty declared and sat back in her chair with finality.

"He's not weird..."

"Maybe he's gay!" Marshall exclaimed. "Can I have him?"

The smug surety in Liberty's face withered a bit. "You always think everyone is gay until proven otherwise."

"I'm just using the opposite paradigm you straight people set a million years ago."

"Which is?"

"Assuming *no one* is gay until proven otherwise."

"How regressive of you."

Natalie retreated into silence as her friends continued their bickering, her static love affair defeated by their own. They didn't bring up Julian again and neither did she. After an awkward cab ride home, Natalie stepped out and said her goodnights. Marshall walked her to the white iron gate in front of her place.

"Never let it be said that I am not as gallant as Sir Julian."

Natalie kissed him on the cheek. "Never."

"And I'm happy for you," he said in a rare, quiet tone. "If you're happy then I'm happy."

"I am," Natalie said.

"Good," Marshall said. "But when you *do* bang his brains out, I had better be the first to know." He cocked his head. "Wait. That came out wrong."

Natalie laughed and gave him a playful shove.

Liberty stuck her head out the taxi window. "The meter is running, not that you care. I'm not spending a dime over ten bucks, Mr. Moneybags."

"She's a delicate little flower, isn't she?" Marshall winked. "Mustn't keep her waiting."

Natalie watched him hop back into the cab and wave good-bye to her from inside its darkened confines. "Too late."

***

Julian was absent from Niko's for three excruciatingly long days, finally returning on Monday night. Natalie watched him approach with apprehension. Their last encounter had ended strangely and he'd left so abruptly. She vowed not to talk about Mendón with such fanaticism again; it was clearly off-putting. *If Julian's an author too, maybe he's got one of those fragile writer egos.* The notion didn't seem to fit, but then Natalie realized she didn't know him well enough to say for sure.

A few minutes after ten, when the café was empty, Julian set down his pen, stretched his fingers, and went up to the counter. "I would like it if you joined me again." He wore that inexplicably shy smile. "Unless you have to work or…"

"No, no." Natalie endeavored to keep her voice in a normal octave range. "I mean, no, I don't have work to do now. I could…uh, join you."

Once again she picked out a pastry and once again he paid for it, carried it to the table for her, and pulled out her chair, not sitting until she had. A silence fell at once. She didn't want to press him on a subject he didn't want to talk about but was at a loss for anything else.

"How is…how's your hand?" she asked lightly. "Working hard, from what I can see."

"Hard enough." He smiled dryly—he seemed to know how vague that sounded—and ran his fingers through the loose black curls of his hair. "I'm sure you've already decided I'm a rude bastard for not talking about my work. I never talk about it. With anyone. Not until it's finished. A writerly affectation, I guess."

"I had wondered."

"It's nothing personal," Julian said quickly. "I feel like if I talk about it while in the process, it disturbs it. Disrupts the flow. I know that sounds a bit ridiculous, but it's true."

"Not ridiculous," Natalie said, "but is that what you do for a living?"

Julian gave a half-nod. "And you go to State? What are studying?"

"Accounting," Natalie replied. It hadn't escaped her that he changed the subject with amazing alacrity. *He doesn't want to talk about it. Let it go.* "Niko, my boss, got me started."

"How so?"

"You sure you want to hear this?"

"Absolutely."

"Well, um…okay. Three years ago, Niko fired his accountant. The guy hadn't been doing much of anything but coming in for a few hours once a month, fiddling with papers, and helping himself to lots of free coffee. The café's books were a mess and I offered to help."

"And it was then your knack for numbers manifested."

She smiled. "Something like that. Niko appreciated my offer though neither of us had great hopes I could do much. But I was able to get the registers in order, and I was glad to tell Niko his accountant hadn't been a thief. And Niko, being the overly generous man that he is, gave me a bonus in my next paycheck. That I promptly spent on books." Natalie picked at her blueberry muffin. "I wasn't doing much else but reading, so when Niko suggested I go to school for accounting, it just made sense. Anyway. Turns out I really like it."

"That's a gift," Julian said.

"A gift?"

"Knowing your life's passion and pursuing it."

"I don't know that it's a passion, but it's definitely what I want to do after college. It seems safe…"

"Safe?"

Natalie's cheeks burned. The words had slipped out. "Nothing. Anyway, I have Niko to thank for a lot of things. He owns this whole building and when I applied to rent from him three years ago, the job here practically came with it."

"He seems like a good man."

"Yes, he is. Him and his wife, both."

"Why does that make you sad?" Julian asked gently.

"Does it? No, it doesn't. I'm just…tired maybe." She smiled faintly. "Long day."

She waited for the next comment or question, something about how her parents must be proud, or if her family lived nearby. But he said nothing and another silence descended.

She nibbled at her blueberry muffin and he took a bite of his croissant. A little flake clung to his lower lip. *Such a beautiful mouth.* A sudden urge to lean over and run her thumb along his lips came unbidden, and she flinched hard enough to upset her plate. The muffin rolled across the table.

Julian caught the pastry and returned it to its plate. "Are you okay?"

Natalie flushed to the roots of her hair. *Did that just happen? Seriously?* "I just…you have something…on your lip."

He wiped his mouth with a napkin. "Got it?"

"Uh, yes," Natalie said. "I'll try to tell you next time instead of throwing my food at you."

He laughed loudly, and she laughed with him, her embarrassment evaporating. *How does he do that? Make me feel perfectly at ease and absolutely thunderstruck at the same time?*

"I really enjoy talking to you," he said. "If you don't mind me saying."

"No, not at all," Natalie replied. "I like talking to you too." A silence fell and after a few moments she held up her hands. "But jeez, we're terrible at it!"

Julian grinned. "Cicero said 'silence is one of the great arts of conversation.'"

"Then we must be masters of the form."

"No, no, we're just rusty when it comes to talking to new people. We can do this. Think of a topic, quick."

"Ummm, travel."

"Travel, brilliant. Here we go. Natalie Hewitt, do you travel?"

She grinned at his playfulness. "Julian Kovač, no I do not."

"No? Are you sure?"

"Yes. I think I'd remember."

"All right, let's say I believe you."

Natalie laughed. "Oh, that's very kind of you."

"*Why* do you not travel?"

"Not by choice. It's just not in the budget at the moment."

"Gotcha." Julian held his arms out. "See? This is easy. We're on a roll."

"We are!" she laughed. "I even have a question for you: your last name is Croatian but your accent is…Spanish?"

"*Correcto,*" he said quickly. "But the subject is travel, and the question is—don't think, just answer—if you could go anywhere in the world, where would you go?"

"Venice."

"Venice Beach?" He fished around in his pocket for his cellphone. "I'll call you a cab. You could drive there tonight. Be there in the morning…"

"Oh stop," she laughed. "Italy. Venice, Italy."

"Mmm, that's a bit more complicated." He dumped his cellphone on the table—the latest iPhone, Natalie noticed—and leaned in. "Why Venice?"

"Because it's…Italy. It's pretty…and…" She waved her hands. "No, I'm not going to tell you why Venice."

"Why not?

"Because. I just can't. You'll think I'm a sap. Or that I've seen too many romantic movies."

"Ah, so it's a romantic inclination." Julian grinned innocently. "What, pray tell, is romantic about Venice, Italy?"

She tossed her napkin at him. "Oh, jeez, let me think…"

"You're not supposed to think. Just answer." He held out the napkin. "And I believe you dropped this."

She burst out laughing and he watched her, as if he liked the sound of it. When she had subsided, he cocked an eyebrow at her expectantly. "Well?"

"Trust me, you don't want to hear it," Natalie said, the laughter fading from her voice. "I'll get all wound up and start babbling away. Again."

"What's wrong with that?"

"The other night I rambled on about Rafael Mendón and you just…Well, you left." Natalie cleared her throat. "You seemed uncomfortable."

Julian's playful expression turned pained. "I'm very sorry if I left you feeling self-conscious. That was not my intention at all. I was just…thinking of other things. Stupid things that get in the way. But what you said…Your passion for…the writing. I liked that very much."

Natalie felt a warm glow bloom in her stomach for the way he was looking at her. "Even so, I tend to get carried away. I know that."

Julian tapped his fingers on the table. "All right, I confess I have ulterior motives for asking you about Venice."

"Oh?"

"I want to hear you talk about something the way you talked about your favorite author."

Natalie swallowed. "You do?"

"My mother once told me that you can see into the soul of a person when they speak of the place on this earth that means the most to them. Whatever the reason, having been there or not."

Natalie felt the warm glow intensify. "So you just asked me a very personal question then, didn't you?"

"Yes, I suppose I did."

"Okay." She rested her chin on her palm, a small smile on her lips. "You first."

He sat back in his chair with a small laugh. "I suppose that's fair."

"I think so."

"Rijeka, Croatia," he answered after a moment. "A northern seaport city where my father was born. He worked in the shipyards before coming to America. I've never been there but have always wanted to go. I feel I *need* to go. He abandoned my mother and me when I was three years old and then reappeared when I was ten, only to die a month later."

Natalie swallowed hard. "I'm so sorry. I had no idea…"

"How could you?" he asked gently. He turned his stunning blue gaze to the window. "I always thought that I was missing a piece of myself with his absence. More than a piece. There is half of me, my blood, my history that I don't understand. I think that if I go to Rijeka, I will find those missing pieces, or at least the remnants of his spirit there, and perhaps fill in the holes."

"Why don't you go?" she asked softly.

"Because I'm afraid of what I will find."

The silence that fell then was a thick one, full, but not unpleasant. Natalie had never met anyone who spoke like Julian did. Who thought about the world the way he did, and she suddenly had an overwhelming urge to read whatever it was he was writing.

"Your turn," he said.

"My turn," Natalie agreed. She heaved a breath. "I want to go to Venice because I saw a picture of the Grand Canal in a travel book once. The photo was taken at dusk, and the water was an amazing, brilliant blue. As blue as…" She looked at his eyes that were watching her intently and cleared her throat. "Uh, well, a stunning color. Lamps from the restaurants and cafés that lined the water cast this perfect golden hue along the edges. In the middle of the Canal there were a handful of gondolas, each with a lantern glowing at the front. The gondoliers who poled them wore their black and white striped shirts, and there were couples in each boat, huddled together.

"And there was one gondola sort of at the front. It had two men sitting in it, one playing an accordion, one with a violin under his chin. In this photo, the gondolier's mouth was open and I just know that he was singing. I could hear the music and feel the warm air, and smell the water, and this man's voice… it was beautiful. I want to go there and experience that beauty, surrounded by history and art. I think it would be…"

"Sublime?" Julian offered.

"Yes, exactly." Natalie huffed a breath and wiped her eyes. "And there's something else to know about me and that is I cry at the drop of a hat and it's really embarrassing but I can't help it."

Julian's smile was wistful and comforting at the same time. "My mother also said that tears flow when the soul experiences an emotion so potent the body can't contain it."

"That's such a nice way of putting it," Natalie said. "I've only ever been embarrassed. She sounds like a poetic woman, your mother."

"She was." Julian glanced at the clock on the wall. "Closing time. I'll walk you home."

He waited for her while she locked up the café, and again while she unlocked the gate to her stairwell.

"Goodnight, Natalie. I'll see you tomorrow."

"Goodnight, Julian."

She hesitated for as a long as she dared, and when he did nothing she slipped inside the dark passage and watched him walk away.

CHAPTER SEVEN

October both raced and dragged by. The days of Julian's absence from the café slowed time to a crawl. More often than not he was there, writing and then talking with her, but he'd also stay away for days at a time, no rhyme or reason to his schedule that Natalie could see but to torture her with his absence.

Marshall and Liberty begged her to come with them to an "epic" party on Stanyan Street on Halloween night. She declined and was mortified when they showed up in the café that night anyway.

Marshall was dressed as Gomez Addams, Liberty as Morticia. Liberty had made the costumes and done their make-up, and Natalie thought there must be a costume contest somewhere waiting for them to pick up first prize. Neither hid the fact they were looking for Julian. They blatantly inspected each customer, speculating over the young male patrons. Julian was late. Or he wasn't coming. Natalie hoped it was the former and that he would arrive with serendipitous timing: right after Marshall and Liberty departed.

"Well?" Liberty tossed a lock of stiff black wig hair over her shoulder. "Where is he?"

Natalie shrugged. "Not here."

"Not here," Marshall said. "Therefore he's *not* around to *not* ask you out on a proper date. Ergo, you are free to meet up with us after you're done slinging joe."

Natalie wiped the counter with a rag. She had no retort. It had been a colossal mistake to tell her friends about Julian. Marshall was right: he hadn't asked her to go outside the café; hadn't made any romantic overtures of any kind. And yet, his attention to her was rife with warm, sweet emotion. The nights he came to the café were rich with delicious conversation and every moment at her apartment gate was filled with possibilities. *This* would be the night he asked her to dinner or a movie or perhaps…something more. But he did none of those things and she was too paralyzed by her own shyness to do anything but let the moments pass. He told her good night and she closed the door behind her, to be rewarded with a dark, empty stairwell, an empty apartment, a cold bed…

"I don't feel up to it," Natalie said now.

Liberty's expression was compassionate under layers of black kohl and white paint. "Honey, come with us."

"I can't just leave the café. I'm working."

"You're off at eleven, right? For a party of this magnitude, you'll be right on time. Come. Be our little Wednesday. You've got the big sad eyes for it." Liberty smiled brightly and took a new tack. "You'll meet some new people! Forget about that Julian guy for a bit. I think that might be good for you."

"No, you two go ahead. I'm going to take a bath and get some sleep."

"Are you sure? Getting plastered might put things in perspective."

"I don't want to get drunk," Natalie said.

"Why not? Afraid you'll drunk-dial him?"

"No, I can't. I…"

"What?"

"Nothing." She glanced at them sideways and saw Liberty and Marshall exchange incredulous looks.

"You don't have his phone number, do you?"

Natalie wiped a ring of old moisture off the counter.

"Girl, forget that freak," Liberty screeched. "He's either a serious closet case or he's stringing you along. Either way, he's no good."

"No good?" Natalie twisted the rag in her hand. "How could you even…? He's more than good. He's wonderful. You have no idea. I mean, there can be…*levels* between meeting a guy and…and sleeping with him."

"Not *this* many levels," Marshall muttered.

Liberty crossed her arms, the tattered black sleeves of her dress billowing and then settling around her. "You're deluding yourself over something that's never going to happen and I don't think it's healthy."

Natalie met her friend's eye, struggled not to look away. "Funny. I feel as if I could say the exact same thing about you."

Liberty colored under her pale make-up.

"Now, ladies," Marshall intervened. "Kiss and make up before the claws really come out and someone gets scratched. Namely, me."

"Come on." Liberty tugged Marshall's arm. "Let's go."

Marshall made an imploring face at Natalie but she just shook her head. He let himself be dragged out of the café, miming "I'll call you."

Natalie watched them go, her hands shaking and tears stinging her eyes. She attended to her customers and waited for Julian to come. He never did.

***

Julian's absence stretched into days. Natalie wanted to be angry but she reminded herself she had nothing to be angry about. He owed her nothing. He could come and go as he pleased, no explanation needed or required. Despite their intimate conversations, he was, for all intents and purposes, just a customer.

Natalie wondered if Liberty (with whom she made up the moment Liberty recovered from her Halloween hangover) had been right after all. Perhaps Julian was already in a relationship. Or that he was toying with her. Neither notion felt true; he never spoke of another man or woman in his life, and he seemed to enjoy her company. But even *friends* exchanged numbers, socialized outside of work. *Maybe we're not even that.*

She cursed her own weakness. *Jane Austen's heroines were more progressive than you are,* she thought. *Take the initiative!*

It was a slow night and Natalie was reading behind the register when Julian returned. He was dressed impeccably, as always: a wool coat over a black cashmere sweater and stylish jeans. She quailed at the idea of putting him on the spot, but there was a dearth of equilibrium between them that needed to be remedied.

But instead of sitting him down and having a serious conversation about what—if anything—was between them, the night progressed as it always had. He wrote furiously for two hours and then they shared a pastry while chatting about everything under the sun except for *them.*

For the first time, Natalie began to fear that *them* was nothing.

CHAPTER EIGHT

On the fifteenth of November, Natalie came into the café a few minutes early for her shift. Niko was at a table, laughing and talking loudly with a customer. She waited, shuffling her feet and tapping her fingernails on her teeth until he was finished.

"Natalia! Such a good girl!" Niko took her cheeks in his thin, tough hands and gave her a playful shake. "I was hoping to sneak out a bit early to get Petra a bucket of flowers? She tells me I'm no romantic. Pfft. I go, yah?"

"Yah…uh, yes. As soon as you say yes to my request." The smile on her face was so plastic she could practically feel it try to slide off.

"Uh oh." Niko's exuberance dimmed. He crossed his arms over his apron. "You have that look on your face. That one you wear when you don't want me to worry. And you know what it does? It makes me worry."

"You don't have to."

Niko rubbed his chin. "Mmm. Well? What is this request? That you work sun-up to sundown? Until you drop from tiredness? Eh? Is that what you want?"

"Yes," Natalie said. "I have four days off from school around Thanksgiving, and I have practically the entire month of December off."

"Natalia…"

"I'll take as many double-shifts as you'll give me. Let Sylvie and Margo take whatever time off they want. And you can take Petra somewhere on a romantic vacation and prove her wrong."

Niko sighed. "The holidays is hard for you, I know this. But Natalia…"

"Just say yes, Niko. Please."

"Maybe I don't want to say yes, eh? Maybe I want you to have Christmas with us. And Thanksgiving too. Come on! Greek-style! We'll have homemade spanokopita, some paidakia—grilled so nice—and tzatziki instead of stuffing. All your friends be jealous."

Natalie braced herself against his generosity, arms crossed over her chest, eyes cold and unblinking. She felt herself leaning towards him, longing to be engulfed in his fatherly embrace. Impossible. She'd start crying and wouldn't stop and then Niko would be late for his date with his marvelous wife.

Niko wilted. "Okay, you win. I'll have Petra write up the schedule and post it next week."

"Thank you, Niko…" Natalie began but the kind man gently took her chin in his hand and tilted her face to his.

"I do this for you, Natalia, for the last time. Next year, you eat with friends or you eat with us. And Christmas too." His smile was sad. "This pain in your heart stays so long, my girl, because you are holding on to it so tightly."

He released her chin with a pat on the cheek and left her standing alone behind the register. She jumped when a customer approached, bumbled his order, and spilled his coffee when she set it down.

***

After four years, Natalie thought she had the holidays pretty well in hand. Or as well as could be expected. Thanksgiving wasn't that difficult. Only one day and generally celebrated behind closed doors. Natalie worked from eight in the morning until eight at night (Niko refused to allow regular hours if she insisted on working on a day he normally would have closed up shop). There were few customers. Julian didn't show up—a fact that was equal parts relief and disappointment. She wondered where he was, with whom he was dining. His family? A lover? No one?

Natalie closed the cafe, went upstairs, and fired up a microwave dinner. Both Liberty and Marshall called and left careful messages on her machine that she erased the moment they finished playing. She watched *Manhattan Murder Mystery* on her tiny TV and when it was over, picked up Rafael Mendón's poetry collection, *Starshine*. She cried a bit—but not too much—and went to bed. All in all, she considered it a pretty successful Thanksgiving.

Christmas and Hanukkah were worse, however. They were inescapable. Television commercials were an assault on her grief, with their endless portrayals of the family unit, either madcap or sentimental. Natalie shut off her TV and left it off for the entire month of December. School came to an unmerciful break and she worked her six double shifts per week—three more than Niko was comfortable with—letting the hours pile up, putting one day after the next. Julian still came to the café three or four times a week in the evenings, though Natalie never let on that she had been there all day and would be there the next. Never let on that she was struggling hard to make it out of this tunnel, to the innocuous dazzle of New Year's.

One night, they sat together under the paper cut-out snowflakes the day baristas had made. The paper twisted in the soft currents of the café. Julian remarked about how tired she looked.

"It's been a long day," she said.

"Yes, this time of year can be exhausting," he said. "Christmas is coming. Or...Hanukkah?"

"Both," Natalie said, her stomach clenching. "Hanukkah from my mom, Christmas from my dad."

"You must be leaving soon? To visit them?"

Here it was. She sat back in her chair, thinking how to navigate away from the question. Instead, she heard herself blurt, "They're gone."

She watched his face as he made the same inevitable calculations everyone else did: it was the holidays, no family, she would be alone. She braced herself for chafing platitudes of pity but instead he said, "I was in this area yesterday morning. I saw you here, behind the counter."

"Niko needs the help and I could use the money."

Julian said nothing. He ran his finger along the rim of his cup.

"Don't feel bad for me," Natalie told him. "It happened a long time ago and I don't want to talk about it."

He met her eyes. "I know the feeling."

"Which feeling?" Natalie demanded. "There are so many, I hardly know where to start."

"All of them. They're undoubtedly of different tones and tenors, but I'm amazed at how many events in our lives are striking the same chords."

There was a silence then, and Natalie heard her words rush out. "My parents are dead. Car accident. Four years ago," she said in single bursts, like a machine gun. Her eyes were full and challenging as they bored into his. He accepted.

"My father when I was ten, as I told you. My mother eight years later. Heart attack and cancer. One fast, like lightning. One slow, like a merciless poison."

"Mine were both fast, like lightning." Natalie could hardly whisper the words. "Which one is easier?"

He cocked his head and smiled sadly. "Which one do you think?"

"Neither."

He nodded.

"I'm sorry," she said, wiping her cheek.

"Me too."

They sat in silence under the snowflakes that hung above them, twisting lazily but never falling.

***

Niko had insisted that the café would be closed on Christmas Day but the Barbos family was in Florida for the holiday and Natalie had the key. She didn't mark her time card, but opened up at eight a.m. and by noon had served only three people—each amazed at their luck on finding something open. No one came in for hours after that and Natalie began to wither. Her book couldn't hold her; the pastries and coffees were stale with familiarity. It was ridiculous to stay but she couldn't go back to her empty apartment either. The silence would be too much to take.

"I miss them," she told the empty room, and soldiered on.

At two o'clock, the door chimed. Her book nearly slipped out of her hands as Julian walked in.

"I had thought the café would be closed," he said. "But I also guessed it wouldn't."

The quiet of the café had been on the verge of unbearable. His voice was music and the beauty of him like a vibrant painting after staring at gray walls. Natalie valiantly fought against the tears of relief that threatened to flood her. "What are you doing here?"

"I was coming by your apartment. I thought maybe you'd like to go somewhere with me. I'm not sure what might be open," he said, wearing that shy smile that still had the power to disarm her. "I didn't think anything through."

It's happening. It's finally happening. Natalie took another deep breath, and the knot of pain in her gut relented to the sheer joy of seeing him. "I'm so glad you're here."

"So am I."

50

There was little to clean or tidy up; Natalie had the café dark and locked five minutes later. She threw on her coat and then she and Julian stepped out onto the street together.

Natalie inhaled deeply, feeling as if she'd just emerged from a stale, airless container, into the world. The chill wind was bracing and lovely. "Well?" Her smile split her face. "I think I would love to get out of this neighborhood. Can you stand to wait in the cold for a bus?"

"We could wait for a bus," Julian said. "Or we could just take my car."

A sleek black Mercedes sedan was parked at the curb.

"This is yours?" Natalie asked.

"It's from a service."

"Oh, well then I'm not as impressed."

He laughed. "I don't want you to be impressed; I want you to be warm."

He opened the door for her and Natalie bent to get in, but stopped. "Wait! I forgot something. I'll just be a minute."

She fumbled her keys out of her purse, unlocked the gate, then raced up to her place. On the coffee table was a square package, wrapped in white paper. A smaller oblong box sat atop the first, also wrapped in white, and both tied together with a red ribbon.

Natalie reached for the presents, but once in her hands, she hesitated. The three black and white composition books were more of a tease. The pen, however, had cost her a pretty penny at an antique shop. When she saw it, she realized she couldn't leave the store without it; it was too perfect for him.

Now, with a luxury car waiting downstairs for her, the books seemed silly and the card...She flipped it open. *Love, Natalie* in her neat, slanted script. She bit her lip. It was too obvious. It was all wrong. Julian hadn't even told her what he was writing and here she was giving him books and pens...

"You have nothing else," she said aloud. Her words echoed hollowly in her empty apartment. She stuffed the package into her bag and raced back downstairs.

Julian was still standing outside, his breath pluming before him in the cold.

"Oh, gosh, you should have waited in the car," she told him.

"What kind of brute do you take me for?" He grinned and opened the passenger door for her.

The seats were soft leather and she felt fading warmth emanating through the cotton of her dress as she sat down.

"Heated seats? Okay, I'm *mildly* impressed."

He started the engine. "They'll warm up more in a moment," he said. "I'm a little unprepared. I didn't plan anything…"

"You know what? I'm actually really hungry," Natalie said. "I skipped lunch. What about you?"

Julian tapped the steering wheel. "I think I know a place that's open."

"Anything but a coffee shop."

CHAPTER NINE

Julian navigated the car through light traffic from the Sunset District to the Financial. Natalie had remembered from one of their talks that he lived in this part of town. She watched him drive, biting back a smile. *The car commercials are right*, she thought. *There's something sexy about a man driving a stick shift.* He pulled the car under an old-style electric sign that read Tadich Grill.

"Do you like seafood?" Julian asked, handing the car keys to the valet. "I think you mentioned you did once before."

Natalie laughed. "You know I do. I have three obsessions: reading, numbers, and grilled halibut. In that order."

He opened the front door for her and Natalie saw that the Tadich Grill was a "nice" restaurant. The kind where her father would have reminded her to put her napkin in her lap and keep her elbows off the table. They stepped up to a long, narrow bar, where a bartender in a white smock was polishing a glass and eyeing them as though they had barged into his home during dinner.

"Well?" the bartender demanded. "Bar or table?"

"Table," Julian replied.

The man sighed as if they'd had a long-standing beef and pulled out two menus. "This way."

"Do you know him?" Natalie whispered. "He seems upset with us. Is it the holiday…?"

"Nah." Julian grinned. "He's always like that."

The surly man led them into the pleasantly dark confines of the restaurant. Cozy tables draped in white lined the walls. Delicious smells of fresh seafood and steak permeated the air, as did the muted conversations of a dozen or so patrons.

The bartender waited impatiently as Julian took Natalie's coat and draped it across the back of her chair. Her lavender dress was simple and rather plain, she thought, but Julian was wearing only dark blue jeans and a gray long-sleeved shirt—albeit clearly expensive jeans and shirt. None of the other patrons appeared particularly dressed up, either. The bartender handed over the menus with a grunt and returned to his post.

"What a grouch." Natalie laughed. "I like it. I like *him*. Suits this place."

"I think so too."

Her laughter died when she perused the menu and saw the prices. They weren't outrageous, but far more than she could ever afford to spend. Some of the dishes, she noted, had no prices at all. She could hear her mother's knowing tone. *If you have to ask, you can't afford it.*

The waiter appeared. He rattled off the day's specials and Julian ordered a bottle of cabernet from a long list full of old-sounding French titles. When the waiter returned to present it, the label showed it predated the Cold War.

"I thought we're supposed to drink white wine with fish," Natalie managed. She was no connoisseur but the bottle had to cost half a month's rent.

"You hate white wine," Julian said. He tasted the small sip the waiter offered, and nodded. The man poured and left them.

Natalie laughed weakly. "Ah yes. Everything I told you of my likes and dislikes is paying off exactly to plan."

Julian grinned. "Is it?"

"How else would I get my fix of..." she turned the wine bottle to face her, "1947 Chateau Gruaud Laros?"

"A real mastermind."

"A girl's gotta drink."

They laughed again as the waiter returned to take their order. Julian caught Natalie's dismayed expression. "Shall I?"

"Yes, please."

He ordered appetizers, entrees—Alaskan halibut for her, red snapper for him—and sides of sautéed mushrooms, pasta, and grilled asparagus.

"Okay?" he asked.

Natalie nodded. "Okay."

The waiter winked. "Okay."

***

Over a Dungeness crab cocktail, Julian asked her about her studies. "How are they going? Nearly done or have you time yet?"

"Nearly done," she said. "I'm set to graduate in June."

"Congratulations," he said. "And have you decided what to do with your degree? Personal accounting or... something else?" He laughed. "I know nothing about the subject myself. David handles all that stuff for me."

"David?" Natalie asked, keeping her voice light. "You haven't mentioned him before." She dipped a wedge of crab into a little dish of melted butter calmly while her thoughts took off. *Marshall was right. He's gay. He's gay and has a boyfriend named David...*

"David is a good friend of mine, as well as my personal assistant. He manages my trust fund. I hate talking about that—the trust fund. It makes me sound useless and spoiled, and besides we were talking about you and what you're going to do with your degree."

Natalie toyed with her under-sized fork as the topic of his money whizzed by like a runaway train. *Like whatever he's writing, it's his business,* she told herself. Besides, it was too good to see him like this, sitting across from her at a table that wasn't at Niko's. She bit back a smile. *And David is only an assistant.*

"I haven't decided yet," she answered. "I don't have to pick my focus until next semester. Personal accounting seems a bit too simple while investment banking is too…"

"Cutthroat?"

"I was going to say 'irresponsible.' I mean, it may sound stupid—I'm probably in the wrong business—but I don't want to sit around counting other people's money. I'd like to do something meaningful. Working for a socially-conscious nonprofit would be ideal."

"Sounds like a noble use of your talents."

"I don't know about noble. It may be a huge mistake. Most of my classmates are going on to grad school to become hedge-fund managers, or try to shoulder their way into a big corporation." She made a face. "The simulations are close enough to that for me."

"Simulations?"

"We use a company's financial data and current economic trends to mock up portfolios for imaginary investors. Over the course of the semester we have to show the profits and losses, and calculate earnings, dividends, that sort of thing. I was assigned a huge, soulless corporation with a fat carbon footprint and no social conscience to speak of. EllisIntel, it's called."

"EllisIntel." Julian frowned. "I believe David's invested in them for me. How bad are they?"

"Well, right now they're in trouble overseas for factory worker violations. They've almost single-handedly ruined a river in Venezuela, and *now* there's talk they're going to partner with some big fracking company out of Oklahoma." She waited until the waiter finished removing their appetizer dishes. "On the other hand, they make money for their shareholders like they were printing it. You could stand to lose a considerable fortune, if you decided to sell."

"Sounds like it would be worth it."

Natalie started to reply when Julian's cell phone chimed from inside the pocket of his jacket. She realized she'd never seen him take a call before.

"Sorry," he said, and pressed a button to silence the ring. "That was David, actually."

"Might it be important?"

"He can leave a message."

The waiter returned with their main dishes and Natalie swooned at the gorgeous slice of fish on her plate. "I haven't had halibut since Mexico."

Julian cocked an eyebrow. "I seem to recall you telling me you didn't travel."

Natalie smiled faintly. She hadn't meant to mention Mexico; it just popped out. "It was a long time ago. Seven years ago now. Puerto Vallarta."

"With your parents?" he asked gently.

"Yes," she said, casting her gaze to her plate as the memory swam up at her. "I was sixteen. My dad let me drink a little bit of his margarita, which somehow turned into *a lot* of margarita, and the next thing I knew I was rolling under the table, laughing my head off. And my mom was *pissed*. She was still yelling at my dad all through my first hangover." She smiled at the memory and then looked up to see Julian watching her with soft eyes. "Anyway," she said, "this looks amazing. Shall we?"

"Yes, but I have one more question."

Natalie twisted her napkin under her lap, bracing herself. She'd had too much wine to be talking this much about her parents. "What is it?"

"Why accounting?"

Natalie blinked. "What? Oh, why did I pick something so boring?"

"No," he said. "Why did you pick something so solid and exact, when you are so fluid and luminous?"

Natalie felt his compliment wash over her like soft, warm water. "I...I'm not..."

"You are." He was looking at her in a way that made her want to tell him everything, anything...

"Accounting is safe," she answered when she'd found her voice. "The numbers don't change. I mean, they can be moved around and manipulated. But four plus four will always equal eight, you know? They're emotionless. After my parents...Well, I have my books to provide me with all the emotion I can take. I want a profession that will never, ever remind me of something I don't want to be reminded of." She heaved a breath. "So that's the long answer. Short answer: I also enjoy it. Go figure."

Julian's smile was sad, warm, and brilliant all at once. He held up his wine glass. "To the socially-conscious nonprofit that will be lucky enough to find you walking through its doors in about six months."

She raised her glass with his, struggling to find some pithy toast for him. She couldn't think of one single thing but that he was absolutely beautiful, and that she managed to keep to herself.

***

The lunch was exquisite, the wine perfect, and the conversation danced from one easy topic to another. After dessert Natalie felt giddy, and reached into her bag before she could talk herself out of it.

"Merry Christmas," she said. Julian appeared genuinely touched. He opened the card and her stomach twisted. "Open the bigger one first," she said, hoping to distract him, and wishing mightily that she had written *Merry Christmas* instead of *Love, Natalie,* but it was too late now. Julian smiled as he read it and she took a long swallow of water.

He opened the first gift and admired the composition books appreciatively. "I thought I might be short a book or two. Thank you."

"Um, sure," she said, and watched him open the antique fountain pen, her heart in her throat.

He said nothing but turned it over in his hand. Its warm wood gleamed, and the pewter nib, with delicate art deco etchings, glowed in the candlelight.

Natalie cleared her throat. "The clerk told me it once belonged to John Steinbeck, but I'm sure that's not true."

"It's beautiful," Julian told her. His eyes were like blue velvet in the dimness. "It's perfect. Again, thank you."

She eased a sigh of relief and then choked a second later as he pulled a flat, rectangular box out of his jacket pocket and held it out to her wordlessly.

"As if this wasn't enough?" she said, indicating the restaurant.

"You need something to open."

She took the gift quickly, so he wouldn't see her hands tremble, and opened the delicate wrapping and the box inside. A micro mosaic pendant lay against the black velvet. A willow tree in pale jade swayed over a lapis lakeshore. Mother of pearl and garnet accents decorated the edges. The chain was long and gold. A lot of very real gold.

"Julian…" she breathed.

"Do you like it?" He toyed with this dessert fork. "I saw it and thought it suited you. If you don't like it, I can take it back."

"Oh, hush." She slipped it over her neck. The pendant lay beautifully against her blouse. "It's just stunning. Thank you."

He started to smile and then frowned. "There was a card…" He fished around in his jacket pocket. "It's a little late now."

Natalie held out her hand, eyebrows raised.

Julian laughed shortly and gave it to her, looking away as she read it.

Merry Christmas and Happy Hanukkah, it read, and Natalie felt that soft water warmth all over again at the last words.

Love, Julian

***

He parked in front of her building, shut off the engine, and then sat with both hands gripping the steering wheel. Natalie curled toward him, warmed and drowsy by the heat emanating from the leather seats, and more than a little tipsy from the wine. The day's sublimity was making her bold; she had a sudden image of standing before him in her apartment wearing nothing but the pendant. Her skin flushed hotly at the thought. She'd never felt this way before, could never have *imagined* feeling this way about anyone. But not even her ingrained shyness could stop her from reaching out and taking Julian's hand in hers.

It surprised him, she saw, and he turned in his seat to look at her, to watch her hold his hand in both of hers. His eyes were full of warmth and longing. He leaned closer and the nearness of him was more intoxicating than any wine. The scent of his skin and his cologne, the sweetness of his breath…She even savored the scent of his fine clothing that smelled new and clean. And his eyes…the blue of his eyes was a tropical sea and she fell into them, became submerged in their depths.

"Natalie…"

"Yes." She smiled drowsily even as her pulse quickened. It was almost as if she'd become accustomed to how he set her at ease and completely undid her at the same time.

"Ah, god, don't look at me like that," he said, his voice thick.

"Like what?"

"Seductive."

"No one has ever called me seductive before."

"Impossible," he said gruffly, and before she could draw a breath, he took her face in both of his hands and kissed her.

Natalie was thankful she was already sitting down; she felt herself falling away, dizzy and drunk for this, the first kiss, that she had been dreaming about for months.

His lips were gentle, caressing hers, sweeping over them. She could do nothing at first but tilt her head back and let him do as he pleased until his tongue ventured to touch her. A gentle invasion, a *wanted* invasion. She parted her lips wider to accept him, let him explore her, and then kissed him back, stroking the warm velvety wetness of his tongue with hers. *Oh god, delicious.* He tasted of the Crème Brule they'd shared for dessert, expensive wine, and beneath that, his own delectable sweetness.

Natalie heard a little moan escape her. She pushed out of her seat toward Julian, wanting to feel more of him, and slipped her hand into the curls of his hair that felt just as soft and silky as she had imagined them to be. He moved closer, grazing her lower lip with his teeth before covering her mouth completely with his. Their tongues danced and stroked and slid along each other until Natalie lost all sense of time and place. There was only this incredible sensation, and the *want* it was building inside her.

Julian shifted, trying to maneuver closer in the enclosed space of the car. A short blast of the horn startled them both and they flinched away. Natalie laughed nervously, while trying to catch her breath. Julian did not.

He looked about, like a sleepwalker awakened, and put his hands back on the steering wheel.

"Julian?" Natalie started to reach for him but suddenly felt she shouldn't.

"I…" He twisted his hands around the wheel, not looking at her. "I'm sorry. I didn't mean to start anything until…"

Natalie bit her lip where she imagined she could still feel his touch, fading now. "What is it?"

"I have something to tell you."

He sounded hesitant, agitated, when a moment before he had been lost in the kiss with her. *Hadn't he?* She sat back in her seat, bracing herself. The warm flush of desire he'd kindled in her was rapidly vanishing. "Okay," she said slowly. "I'm listening."

"I should have told you sooner," he said, his gaze still on the nearly empty street outside the windshield, "but I didn't know how. Not without leaving you thinking I'm a lunatic or that I'm playing a horrible, cruel joke. Even at this moment, I fear you will think that and hate me."

Natalie's heart began to clang dully against her chest. The contentment, the pure joy of the day was seeping out of her moment by moment, leaving her cold. She waited for him to say more and when he didn't, the silence became unbearable.

"Is it…that you're seeing someone else?" she ventured. "Oh, not someone *else,*" she added quickly, her cheeks burning, "because you and I…we're not really seeing each other. Are we? I mean…we haven't…until today." Her hands trembled and she clutched them tightly in her lap. "We just talk. Five months…off and on, and our talks are so nice, *more* than nice. They're incredible. But I just…I'm not sure what we're doing."

"That's my fault," Julian said, turning to look at her finally, his expression pained. "All of it. My fault. I know my behavior must seem strange, but please believe me there's a reason for it."

Natalie nodded though she was more confused than ever. And afraid. *Is he breaking it off?* "What is it?"

Julian held her gaze a moment, a thousand thoughts behind his eyes, words forming in his mouth…And then he abruptly sat back in his seat.

"It's uh…well, it's complicated. Too complicated to discuss here, in the car." He closed his eyes and shook his head. "This is all wrong. I'm making a mess of everything. The very last thing I want to do is hurt you."

Though her heart might shatter with his next word, she had to know. "You can tell me. Please. Tell me."

"Yes," he said, firmer now. "Yes, of course. I should. I will. But…not here. Let's go—"

Julian's cell phone rang from the pocket of his jacket, its insistent chiming filling the car.

"I'm sorry," he said, and fished it from his pocket. He glanced at the screen, frowned, and jabbed a button. The chiming ceased and he tossed the iPhone onto the dash. "What was I saying? Nothing that makes any sense, I'm sure."

"You said we should go—"

The chiming came again and Julian scrubbed his hands over his face. "*Maldita sea al infierno*," he swore and grabbed the phone from the dash. "It's David again. I don't know what he's calling about." He jabbed the button again and then flipped a tiny switch on the side of the phone. "Muted," he said but before he could put the phone away, it vibrated in his hand. He bit off another curse. "Natalie, I'm so sorry. Let me…" He put the phone to his ear.

Natalie sat back in her seat, her hands twisting in her lap.

"What?" Julian demanded into the phone by way of greeting and then listened for a moment, his beautiful features twisted by irritation. "*What?* Why would they think…?" She saw him glance at her, and then he turned away, lowering his voice. "Yes, of course it's my charge. This is ridiculous."

Natalie's stomach twisted, feeling certain Julian and his assistant were talking about her. She quickly turned her gaze on the quiet street. *Today had been so perfect.*

"Authorize it, David," Julian snapped into the phone, angry now. "*Authorize it.*" He hung up and sat with the phone turning over and over in his hands, his expression stony, his voice tight. "Natalie, I'm so sorry. This isn't how I wanted today to end, I promise you."

She forced a tremulous smile. "It's okay." Her fingers blundered over the door handle. "I understand," she added, though nothing could be further from the truth.

"No, Natalie, wait—"

"I should go," Natalie opened the door. "Maybe we're not ready yet...or I don't know. Thank you for the lovely lunch and...for everything," she managed before tears choked her completely, and got out of the car, fumbled her keys into her own door and disappeared behind it without looking back.

Upstairs, in her empty place, she stared about vacantly. She worried that she had overreacted by getting out of the car; but she couldn't withstand the crushing confusion a moment more, not when things between her and Julian had seemed to be progressing—finally—toward something more. His kiss, his magnificent kiss, was like a promise that her loneliness was over; a bright and shining gift dangled before her and then vanishing the moment she touched it.

Below, she heard the angry squeal of tires on concrete, and the roar of a high-powered engine that quickly grew distant and faded away. She touched her fingertips to her lips, where Julian's mouth had swept over hers so sweetly, one question turning over and over in her mind.

Why had it all gone wrong?

CHAPTER TEN

With a satisfied smile, David Thompson pushed "end" and dropped his cell phone into his jacket pocket. He got out of his car and jogged to the elevator, pushing his brown flyaway hair out of his eyes, his footsteps echoing hollowly in the cavern of concrete of the underground lot. He keyed in a security code that allowed the elevator to take him up, past the lobby, to the residences. At the fifteenth floor, he keyed in another security code that granted him access to Julian Kovač's penthouse apartment and stepped inside. A cold, gray light illuminated the living area, ushered in from the immense windows that overlooked the city and bay. The sky was leaden. He flipped on a light.

The apartment was stark. Elegant. Cold. Just as David liked it. No sign of the holidays anywhere to ruin the perfect, stylish aesthetic. Why bother with tacky decorations, David had hinted carefully to Julian, when he would be alone anyway?

But Julian had countered that by taking that Natalie woman out. She hadn't any family and Julian didn't want *her* to be alone. *What about me?* David thought. *He's* my *family; my true family. After six years you'd think he'd realize that.* But lately, Julian's thoughts revolved only around Natalie Hewitt.

David's ulcer had flared on that summer night last August when Julian confided in him about the coffee shop in the Sunset District and the girl behind the counter. Julian had discovered what he thought might be the perfect place to write his next book, but it was clearly the girl he was intent on. When he began going to that café four or five days a week, the acidic burn in David's gut burrowed deeper—the same sort of anxiety he'd had when Julian brought his last girlfriend, Samantha, home for the first time.

But this was worse.

Julian hadn't spoken about Samantha in the same way, or as warmly as he talked about this Natalie woman. He hadn't worn strange, funny smiles, or tuned out of conversations with faraway expressions on his face. Over the last few months, David had done his best to subtly caution Julian not to get involved, to remember the disaster that Samantha had turned out to be. But time and again Julian said, "I think this could be different," in a soft, blissful way that made David very nervous.

Now Julian was on a date with the girl. The fact that it had taken him nearly five months to arrive at that event was David's sole consolation. *That and an ill-timed phone call or two.* A small triumph, but it was time to get down to the serious business.

He went to his office off the hallway behind the kitchen, and turned on more lights and the computer. He thought about brewing coffee, but decided he wouldn't stay long enough to need it; his true purpose for being there wouldn't take but a moment. His gut twisted at the notion as it had every month for the last eight months. And again, he had to quell the queasiness by reminding himself that there was no other way to keep Julian safe.

No other way.

David checked the security console. There was one mounted in every major room of the apartment. Above the keypad were three lights, two of which were dark. The third light shone orange. It meant the system was armed but someone authorized—himself—was in the residence. It would flash red when someone approached the front door and then green if they had the code. No other lights came on; he was alone. At the computer, he opened up Julian's bank accounts and investment holdings, keyed in usernames and passwords. He dragged the screens so that they were side-by-side, their activity and totals all before him.

In the monthly expense account was the money to pay the regular bills, and the Home Owners Association fee on the penthouse that looked like a mortgage payment in and of itself. David paid all of this electronically, and wrote a check for Esther, the cleaning woman—whom Julian paid *far* more than was reasonable, in David's mind—setting a clean slate for January, and leaving Julian plenty of money for anything minor he might want or need.

His second duty was to handle the Platinum Amex credit card bill, and this month's balance was massive—much more than Julian usually spent—with holiday shopping. The card carried a top-of-the-line set of golf clubs for his editor, Len Gordon, and a gift basket of wine, chocolate, and a cashmere scarf for Len's wife. It also bore a huge charge for the gold-and-diamond Bulgari watch that now glittered on David's wrist. His heart fluttered with joy that Julian had spent so much on him, but a sour look crossed his features at the next item.

Julian had spent a ridiculous amount of money at a boutique jewelry store. A present for Natalie. Some trinket that cost less than David's watch, but still too much by half. *The little coffee shop tart isn't worth that much.* He'd known about the necklace, of course. No dollar spent escaped David's awareness; it was part of his job to manage and protect Julian's wealth. *I protect him in all things,* he thought, and paid the bill off.

He looked at the investment accounts and stock holdings in which the bulk of Julian's fortune was doing them both some good. David beamed to see the numbers for EllisIntel LLC, especially. It was the kind of company that made Julian's eyes glaze over with disinterest at the mere mention. He'd only agreed to invest at David's urging, and never even thanked him when the company skyrocketed.

"One cannot live on royalties alone, my dear," he muttered. At least not without sacrificing some of the lavish lifestyle David had established for them. But EllisIntel wasn't just a moneymaker. Eight months ago, it became a lifesaver. *Mine and Julian's, though he doesn't know it.*

David pulled an envelope from his jacket pocket, fresh from yesterday's mail. It was addressed to Mr. Julian Kovač, sent from EllisIntel Holdings. The quarterly dividend check. Money Julian didn't know about because as far as he knew, EllisIntel didn't pay dividends.

Oh, but they do.

David's heart thudded dully in his chest as he opened the envelope. He already had an idea how much it would be by tracking the company's stellar performance in the markets, but he still nearly wept with relief to see $63,890 in black and white.

"Sixty-three thousand…" He clutched the check to his chest. He'd have enough to keep Julian safe from those blackmailing thugs for another three months…just in time for another dividend check to arrive in March. "God bless EllisIntel."

David shot another glance at the security console, and even peeked over his shoulder, as if Julian could materialize behind him like a ghost. Bile rose in his throat and sweat broke out on his forehead. It never got any easier. With fingers that trembled with reluctance, he took out his smart phone, brought up a banking app, and took a picture of the check.

"Like magic," he said sourly.

Sixty-three thousand dollars Julian didn't know was his was now safely deposited in a savings account he didn't know he had. David took the check, and instead of filing it in with the other financial documents in the cabinet beside his desk, tucked it back into his inner jacket pocket to take back to his own apartment.

Then, as he always did, David whispered, "I'm sorry," to the computer and hurriedly signed out of all the accounts.

The job was half-done. The second part of his task was infinitely worse than the first, but the banks were closed. The delivery would have to wait until tomorrow.

He took a deep breath and ran both hands through his unruly brown hair. The empty silence of the apartment began to pull at him, enticing. Julian wasn't here, and yet he was. The very air was tinged with his scent: the remnants of soap and steam from his shower; the cleanliness of his fine clothes, his cologne... David could almost sense what routes Julian had walked through the house earlier that day. The kitchen was cold, but David smelled ribbons of coffee, eggs, and chorizo hanging above the counter, dissipating slowly. Julian was everywhere. David wanted more.

The desire rose fiercely this time, taking him by surprise. The thievery hurt and so his devotion to Julian surged to assuage his guilt, to reassure his conscience that what he did was out of love. And it wasn't often he indulged his hungers, but it was Christmas Day, he reasoned. A gift to himself.

David drew a duster from a cabinet in the kitchen if Julian happened to come home and catch him unawares. It was a meager excuse and hardly necessary in any event. Julian's trust was David's best defense.

He meandered toward the back of the apartment, twiddling the duster here and there, until he arrived at Julian's bedroom. He let out a little gasp. Julian was fastidious, but not obsessive: the bed was made but the towel from his morning shower lay over the comforter, like a gift left for a lover.

Left for me. David swallowed hard. *Save it,* he thought, and kept to his usual route.

First the bathroom. Quartz counters with gleaming chrome fixtures, marble walls veined with silver, dark gray ceramic tile floors. Coldly beautiful. Masculine. David trailed his fingers in the little puddles of water left on the sink from Julian's morning ablutions, and picked up Julian's toothbrush. It had been in his mouth, had been past his lips and along his tongue… David chuckled to envy a toothbrush and set it down.

The bedroom was brighter but no less elegant. The hardwood floors were dark, the walls pale, the furniture modern Italian with asymmetrical designs in beige and gray. David thought it all beautiful and perfect, but then he had been in charge of the design renovation while Julian had been working on a book, so of course it was beautiful. He made certain Julian had only the best.

David turned next to the walk-in closet. Usually on the rare occasions he indulged in one of these covert excursions into Julian's private chambers, he saved the closet for last. But there was a bathroom towel on the bed…

The closet doors glided soundlessly open and the feather duster fell from David's fingers. There was nothing to dust here. If Julian caught him, he'd make up a story about wanting to take inventory before making a new purchase. It was one of his favorite tasks—ordering Julian's clothes. Julian cared little for styles or labels, so long as he appeared neat and comfortable. David took that indifference and made the most of it, dressing Julian as if he were a doll, taking great pains to see that his clothes were elegant and tailored to his body. David had his measurements memorized, and he delighted in finding expensive clothes from Milan or New York and imagining how the rich fabric would lie against Julian's dusky skin, or how they would accentuate his fit frame.

David went to the hanging shirts and coats, embraced them, inhaling deeply. L'eau Serge Lutins, Julian's preferred cologne, filled his nose with its clean, crisp scent. David would have preferred something with more personality, but Julian never wore anything else. It was his signature scent, and now David appreciated it for how it immediately conjured Julian in his mind.

The third wall, the wall opposite the door, was his favorite. A mahogany dresser held socks and underwear in the bottom three drawers. Stored on the top: cufflinks, tie pins, watches, and other personal treasures from his past, such as foreign coins and photos. David never touched the items in the top drawer. He was not a thief by nature, no matter that those horrible men forced him to be one. He respected Julian's privacy and only opened the drawer, never touching what lay inside.

Someday, he thought, he would be in the top-drawer of Julian's life, loved and protected just as David loved and protected him. And he was close—so close—to that love. He was sure of it. Julian trusted him completely, had handed him the greatest secret of his life and asked him to guard it with his own. The sting of his one little failure bit at him, but he brushed it aside. It was minor and he had it under control. He would never let anyone hurt Julian. Never.

David took a deep breath that quavered when he exhaled, and left the closet. On the bed, the towel was waiting for him. It was still damp.

He sat on the bed, holding the cloth to him, inhaling its scent and touching its softness to his cheek. It had touched Julian's wet skin, kissed it and left it dry and warm. Julian had held it in his hands and used it over every part of his body, and then discarded it without a thought. David shuddered. To be used so...

He squeezed his eyes shut and hugged the towel to him, curling his legs around it. He let his imagination go, and it began with soft, loving caresses and long, lingering kisses that he could feel in the pit of his stomach.

He pressed the towel between his legs, inhaling its scent again and again. His body rocked and he moaned. The phantom of Julian's body was over his, his tanned skin taut with lean muscle. His hands, long-fingered and deft, touched David—he reached his hand under his waistband—with strong, hard strokes.

"Yes..."

He was writhing now, the towel clenched between his teeth and Julian was riding him mercilessly, driving into him with hard, impassioned thrusts. David cried out, a half-laugh, half-sob, and his hand was full of his own sticky wetness. He buried his face in the towel. "I love you."

It was dangerous to forget himself like that, but sometimes the desire was too much. The constant, day-in, day-out of it granted him no peace or rest. If he didn't indulge from time to time, he thought he'd go mad from the sheer relentlessness of it. He closed his eyes and as his breath became deep and even, it drew him into a relaxation made all the more wondrously heavy and deep by his pleasure.

He started drifting toward sleep, hoping to dream of impossible blue eyes and whispered promises that he would never be alone when the alarm panel by the bedroom door *beeped*. Panic pierced his heart. Julian was home.

David jumped to his feet and smoothed his rumpled clothing. He didn't think Julian would remember what he'd done with his towel that morning; he wiped his hand on it and tossed the towel into the clothes hamper. He could hear Julian moving about in the living room.

David rumpled his hair up on one side and walked into the living area, stretching and pretending to yawn. "Oh, I didn't hear you come in."

"What are you doing here?"

"I came in to do some year-end account cleanup." He offered a sheepish smile. "A good excuse anyway, for escaping the terminal dysfunction of my family around the holidays. I must have fallen asleep at my desk. What time is it?"

Julian said nothing; his gorgeous eyes were on the cityscape around him. He looked extremely displeased. *Did my phone call do that?* He thought it just might have. Julian stood in his customary stance that meant he was trying to regain control of his fiery temper: stiff and still, like a statue. David knew it well. Julian was a passionate, emotional man. He had to be, David supposed, to write as well as he did. His temper was slow to burn but when it flared, he used his talent with words to cut the object of his anger to ribbons. He struggled painfully with it, and, David was pleased to note, he was struggling now.

"How uh…how did your date go?"

"Not well, thanks in no small part to your incessant phone calls." Julian's blue steel gaze could have frozen boiling water, but David had his defense planned and prepared. "What the hell were you doing, David?"

"I know," David said, all contriteness and regret, humbling himself like a groveling dog. "I feel terrible. I absolutely loathed interrupting your date, but the credit card company has never been so insistent before."

Julian's rigid posture didn't bend an inch. "It was humiliating."

Music to my ears. David's face was a perfect mask of agony. "Oh Christ, Julian, I'm so sorry. I thought that might happen but I worried they'd cut you off and you'd be *more* humiliated trying to use the card and be denied with—Natalie, was it?—standing right there." He held up his hands in a helpless gesture. "Lesser of two evils."

Julian remained stony for a moment more and then released himself from the prison of his rigid stance and sank onto the couch, his back to David, his voice ripe with defeat. "I can't lay all the blame at your feet. Or any of it, really. *I* thoroughly wrecked the date at the end. Until then, it had been exquisite."

David bit back his smile of triumph. "What happened?" he asked. "If you want to talk, I mean…"

"What the hell am I doing?" Julian said. "Five months. Five months and I finally work up the nerve to ask her out and then I spoil it with more hesitancy and awkwardness."

David sat in the chair across from Julian, keeping his face open and sympathetic. "You're being cautious. There's nothing wrong with that."

"Cautious?" Julian snorted. "I'm being insanely defensive. She's going to think I'm a lunatic, if she doesn't already."

"Julian, in light of what happened with Samantha—"

"This is different," he snapped. "I think Natalie cares for me. I know she does. But I'm too pessimistic to believe she feels as strongly for me as I do for her."

"You feel…strongly about her?" David's stomach began to twist the triumph of his interference right out of him.

Julian hung his head between his hands. "I'm in love with her."

David was proud he managed not to flinch, given how Julian's words slapped him.

"But I've likely ruined it."

A ray of hope. "What happened? I mean…aside from my terribly uncouth interruption."

"I wanted to tell her everything. I owe it to her, before we start anything. But she loves the writing so much." Julian carved his hands through his hair. "Guess who her favorite author is? And not her favorite the way someone prefers blue over red, or cats over dogs. She feels spiritually connected to…*him*. I thought if I told her the truth she'd feel trapped in the car with a madman, and I just…I bumbled everything. I couldn't speak. I'm supposed to be so deft with words," his voice dripped sarcasm, "and I couldn't find any to properly explain myself. So she left— escaped, really—and I don't blame her."

David hadn't heard much after, *I wanted to tell her everything.* After those words, his blood had turned to sludge in his veins. "The secret keeps you safe," he managed. "You know that."

"Maybe. Or maybe not. I feel as though some horrid twist of fate is testing me and the vow I made to my mother. I'm telling you, David, I was ready to throw it all away." Julian sighed. "But I have to finish the book. It's nearly done and it needs to be completed at that café, with her."

David had never pretended to understand Julian's artistic process and he never cared to. His books were good—astonishing, if one believed the critics—and he was glad for that. They assured Julian more money with each publication. The money, invested properly, assured David of continued employment. To him, the novels—which he'd never read—were the means by which he could stay close to Julian, and for that reason alone, he cherished them in a way no one could understand.

"Why there?" David asked. "Why not just work in your library, free of distractions?"

"It's just…how it is," Julian said. "The book demands it. If I were to leave the café, the whole structure would fall apart. If it didn't have Natalie's presence it would wither and die like a plant shoved in a closet. I can't let it perish like that." He looked at David. "I think it's the best thing I've ever done."

David sat back in his chair. This was more complicated than he had thought. The fact Julian thought he was in love with this silly girl was surmountable; he could poison his thoughts against her given time, as he had with Samantha. But Julian was caught up in some ridiculous notion that his writing was connected to Natalie, as if he couldn't find some other dingy café in the city to write in. What possible difference could one make over another? David couldn't fathom it.

"I'm happy for you that your book is going well. But maybe it's best if you give yourself a break from that girl and try to finish it here. A change in perspective might do you some good."

Julian rose and rested his hand on his shoulder. David's skin tingled pleasurably at the touch.

"I know you think I'm afflicted with a crazy eccentricity, but it is what it is. I have to go back. I can't live like this anymore."

David's throat went dry. "Live like what?"

Julian didn't answer, but smiled ruefully. "Merry Christmas, David. Go home now," he said as he retreated to his room. "Your family will think I'm a tyrant to have you work on the holiday."

It wasn't fair, David thought with a curse, as he left the penthouse and keyed the code behind him. He was working so hard to protect Julian. It wasn't fair that it should be this difficult, or that Julian's love should be spent on an unworthy nobody instead of on him. The elevator took him down, out of the heights of the city, to the street.

He got into his fire-engine red Audi Quattro—Julian paid him well—and drove with sullen lethargy back to his parent's home in Colma. A city decorated with graveyards. A city where the dead outnumbered the living. David shuddered as he drove past row after crooked row of headstones, imaging his own: neglected and flowerless if he failed. It was a strong reminder that coffee shop Natalie was the least of his worries.

CHAPTER ELEVEN

The following day David went to United One Bank and asked for ,Choi. She smiled warmly at him as she prepared the envelope. "I trust the homeless shelter had a wonderful Christmas?"

David blinked. "What? Oh, yes. They did."

She passed him the withdrawal form and a pen. "Thanks to your generosity."

Her smile made his teeth ache. "And now I'm hoping they have a Happy New Year as well," he said.

"I'm sure they will." Grace Choi discreetly, with a security guard behind her, counted two thick stacks of one hundred dollar bills, which David tucked into a manila envelope, and then his briefcase. "You're doing a good thing," she called after him when he strode for the exit.

He shoved open the glass door. "I know."

***

It was early for the club to be open. Sharp shards of cold December light pierced David's eyes as he drove along Mission Street. It wasn't even noon but he recognized Cliff's white pick-up in the Club Orbit's tiny back parking lot. David's heart thudded dully in his chest. He pulled up next to the truck, glass crunching under his tires. If he pulled a nail out of one of the Audi's tires later, he thought, he'd be pissed.

From behind, Orbit looked less like a nightclub, and more like a run-down, one-story business that might sell siding or do car detailing. Dirty white walls tagged with unintelligible graffiti faced the parking lot. Adjacent to a shuttered, barred window, was a backdoor that sealed the place shut. David knocked on it smartly and squared his shoulders. It was humiliating enough, what he had to do. They didn't have to read it on his face.

Cliff Tate answered the door himself. His brother, Garrett, the ugly blond beast of a bouncer, must not be in yet. Cliff was a fatter, older version of Garrett, and the owner, proprietor and bartender of the club. It was to this odious man David had inadvertently spilled Julian's secret. *To have that day back...*

Cliff blinked into the sunlight. "What? Oh, it's you." He held out his hand in an indifferent, presumptive manner that made David bristle.

David handed over the envelope. "January's payment," he said coldly, as if he were the one collecting.

Cliff peered into the envelope and flipped through the bills with his thumb. He nodded and started to shut the door on David. "See you next month."

"Cliff, wait."

The man halted at the door, not bothering to conceal his irritation. "Yeah?"

David swallowed. "How many more? It's been eight months. I can't keep doing this…"

Cliff heaved a sigh. "Every month, Dave. Every month you give me this tired song and dance about how you can't keep doing this, and every month you keep doing this. So let's just spare each other the spiel. You *will* keep doing this so long as I tell you to. If you want your boy to keep his cover—and his brains—intact, that's all you gotta know. There. Feel better? Okay, bye-bye now."

The door closed and David heard the clicking and sliding of at least three locks. He clutched his stomach as the burn of his ulcer flared. "It's not fair. Not fair at all."

He sped from the driveway, his tires spitting gravel and glass in a satisfying hail against the side of the club. "Serves them right," he muttered.

When he reached his apartment in Bernal Heights, the right front tire was flat.

CHAPTER TWELVE

In mid-January the three friends met up in Liberty's favorite bar in the Mission where they sipped margaritas under the watchful gazes of Carmen Miranda and James Dean. Cuban music filled the darkened spaces, and the *crack* of a pool game starting sounded from behind them. Liberty and Marshall bickered and gossiped as per usual, both seeming to have forgotten about Julian. Natalie thought that was appropriate.

"I'm going to get drunk," she announced.

"I second that." Liberty leaned over the bar and hailed the bartender who knew her by name.

Marshall cocked a brow at Natalie. "You okay?"

"I survived the holidays."

He watched her. "If you say so."

Liberty procured another round of cocktails but instead of fulfilling her vow to get drunk, Natalie sipped slowly at her margarita and listened to her friends' good-natured griping.

"What happened to New Year's?" Marshall wondered. "Came and went. Just like that."

Liberty sighed. "Yeah, it sucked."

"I was stuck at this ridiculous party in Newark, New Jersey for god's sake." Marshall punctuated his words with a sloshing cocktail. "And this guy, an ex-cast member of Rent, plants one on me at midnight. I said, 'Honey, just because we're the only two gay men in *Newark* doesn't mean we have go and make some sort of *statement.*"

Liberty scowled. "So you socked him one?"

"Oh, no, we made out like bandits," Marshall said. "You have to remember, I was in *Newark* for god's sake."

"And what about you, Lib?" Natalie asked. "Kiss anyone?"

"I don't kiss and tell, New Year's or not."

"That would be a 'no'," Marshall said.

"Shut up."

Natalie toyed with her swizzle stick until she realized her friends had gone silent and were watching her. "What?"

"Spill it, girl," Liberty said. "What's with the manic depression?"

"What…What do you mean?"

"Until, like, *this morning* you haven't answered my phone calls or emails or texts or Facebook messages—"

"I'm not on Facebook."

"A rare and endangered specimen of humanity," Marshall commented.

"Whatever," Liberty scoffed. "The point is, getting you here was a minor miracle and now you've clammed up. It's one thing to be a little mopey; hell, my PMS would kill a lesser woman. But this is different. What gives?"

"Okay," Natalie said with a sigh. "But let's sit somewhere quieter."

The bar had a patio out back; they took a wooden table in a corner, and Marshall and Liberty sat to one side, to give her room. She offered a grateful smile but it wavered and quickly vanished. "I had a date with Julian."

The responses were simultaneous.

"What?"

"Who?"

Liberty elbowed Marshall. "You know. Julian…from the coffee shop. The creepy weird one who hangs out all night, *journaling.*"

"There's nothing creepy or weird about him," Natalie said tiredly, but Liberty didn't seem to have heard.

"Hold up. You had a *date?* When?"

"On Christmas Day. He took me to a nice restaurant—"

"Christmas?" Liberty snapped. "That was ages ago! *Last year,* if you want to technical about it."

"Liberty…" Marshall said in a low voice.

"I'm sorry, I just *assumed* that friends would share this sort of information as it happened." She lit a cigarette with a huff.

Marshall was more conciliatory. "Why didn't you tell us, honey?"

"Because there's nothing to tell. We had a nice lunch and…that's it."

"What do you mean, that's it?"

"Just…nothing happened. We kissed and—"

"You *kissed* him?" Liberty's eyes flashed. "What the exact hell, Natalie?"

"Liberty, for chrissakes, let her tell the damn story."

"I'm just trying to figure out how all this happens without so much as a phone call."

Natalie put her hands over her eyes. "I couldn't call you. It's too embarrassing."

Liberty tamped her cigarette out and asked in a stubbornly softer tone, "What happened?"

"I don't know," Natalie said miserably. "Everything was just lovely and then it all fell apart. He had something he wanted to tell me but was afraid, and I was afraid to hear it. The date ended about as awkwardly as you can imagine—even by my standards—and I just...I ran away and I haven't heard from him since. Okay? Happy? Because I'm not." She shook her head, disgusted with herself, as tears began to well up. "And of course I have to cry about it. Again. Because all I do is cry. Instead of talking and figuring stuff out, I cry. So there you go."

"I didn't realize you liked him so much," Liberty said. "Are you going to see him again?"

"I don't think so. I'm pretty sure he wanted to tell me he didn't want to see me anymore."

"That doesn't make sense," Marshall said. "You two kissed—"

"Yes, but that's when it got so weird. Maybe I'm a terrible kisser. God knows I'm out of practice." Natalie waved her hands. "Anyway, it's been two weeks. He hasn't been back to the café since." She dabbed her eyes with a cocktail napkin. "That means it's over, right? I think it's over."

Liberty pursed her lips. "We need shots. Tequila. Stat."

"God no, not tequila."

"Tequila is just the thing. The guy's obviously a nutjob. Get good and plastered and forget all about him."

Natalie started to protest but she hadn't the energy. Marshall brought a round of tequila shots to the table and he held up a little glass of the golden liquor. "The eternal sunshine of spotless minds."

"To forgetting him," Liberty said, and downed her shot as though it were water.

"To forgetting him," Natalie said dully.

She held her shot a moment, turning it in her hand, then tossed it down. By the end of the night, she was as good and drunk as she had first promised herself, but nowhere near close to erasing Julian from her thoughts.

I don't want to erase him, she thought, her heart aching. *I love him too much.*

CHAPTER THIRTEEN

The book had taken on a life of its own.

Julian didn't know at what point he had stopped writing it for the sake of the story and when he'd begun to write it for Natalie. Not even halfway, he guessed, given how the arcs had progressed. It was infused with Natalie; she inhabited its pages so that Julian sometimes felt as though he were merely a vessel, that some other power were using him to capture her spirit. His more practical side had a simpler explanation: he was madly in love with her. Her spirit inhabited *him*, infused *him* so that his writing—like his every thought—couldn't help but be saturated with her.

Whatever the reason, I have to finish it. For her.

He sat in the car outside Niko's that late January night, dreading how selfish and pigheaded he must seem, but it couldn't be helped. If he blurted out the truth without plan or evidence, she wouldn't believe him. She'd evict him from the café—and her life—for good.

Steeling himself, he tore out of the car and strode toward the café before he could change his mind. She was alone, sitting behind the counter, a book in her hand, though he could see from the street that she was preoccupied. His heart ached for the disquiet on her delicate features, and shame burned him to know he'd put it there.

It's almost finished. Then I'll tell her everything, and pray she'll forgive me.

The bell tolled above him—a discordant jangle that set his nerves on edge. Natalie's face lit up at the sight of him and then dimmed almost immediately. He cursed himself. *You did that. You and your fumbling cowardice.*

"Natalie," he said. He ached to tell her how beautiful she was, how her kiss on Christmas Day had been the most exquisite thing he'd known in so many lonely nights, but it wouldn't be fair. "I have to finish the book," he told her in a quiet voice. "After it's done, I'll—"

"Okay, Julian," Natalie said quickly, fanning her hands in front of her. "Just…do what you need to do and then…I don't know."

"Natalie…"

"Here." She rummaged in her sweater pocket, and then held out her hand. She dropped the mosaic pendant into his.

"But it's yours."

"No. Someday, maybe…"

He nodded. *You have no right to expect anything more.*

The door chimed. Natalie wiped her eye. "I have customers."

Julian went to his customary table and got to work. He wrote in a constant, unbroken stream, marveling that the words could flow so effortlessly—and the story retain its hopeful cadences—despite the circumstances between them. There was no conversation that night and when she locked up, he waited a respectful distance away.

"Good night," he said. He had thousand more words behind those, but she slipped quickly into the shadows.

"Good night," she said, and let the gate close on its own.

***

February brought constant rains, and the café was quiet most evenings. Julian wrote furiously, driving the novel to its crescendo without looking back. The sense of being only a vessel came over him again, as he hardly had to think or ponder. He only needed to set pen to paper and the words came; the exact right words aligning in the exact right order. He'd experienced this before on other books, but could never sustain the euphoria—the pure submersion—of the work for so long. *It's because of her. It's all for her.*

Natalie was so patient. So kind. If anything could distract him from the writing, it was the urge to sweep it all to the floor and hold her in his arms instead. But he knew his limitations. His urges. It would be so easy to forget everything and lose himself in her as he had on Christmas Day. But he had to tell her first, and once he told her, there would be no going back. Revealing his secret was a distant second to letting himself love her as much as he did; laying his heart bare before her the much more dangerous endeavor. *I love her too much,* he thought, watching with an almost detached fascination as his pen—the pen she had given him—flew over the pages.

And then the book was finished.

A quiet, empty Tuesday night. The sky was heavy with rain, the air charged.

At quarter to ten, Julian wrote the final words and shut the composition book—one of five others that comprised the whole. He set down the pen and put his hand to his mouth, contemplating

what he had done. *It's ended and now we can begin.* He looked at
Natalie perched behind the register as usual, a book in her hand.
She'd been watching him; she knew what he'd done. *Did you wait
for me?* Julian wondered, and wasn't surprised to see her nod in
reply.

The sky broke open.

The rain fell in sheets, sounded like shattering glass as it
struck the pavement. The power went out without a flicker, and
the shop was plunged into blackness. Julian stood at the window,
held out his hand to her. Natalie wended her way through the
darkness with ease, and Julian steeled himself as her hand slipped
into his. Even that simple, chaste touch quickened his pulse.

They stood side by side, hand in hand, watching the raindrops
explode against the cement in silver bursts. The storm raged,
having swept the streets empty; Julian felt as though they were the
only two people in the world. Beside him, Natalie recited quietly:

"The earth turns her face up to meet the tears,
drinks them
And creates days from the sky's sorrow.
Between these implacable forces
We, little creatures
In shells of flesh and bone,
Dance…"

"…and beg for mercy," Julian finished, closing his eyes. His
words in her mouth…they finally sounded as he'd meant them to.

She turned to him, gasping. "You know it? From *Starshine.*
So beautiful, isn't it?"

"Not half so beautiful as you." He brushed a lock of hair
from her eyes. "I hope you can forgive me."

She leaned close to him; he could feel her heart thundering
under the soft cotton of her dress. "Breaking through old
routines…" she said, "it's not easy."

"No. But there are so many things I have to tell you." He said
this to himself as much as to her, to remember restraint.

"I know," she breathed. She slipped her arms around his
waist and tilted her chin.

"Natalie…Wait." Julian held her by the shoulders, his voice
hoarse with want. "When you look at me like that, I can't
think…"

"Don't think," she said. She leaned close, stood on her toes to reach him, her lips brushing his with every word. "Kiss me, Julian. Kiss me…"

Just one kiss, he thought before rational thought abandoned him completely. He slipped one hand to the back of her neck, the other to her waist, and in one swift motion pulled her to him like a drawstring closing, engulfing her completely.

Outside, rain and wind battered the windows. Inside, Julian felt Natalie's vitality, powerful and potent, sweeping him up in its own storm. He kissed her hard, with lips and tongue and teeth, pressing his hips against hers, until he was desperate to satiate the heavy need between them. She responded with equal passion; her hands slipped around his neck, holding his mouth to hers with her own fervor that was somehow ardent and gentle at the same time.

He groaned at her touch and surged against her, driven by a sublime, absolute synthesis of love and lust. One hand wound into her hair and pulled gently, exposing her neck to his mouth. She let out a half-cry, half-sigh of want that stirred his blood into a frenzy. He trailed kisses down her throat as his other hand slipped down to cup one small breast; it filled his hand perfectly, and she arched her back into his touch.

Desire whipped him again; he backed her against a table, pressed himself between her knees. She clung to him, wrapped her legs around his waist. He thought he'd go mad if he didn't have her then. An animal need was taking over, turning his hands greedy, his kisses savage. A vague, half-formed thought warned him that they were nearing the point of no return and he still hadn't told her anything, when lightning flashed outside, breaking their kiss, and saving him from his own unthinking lust.

"Your heart is racing," Julian said, breathing hard, the physical world rematerializing around him from a red haze of want. "Mine too. We should stop. We have to stop…"

"No, no," Natalie said, her own breath fluttering on every word. "I don't want to stop. It's okay…I'm ready."

"Natalie…"

"But…we shouldn't do this here," she continued, her face flushed and her dark eyes cloudy with passion. "And I should tell you now…I've only ever…once before. A few years ago." Her hands gripped the front of his shirt, twisting and untwisting. "I mean…I'm not a virgin but may as well be. I sort of feel like it, it's been so long. So I want it to be perfect…and now I'm babbling. God, I'm so sorry…"

"Don't say that," he said quickly. "Don't be sorry. For anything. It's better if we stopped. Natalie, I—"

"No…" she said and took a deep steadying breath. "I don't want to do nothing, Julian. We've done nothing for long enough."

Julian felt the tenor of his heartbeat change from the fiery pulsing of lust to the nervy stutter of worry and doubt. *She's right. And now you're going to stop again, hesitate again.* Engañar, *you let it go so far…* He held her hands more tightly, as if he could keep her from running away. "I can't. I want to, god, so badly Natalie, believe me, but not yet. I have to be honest with you. I have to tell you—"

"No." The open sweetness of her face began to fold, close down. "Not again," she whispered. "Don't do this to me again."

"Natalie, I'm sorry. I didn't mean for it to go so far. It's just so easy to become lost in you. The way you were looking at me, I—"

"So this—whatever it is you're doing—is my fault? I don't understand. What is happening? *Again?*"

"*Nothing* is your fault. No…Please, don't cry." He tried to touch her face but she pulled away. "I want nothing more on this earth than to spend the night with you. More than that; I want to be with you every moment of every day. I want to share my life with you, and now that the book is done, I'm ready. I'm ready to tell you everything, and I'm so terribly sorry I put you through such a strange, fruitless courtship." He cautiously stepped close and held her gently by the shoulders. "But it all pales in comparison to the betrayal you'd feel if I made love to you before you knew the truth."

She nodded and swallowed hard, her voice small and tremulous when she next spoke. "You're married, aren't you?"

He nearly burst out laughing at the absurdity but didn't dare. "No, I'm not."

Relief flitted over her delicate feature and was gone again. "Are you gay? Are you dying? I just don't…What is it?"

"I can't tell you now. Not here. Tomorrow night. At my home, where I can show you—"

"What? No. Tell me now."

"I can't, Natalie."

"Why not?"

"Because, my love," he said, infusing each word with as much truth as he could muster, "*you would not believe me.*" He could see the import sink in but he said it again. "You wouldn't believe me. I could quote a thousand poems, I could show you what's in those books—" he indicated the black and white comp book on the table, the last of his now-finished novel, "—but it wouldn't be enough. You'd think it all a terrible, manipulative ploy. I have to do it right. This is hard for me too, I promise you."

She blinked hard, her eyes glittering. "I don't understand. *Why* is it so hard to tell me? Why has it taken so long?"

He moved closer to her, cupped her face in his hands. The desire to kiss her again was fierce but giving in again would be unforgivable.

"Sometimes the mind shrinks away from what the heart wants because what the heart wants is so good, so impossibly extraordinary, that to keep it forever would be a miracle. The mind can imagine losing everything, while the heart can't. It only wants what it wants."

He felt her melt into his touch. "Am I…that? To you?"

"More than that." He stroked her cheek. "Come over tomorrow night. I'll make you dinner and tell you everything. Please."

Natalie nodded. "Okay," she whispered. "Okay."

He could've wept with relief. "Thank you."

Julian was grateful for the storm. There was nothing romantic about the cold, glassy pellets that stung his cheek, or the icy wind that dampened his ardor. He shielded Natalie from it with his coat as she locked up Niko's and then unlocked her gate. The concrete stairwell to her place was hollow, and gritty with tracked in mud. And dark. He loathed the idea of watching her make that ascent alone yet again, as much as he loathed the idea of returning to his own empty place. *Only once more,* he told himself as she slipped behind the wrought iron gate. *Once more and then we'll be free.*

CHAPTER FOURTEEN

"Are you sure you can handle all this mystery and intrigue?" Liberty asked.

Natalie could hear soft music in the background that meant her friend was at work. "No," she said. "Yes. I don't know." She plucked at a stray thread on her couch cushion. "I just thought I'd call and tell you…"

"In case he's a serial killer? Not that I'd be able to help since you *don't know where he lives.* "

"Financial District."

"Oh, that narrows it down."

"Look, I trust him. At least as much to know he's not going to kill me." Natalie smirked at the absurdity of those words. "I trust him," she said again. *He called me his love.* Her cheeks warmed at the thought.

"Then why are you calling me?"

"Maybe because it feels crazy if I keep it in my head."

"Mmmm," Liberty mused. "I wonder what the hell it is he's going to tell you. Aren't you dying to know?"

"Not really. Honestly, I just want it to be something that explains all the coming and going. Something normal."

"With men, there is no such thing as *normal.*" Liberty took a sharp intake of breath. "Oh my god, I've got it! He's got a kid. You know, like, from a previous marriage or something. And he doesn't want to bring any woman around until he's sure she's the real deal."

"Liberty, you're a genius!"

"Right? It explains everything. Those long stretches when he doesn't show up? That's when he's got custody."

"That makes the most sense. I knew it couldn't be something awful. I knew it."

"So now the real question is, are you okay with that? With being the Not Mommy in some kid's life? You'd be going from first date to instant family."

"No, that's not what still bothers me. Even if that's the reason, it's been *months.* I can't tell if I'm being reasonable or…"

"Taken advantage of?"

"Something like that."

There was a pause and when Liberty spoke again, it was in tones gentler than Natalie had ever heard. "Honey, you really like him. Maybe in love with him, and I think you're calling me to ask if that's all right."

"I don't need permission—"

"Not permission. Checking in. You're sort of new to this relationship stuff, so you want to make sure that you're not doing something gullible because he's *extraordinarily* good-looking. Am I right?"

Natalie smiled and hugged the pillow to her. "Maybe."

"Maybe, yeah." Liberty chuckled. "I'll say this: if I were in your shoes, I would totally get in the car and go to dinner at his place, and hear whatever crazy-ass secret he's got. But Natalie?"

"Yeah?"

"If it's not enough, then it's not enough and you let him go. Okay?"

"Okay."

"I gotta go. My next client's here."

"Love you, Lib."

"Love you, too. Oh, and Happy Valentine's Day."

"Oh my god, I totally forgot!" Natalie clapped her hand over her mouth. "I've never had reason to pay much attention to it before…"

"Uh huh. I've changed my theory about his big secret." Natalie could practically see her friend's knowing smile. Liberty hummed a few bars of the "Here Comes the Bride", laughed, and hung up, leaving Natalie to scowl at her old phone.

"That's ridiculous," she muttered. She rose to get dressed, buttoning buttons on her dress with hands that inexplicably trembled.

***

The car Julian sent to retrieve her was punctual to the minute. Natalie saw the black sedan pull up to the curb in front of Niko's at seven o'clock. She smoothed imaginary wrinkles out of her dress. A vintage find, as was most of her wardrobe, this one a pale blue that cinched in at her slender waist, flared above her knees.

It seemed pointless to make the driver come up the stairs since she had seen him, so she grabbed her purse, sweater, and old cell phone and dashed down to meet him. He tipped his cap to her and opened the rear door.

"Good evening, miss."

"Good evening."

The car's interior was impeccably sleek, with rich, gray leather seats and polished wood trim. A phone nestled in a console above her head, and a mini-bar sat tucked between the front seats, facing backwards for her use. On the seat beside her was a bouquet of velvety red roses in a bed of delicate ferns. Natalie's hand trembled as she pulled the little card, so white against so much green and red, and read Julian's tiny, precise script, almost like typeset.

Thank you for coming,
Love, Julian

The flowers were beautiful and filled the car with their rich scent. Natalie suddenly felt too plain. It was on the tip of her tongue to ask the driver to wait while she ran upstairs for a little more makeup perhaps, or a more flattering hairstyle. But the car was pulling away from the curb and she firmed her resolve to not give in to Julian until she had heard whatever it was he was going to tell her. She looked fine. She looked herself. If that wasn't good enough, so be it.

"Do you work for Julian? Uh, Mr. Kovač?" she asked the driver.

"No, ma'am. I work for a service." He pointed at a card mounted on the dash that displayed his photo, name and license information.

She wanted to ask him where they were going but thought that might sound strange. Instead, she bit her thumbnail and watched the city glide by outside the tinted windows.

The driver took them along Geary and then to Market where the traffic was heavy. A caravan of white-yellow lights passed them in the deepening dark. Tall towers rose around her and the Transamerica building stabbed the sky.

Natalie craned her neck to admire the architecture of one fine complex, and then marveled as the driver pulled into its circular, hotel-like drive.

"We're here, miss."

Natalie blew out her cheeks. "Of course we are."

The driver opened her door and took the flowers for her. She followed mutely as he went to the front of the building, to a doorman who wore a dignified grey uniform and a nametag that read Bernie. Bernie smiled from within old-world style muttonchops, took the bouquet, and ushered her inside.

"This way, miss."

Bernie led Natalie across the marble-floored lobby. A set of richly upholstered couches and chairs took up the middle space, and live potted plants added warmth to the austere décor. A security guard sat ensconced behind an immense mahogany desk, his uniform a sedate blue bearing a large badge on the front. A desk lamp with a green glass shade illuminated a leather-bound tome.

"Miss Natalie Hewitt to see Mr. Kovač."

"How did you know?" Natalie asked.

Bernie's smile was grandfatherly. "Mr. Kovač told us to expect you."

"Standard protocol, ma'am." The security guard lifted the great book and rested it on the upper surface of the desk. "If you would just sign in, Miss Hewitt."

Natalie did so, hoping she didn't look as half out of her element as she felt.

"Thank you, Miss Hewitt. Would you, Bernie?"

The doorman beamed. "Of course. Come, my dear."

The security guard bid her good night as Bernie led her to the elevators across from the desk. When the doors opened, he gestured for her to step inside and then handed her the bouquet.

"Have a lovely night, Miss Natalie."

Natalie felt a bolt of panic as she realized she didn't even know what floor Julian was on. But before the doors could close on her, Bernie punched a button. Natalie blinked as the little disk marked "15PH" lit up.

"Thank you, Bernie," she murmured as the doors closed.

The elevator glided upward until a gentle, refined *bing* announced her floor—the fifteenth floor penthouse. The doors parted and Natalie was confronted with a small anteroom with lush carpet and an elegant mirror hanging on the wall. At the end of the hall was a door left ajar. Julian stepped out.

"I thought I heard the bell." Julian's faint smile slipped. "The driver was supposed to give the flowers to you at your door."

"I met him downstairs before he could come up," Natalie said. "They're beautiful,"

"They make a poor showing next to you."

"Thank you."

"Come in. Please."

Julian took the flowers and kissed her cheek—an awkward, nervous peck—as Natalie stepped into his home.

A sense of disorientation swept through as she looked about his apartment. The ceiling in the anteroom was deceptively low. Here the walls—in a muted beige color—stretched up to vaulted ceilings so she felt as if she'd stepped into another building altogether. A gorgeous chandelier of downturned glass pillars, each with a small light glowing in its base, hung from the juncture of ceiling angles. To her right, a formal dining room sat in the dark, looking as if it hadn't been used in ages. The main living room was expansive and curved toward a kitchen of cherry wood cabinets and a gray granite-topped bar. Her shoes clopped on dark hardwood floors, and one wall was entirely comprised of windows that glittered with the panorama of the nighttime cityscape.

Behind the kitchen, the apartment kept going into unknowable reaches; if there was a child's room it would be there, but the space as a whole showed no signs of a child's presence. In fact, Natalie thought, there was no sign of *Julian* here either. The apartment was beautiful, but austere. Every piece of furniture, every design piece, was modern and sleek and didn't reflect Julian's warmth in the slightest. *It's a textbook example of 'bachelor pad,'* she thought, and rubbed her shoulders.

And then she came around the front entry and saw another space, open to the living and kitchen areas.

"Oh, wow."

Where there might have been a sitting room or office, there instead was a library. It had no door but seemed as though it should, as if it didn't belong with the rest of the house. The warmth that was lacking everywhere else was here in abundance. Bookshelves of rich mahogany stretched upward on three walls, their shelves replete with a library's worth of tomes. The floors were the same dark hardwood, but overlaid with a stunning rug of an ornate floral pattern in green, gray, and blue.

The centerpiece of the room was an antique desk—old, scratched, worn with time and care—and a plush chair that appeared chosen for comfort rather than beauty. On the desk stood a small Murano glass desk lamp, its multicolored shade glowing warmly in the dimness. Its light illuminated a stack of black and white composition books, bound together with a rubber band. *The café book*, Natalie thought absently as she moved to peruse the bookshelves.

The books that resided on the polished ledges were in all makes, shapes and sizes. Leather-bound volumes cozied-up beside paperbacks. Hardcovers flanked yellowing antiques, the ordering force being the authors' names. It was clear Julian felt every book in his collection was worthy of sharing space with its conditional betters. Natalie stared in open-mouthed wonder.

"If I had money, this is how I would spend it," she murmured, then snapped her mouth shut, realizing she'd voiced her thought aloud. She glanced at Julian, her cheeks burning. But he apparently hadn't heard. He was busy setting out a bottle of red wine and two glasses on the kitchen counter. Natalie cleared her throat.

"Dinner smells wonderful," she said. "What are you making?"

"*Bandeja paisa y crema de platano verde.*"

She felt her cheeks grow hot; his accent had to be the sexiest thing she'd ever heard in her life. "What does that mean?"

"Creamy plantain soup to start, and the Paisa platter is a variety of different things…both Colombian dishes." He pulled the cork free and poured the wine into two glasses.

"Where did you learn how to cook Colombian food?"

"From my mother."

"Not too spicy, I hope," Natalie said.

"No, I remember you don't care for spicy food." He approached her with a glass of wine. "Please. Make yourself at home."

She took the glass, conscious of his nearness. The mere presence of him made her breath quicken. "Thank you."

"Of course," he said, and then returned to his post behind the kitchen counter, as if it were some sort of protective barricade. Natalie had never seen him like this before. So out of himself. But then, she felt just as disoriented. *This place, but for the library, is not like him.* Another thought suggested that maybe she didn't know him quite as well as she thought she did. *You don't know him at all, do you?*

Natalie retreated to the books.

She hadn't noticed at first but the library was decorated with sculptures, paintings, and a small handful of exotic-looking knickknacks, artfully arranged. African wood carvings shared shelf space with brightly-colored porcelain animals that brought to mind South America. A sumptuous oil painting of a man and a bull, high above one bookshelf, appeared vaguely Eastern European. *Croatian,* she guessed. *And his mother is Colombian.* She smiled faintly. *Maybe from Cartagena, like Mendón.*

A figurine on one of the bookshelves caught Natalie's eye.

It was a bright blue pony—electric blue, like a pure summer sky—done in delicate porcelain, and big enough to hold in two hands. Swirls of yellow and white dotted its body in nickel-sized spirals, and it wore a saddle and bridle of melted gold. Natalie recognized it instantly.

"Oh, hey!" she laughed. "This is exactly like the pony figurine Karina buys at that Argentine market in *Above.* You know, that Mendón book I love so much?"

Natalie ran her finger down the horse's muzzle. Out of her periphery, Julian had frozen and was watching her intently.

Natalie looked beyond the figurine to the books behind it. "*Exactly* like the one Karina..."

She cocked her head and peered at the items on this particular shelf. There were no regular novels but sets of black and white composition books, bound together with rubber bands. Seven sets in all. Each collection of notebooks had a label taped across the spines. *The Common Thief,* read the label on the group of six books Natalie stared at now.

"What...?"

She read the other labels. *Red Water. Lira and Jamie. Starshine: Collected Poems.* Her heart clanged in her chest until she got to *Coronation*—that one made her heart stand still. And the oldest, most worn collection of books with a faded label...

"*Above.*"

Natalie set her wine glass down on a different shelf and carefully drew forth the collection of five composition books. With trembling hands, she slipped the old rubber band off the set, and opened the first notebook. Tiny, typeset-sized script filled the page in blue ballpoint pen, its neatness marred by alterations. The second sentence crossed out and redone. Notes in the margins. Messy scribbles that canceled one word in favor of another. And in between these corrections, the words she knew by heart, words that began the journey she had taken so many times to escape her own static, grief-stricken life. She spoke them aloud, reverently and with awe, for here was their birth.

"*'He's gone, Javier.' Her voice was old. She sounded like* Abuela. *And* Abuela*'s abuela. Layers of voices; generations echoing down to him from the place where dead weeping wives still sew and cook and mend, gnarled fingers flying because hunger and illness run faster than idle hands, and they curse their inconstant men but never loud enough for the children to hear. 'He's gone, and if you are a man and not a boy, you will find him and bring him back.'*"

Natalie closed the notebook and held them all to her chest for long moments. A peculiar sensation gestated deep within her, unfurling at a rapid, eye-blink pace; an amalgam of shock, exhilaration, and something akin to panic. Her heart pounded so loudly, she could hardly hear her own thoughts. One word resounded again and again. *Impossible.*

She turned her head, intending to ask Julian…something. Why he would pull such a terrible prank. Why…?

Julian studied the counter before him, rubbing it aimlessly with a cloth. He didn't meet her eyes, couldn't look at her, and Natalie's body began to tremble. She looked back at the composition books in her hands and returned them to their place on the shelf. The sweet smell of the soup wafted to her. A Colombian dish, he'd said. Natalie almost laughed but she was too close to tears.

"Oh my god," she breathed. She turned to him, imploring.

Julian raised his head with a sheepish, half-smile. "Dinner's ready."

CHAPTER FIFTEEN

Natalie took several halting steps from the bookshelf. In her mind's eye, the days and weeks of her time with Julian at the café returned to her: bits of conversations, strange comments, questions unanswered and topics diverted. A pointillism painting she'd been standing too close to; none of it made sense. Now, if she stepped back...

"No," Natalie whispered as Julian came from the kitchen to stand before her. "It's impossible. You're...him?"

"Yes." Julian eased a sigh—a long exhalation—and shook his head, incredulous. "*Maldita.* I feel like I've been holding my breath for ten years."

She marveled that he could look so relieved. Her own heart churned with a turmoil that left her certain she'd never feel something as simple as relief ever again. She moved on shaking legs to the couch and sat down hard. "You expect me to believe...*No.*" She shook her head. "Mendón is in his forties. You're twenty-eight years old. It's not possible..."

He sat down beside her on the immense couch, but far enough away to give her space. "Most of what you've read about me is false. A diversion—"

"*Above* came out ten years ago. You would've been *eighteen* when you wrote it."

"Seventeen. I turned eighteen the summer it was published."

She stared, open-mouthed. If he was lying he had zero compunction about it. His expression was open, his eyes met hers unflinching. *You saw the notebooks...* Her gaze strayed to the library where the handwritten *Above* sat on a shelf with handwritten versions of every other Mendón novel she'd read a hundred times. *Not versions. Rough drafts.*

A thrill shot up her spine and then morphed into panic. She trembled, shell-shocked by dual emotions: euphoria and fear, hope and humiliation. She clapped her hand over her mouth, not sure if she were going to laugh or burst into tears. "You...you should have told me. Right away. You should have told me the first time I mentioned him."

"I couldn't. I haven't. Not in ten years. Only David and my editor, Len, know the truth."

"But...why?"

He sighed. "I made a vow to my dying mother and kept it, long after its usefulness had expired. By then, so much time had passed..." He shrugged. "Call it habit or cowardice...fear of breaking out—"

"Fear?" She rose to her feet, carried on a tide of something that felt close to hysteria. "What could you possibly be afraid of? You're wealthy, talented—a *genius*..."

He stood up too, held out his hands to steady her. "Natalie, wait—"

She tore away from him. "No! I feel all turned inside out. I don't...You lied to me. For six *months*. Every day, every time I saw you, you were sitting there, lying to me."

"I didn't lie to you—"

"Didn't you?" Natalie cried. "I seem to recall something about a trust fund..."

His arms dropped to his sides with a sigh. "Okay, yes, but that—"

"But that's not the worst part," Natalie said, her voice thick with tears. "I gushed about Mendón—about *you*—like a lovesick idiot and you said nothing. You let me talk and talk and talk, and all the while I never knew, never could have guessed."

"Natalie, please..."

"Every word I've ever said about him—about *you*! It's all ringing in my head like some clown's bell. But that's not bad enough. No, the worst part is that I used *your* books to try to get over *you* when you left."

"Of course you did!" Julian cried. "Of course you did," he said again, gentler. "Natalie, that connection you have to the writing? It's my writing. It's me. Everything that I am is in those books. And you found them. You found me, and by some miraculous twist of luck or fate, I found you. Or maybe it wasn't luck at all. We were drawn to each other. I walked into that café because I was searching for you." He smiled, his eyes shining. "My work is your refuge? You are mine, Natalie."

She sucked in a breath as the truth of his words finally broke past the shock and confusion; shattered the fear of believing that something so impossibly good could be real. "Really?" she said, her voice watery. "Are you really...? Those are your books?"

"My books," he said, smiling softly. He moved closer to her. "*Above* and *Coronation,* and all the rest. And that one," he gestured to the stack of composition books on the desk in the library. "That one is for you."

"For me. Rafael Mendón wrote a book for me." The half-laugh, half-sob escaped her, and she fell against him, the tears coming in earnest when she felt his arms go around her.

"I'll write you a thousand more if that's what you want."

Natalie said nothing but held him and let herself be held. Finally, she lifted her tear-streaked face and looked to the new stack of composition books. Taking Julian by the hand, she went to the desk and rested her hand on the topmost book. She imagined she could feel its pulse, but it was only her own.

"What is it called?" she asked.

"I don't know yet."

"What is it about?"

"You. It's your book, Natalie. It doesn't exist without you." He pulled her close. "I love you."

She laid her hand over her heart that suddenly felt wondrously heavy and full. "You do?"

"I do."

She raised her head, smiling through her tears. "Say it again."

"I love you, Natalie. So much."

She nodded. "I want you to know that I love you, Julian. I loved you before I knew. Remember that, okay?"

"Okay."

She slipped her arms around his neck and as his mouth met hers, as he kissed away her tears, a thrill of pure joy suffused her. The last vestiges of pain and uncertainty evaporated. He was everything she'd hoped he would be and, when she was ready to confront it, he was so much *more.* She smiled into his kiss, feeling as if she'd just won the lottery and then turned around and won it again.

He held her and kissed her for what seemed a long while, and she knew he was giving her time. "Would you like to eat dinner now, or—?"

"No," she said, over the thundering of her pulse. "After."

He grinned, though his voice was husky. "I was hoping you'd say that."

She felt another laugh try to burst out of her. She kissed him instead, infusing it with all the joy and euphoria that was welling up in her, moment by moment. *This is real. At long last...*

The kiss deepened, became sweeter, then harder. She melted against him, and could feel the desire coiling in him, feel it humming under her hands where she touched him, emanating from him like heat. She marveled that she was the object of such intense desire…and that he could kindle the same in her. No more stops. No more hesitations. A thought whispered that this was Rafael Mendón in her arms, but she brushed it aside. *No, this is my Julian…*

He lifted her easily and carried her past the kitchen where the dinner he'd prepared sat, cooling and forgotten, and down the hall to his bedroom, kissing her always. Natalie was vaguely aware of more austere colors and furnishings, a bed that was an ocean of gray linen made silver in the light streaming in from the window.

He set her down and kissed her gently, touched her slowly, assuring her that he wouldn't rush anything. But she felt as though she were burning from the inside out. She wanted to tear his clothes off and feel his skin on hers more than she'd ever wanted anything, but she didn't trust that her shaking hands could do anything besides reveal her own inexperience.

"It's okay," he breathed, "let me."

He pulled her sweater off and let it slip to the floor. She shuddered as if a live current surged through her while he undid the top buttons on her dress and bared her shoulders. He bent and put his mouth to her naked skin, grazing his teeth lightly over the sensitive flesh of her neck while the buttons opened, one by one. The dress fell away, pooled at her feet.

"So beautiful," he murmured, taking her in. "My god, Natalie, you are so beautiful."

He kissed away any reply she might have had—she had none; it was all she could do to keep breathing. He trailed his mouth down her neck, between her small breasts. She gasped; the feel of his hair against her bare skin, brushing her collarbone, was a kind of ecstasy all its own.

He pulled away long enough to tear off his sweater, but she stopped him before he could remove the t-shirt underneath.

"Let me," she said, echoing his words. Her hands found the edge of his shirt and lifted. The meager moonlight found every hard line of his body, filled in every cut of muscle. His elegant clothing had hinted at his physique but hadn't prepared her for the reality or what it did to her.

"God, Julian…" she encircled him in her arms, wanting to feel that body pressed to hers, a moan escaping her when it did. Soft skin and hard muscle enveloped her, the scent of his cologne stronger now and she closed her eyes, reveling in being this close to him. And then she wanted much more than to be held and kissed. *I want him, right now.*

"Take it off," Natalie whispered. "Take it all off."

Her words were the permission he must have been waiting for. He kissed her again, demanding and hard, his breath rasping in his nose. He undid the clasp of her bra and slid it off her arms to toss it aside, relinquishing her mouth in exchange for her naked breasts. She moaned at each touch; the light bite of his teeth, the pull on her nipples as he sucked and licked. Shards of electric heat radiated from under his lips; she'd never been touched like this, never imagined it could feel so good and perfect.

He encircled her waist with one arm, lifted her easily, and laid her on the bed. She sank into the softness, cool silk on her back and Julian's warm skin everywhere else. His mouth found hers again, and their tongues slid against each other deliciously.

Clothing fell away, warm skin pressed against warm skin; they kissed and touched until the passion burning between them demanded more, demanded everything. A fresh swell of desire crashed over Natalie when she thought of what was coming next.

"Wait." He pulled back, his voice haggard with want. He fished a condom from a box in the nightstand drawer and was deft about its application; she was hardly aware of an interruption. And then he was over her again, holding her face in his hands. She exulted in the beauty of him this close, his eyes that were filled with only her.

"My love…"

Their lips touched again, grazed and tasted and parted. And then he kissed her—the sweetest kiss of her life—as he slid inside.

She gasped at the pressure, the exquisite heaviness that filled her completely, and clung to his neck as he pushed deeper, until there was no space between them. His face crumpled with agonized restraint. "Oh god, Natalie…" he groaned and rested his forehead against hers for a moment, as if mastering himself. "Are you okay?"

She nodded quickly. "Oh yes. More than okay…" And then words failed her, thought failed her, as he began to move.

Slowly at first, a gentle rocking, a smooth rolling of his hips. More kisses, long slow kisses that mirrored the rhythm of his thrusts. Natalie luxuriated in every sensation, the heat of his mouth, the warmth of his skin, the weight of his body on hers. And between them, at their joining, a pulsing ache of pleasure that grew stronger, more potent with every movement.

Julian kept the gentle pace but she could feel the urgency in him simmering, ready to be unleashed. It mirrored her own. She returned the kiss, opened her mouth wider, wound her fingers into his silken curls to pull him to her. He drove deep inside her now, fast and hard, unbridled, free of the constraints of his conscience. He held nothing back. It was as if she could feel his every emotion and they all belonged to her.

Natalie's own desire became ravenous; he was giving himself to her and she wanted all of him. She spread her thighs wider, tilted her hips so that he was deeper, and held him tightly as he rocked against her. Words and passages from his books floated in and out of her thoughts, whispering that all that beauty was hers now in a way she could never have imagined. It was almost too much.

They shared the same breath, his sweat mingled with hers, the ecstasy building between them like a small sun. He shuddered and thrust a final time, and the heat between them was searing.

She may have screamed or called out his name—she was too delirious to know for sure, but as the rolling swells subsided, something inside her broke loose and the damnable tears threatened again.

Julian started to move off of her, but she held him tightly, savoring the weight of him over her and inside her, strong and substantial and real.

"I'm too heavy…"

"Just for a moment," she said quickly, but the thickness in her voice gave her away.

"What…?" He lifted his head to look at her. "Oh, my love, it's all right. It's just…release. I feel it too."

She nodded, breathing deeply until she trusted herself to speak. "I just…I've been alone for so long."

He smiled and kissed away her tears. "Not anymore."

CHAPTER SIXTEEN

Moonlight cast a silvery slant over the bed and the city seemed to be sleeping outside the immense windows; the quiet was so thick. The soft susurration of Natalie's breathing broke the silence. Julian thought he would fall asleep with her; his body felt heavy and sated. But it was too good to have her there, in his home, in his bed.

And to think I almost ruined this.

He nestled closer. Her petite frame curled against him perfectly. Her softness against his hardness. His musculature was slender and lean as opposed to big and bulky, but her delicacy made him feel even stronger, more powerful, and awakened a primal desire to protect her.

He kissed her shoulder, but softly so as not to wake her. Her skin beneath his lips was soft, porcelain smooth, and very warm. Such an ecstasy to be enveloped in that warmth; the warmth of her mouth, her arms, the nexus of her legs. But especially her mouth. Making love to her had been as phenomenal as he could have hoped, but he wanted to kiss her all day, every minute. Her lips were more flushed than her skin, the color other women needed glosses to achieve. He loved kissing those lips; tasting them, biting and sucking them until he was half out of his mind for her.

He felt a stirring between his own legs at such thoughts, and took a steadying breath. But he couldn't stop admiring her, and wound a lock of her silky hair around his finger. A gorgeous chestnut color, almost as rich as her eyes that were the color of melted chocolate and alit from within with intelligence and wit and a passion for life that stole his breath. He knew he was waxing rhapsodic, but couldn't help it. He'd lost himself in the velvety brown depths of her eyes too many times in the cafe, listening to her talk about her dreams, her desires, her books…and him.

He brushed that last aside. What she'd said about his writing revealed more about her than anything else. The spirited, profound ideas she'd set forth had shocked him. She was too vibrant, too passionate a person for an empty café and nights spent alone, talking to no one. She was shy, but she also wasn't. She was bursting with ideas, with observations, lacking only a person to share them with. The idea that he could be that person…It thrilled him entirely, but the responsibility of it had frightened him too.

He sighed again, this time in relief. He had almost ruined it, but somehow here she was. The sweetness of her, her generous heart, and her love had saved them both and he vowed he would never do anything to jeopardize her happiness again. Never.

She stirred and opened her eyes. "Hi."

"Hi."

"What time is it?"

Julian glanced at the digital clock on his bedside table. "A little after midnight."

"I slept so well, I thought it must be later."

So beautiful…He started to kiss her, but pulled back, shaking his head sheepishly.

She laughed. "What was that?"

"I love kissing you, more than anything. But I don't want to wear you out over it."

"As if that were possible."

Thank God. He kissed her thoroughly while her fingers slipped into his hair.

"Mmm, that's my weakness," she said. "Your hair. I've been wanting to do that for months."

"Don't let me stop you."

She raked her fingers this time, sending shivers of pleasure down his back while he indulged in another kiss with that exquisite mouth of hers.

"As tempting as it is to spend the rest of the night right here, dinner is languishing. Are you hungry?"

"Yes. And you need to fuel up."

"Do I?"

He watched her face turn scarlet with mortification. "Oh my god, I meant because I want to hear all about you and *Above* and not because of…other…things."

Julian pulled her hand from her eyes, laughing with her and kissing her again until they were in danger of losing the night altogether.

***

Ten minutes later, in the kitchen, he heated up the dinner he'd prepared for her when Natalie emerged from the bathroom. She wore the t-shirt he usually slept in, while he wore another shirt and soft pants. *Such a cliché*, he thought, but the sight of her, in only a shirt and panties, the outline of her breasts barely hinted at...

"You have to stay on that side of the counter," he told her. "If you come near me looking that cute and sexy, I'm liable to burn the dinner. Or myself. Or both."

She took a seat on the barstool, her cheeks blushing prettily. "No one has ever called me sexy before."

"*No one* is a raving lunatic," Julian said, and she laughed. He loved to make her laugh, to see her smile. She did both so easily, but there was pain locked behind her eyes, the pain that she wouldn't let go of. *She will in time,* he thought. *Just love her and be there for her so when she's ready, she'll know it's safe.*

"There are lots of firsts happening here," she was saying, her gaze downward. "Lots of things I've never done before. I'm sure you've noticed."

Julian stirred the soup as it heated up again, and smiled at her. "There are lots of things *I've* never done before."

She arched a brow. "You know what I mean. I worry that I'll seem too clumsy to you, or...I don't know."

He marveled at her, how honest she was and how forthright, despite her bashfulness. *I'll make it easy for her,* he thought and another on the heels of that; *I'd do anything for her.*

"I have been with a grand total of five other women," he said, pouring a glass of wine for her, and one for himself. "I was nineteen, alone in New York City...This was right after *Above* came out and started to make some money. I had a strange, off-and-on relationship with a performance artist. I never had to worry about my secret with her; neither of us were interested in anything other than sex, to be honest. It was an educational relationship and, if I'm being *very* honest, a rather fun one."

Natalie smiled at this, not a shred of jealousy lurking in her eyes.

"At twenty-two I moved to San Francisco and briefly dated three other women before I met Samantha. She was the most serious of any relationship I'd had; we were together for about a year. But it ended badly. She knew there was something I wasn't telling her—of course she knew—so in the absence of truth, filled in her own fact: that I was a cheat and a liar. That was a year ago."

He watched her absorb this as he set a bowl of creamy soup before her.

"Did you love her?" Natalie asked gently.

"No," Julian said. "I thought I might, given time, and for a while I mourned the break-up for just that reason. But then I met you and I realized how shallow my feelings for Samantha were, how artificial. I don't mean to speak ill of her, but trying to love her took effort. Falling for you was the easiest, most effortless thing in the world."

Natalie's cheeks colored again and her eyes shone. "Thank you for saying that. And I know you mostly did to make me feel okay about telling my sordid story. So thank you for that too."

"You don't have to tell me anything you don't want to," Julian said. "Or, when you're ready—"

"I want to," she said, shifting on her seat. "I just…need to."

"Okay," he said gently. "Then I'm listening."

She smiled briefly and took a long pull on her wine. "Before you, I've been with one man. I think I told you before…or at least babbled about it the night we…we almost…" She waved her hands. "Anyway, when my parents died I was eighteen and received some insurance money. Not a lot, but enough. We'd lived in San Diego but I couldn't stay. Too many memories. So I drove north, stopping in coastal towns for weeks or months at a time, trying to find one that fit. But I was aimless. Lost."

Julian could easily conjure her on that journey; alone, grief-stricken, and so very young. His chest tightened.

"I stayed in Santa Barbara the longest, working as a waitress in a restaurant by the beach. For two years, I lived there, hardly talking to anyone, all my time divided between working and reading on the beach. It sounds sort of like a vacation when I put it that way, but it really wasn't. It was…terrible. I've never been so lonely."

Julian longed to go to her, but she wouldn't want his sympathy. *She's stronger than she realizes.*

"I felt like a child wandering on her own," Natalie said. "And being a child was too painful. Children have parents to take care of them. I felt like I needed to shed the first half of my life, my home, my city…I thought if I did that, just cut it all off, like a rotting limb, the pain would fall away with it."

She sighed and gave a kind of half-smile. "I wanted to shed my virginity because it was part of the old life, which is kind of sad when I think about it. I wish I hadn't. I wish that I waited." She glanced up at him. "For you."

Julian felt the ache in his heart grow heavier. "I'm honored," he said quietly and watched her blush and look away.

"But that boy…he was kind," she said quickly. "More so than I had counted on. He wanted to see me again, take me out for a proper date. But no…I thought I would know everything there was to know about him in a week. I left Santa Barbara two days later."

She huffed a breath. "So that's the extent of my sexual escapades. A brief one-night stand and not much else. I never had a boyfriend in high school, just boys that were friends."

"Okay," he said.

"And I'm on the pill. Because my periods are sort of out of control and…so that's for future reference. Oh, god, I'm babbling again, but I just wanted you to know all this so that you don't confuse any hesitancy on my part with a lack of…um, desire…for you. Because I have a lot… of…that." She covered her eyes with her hand. "Stop me at any time if my eloquent seduction is too much for you."

Julian burst out laughing and came around the counter to slip his arms around her waist and kiss her. She tasted of wine and below that, her own addictive sweetness he couldn't get enough of. "Everything about you is an eloquent seduction."

Her fingers wound into his hair and she drew him close for another kiss that had the potential to send them back to the bedroom until she pulled away. "Our food is going to get cold and it smells too good to ignore a second time. And I want to hear about your life, about your mother. And your father. Whatever you feel you want to tell me. Maybe," she smiled coyly, "a little bit about the books?"

"Curious about that, are you?"

"Eh. I only have about a *billion* questions. No biggie."

"The story of my early life is how *Above* came to be written. Will that suffice for now?" She nodded dumbly, and he could see the weight of his revelation striking her again, erasing her levity. "It's okay," he told her. "After I'm done, it won't seem so strange."

She smiled faintly. "Says you…Rafael Mendón."

CHAPTER SEVENTEEN

They retreated to the couch. Julian smiled to see Natalie tuck her legs under her, an attentive expression on her face, but he hesitated. He mentally scrolled over his own life history, organized it, and wondered how painful it was going to be to bring it into the light of day. *It doesn't matter,* he realized. *Natalie's owed every truth and my mother deserves to be remembered.* But his story started with his father. He took a long pull of wine and then began.

He told her of how Kristoff Kovač had been afflicted with wanderlust from a young age, and how he'd landed in Colombia where he met Alaina. Three years of nomadic bliss, before she became pregnant and wanted to settle down, something Kristoff could not, or would not, do.

"He was gone for long stretches of time, wiring money when he could or was inclined to. And then one of those stretches kept stretching until it was clear he wasn't coming back. The wires stopped. We didn't hear from him for six years. And yet my mother refused to let anyone speak a sour word about him in my presence. She believed it was a sin to blacken the impression of a parent in the mind of their child. But I knew. From my earliest years, I knew. I could hear her crying at night."

Julian took another sip of wine, hardly tasting it, and spoke of the day his father came back, ill and ashen. "I was ten years old, and I thought it meant we'd be a whole family again, but he wasn't well. A month later, his heart gave out and he was gone."

"Fast, like lightning," Natalie murmured. She gave him her hand and he squeezed it gratefully.

"During my father's long absences and after his death, my mother worked in housekeeping at various luxury hotels in San Juan, Puerto Rico. She kept long, hard hours while I went to school, and she was determined that I get good grades and go to college. I came home from school to our shabby four-room apartment, did my homework, and then wrote. I was alone most afternoons and into the evenings, and so I created worlds that were not so empty. By the time I was in middle school, it had become evident that I was—"

"A genius?" Natalie put in, with a small grin.

"I was going to say 'ahead of my class'," Julian said. "But my mother couldn't afford a private school, and scholarships for children of that age were few and far between. The public school I went to wasn't a terrible one, anyway. One benevolent teacher — Mrs. Ruiz, in the sixth grade—bought me a stack of black and white composition books and I've never used anything else for the first drafts of my novels. I can't. It may sound strange but I don't want to change much of what began when my mother was still alive. I don't want to lose any more of her than I have already."

Natalie wiped her cheek. "That's not strange at all."

Julian nodded, cleared his throat.

"I didn't stay in school long. I took the GED as soon as I was able so that I could work. We were living in Tampa Bay at the time and until then, she had forbidden me from working, saying I needed to concentrate on my writing. It was evidence of her encroaching illness that she did not protest when I finished school to work, but patted my hand and told me I was a good son to her. But I felt I wasn't doing enough.

"I've heard you shouldn't write—or make art—solely for the money. I understand the gist; writing is something I have to do. I would do it for free. But not that first book. That first book was both a story I needed to tell and a way to make money we desperately needed. Or so I hoped. That's when I wrote *Above.*

"I worked all day at a grocery store, bagging groceries and stocking shelves, and at night I wrote obsessively, furiously, through blisters and burning eyes and headaches; fueled by resentment toward my father for leaving us and a panic that time was slipping away. And it was. When it was finished, my mother's cancer had progressed to the point where doctors begin speaking in weeks instead of months. It was in her lungs despite the fact she'd never touched a cigarette in her life."

Julian heard his voice grow hard with bitterness.

"I walked into the offices of Underhill Press in Tampa and slammed the five notebooks on the desk of the man who is still my editor to this day, and I said, 'How much will you pay me for this?' Naturally, he thought I was insane. I was seventeen years old, wearing a grocer's apron and had dirty fingernails. But Len—Len Gordon is his name—told me later he saw something in me that intrigued him. I left him the books and my phone number and walked out.

"Len called me that same evening, at the hospice, and offered me a contract right there, over the phone, provided I could prove I wrote it myself. I quoted him whole passages at his discretion and he was sold. Or rather, *Above* was sold."

"For a huge pile of money, I hope."

"Huge to my mother and me. Len came over two days later with a contract. Underhill Press offered me a thirty thousand dollar advance—an astonishing sum for a debut novel by today's e-book-friendly standards, and enough to give my mother a few weeks' or months' peace and luxury.

"Between the contract signing and the release of the book, I took her to the Bahamas. There, she sat by the beach or the pool in a fancy hotel reading *Above* while others waited on her, hand and foot. It was the best and worst time of my life, as I could see she enjoyed the sun and rest, but it was too little too late. She didn't have the strength to stay longer than a handful of days. We returned to the hospice and she…"

Julian felt as if he'd been suddenly dragged backward through time. He saw everything clear as day; the dingy room, the smell of the air freshener the hospice used to cover the scents of disinfectants and illness but never could manage to conceal entirely, and his mother's bone-thin body on the too-big bed. He heard her every word, echoing across ten years, in a wasted voice that had once been rich and full.

"She pulled me close to her and said, '*Mi hijo*, you have to be very careful. You are only a boy and soon I will not be here to take care of you. Your book is going to splash on the world and make a tidal wave. You have to keep yourself safe. You are so very young. Low men will try to take advantage of you, steal your money. Women will want you for your name and not your soul. Promise me you won't pollute your beautiful mind with drugs or liquor; that you won't let money turn you into something that you are not. Promise me you will tell no one that you have made this book. Promise me, so that I may leave his world in peace.'"

He looked at Natalie. "Of course I said yes."

"Of course," she said, her eyes shining.

"This didn't sit with Len," Julian said, clearing his throat. "He thought he had a prodigy on his hands and the publicity to go with it. But he acquiesced on the condition that it would not be published anonymously. We had to give him a name.

"Out of anger with my father I had been going by Rafael since I was four. But my writing was for my mother, so I chose the names she had given me for the world to hear, and used my father's names in life, where I was alone and no one knew me."

"They're all beautiful names," Natalie said in a small voice. "Your mother must have been touched by the gesture."

"I'd like to think so. By then there wasn't much left of her. She…she died. She died before she saw *Above* in print, before it became a bestseller or an award-winner, before it made me enough money that I could have taken her anywhere in the world, or gotten her better medical care, or bought her anything she wanted, or…"

He wiped his hands over his eyes, and took a deep, fortifying breath. He heard Natalie sniff and couldn't look at her.

"So there it is. Not a very glamorous story, but I'm glad you know it. I'm glad to have told you about my mother, so that she doesn't exist solely in my mind and heart."

"No, now she lives in my heart too," Natalie said softly.

Julian's chest tightened and he turned to the cityscape outside the windows. The brilliant spread of lights blurred in his vision.

He felt Natalie slide onto his lap, felt her arms go around his neck and she held him. He buried his face in her hair that smelled like cinnamon and flowery shampoo and even his own bed sheets from when she'd lain with him. She pulled away enough to kiss him. Her mouth was soft on his, and so very sweet.

"Thank you," he said hoarsely. "I needed that."

"There's more where that came from," she said in just the right playful tone to pull him from the melancholy of his story. She got to her feet and tugged his hand. "Come on. It's late and we still have unfinished business."

"We do?"

"We do."

CHAPTER EIGHTEEN

Natalie lay back on Julian's pillows, her thumbs flying over the keypad of her old flip phone.

"What are you doing?" Julian asked, drawing on a pair of jeans. "You're not selling my story are you? Already? It's not even eight o'clock in the morning."

"Of course I am. It's been my plan all along."

"Damn. I feel so used and dirty. And not in the good way."

"I'm texting my friend Liberty to let her know that you're not a serial killer after all."

"A serial killer? That was on the table?"

Natalie giggled. "We had our suspicions."

His secret isn't that he has a child, she wrote. *It's better than that. It's better than anything I could have imagined.*

Natalie hit "send" then flipped the phone shut and set it down on the nightstand. It immediately chirped an incoming text, and she giggled again, feeling slightly guilty for not answering it. Slightly.

"I didn't tell her who you are, even though I'm bursting to do so."

"I'm not as worried about that as I once might've been."

Natalie sat up, her knees to her chest. "Does that mean you're going to go public?"

"I haven't decided. The promise I made to my mother was to keep from being reckless and arrogant with my good fortune. But I'm no longer the eighteen-year-old kid she wanted to protect. I feel as if I should just let it go and move on. Even so, I don't like all the other stuff that comes with it. The press and the questions…"

"Questions about you or the writing?"

"Both."

Natalie frowned. "You don't want to talk about the books?"

He sat beside her on the bed and took her hand. "With you, yes. You can ask your million questions and I'd never get tired of it. But with total strangers?" He made a face. "And in the grand scheme of things, it can't make that big of a ripple, can it?"

Natalie thought he was understating it—that the literary world, at least, would go mad for him—but she said nothing.

"And David wouldn't be happy about it," he said. "Not at first."

"David? Oh, your assistant? What difference would it make to him?"

"He's protective. And maybe a little worried he'd be lost in the shuffle should I go public. He's a bit…neurotic but a good guy. You'll meet him soon."

Natalie slipped her arms around Julian's neck; it thrilled her that she could touch him whenever she wanted. "You don't have to decide right away. And whatever you do, I'll support you." He smiled and started to kiss her, but she pulled back. "But can I tell my friends? I think I'll explode if I don't."

"Can they be trusted not to spread it around?"

"No, but they're both so dramatic, no one would believe them anyway."

"I'd be more concerned that they don't believe *you*. I'd be wary if I were you, but if you trust them, tell them." He kissed her gently above the ear. "I shouldn't care either way, now that I have you. You're all the good fortune I need. Everything else can go up in flames tomorrow and it won't matter."

Natalie nestled against him, basking in the warm glow of his affection. His love for her. *How did this happen?* She looked at Julian, at his blue eyes that held within them the intelligence and observation of an artist. Her favorite artist, the poet she had been waiting for, though she knew that if he never wrote another word she'd be happy so long as he was hers.

He gently wiped the tear that escaped the corner of her eye. "What is this?"

"Nothing," she said. "Just…happy."

"Me too. And that, my love, is the grandest understatement of the century."

***

Over breakfast, he answered her questions and promised to answer the thousand more left waiting in the wings. When they'd finished, he took her in his arms and held her close.

"I want you to spend the weekend with me," he said. "Until Monday."

"This weekend?" Natalie bit her lip. "I have to work. It's Thursday now. Too late to cover my shifts with such short notice."

'"Next weekend, then," he said. "I don't particularly want to wait that long but on second thought, it'll give me time to plan something nice for you."

"I sincerely doubt anything could top this Valentine's Day."

He laughed. "Sounds like a challenge to me."

Natalie thought it over. She'd never taken so may shifts off in a row before. Not in three years. She wondered if Niko would be okay with it, and then realized he'd probably kick her out the door to know she was taking time for herself.

"I'd love to."

"Excellent."

"But Julian," she said, "nothing crazy or fancy. Promise?"

He gave her a 'who me?' smile and then kissed her until she'd forgotten what she'd asked.

CHAPTER NINETEEN

Club Kyrie was dark and silent except for the tinny, tinkling chimes of a music box. Another song from *Cabaret*—Liberty's theme for the season. All faces were rapt, shadows dancing over them as little table candles flickered. Tendrils of illicit cigarette smoke twisted upwards in graceful spirals. No glass clinked. No one talked or even coughed.

On stage, Liberty stood frozen atop a black pedestal. Her arms were bent at stiff angles, her head cocked to the side. Her dress was that of a child's: a billowy but tattered and torn white tutu, ripped stockings, and black Mary Janes. Her cheeks were perfect red circles dotted with large black freckles. Her hair dangled on either side of her frozen face in two raggedy pigtails. The rigid smile on her face was clownish and too big, her eyes vacant.

The scratchy and tinny-sounding music filled the small club, another woman's voice sang in German. Liberty began to move like a wind-up doll and the pedestal spun slowly. Her Barbie-bent arms moved up and down; she tilted at the waist and cocked her head, her expression never changing.

The song ended but the music started again, and Natalie watched, eyes shining, as the stiffness left Liberty and her doll began to slump, defeated. This time, she sang the song in perfect German, each lyric thick with emotion as she implored the audience with her sad, doll eyes. As the last note faded, she froze again, hands outstretched, beseeching. There was a moment of stillness and then a shrill whistle pierced the silence, causing everyone in the club to jump; Marshall nearly spilled his cocktail.

Two men in S.S. uniforms goose-stepped onto the stage. The red swastika armbands were obscenely vivid. Liberty was frozen, on her knees, her hands outstretched stiffly and perfectly still. Natalie watched in amazement as the officers took the "doll" under its arms and lifted. Liberty's pose didn't change. Like a piece of furniture, the men carried her off stage, her white oval face in a motionless plea, and then everything went black.

The crowd erupted. Marshall tried to conceal his shining eyes. Natalie didn't bother.

***

Liberty was in her silky kimono when she joined Marshall and Natalie at their table. Patrons applauded her again as she sat down, and Natalie thought her friend handled the praise gracefully. Marshall kissed her cheek, shaking his head in mute admiration. Liberty lowered her eyes and cleared her throat.

"I have a few minutes before the next act," she said. She grabbed Marshall's cocktail, took a long pull, then turned to Natalie. "So speak."

"Liberty...your show..."

She waved a hand dismissively and lit a cigarette. "My show will be here tomorrow night and the next, until they kick me out. You, on other hand, had sex. On Valentine's Day, no less. That takes precedence."

Marshall's adoring gaze for Liberty swung around to Natalie. "Whaaaaat? It's been a whole week and you didn't tell me! Sir Julian? Really?"

Natalie felt her neck grow hot.

Liberty rolled her eyes. "Look at her. She's flush, happy, *alive*...It's depressing. And infuriating. Your morning-after text was not funny, missy."

Marshall clapped his hands together. "I'm so proud of you!" He frowned. "Wait. Why does she get a morning-after text? What about me? Oh, who cares! You had sex! Miracles do happen; you're living proof."

Natalie brushed aside his hands as he tried to cup her cheeks like a proud father. "Thank you, Marshall, but I'd feel better if you weren't so surprised."

"I'm not surprised, I'm shocked to the very core of my being."

"Tick-tock," Liberty said. "I don't have much time and I want details. Lots of them."

"No details," Natalie said. She thought of the way Julian's mouth moved over hers when they kissed..."No...just, no details."

"Look at her face!" Marshall cried. "She's glowing like a torch. Don't torture us like this, darling. Some of us have been going through what you might call a *dry spell,* and by some strange, insane twist of fate, *you* are the one enjoying a sexual extravaganza. It's your duty to let us live vicariously through your exploits."

Natalie laughed. "No, no. You'll have to use your imaginations…"

"Honey, I'm an accountant. I have no imagination."

"And is that your Valentine's Day present?" Liberty reached over and examined the micro mosaic pendant hanging from Natalie's neck. "Wow, that's gorgeous."

Natalie beamed. "No, that was Christmas." *Julian was my Valentine's gift.*

"Some gift," Marshall commented. "That thing's Victorian. Not just the *style.* As in, from when Queen V's bony old butt was perched on the throne. Got to be worth six grand, easy."

"What? No!" Natalie studied the pendant. "I know it's old, an antique, but surely not…"

"Surely *yes*," said Marshall. "Don't you ever watch *Antiques Roadshow*? Your man's got taste. And money." He heaved a sigh. "So unfair."

My man, Natalie thought and felt her skin warm again. "Yes, he's wonderful. And you may be pleased—or shocked—to know that I'm taking time off from work this weekend. I'm going to spend it with him."

Liberty smirked. "Translation: you're going to spend the weekend having sex until you can't see straight."

"Now she's just rubbing it in." Marshall pouted. "Is that why you're able to grace us with your presence this Thursday eve?"

"Yes," Natalie said. "I took tonight too. I didn't want to miss Lib's show and…there's something else. Something I had to tell you both before I burst. You won't believe this…I get shivers just thinking about it, it's so amazing."

"Is this about his big bad secret?"

"Yes." Natalie's smile split her face. "But you both have to swear you won't tell another soul. Promise me."

They exchanged dubious glances, but Natalie was too excited to be annoyed. *I can't wait to see the looks on their faces…*

"Okay, we swear," Marshall said.

Liberty nodded. "Well?"

Natalie heaved a breath. "Julian is a writer. A published one. A very highly respected and adored one. One whom I've read before."

Marshall wagged his hand. "Lord, girl, that's nothing. You read everything. I wouldn't be surprised if—"

"He's Rafael Melendez Mendón."

Liberty and Marshall stared at her, motionless, and then almost simultaneously burst out laughing.

"Oh, sweets, you had us going there," Marshall choked.

Natalie felt the blood drain from her face, taking all of her excited joy with it. It rushed back to burn her cheeks when her friends ceased laughing and exchanged another pair of looks.

Liberty studied her through narrowed eyes. "Wait, wait, wait. Nat…You don't really…I mean, did he *tell* you that?"

"Of course," Natalie said. "How else—?"

"And then you slept with him," Liberty continued. "He told you that he was your favorite author…aaaand then you slept with him."

Another pair of glances went between her friends, and then Natalie could barely see for the blinding humiliation and fury that swept over her.

"It's not like that. I've seen the books…He told me…He…" *He warned you this would happen,* she thought. And he was right but he couldn't have known how badly their derision hurt. "I…can't…I have to go. I'm going…"

She stood on shaking feet and snatched her purse off the back of her chair. They called her back but she ignored them, stumbling to the door and up the stairs. Outside, the icy chill of winter still hadn't left the air yet and it cooled her burning cheeks. She walked down the street, heedless of direction, clutching her coat around her. Running footsteps followed her and then Marshall caught up, took her by the arm. She tore out of his grasp and faced them.

"Natty, we're sorry," he began.

"It's just too…serendipitous," Liberty said behind her, shivering in her kimono.

"So I'm an idiot, then?" Natalie said. "You two, with all your worldly wisdom and experience can't believe it so therefore it must be a lie? The only explanation is that I'm some empty-headed naïf?"

Another knowing glance between them and Natalie turned on her heel. She took three steps before whipping around again, her purse slapping painfully at her thigh.

"Why do you hang out with me? To feel better about yourselves? To feel superior? Or is it just good old-fashioned pity?"

"Are you kidding me?" Liberty snapped. "You honestly believe that some rich schmuck who's been hanging out at your café for six months is a prize-winning author? And not only that, he just *so happens* to be utterly gorgeous? And he just *happens* to be your favoritest author in the whole wide world? And he just *happens* to really, really love you too?"

"Shut up, Liberty," Marshall intoned.

"Yes, I do," Natalie said. "But I'm not going to explain it to you. Or tell you what I've seen to make me believe it. You both think I'm so pathetic? Look at you, Liberty. You can't have what you want but you don't change anything. You don't do anything different. Just sit around in bars every night. You don't even put yourself out there—"

"I don't put myself out there?" Liberty screeched. She flapped her silk-sleeved arm back toward the club. "I *put myself out there* every goddamn night on that goddamn stage. You, on the other hand, fucked a guy who's playing you like a fiddle. Congratulations. Welcome to the real world."

Natalie recoiled at Liberty's anger but stood her ground. "He is who he says he is. I'm not going to let you try to ruin something perfect with your insinuations—"

"Oh, so he's *perfect* now?" Liberty snorted an ugly laugh. "Don't make me puke."

Natalie's throat tightened. "I feel sorry for you." She wanted to say more but was afraid of sounding petulant. Instead she said, "Don't follow me," and walked away.

"Don't worry, I won't."

Natalie heard the clip-clop of heels going the other way from her, then the release of chatter and music as Kyrie's door opened and then slammed shut. Natalie tried to hold them back, but the tears fell anyway.

"Natalie, wait," Marshall called after her in a forlorn voice. He caught up to her and his arms went around her. "We're pigs."

"Yes, you are."

"It's just a pretty huge, astronomical coincidence…" Natalie started to pull away but he held her tight. "But, I believe you. At least I think I do. And so does Liberty. She's just bitter because…well, she's just bitter."

"She's bitter because she loves you," Natalie said. "And you know it."

"What? No…"

"Marshall…"

He met her gaze for a moment, his lips pursed. Then he flung his hands in the air. "What am I going to do? I love the woman, infuriating though she may be. I think she's talented and gorgeous and I want to spend all day with her. I just don't want to fuck her."

Natalie breathed a hiccupping sigh. He handed her his handkerchief. "Thank you." She dabbed her eyes. "What *are* you going to do?"

"I haven't a clue, but it doesn't matter right now. This was supposed to be your night and we screwed it up." He put his arm around her. "Is it really him? No joke?"

She nodded.

"But wait, I thought Mendón was over forty." He raised a brow. "So he's…an older man?"

"He's twenty-eight. All that stuff about his age isn't true. For his privacy."

Marshall gave her a look. "You have to know how convenient that all sounds from where we're standing, Nat."

"I don't care. I know the truth."

"We're just trying to protect you. Liberty too, in her own way."

"I don't need protecting, Marshall," Natalie said. "Not from him. All this is just making me feel stupid. I have to go now."

"No, don't. I won't be able to sleep tonight knowing you're this upset. Just…tell me everything and start at the beginning."

"I don't want to now," she said, leaning her head on his lapel. "I'm sorry."

He squeezed her tight and sighed. "Me too."

***

"I'm here to see Julian."

The security guard—Hank, she remembered—smiled warmly. "Of course, Miss Hewitt. Let me see if Mr. Kovač is in this evening."

Natalie blew on her fingers. They were cold though her face felt flushed and hot, and when Hank allowed her access to the elevator, she had to hold herself back from running.

The elevator opened on his floor. Julian was waiting at the door for her.

"I wasn't expecting you until tomorrow—" He stopped, his pleased expression morphing to concern. "Are you all right? Natalie, what is it? It's happened, hasn't it? You told your friends…"

She burst into tears. "And now that I'm here, I know it's all true. And I'm so ashamed…"

His arms went around her, his voice rumbled against her ear. "Don't be ashamed. I understand. It's precisely why it was so hard to tell you. It would be different if you didn't love the writing so much. But you do, so there's much more at stake."

"Even so. I feel terrible."

He said nothing but took her hand and led her into his bedroom, to the walk-in closet that was the size of her entire kitchen. It smelled of fine clothing and his cologne she loved so much. He crouched on his heels and pushed aside a hanging row of slacks to reveal a wall safe.

"Not even David has the combination," he said.

Natalie knelt beside him as he turned the dial of numbers and opened the safe. He withdrew a leather portfolio and handed it to her.

"These are my contracts with Underhill Press," he said. "The first, for *Above*, is on the bottom."

Natalie opened the portfolio, shame burning her cheeks even as a thrill shivered over her skin. *It's like buried treasure*, she thought, and that notion felt even truer as Julian held two golden medals out to her.

"National Book Awards for *Above* and *The Common Thief*," he said.

She took them and held them in her lap. *So heavy…* She let her fingers trace the engravings.

"I have other papers…the certificates for the Awards, galley prints, early drafts of the *Starshine* poems…Whatever you want."

Natalie looked up at him. "I'm so sorry."

He smiled and cupped her cheek. "Don't be. The certainty feels better than any shred of lingering doubt, *sí*?"

She nodded. "Thank you for understanding. My friends…they make me feel like I'm a stupid, silly child sometimes. Maybe they're right. I've missed out on so much. I want to experience all of it. Everything I've missed. I want it with you."

"Okay." He held her face, his impossible blue eyes taking her in, his thumb stroking her cheek. "I'm here."

He kissed her then and she felt his love for her, as real as the gold in her lap and a thousand times more precious.

CHAPTER TWENTY

The following morning, Natalie sighed and watched the sunlight stream through Julian's bedroom window. It fell over his dusky skin, played over the long lines of him, as he lay naked on the bed beside her.

"At the risk of sounding like a bastard, I need to send you home," he said. "I have more to plan before our weekend starts."

"You do?" Natalie frowned. "I thought we agreed on nothing fancy."

"How about a little bit of everything? I have you until Monday morning. We've got a lot of time to make up for. Six months' worth of dates I should have been taking you on…"

She silenced his regret with a kiss. "Will you call me a cab? I said I wanted to experience all of it, but a walk of shame isn't what I had in mind."

***

Julian didn't call her a taxi, but a car from the service he favored, and stood with her as it pulled into the circular drive.

"Bring at least one pretty dress. I want to take you out on a proper date. Like the one we had on Christmas, but with a better ending."

"Okay. But nothing too fancy, seriously, Julian. You don't have to spend money on me."

He pulled her close. "I want to. I'm *going* to. I love you, Natalie," he said when she started to protest, "and I'm dying to lavish you. I won't go overboard, I promise."

He kissed her long and languidly, oblivious to the driver holding open the back door of the Mercedes sedan for her.

"I'll see you soon."

***

In her apartment, Natalie showered, then packed a small bag of clothes and sundries for the weekend. She laid her one "good" dress over it. It was her best vintage find, and not something she'd bought at a consignment shop. The black velvet dress had a gathered waist, ruched sleeves, and flowed to just above her knees. Faded lace trim at the neck and sleeves revealed its age. She had purchased it on a whim, from an online retailer, for $110, which was far more than her budget allowed. But she'd fallen in love with it and had to have it. It fit her petite frame to a T, but she'd never had a real opportunity to wear it until now. The pendant Julian gave her would compliment it beautifully she thought, and then bit her lip.

Marshall thought the pendant cost $6000. And now Julian wanted to spend even more money on her. Part of her thrilled at the notion; not for want of any gifts, but for the experience of venturing out into San Francisco on his arm. Perhaps a fine dinner and delicious wine. Maybe a swanky club, cocktails, and dancing. The thought made her giddy. As for gifts... *He promised not to go overboard.*

The sedan returned at 6 p.m and the first thing she found when she climbed inside was the small-ish rectangular box sitting on the seat beside her. Natalie shook her head and read the card on top.

Don't shake your head at me. Just open.
Love, J

Natalie burst out laughing and opened the wrapping. The gift was an iPhone, the latest model, white and sleek. The box had already been opened and the phone set up for her. The only number in it, so far, was his.

"You promised!" she said when he picked up with an innocent hello.

"A new phone is not overboard. Not even close. Have you *seen* your flip?"

"I like my flip!" Natalie laughed.

"So did the '90's. Listen, did you bring a jacket?"

"This is San Francisco, right? I have a sweater and jacket, both."

"Perfect. We're on a time crunch here."

"We are?" Natalie took in the lush interior of the luxury car. *Maybe we are. Maybe this coach will turn into a pumpkin at midnight...*

"We are, and I'm extremely busy right now. Can't talk. I'm going to text you a number and I need you to call it for me."

"What? Who am I calling?"

"Okay, perfect, thanks very much. Love you. Bye."

Natalie held the phone in her lap, smiling at it as if she were smiling at him. It chimed twice with the promised text. She tapped the screen, grudgingly pleased with how fast and efficient it all was—light years ahead of her old flip. The text was a phone number, underlined. She pressed it and the phone asked her if she wished to call it. She hit "yes" and put the flat rectangle of a phone to her ear.

"Golden Gate Charters, may I help you?"

"Um…hi." Natalie said, mentally shaking her fist at Julian. "I…uh…"

"Do you wish to confirm a reservation?" the woman asked, and Natalie could hear the knowing tone in her voice. *She's in on it.*

"Yes, I do," Natalie said boldly, and the faltered again when she realized she had no clue what to say next. *Damn him.*

"Very good, Miss Hewitt. You and Mr. Kovač are confirmed for this evening, seven o'clock."

"Uh, thank you."

"Thank *you*."

Natalie hung up and switched to the text screen. *Charter?*

The reply was quick. *Charter? I don't even know her!*

She rolled her eyes, laughing. *Yuk yuk.*

You look beautiful.

Natalie looked up. The sedan had stopped at Julian's building and he stood on the curb, phone in hand. He opened the door, but instead of handing her out, he started to climb in.

"We're going out now?" Natalie asked, sliding over the leather seats to make room. "My things…"

"Safe in the trunk, right Bruce?"

The driver nodded. "Yes, sir."

Julian grinned, his eyes sparkling like blue topaz. "See? We're all set."

Aren't we just?" Natalie laughed. "Our reservations are confirmed tonight for seven. Whatever they may be."

"Excellent. We'll be just in time. Are you hungry?"

Yes, for you, she thought and her cheeks grew hot. *He's turning me into a fiend.* "Maybe. First we need to talk about this." She held up her new phone.

"That's nothing. Something you needed. It doesn't even count."

"Doesn't it?"

"Nope."

"Julian, it's not just the phone. It's the plan, the cost of the data and all that—"

"Don't worry about it. I've got it covered." He turned in his seat and faced her, his expression serious. "Please let me indulge a little. I have all this money but what am I using it for? I have all the stuff that I need. I don't need more *stuff*. I want to take you out, buy you pretty things. Please let me, okay?"

"I don't need *stuff* either, Julian. Experiences, yes. And you. That's all."

His mischievous expression returned. "All the experiences you can handle and a few gifts besides. Sorry. Comes with the territory."

She smiled despite herself and laced her fingers with his as the car took them through the city.

There were no more gifts that night, but an experience Natalie knew she would never forget. The reservation she had unwittingly "confirmed" was for a private yacht that took them out onto the bay at sundown. There was champagne, finger sandwiches, entrees of exquisite seafood, and delicate desserts. After, they slow danced alone on the deck with the city glittering behind them and the lights of the Golden Gate Bridge glowing over them. On the way back, they huddled under a blanket together at the prow, her back to his chest and his arms around her.

This is perfection, she mused, while a tiny voice whispered that she loved him too much. That this sort of bliss could be taken away, like a rug swept out from under her feet, and the gaping hole that remained would be too deep and dark to crawl out of. But back at his apartment, he kissed her in front of the city panorama and made love to her, slowly and languidly on his soft bed, and the voice was silenced, buried, its words forgotten.

CHAPTER TWENTY-ONE

The next day they had lunch at a dim sum restaurant called Yank Sing, south of Market, and Natalie thought she had never had a more delicious meal in her life. As they sat sipping tea, she watched that sly smile come over his face again.

"I hope you've nothing more planned for this afternoon than a nap," she said. "I'm stuffed."

"No naps. No time. I'm taking you shopping."

Natalie pursed her lips. "What, for clothes? Like in *Pretty Woman*?"

Julian grinned. "Not quite."

***

The sedan pulled up in front of City Lights Bookstore, and Natalie felt her heart stutter excitedly and then slow with a clang of uncertainty. "Julian, no…"

"*Yes.*" He turned to her once again. "Let it go, Natalie," he said gently but firmly.

She looked down. "I'm just not used to it. It doesn't feel wrong, exactly. Just…strange."

He didn't answer right away. She heard him sigh and a quick peek revealed him staring out the window.

"My mother worked her fingers to the bone raising me by herself," he said, his voice hard. "Folding laundry, cleaning hotel rooms, cleaning *toilets*. The cancer got her before she could retire and enjoy one iota of rest."

He turned to her, lowered his voice so the driver couldn't hear. "I told you that I took my mother to the Bahamas with the advance for *Above*. There, people did *her* laundry, and cleaned *her* hotel room, and brought *her* fresh towels and food and frothy drinks on the beach. That money was the best I've ever spent. A close second is what it cost to charter that yacht last night and see the city's lights reflected in your eyes." He held her face in his hands, his tone softening. "Both sums are a pittance from where I'm sitting. Okay?"

"Okay. But Julian?"

"Yes," he said, wary.

"I hope you brought enough money for a forklift. Or maybe movers? I'm likely to clean out the entire store."

He relaxed and kissed her. "Now you're talking."

In the bookstore, Natalie inhaled deeply. The night before, Julian had showed her the ins and outs of her new phone, one perk being she could read books on it. Convenient, she thought but nothing could ever replace the weight of a real book in her hands or the smell of its pages. And City Lights was the crown jewel of bookstores. She shivered in delight as they crossed the threshold and stepped onto the black-and-white checkered floor.

Natalie's heart leapt to see that a small table near the front was dedicated to the works of Rafael Melendez Mendón, with *Coronation* front and center. She elbowed Julian, but he made an inscrutable face and walked past. Natalie lingered, trailing her fingers along a copy of *Above*, thinking of the black and white comp books that bore the same title. A smile touched her lips as she found an employee recommendation for *Coronation* that read in part:

"I wish Mendón would materialize from his seclusion just long enough for me to thank him for *Coronation*, that's how incredible this book is."

She contemplated showing that to Julian but he had disappeared into the stacks. *He's not ready yet.*

Natalie soon became lost amid the shelves herself. Book buying had always been an event for her, something she worked hard to save for. Libraries filled in the gaps, but she wanted the new releases of her favorite authors on her own shelves, and hardcovers were a luxury she couldn't often afford. Now, she could choose whatever she liked but despite Julian's assurances, she still felt reluctant and picked out only five books. The first four were at the top of her lengthy To Read list: *The Goldfinch* by Donna Tartt, *All Fall Down* by Jennifer Weiner, *The Children Act* by Ian McEwan, and *The Bone Clocks* by David Mitchell. The fifth, *A Prayer for Owen Meany* by John Irving, she'd read at least fifteen times but she had lent her one and only copy to Liberty who had promptly forgotten it on the Muni.

Julian frowned at her selections. "Only five?

Natalie affected a thoughtful expression. "Well, I could pick out fifty and spend every spare moment reading. Or I could be judicious, and spend that time with you. In your bed. Naked."

"You win."

He carried her books to the check-out, along with his selections: *Across the River and into the Trees* by Ernest Hemingway and some sort of Italian travelogue.

While they waited in line, Natalie watched a young woman approach the Mendón table and pick up *Above*. The woman flipped it to the first page and fell in; Natalie saw it happen, and she had to squeeze her lips together to keep from squealing with delight.

She nudged Julian. They watched as a slow smile spread over the woman's face, an intensely intimate expression of satisfaction. Julian looked away, fixing his gaze straight ahead.

Natalie squeezed his hand. "That's what happens."

"It's not why I write," he said under his breath. "I don't do it for her. For you, maybe, even when I didn't know it…"

"Oh, love," Natalie said, "that woman *is* me."

***

That night, Julian kept things casual. They ate burgers at Mel's Drive-In and then caught a movie. Natalie thought it was almost as fantastic as the yacht ride, just to stand in line waiting to buy tickets, Julian behind her, his arms around her, talking and laughing in her ear. A date. Dinner and a movie. She'd never had such a simple thing. The tiny voice whispered again in her ear that this kind of bliss couldn't come without a price. But it seemed far away as he kissed her in the dark of the theater. She could taste the salt and sweetness on him, French fries and vanilla shake, and below that, his own delectable flavor that made everything bad and ugly seem so far away.

They walked along Market Street after the movie, sat at a café and talked like they used to when he was coming to Niko's and writing.

"I miss you so much at the café," she told him, her fingers laced in his across the table. "It's not the same."

"I worry still," he said. "I don't want you to work alone at night. Not anymore."

"I'm okay."

"I can still come. Not to work, but to see you. The book needs time to breathe before I look at it again and start editing."

"Time to breathe? Like a fine wine?" Natalie smiled. "Doesn't sound too far off the mark."

"If I let it alone I can come back to it with fresh eyes later. It puts distance between it and me so I can be a more ruthless editor."

"I can't wait to read it," Natalie said. "And I'm not alone. You have a lot of fans, love. Like that woman in the bookstore." She thought of the employee recommendation card and its fervent wish. "So are so many people who'd love to meet you."

Julian frowned and turned his cappuccino cup in circles. "You think I should reveal myself?"

"Not unless you're ready. Not if it's going to make you unhappy…"

"I just don't see the point. I can't imagine giving interviews and yammering about myself for an hour, or sitting at a table signing books. It seems so arrogant."

"Not arrogant at all." Natalie leaned over the table. "You don't do all that stuff for yourself. You do it for us. The people who've read you and love you and want to thank you for what you've given them." She hesitated, already feeling tears sting her eyes. "*I* want to thank you."

"For what?" He leaned forward, alarmed. "What's wrong?"

"Nothing, I…" She looked at him, held his hand tightly. "How do you do it?"

"Do what?"

"Write like you do?"

"I don't know, love. I can't answer that. I just put one word after another…"

"No, it's more than that," Natalie said. "It's magic. That's what it feels like, and I know you don't want to hear this stuff, but I have to tell you…" The tears were building in her throat. "Jeez, I can't even say anything without all this…old pain bubbling up."

"It's okay," he said quietly. "You can tell me."

She nodded. "Okay, well…When my parents died I was lost. I still feel like that sometimes. Alone. Or no…untethered. We had no other family but some distant cousins somewhere and so it was just us. And then my parents were killed and it was just me. I wandered aimlessly, and then I found your books. They helped me get through the worst days where it just seemed like the grief wouldn't end, and they help me even now, when I have bad days…"

Julian silently offered her a napkin and she took it to dab her eyes. She heaved a sigh and rushed her words, trying to get them out before the sobs crashed in. "And your characters were my friends and my family when I didn't have any, and when I had nothing and no one to talk to, I had your books, and I just want to thank you for that. Thank you," she whispered, smiling through her tears. "Thank you so much."

He came around to her side of the table and held her wordlessly, his chin on her head. She cried hard but quickly, like a rainstorm that bursts and then passes on. She felt better; as if some of the wound's infection had been purged.

"I guess it's official," she said, pulling away and drying her eyes. "All I do is cry." Julian didn't reply but kept his eyes averted. She watched him return to his seat and turn his saucer around and around. "And I've made you uncomfortable."

"Yes," he agreed, his smile gentle for her, "but in the best possible way."

CHAPTER TWENTY-TWO

The last night, Sunday night, Julian pulled out all the stops. After a late breakfast, and an afternoon spent strolling through Golden Gate Park, they returned to his place to shower and change.

Natalie stepped into the amazing glass enclosure and let the rainfall drench her as if she were caught in a summer storm. She'd wondered if Julian would join her, but he did not. Throughout the day, he'd kissed her numerous times but never let anything progress. Every touch was charged with electricity, building but never releasing; an unspoken promise that the end of the night was going to be spectacular. The water falling over her was hot, but she shivered in pleasant anticipation.

She dressed in her vintage black velvet, and styled her hair as she sometimes did for Kyrie. She drew elegant stockings over her legs, making sure the black seam in the back was straight along her calves, and buckled the little strap on her cream and black Mary Janes with a four-inch heel. She put on red lipstick and black eyeliner, and then slipped the pendant he'd given her on Christmas around her neck. She studied herself in the mirror, pleased with the result but nervous that it wasn't fancy enough for whatever he had planned.

She left the bathroom just as he emerged from his walk-in closet. Her breath caught at the sight of him, while her heart seemed to stop for a moment and then gallop to catch up.

He wore a black suit in a modern style—cut close to his toned physique—and a white shirt and a narrow black tie, loose at the neck. He'd tamed his curls with gel that enhanced the sleek, dark look of him. The sharp lines and angles of his face stood out in contrast to his broad mouth and full lips. And his eyes...*Dear god, he's stunning.*

He stared at her with those radiant eyes of his, drinking her in.

"*Usted es la mujer más hermosa que he visto.*"

"What does that mean?"

"It means I've never seen anything so beautiful in my life."

"I was thinking the exact thing about you." She smoothed her dress down. "Is this all right? I feel like it's too simple. Or like a costume..."

"It's perfect. It's you. You belong to that era but I have you now. I have you..."

He leaned close and kissed her cheek, taking his time. She closed her eyes and felt him lay another kiss near her ear, then another at the corner of her eye. His breath, warm and sweet, wafted over her as he moved his head and kissed her other cheek. His lips brushed her skin, sending shivers of pleasure skimming along her neck and over her arms.

"Julian..." Her eyes fluttered closed. "What are you doing?"

"Nothing. Just kissing you. *Sólo besos, mi amor.*"

He found her earlobe next and he drew it between his teeth, grazing her flesh, before he laid his mouth to the hollow beneath her ear.

The sensations sapped the strength from Natalie's legs. She clutched his arms at the elbows to steady herself, a soft mewling sound of want escaping her. He continued slowly—agonizingly slowly—down her neck, now flicking his tongue in soft, feather-light touches as he went. He circled her, lifting her hair so that he could trail kisses around the back of her neck. She gasped sharply and arched her back, as his touch there sent sudden, powerful shards of electric ecstasy radiating out, down her spine.

"God, Julian..."

"An erogenous zone," he whispered between his kisses. "I'll have to remember that."

He continued his journey around, his lips moving gently, up her neck and along her jawline, until he reached the corner of her mouth that was open and waiting. She tilted her head so that he might kiss her lips...and then he pulled away.

"Wouldn't want to ruin your lipstick," he said, smiling slyly, though his voice was thick.

"Oh, you scoundrel." Natalie clutched his arm until she could get her bearings. "No fair. No fair at all..."

"I know," he said. "I can hardly see straight, but it's time to go."

He offered his arm and she took it but before she let him take a step she said, "I love you, Julian, scoundrel that you are. I really and truly do. And I just want to tell you that now since I'm certain to be incoherent later tonight."

He ran his tongue over his lower lip, as if he could still taste her there. "I guarantee it."

***

A limousine instead of a sedan awaited them, and Julian poured champagne from a minibar that wasn't quite so mini.

"I never get this extravagant," he told her as the city glided past them on the other side of the tinted windows. "I've never had cause to, but tonight I figured, why not?"

Natalie shook her head. "I have to be in class *tomorrow*. This will all feel like a dream."

"Don't think about it now. Just stay here, with me. Tonight."

She turned her head to the watch the city go by. *Tonight and forever...*

***

The restaurant was called Saison, and Natalie had never seen anything like it. A gorgeous motif of exposed brick, warm wood, and hard cement, rife with industrial elegance and permeated by mouth-watering aromas coming from the kitchen that opened on to the dining area.

They were seated at a wooden table next to a decorative stand of potted plants and antique-looking books. The maître'd gave them the day's menu and engaged Julian in a brief conversation about wine pairings and other particulars Natalie didn't quite understand.

Then the maître'd bid them have an enjoyable experience and retreated, taking the menu with him.

"Wait, don't we need to order?" Natalie asked.

"Not necessary."

Natalie frowned. "What do we eat?"

"Everything."

She soon understood what he meant. This restaurant was above and beyond anything she had ever encountered. The meal unfolded as a series of small courses in which they tasted everything under the sun, food Natalie would never have known to order in a million years. A different wine accompanied every dish and she thought the presentations were almost too beautiful to ruin with her fork. Abalone with a nettle puree stood out as her favorite, though every bite was extraordinary.

It took hours to complete the dinner and when they stepped outside to wait for the limousine, she was sure it was midnight.

"Only nine o'clock! We've been in there for ages."

"Did you enjoy it?" he asked, unsure. "I know, it's a bit much..."

"It was amazing. Everything I eat from now on is going to seem bland and naked after that." She snaked her hand into his. "Speaking of which…"

"Oh no, not yet."

"What? There's *more?*"

The limousine took them back down Market Street, and Natalie clapped her hands together when the glowing sign came into view.

"Café du Nord! Julian, how did you know?"

"How did I know you'd like a throwback speakeasy that plays swing? Hmmm, let me think."

She gave him a playful sock in the arm and he laughed and led her inside where Natalie swooned to see Lavay Smith and Her Red Hot Skillet Lickers on the stage, playing before a full crowd—even for a Sunday night. Couples danced on an oval-shaped dance floor. Julian bought her a cocktail—a White Russian—and they watched the couples swing and Lindy Hop before them.

"I'm sorry that I don't know how to swing dance," Julian said into her ear.

"It's okay," Natalie said, concealing the twinge of disappointment. Swing wasn't the kind of dance that was easy to ad-lib. The man leads and has to know what he's doing. They watched one couple blaze across the floor, head and shoulders above the rest. The man, with spiky blond hair, a white tank, suspenders, and baggy beige slacks, spun and twirled a woman dressed similar to Natalie, in green and white 1940's perfection. Natalie watched, awed, and leaned in to Julian. "They look like professionals."

"Do they?" he wondered, a hint of amusement in his tone.

The song ended, another started up and the dancer in suspenders slid up to Natalie.

"Nattie Hewitt?"

"Um, yes?"

"I'm Johnny." He took her cocktail out of her hand, handed it to Julian, and tipped her a wink. "Let's go."

"Wait, what?" She glanced over her shoulder as Johnny pulled her onto the dance floor. Julian saluted her with her drink, his smile crooked and sly. *I don't believe this,* Natalie thought and then there was no time to think; Johnny took her right hand in his left, clapped his hand on her waist, and they were on their way.

In the deft hands of a pro, Natalie found she was able to dance better than she could have imagined. She sensed his turns, his changes, and didn't think but went with him, spinning, turning, sliding under his arms over and over, until the song ended and Johnny spun her with a flourish, and dipped her over his knee.

"Another?"

"Yes!"

Four songs later, Lavay Smith mellowed the house with a slow song, her rich voice—a voice from another era—spilled into the space. Johnny kissed Natalie's hand. "You're aces, honey, but your old man's cutting in."

Natalie turned and Julian was there. Johnny gave them both another wink and was gone. Natalie slipped into Julian's arms and rested her head on his chest until she'd caught her breath. Then she laced her fingers around his neck, gazing up at him.

"I can't believe you," she said. "How on earth did you plan all this? The cruise the other night, that dinner, the *professional dancer*?"

"I had to grease a few wheels, but for you, love, it was worth it. Are you having a good time?"

"Are you kidding? The only thing that would make this night more perfect is if I were dancing with you."

"I might consider lessons."

"You would?"

"Right now, you could ask me to eat fire and I would do it." Then Julian's smile slipped and a feral, hungry look stole over him. "I loved watching you dance. You looked so hot out there. The way you moved…" He kissed her lower lip, long free of lipstick from dinner and cocktails, capturing it with his teeth and then letting go.

"Let's go," Natalie breathed.

"Are you sure? No, stay. Dance…"

"No," she said. "It's time to go."

***

In the limousine, she straddled him, kissed him, carved her fingers through his hair. He gripped her waist, pulling and pushing her against him. She could feel the hard heat of him pressing against her through his slacks. His hands slid up her thighs, over her stockings, and his thumbs delved into the cleft of her hips.

"Julian...the driver," she said, between kisses.

"I'm sure he's seen worse. But you're right. I'm going to get arrested if we don't stop."

He slowed his kisses and she smoothed down her dress. By the time the car pulled into his building's circular drive, they were both composed—at least on the outside. All of the heat and energy that had been building between them all day—stoked by his maddening kisses earlier—was threatening to unleash itself.

They walked past the night doorman and the security guard in silence, as if speaking could break the tension. At the elevator bank, Julian murmured, "Cameras."

The elevator ride was chaste; they stood side by side, watching the numbers climb to fifteen. On his floor, they walked calmly to his door where he keyed the security code. The console *beeped*, the door opened, and they were in each other's arms, crushing their lips and bodies together, her back against the wall of the entry hall off the kitchen. He tried to guide her to the bedroom but she resisted.

"No, here," she said. "I want..." She swallowed. "I want you here. Now."

Julian nodded, stunned, and his hands surged into her hair. He devoured her mouth with his as she hauled at his clothing, pushing his suit jacket off his shoulders and stripping off his tie. His shirt came off next, leaving him in a white undershirt that accentuated every cut of muscle on his arms and chest.

"I don't want to tear this," he said, his voice haggard, and moved behind her to unbutton her velvet dress. "Lift your hair."

She did, and then gasped as his mouth worked over the back of her neck. Her dress was open in the back, and he slipped his hands around her, to knead her breasts through her bra. Shivers and shards of heat radiated from under his kisses, until he pushed her dress off. It pooled at her feet. She turned around, reaching for him, but he knelt swiftly and laid his lips to the silk triangle of her panties.

"Wait, wait," Natalie breathed, arching away.

"You don't want me to?"

"It's just, I've never...I mean, do you really want to?"

"God yes," Julian replied. "I want to kiss you everywhere."
She nodded. "Yes, okay. Yes."

He tugged the silk off her hips and kissed her, lightly, a feather stroke, and even that was enough to make her dizzy. Natalie fell back against the wall as a surge of pleasure shot through her.

"If you don't like it, I'll stop..." he whispered, and kissed her again, using his tongue this time, and the very last thing Natalie wanted him to do was stop.

He was kneeling before her, almost reverently, his hands holding her from behind as his mouth delved into her, producing sensations she'd never imagined were possible. She arched her back against the wall as Julian brought her quickly to a climax that rocketed from between her legs and through her body, leaving her trembling.

"Oh my god," she breathed, as he began working his way back up her body, trailing kisses over her stomach and then between her breasts. Her body wasn't sated, but asking for more, and she could feel the tension in his, the want. He kissed her again, hard, driving her back against the wall and holding her there with his body.

"I need you now, Natalie," he said. "*Right now.*"

"Yes, now," she said over the thundering of her heart. "I want...I want you inside me, Julian."

She couldn't believe that had come out of her mouth, but it was exactly what she meant. Her words spurred Julian like a whip. He attacked her bra; cool air swooped in until his mouth was there, then his hands. He mauled her breasts until she pushed him away enough to open his pants.

"Tell me what you're going to do to me," she breathed, her lips brushing his with every word. She slipped her hand inside his pants and squeezed the hard length of him. "Tell me," she demanded, stroking him harder and pushing his slacks down to his knees.

He gripped her wrists in both hands and slammed them against the wall over her head. He filled her with his presence, captured her, so that all she could see and feel was him. "I'm going to come inside you."

His voice was low, feral, his accent exotic and sexy as hell. Natalie closed her eyes at the sudden flood of heat between her thighs that was already throbbing with pleasure. "*Yes.*"

He hooked her leg around his waist and impaled her, pinning her to the wall. She didn't bother to keep from screaming out; impossible not to. She held on to him, her nails digging into his neck. "More," she gasped. "Tell me more. Tell me in Spanish."

"*Te sientes tan bein,*" he said, driving in to her fast and hard from the start. "*Y mojado, oh Dios…*"

"Yes…Julian…"

"*Corre más amplio para mí… así que puedo follarte.*"

She didn't know what he breathed so hotly into her ear but the implications were clear enough. She reached out, found the edge of the wall with one hand, the other gripped the back of his neck and held on for dear life as he thrust harder, over and over again. "I want… I want…"

"*Que me quieres.*"

You want me. She understood that, clear as day. "Yes, yes, god *yes…*"

He silenced her insensible words by crushing his mouth to hers. She clung to him, her back thumping against the wall with the force of his movements and gave herself up to the heavy, hot pressure building deep inside her. It didn't even matter if she came again, she thought. She just wanted this. Him. But she did come, hard, a sudden rush of pleasure that wracked her, surged through her and across her, like a storm sweeping across an already turbulent lake, leaving it in ecstatic turmoil. She clung to him as he tensed, every muscle rigid with his own climax that filled her with sticky heat.

Neither moved but to breathe, forehead to forehead, sweat mingling. She slid down until both feet were on the floor.

"Natalie…" Julian gasped. He kissed her gently, softly, as if to make up for the roughness of their lovemaking. "Oh god…I definitely did not expect that."

"I love you. I feel safe with you." She smiled coyly, confidently. "It helps that you're drop-dead gorgeous."

He swept her into his arms.

She let out a little shriek of breathless laughter. "Where are you taking me?"

"The bedroom," he said, his voice growing husky. "I don't want this weekend to be over yet."

CHAPTER TWENTY-THREE

Monday morning came too soon.

He lay draped over her, naked, his head pillowed on her stomach as she stroked his hair absently.

"I have to go," she told him eventually, sighing. "I have class and then work. I can't afford to skip any more shifts."

"You can…"

"No," she said. "I can't. I don't want you to do that."

"To do what? Help?" He moved to lie beside her, propped up on one elbow. "Natalie, I can make things very easy for you."

"You can make my rent disappear with a snap of your fingers, you mean."

"Well, yes…"

"*No.*" Natalie said. "You told me why it's okay for you to buy me gifts, how it's important to you. Well, this is important to me. I can see myself just getting lost in it all, like how I get lost in your books. I'll just sink into you…your life, your home, your money. What happens to the rest of me?" She stroked his cheek. "You catch my drift?"

He smiled. "I think so."

"This weekend was perfection and I'd love more like it. Not the fancy stuff necessarily, just more dates. Movies, dinner, dancing. You can pay for all of it to your heart's content. I mean, even that sounds presumptuous."

"No, that sounds absolutely appropriate."

"But if I stop working or let school fall away, I won't be much good to anyone and…Why are you looking at me like that?"

"Because you're a gift the universe set down before me, and I don't know what I did to deserve such a treasure."

"Stop right there," Natalie said. "I've been *marginally* good all weekend about blubbering—only one total break down in a café but who's counting? If you start in with your talk I'm going to break my twenty-six-hour-long streak."

He laughed heartily and kissed her shoulder. "Okay. I'll call you a car. You'll let me do that, yes?"

She glanced at the clock. "I have a little time. You don't have to kick me to the curb just yet."

"In that case…" He kissed her again, this time with intention behind it. She felt a thrill surge up her spine…and then the security system beeped.

"That would be David," Julian said. "Not the best timing, but I'm eager for the two of you to meet."

"Does he always come and go as he pleases?"

"Officially, he works four days a week but I've long ago stopped trying to convince him to do less. He takes care of all the things I'm too lazy to do myself. He spoils me, really."

They got dressed but one glance in the bathroom mirror and it was pretty clear how they'd been spending the morning. Natalie ran her fingers through her hair and followed Julian into the living area where a tall, lanky young man in his early thirties stood glancing about uncertainly. He wore a nice suit, if a bit rumpled, and his brown hair looked as though he drove a convertible with the top down. His smile stretched from ear to ear, but didn't touch his eyes in the slightest.

"Hi, there," he said, hurrying over to Natalie, hand outstretched. "Heard voices…didn't want to intrude…Not staying long, just dropping off and picking up…I'm David Thompson."

"Natalie Hewitt," she said. His hand felt cold and dry, his grip harder than necessary.

"Pleased to meet you, Natalie. I've heard a lot about you from the boss here." He glanced at their breakfast dishes from earlier strewn over the counter. "Oh darn. I didn't know you'd have eaten already. I brought you a breakfast burrito from El Gordo." He offered Julian a white plastic bag he'd been holding behind him as if it were a bouquet of flowers.

"Hey, thanks!" Julian took the bag. "I'll save it for lunch since Natalie is abandoning me."

David's eyes lit up. "Oh, you're not staying?"

"No, I have class," Natalie said. "In fact, I'd better get going…"

"I'll call the car." Julian went to the phone in the living room, leaving Natalie and David alone.

Natalie glanced up at him. For the briefest of seconds she found David wearing a dark look, but then he beamed. "So, what do you think of Julian? He's wonderful, isn't he?"

"Yes. Yes he is." She cleared her throat. "And you've been his assistant for…?"

"Six years. Time does fly, though. Doesn't even feel like work. We're more friends than employer and employee."

Natalie had the impression of a jack-in-the-box bouncing on its spring. She smiled faintly. "That's...good."

"Primarily, I handle his accounts and finances," David continued, his tone more subdued now. "Wealth management, investments, that sort of thing. He has a trust fund, you see..."

"He told me who he is," Natalie said, and felt a strange surge of pleasure at the look of dismay that flitted over David's face.

"Oh, he did?" David ran a hand through his fly-away hair and laughed shortly. "Well, that was...impulsive of him."

Natalie thought she could exchange "impulsive" for "stupid" and it would have more accurately reflected his tone. She glanced at the living room and saw that Julian was gone, perhaps to the bedroom.

"He's never told anyone. Not in ten years. You must be very special to him for him to trust you with such an important secret."

"I'd like to think so."

"Are you?"

Natalie balked. "Am I what? Special?

"Trustworthy?"

"Of course," she said, rubbing her arms from the sudden chill that danced over them. "I only want him to be happy."

Julian finally reemerged with her bag and her velvet dress on a hanger. David took the remnants of Julian and Natalie's breakfast to the kitchen sink. "Here, let me." He started water and began cleaning the dishes noisily.

"You know you don't have to do that, David," Julian began.

"No trouble. No trouble at all."

Natalie gathered her purse and sweater from the couch.

"Ready?" Julian said. "I'll walk you down,"

"Pleasure to meet you, Natalie," David called. "I'd shake your hand again but..." He flapped his soapy hands and smiled his ear-to-ear grin.

"I don't like him," Natalie told Julian the instant the elevator doors closed.

"What do you mean?" he laughed. "You were speaking to him for all of two minutes."

"You know what they say about first impressions."

"Oh, come on. David's harmless."

"He reminds me of Uriah Heep. And I don't like the way he looked at me when I told him I knew who you were."

Julian's lips pressed into a thin line. The elevator opened and they walked through the lobby; the day security guard greeted Julian and gave Natalie a warm smile.

"He's no Uriah Heep. That's a harsh comparison, and uncalled for."

"Don't get mad," Natalie said in a quiet voice. "I just…"

Julian took Natalie gently by the shoulders. His smile was strained. "David's been a good friend to me—my only friend—for six years. He's a little bit neurotic and a lot over-protective, but I care for him. Please tell me you'll give him a second chance."

"I'm sorry. I guess I just want you more to myself right now."

Julian's smile lightened. "I know what you mean. I'll ask David to call before he stops over. And you'll warm up to each other, given time. Samantha—my last girlfriend, whom I promise not to mention more than three or four times a day—"

"Four maximum, if you don't mind."

Julian grinned. "Samantha found David to be quite the confidant."

I can't imagine it. "All right. Next time I see him, I'll try to start over. For you."

"I'd appreciate that."

Natalie slipped her arms around him. "I miss you already."

They kissed until the car came for her. Angelo, the door man, cleared his throat discreetly.

"I love you," she said. "Thank you for everything."

He sighed and held her tight. "Oh no, love. The pleasure's all mine."

She felt another blush color her cheeks. "Not all of it."

CHAPTER TWENTY-FOUR

After the weekend with Julian, going back to school and work seemed like drudgery. But Natalie slipped back into her routines, the days brightened now by dates with Julian, nights spent at either his place or hers, in throes of ecstasy or basking in the simple joy of his companionship. Her long, lonely days seemed like a bad dream; one that she never wanted to have again.

Well into March, Marshall called her, and Natalie felt a pang of guilt; she hadn't spoken to either him or Liberty since that night at the Kyrie.

"Call her," Marshall said. "Before it's too late. If you dwell on why you're mad, you'll forget why you were friends in the first place, and then where will I be?"

"She owes me an apology," Natalie said, plucking a thread on her couch cushion. *Doesn't she?* It was getting harder to remember the particulars of their argument, though Natalie recalled she'd said some things she wasn't proud of.

"Just take a photo of Julian's Pulitzer with your shiny new cell phone and send it to her. That'll clear everything right up."

"Over my dead body," Natalie said. "And he didn't win it anyway. Just nominated."

"Only nominated? What a hack."

"I'd love for you to meet him."

"Honey, tax season has me by the balls and won't let go. This phone call is probably costing me three hundred dollars."

Natalie smirked. "I'm sure."

"But how are things with Sir Julian? Or should I say Sir Rafael?" He heaved a sigh. "Secret identities are so hard to keep track of these days…"

"Amazing," Natalie said. "Beyond amazing. He's the prize-winning author but every minute of every day he makes me feel as though *he's* the one who's struck gold."

"That's because he has," Marshall said, "and don't you forget it."

"Oh, Marshall, I love you." Natalie's smiled faltered. "How are things between you and Liberty?"

"Weird. It's like she's afraid to be friendly to me. What you said really knocked her a good one. Me too, I guess."

"I'm sorry for that."

"Don't be," he said, and she heard the smile in his words. "I have an honest-to-god date on Friday."

"Didn't you just tell me you were too busy to even talk?"

"It's possible I'm prone to exaggeration."

Natalie beamed. "I'm happy for you, Marshall."

"Thanks, honey. I'm happy for you too."

***

The following Sunday, her day off, Julian was to spend the night at her apartment. He arrived just as she was checking her mail. She started to lead him up the stairs but he held back.

"I want to meet them. Niko and his wife."

Natalie hesitated, a strange pang of anxiety twisting her stomach. "Okay. If you want." *Maybe they won't be in today.*

To her dismay, both Niko and Petra were in the café. The jolly Greek man nearly shook Julian's arm out of its socket before deciding a bear hug was more appropriate.

Petra pinched Julian's cheeks. "Look at this gorgeous boy, Natalia! Those eyes!" She then pulled his face close to hers and said, "You treat her good, yes? Or I come and find you."

Natalie was mortified, but Julian smiled with genuine affection and they chatted for a bit before Natalie was finally able to extricate him.

"What's wrong?" he asked, once inside her apartment.

"Nothing, it's just...weird."

"Why?"

"It just is."

"They're in love with you. That's obvious. They'd adopt you if they could. If you'd let them."

"I suppose." She sat on the couch and picked up the closest book, flipping it open absently.

"Natalie..."

"Would you replace your mother?" she snapped and then shook her head. "I'm sorry, I didn't mean that. I'm just...I don't want to talk about it."

Julian glanced at the ski trip photo on her bookshelf. "You've never told me about them. About the accident."

"Why would I?"

"To let it out. To lance the wound."

"I can't."

"You can." He sat down beside her on the couch. "Don't let the feelings fester—"

"It's not just *feelings*..."

"It's pain, and I hate to see you suffer it. Let it go." He took her hands. "You can tell me."

"It's not as simple as that, Julian," she said, snatching her hands away. "It's not like they got killed and it hurts and I don't want to talk about it. That's bad enough, but it's more than that. I can't talk about it because not talking about it is what keeps me from remembering."

"Remembering...?"

"I was there," she said slowly. Getting even this close to the memory was dangerous. She could feel the tight knot of it writhe like a nest of snakes. "It's not like I got a bad phone call or a cop showing up at my door. I saw it. I saw it but it's in bits and pieces and if I talk about it, they'll come together. And I don't know what will happen if I see that again."

"You'll be okay," he said. "You'll be better. You'll go through it and come out the other side. I know you will."

"Better," she said. "I can't imagine it. And I'm scared." She met his eyes. "I'm just not ready. Okay?"

"Okay. And when you are, I'll be here for you."

Natalie moved back into his embrace. "Thank you, Julian. That's all I need."

***

On Wednesday—solely because Julian wanted badly for them to get along—Natalie found herself having lunch with David Thompson.

They sat across from each other at a sidewalk table at the Crepevine, her favorite brunch spot in her neighborhood, and chatted, haltingly, about the only thing they had in common besides accounting. But even before their food arrived, Natalie itched to leave and struggled to banish the nervy disquiet that hummed along her skin from being in David's presence.

"Julian is something special, isn't he?" David said. "I'm lucky to call him a friend. And he's lucky to have me, if I don't say so myself." He laughed. "He has no head for numbers—can't take care of his own money at all. I mean, royalties will only get you so far. I made the bulk of his fortune for him with smart investments."

Natalie smiled faintly. "His money's in good hands."

"It is, though I'd like to think I do more than count his pennies. An accountant and personal assistant...Hell, even his interior decorator!"

"*You* designed his apartment?" Natalie sipped her iced tea. *That explains a lot.*

"I did! Do you like it? It needed serious attention and Julian was too busy working on a book. The one about some village queen with a deformed hand?"

"*Coronation*," Natalie said thinly. She thought reducing that masterpiece to one sentence was like saying *The Great Gatsby* was about 'a rich white guy,' but bit her tongue to keep from saying so.

David shrugged and laughed. "Right. He was up to his eyeballs in that so he let me redo the place. And good thing too. Julian thinks crown molding is something that happens at the dentist!" He laughed uproariously.

Natalie managed a smile. "It's very lovely, though not...what I expected he would like."

"Oh, it was all his idea. I mean, I worked on the particulars, but Julian was very clear about the overall theme. He wanted something kind of cold and...aloof."

"He did?" Natalie frowned. "That's weird, since he's neither."

David raised his eyebrows. "Yes, well... He is and he isn't. You haven't known him all that long so..."

Natalie stiffened. "I know him pretty well. We've been talking for months—"

"Sure, sure," David said. "He cares for you a lot. No doubt he's shown you his best side. But there's a lot of baggage there. About his parents. His father abandoning him, particularly."

Natalie felt an unpleasant stirring in her gut. It was wrong to be talking about Julian like this, behind his back. It was on the tip of her tongue to say so, but David continued.

"He's a passionate man, you know? Loving and kind to be sure, but there's anger in him too. It's buried real deep but it's there. I've seen it roar out of him a few times and it wasn't pretty. I was frightened, to tell you the truth."

"What happened?" Natalie heard herself say, even as shame burned her cheeks.

"Well, the first time his editor, Len Gordon, was visiting. I don't know what he and Julian were arguing about—I came in right as Len was storming out. Len Gordon's a nice old guy. One of the nicest you could meet, and whatever Julian said to him left him close to tears. I only caught the tail end of it. It was…bad." David shuddered. "You know Julian's gift for words; you've read his books. Well, it goes both ways. Sharp tongued, to say the least."

Natalie shifted in her seat. *Don't do this. Don't feed this ugly conversation.* And yet she couldn't help herself. "So his anger…it just comes out verbally, right?"

David rubbed his chin, thinking. "Well, the second time I witnessed his temper was when he broke up with his last girlfriend, Samantha. They were real hot and heavy for a while there. But at the end he cut that poor girl to ribbons, let me tell you. And he threw a vase. Not *at* her!" He laughed at Natalie's horrified expression. "At a wall. I'm almost positive Julian wouldn't hurt a fly."

Natalie set her fork down, her appetite having vanished.

"So anyway, he and Samantha didn't end well and I think that's why he had me redecorate his place. To kind of keep future dates at a distance, right? The ultimate bachelor pad!" David laughed again but it died swiftly. "Oh hey, no, don't feel bad. Gosh, I'm an idiot. I know how all that must sound. I'm sure it's different with you."

"It is," Natalie said, struggling now to keep a civil tone.

"And now he's contemplating coming out of seclusion, eh?" There was a thread of tension in his voice now. "That's surprising, given the vow he made to his *dying mother*. I can't imagine what he thinks to gain by breaking his anonymity."

"A normal life. A chance to connect with his readers. To just be himself."

David frowned. "I suppose. He just hates publicity and suddenly he's all for it."

Natalie crossed her arms over her chest. "If you're worried I've talked him in to it, I haven't. He told me he thinks the secrecy isn't necessary. He's a grown man. He can handle it. But I will support him no matter what he decides."

A smile flitted over David's lips and was gone again. "He's very lucky to have you."

***

The Crepevine was in walking distance from Natalie's apartment, and she was thankful for her foresight in choosing that restaurant. The notion of getting in David's car for a ride home made her skin crawl. *But why? He's not...terrible.*

Except that he was, somehow, and she couldn't put her finger on it. *And those things he said about Julian...*Natalie hugged herself as she walked, shivers skittering up her spine. They weren't all true; Natalie would have bet her life on it. Like David himself, his stories about Julian's temper seemed *off.* Perhaps there was some truth to them, just enough to make her worry. *But why? Is he attracted to Julian?* She couldn't blame him if he was, but that wasn't what bothered her. *I don't* know *what bothers me about him, that's the problem.*

There was a bouquet of flowers waiting for her at her front door; her neighbor must have accepted them for her. Natalie hugged the long-stemmed sunflowers to her and then read the note.

> *Thank you for taking the time to get to know David. I hope this second impression erases the first and the two of you can be friends.*
> *Until tonight, all my love,*
> *~J*

Natalie vowed she would never repeat what she and David talked about. Not one word. She put the flowers in a vase and threw the note in the trash.

It had David's name on it.

CHAPTER TWENTY-FIVE

March 18th was the day things began to unravel. That's what Natalie told the police in her report weeks later, when they asked her to recall the beginning, the first incident. Another Wednesday. She had the day off from the café and intended to get some much-needed laundry done.

Natalie walked in the door from her last class when her cell phone rang.

"Hi, love, it's Julian. Are you busy right now? I need a favor."

She looked to the bulging sack of laundry and the neat stack of quarters on the coffee table beside it. "I have a glamorous date with the laundromat, but I might be persuaded to postpone. What do you need?"

"I need your accounting prowess to sort out a problem. Or maybe it's not a problem; I don't have a head for numbers. Can you come over and take a look?"

"I'd be happy to, but what about David? Isn't that his domain?"

"Well," Julian said, "I think the problem may be David."

"You do?"

"But I don't know. I need someone who understands these things to take a look."

Natalie bit her lip. "I'll be right there."

***

Julian kissed her at the door. "It's okay. He's not here. He had some family emergency and I told him to take the day off."

Natalie relaxed a bit without showing Julian that she had. "What's the problem?"

"I'm not sure if there is one," he reminded her, ushering her into the office.

Natalie had never been in the office before; it was unofficially David's area and he had made it more than clear that he preferred to keep it private, always closing the door behind him when she was over.

The first thing she noticed was that it was decorated with the same sleek, austere sensibility as the rest of the apartment but looked much more lived-in. Framed movie posters from old films such as "Double Indemnity" and "The Maltese Falcon" hung from the walls. The small sofa was draped with a pillow and afghan, looking like an unmade bed, the glass coffee table was strewn with old newspapers and mugs half-filled with old coffee. A small closet faced the entry door and inside were several shirts still in plastic from the dry cleaner's and three pairs of dress shoes tossed haphazardly inside. Natalie glanced at Julian but if he was bothered by his employee treating the office like a guest room, he didn't show it.

"Here," Julian said, indicating the desk where a state-of-the art computer rested on polished cherry wood. The monitor was on and Natalie could see account statements from different banks open. From where she was standing, she couldn't see the actual figures but it wasn't hard to see strings of numbers broken by commas on each statement. She looked away.

"Julian…"

"Is it too soon?"

"No, I…I don't know." She looked at him. "You trust me this much?"

"I trust you to treat this as a job. As a professional."

"I can do that," she said but hesitated again. The entire room was rife with David Thompson's energy, as if he were a ghost thickening the air with his presence.

"It's all right," Julian said. "They're just numbers."

Natalie sat down in the chair before the computer and focused her attention on the task at hand. Up close, the figures that were "just numbers" to Julian were staggeringly large to her; larger than she could have guessed. She kept her face neutral, however, and ignored the way her skin tingled unpleasantly when she had sat down in David's chair.

"All right," she said. "Where is the issue?"

"You once told me about a terrible company, EllisIntel, that you're following for your accounting studies."

"What about it?"

"Well, I became wrapped up in the book and forgot about it, even after you warned me off it. Until this."

He handed Natalie a business-looking letter, already open. In it was a check for $61,365.

"It's a dividend check," Natalie said. "A huge one."

Julian rubbed the back of his neck. "David invested some of my money in EllisIntel for me—"

"*Some*? Honey, to get a check this big, the company not only has to be insanely profitable—which it is—but you have to have *a ton* of money invested. A lot more than 'some.'" She met his eye. "Is that the problem?"

"No. Well, maybe. I thought David told me EllisIntel didn't pay out dividends. I could be wrong on that, but I believe that's what he said. It's pretty clear they do."

"They always have."

Julian's expression darkened. "I've been invested for about a year. The problem then, is where are the other checks?" He indicated the open accounts on the computer screen. "I've looked and I can't see where they might have been deposited."

"And you want me to look for them?"

"Yes." He rubbed his jaw. "Looking at it like this…It's not good, is it?"

"I don't know yet," Natalie said. The part of her that twitched at the mere sight of David hoped it was what it looked like: plain old thievery. He'd get fired, maybe go to jail, and be out of their lives for good. But the part of her that loved Julian—a much larger, deeper well of emotion—hoped he hadn't been betrayed by someone he considered a friend.

"It might turn out to be nothing." She smiled up at him. "I'll see what I can find."

"Thanks, love." He kissed her cheek. "I'll make you some tea and leave you to it."

***

The mug of steaming chamomile hadn't even begun to cool when Natalie sat back in the chair, her heart hammering in her chest and her fists clenched.

"Damn him," she muttered at the computer screen, and called Julian in. It wasn't easy to hurt him but he had to know. "I think he's been stealing from you."

Julian pressed his lips together. "Are you sure?"

Natalie showed him the evidence, neatly compiled. "I've found your investment portfolio from Ellis and it clearly reveals that you've been receiving quarterly dividend checks for the last year. Because of the size of your investment they're all roughly as large as this one: about sixty-five thousand dollars. But there's no sign of the other checks. That's about $200,000 missing. I can't find where that money has been deposited…or if it has been at all. There's no record."

Julian stiffened. "What else?"

Natalie took a breath. "In order to get quarterly dividend checks that large you'd have to have a lot of money invested. A lot."

"How much?"

"$2.2 million."

He said nothing, but stood ram-rod straight, his arms crossed over his chest.

Natalie cleared her throat. "Your net worth, near as I can tell, is uh… close to thirty million. To have that much tied up in one company is…well, it's pretty huge. Even if you wanted to sell the stock, you'd get a huge payout, but also an immediate tax liability. The bigger concern, of course, is the missing money."

Julian uncrossed his arms; a thought occurred to him that blunted the sharp expression on his face. "Hold on. Maybe there's some expense that I'm not aware of. Something he's using that money to pay off."

"I've looked." She indicated the computer screen and a small filing cabinet next to the desk. "All of your expenses are accounted for. And even if it's something I've missed, where are the invoices?"

"That's easy enough to remedy. I'll just ask David."

"Ask me what?"

Natalie jumped out of the chair, her heart clanging madly.

David stood in the doorway, his arms laden with his briefcase and a small sack of groceries from a convenience store. His hair stood on end even more than usual and his eyes were wide as they went between Natalie and Julian.

"What are you doing in here?" he demanded after his venomous gaze landed on Natalie. "What are you…? This is my office. My workspace…" He dumped his belongings on the coffee table; Natalie heard a clank of glass-on-glass from something in his bag striking the table. He whirled on Julian. "What is going on here?"

"David, I wanted Natalie to look at some of my accounts," he said. "I found some discrepancies and I thought I'd ask her about them, given that she's an accountant. Or will be soon. That's all."

"Why didn't you just ask me? I could have told you! I could have explained everything!"

"Then why don't you?" Natalie said, surprised at her own boldness. David appeared as though his head would explode. It was almost comical, if it hadn't been so frightening.

Julian's voice was tight. "Natalie, will you wait in the living room while I speak privately with David?"

"Of course." She swept past David without a word. The office door closed behind her and she breathed a sigh of relief. Natalie had the heart for honest confrontation but not the stomach. Julian would handle it—hopefully by firing David—and that would be the end of it. The end of him in their lives for good.

***

David watched the smug little bitch walk out the door, twitching her ass in her tight skirt, mocking him. She thought she was so smart. She thought she could get rid of him that easily. His lip curled in disgust.

Julian was staring at him with those astonishing blue eyes. But now they were like chips of ice instead of the sparkling sapphires David loved so much. He shivered under that penetrating stare.

"The dividend money goes to expenses," he told him, echoing Julian's words he'd been eavesdropping on moments before the outrage had been too much and he'd been forced to speak. "It goes to all those charity donations you insist I make for you. Since they're not an official expense, I didn't want to take them from your regular account. Much easier to just use the dividend money, which isn't like regular earnings. It's like a bonus. I thought it was pretty clever, actually, but I guess not."

"I thought you told me Ellis didn't pay dividends."

David's mind raced. "No, it's Tesla Motors that doesn't pay dividends. Remember? You wanted me to invest in them because you liked their business philosophy? And I kind of tried to talk you out of it because I want to make sure your money is working its hardest for you. Remember?"

David could see Julian's memory going back more than a year. It was all true, what he'd said about Tesla, and David watched with relief as that truth worked to cover the lie about EllisIntel.

"Okay," Julian said. "But if the dividend money is going to charities, which ones? Where's the documentation?"

David blinked. "Anonymous," he said, a split second before his hesitation would have cost him everything. "You have to keep your donations anonymous so it's not like I can write a check from an account with your name on it. I pull out cash and put it right in the hands of the charity directly. They give me the donation statements for your tax deductions and that's it. I've got those around here somewhere. Or maybe at my office at home…"

Julian rubbed his chin, a good sign. He may be some sort of genius in the literary world, but the man had no head for numbers and he trusted David. He wouldn't delve deep enough to parse that David's rationale was utter bullshit, but Natalie would. *Damn her.*

David sat down and went through the accounts on *his* computer. Natalie had meddled thoroughly. He closed all the files she'd stuck her pointy little nose in and vowed to change the passwords to something Julian didn't know; something he should have done months ago. The most careless of all mistakes, left over from the days when he hadn't been stealing from Julian. From when he had nothing to hide. He felt a hand on his shoulder and nearly jumped out of his skin.

"Thank you for clearing that up."

David eased a sigh of relief. But Julian had betrayed him, had hurt him. And David hadn't done a thing to deserve it.

"You should have asked me first," he said. "After six years…I thought you would have asked me first."

"Next time, I will."

"There won't be a next time," David said. "I'll make sure I keep you updated on everything more closely. I'll tell you what I'm going to do before I do it…"

"No, no, that won't be necessary. I'm not going to start policing you."

David was inwardly satisfied. Outwardly, he shook his head morosely. "She's turning you against me. Can't you see it?"

"To what end? I'm the one who called her over."

"Likely because she's planted the seed in you that I'm not trustworthy. She's never liked me. From Day One." He pretended to straighten his desk and muttered just loud enough to hear, "She's probably after your money."

"That is patently untrue," Julian said, "and I don't appreciate the insinuation."

"I'm sorry, but all this talk of you revealing yourself? That wasn't happening until she came around. We...*You* were perfectly happy until her."

"Perfectly happy?" Julian barked a harsh laugh. "*Tú me estás jodiendo!* I was miserable. I don't want to get into this right now. I have a lot to think about. In the meantime, please don't undo all the progress you two made over lunch the other day. I'd hate to think I set you back."

David restrained a snort of disgust. *Don't stress yourself, sweetheart. There was no 'progress' and there never will be.* But if an empty promise was what it would take to make Julian forget about this business with the dividends, so be it.

"I'll do my best, Julian. For your sake."

"Thank you. I appreciate it. And if you would just show me the donation statements from the charities, I'll consider it a closed matter, all right?" He patted him on the shoulder a final time and started out. "Oh, and I want you to sell all my stock of EllisIntel. Immediately."

David swallowed a laugh so it sounded like a gurgle. "Of course. I'll get right on that."

He stared aimlessly about his office until he found the brown paper bag on the table. He'd almost forgotten about the little flask he'd allowed himself to buy at the 7-11. It wasn't a good idea to let it become a habit again. Julian's employment, friendship and love—yes, love; he knew Julian loved him, loved him enough to buy his stupid lies—had set him straight. But the pressure of Cliff's threats and the pain of Natalie's very existence were like huge, jagged boulders, crushing him between them.

He twisted the cap off the fifth of Jack and took a pull. It burned sweetly but a few more and he'd hardly notice. But not here. He had to get out of here. No doubt Julian was fucking that Natalie woman at that moment. He considered taking a peek as he had in the past when Samantha was the nuisance to be weathered. But as he approached the bedroom door, he heard their voices. They most definitely weren't fucking; they were talking about him. Arguing. He heard Natalie say his name. She made it sound like a dirty word.

He started to press his ear to the door but stepped back. After everything that happened today, if they caught him listening in, it'd be all over. That they were fighting was a good sign, though not enough to lift his spirits. He left, head down and feet dragging, wondering with dejected anxiety how long it was going to take him to make up donation statements from charities that had never seen a single dollar of Julian's money.

CHAPTER TWENTY-SIX

Natalie watched the lights on the bedroom's security console flash orange, and then go still in concordance with the front door opening and closing. David was gone.

"Good," she muttered.

"Look, he told me what happened, and I believe him," Julian said from the bathroom sink.

"I'll believe it when I see the donation statements from the so-called charities your money is going to," Natalie said, pacing. "And *cash*, Julian? No one makes cash transactions that large. No one legitimate, anyway."

Julian emerged from the bathroom looking sleek and dark, having run some water through his hair to tame the curls. "I asked him for the donation statements and he said he'd provide them. End of story." He smiled to take the bite out of his words but it didn't warm his eyes.

"If you say so. It's your money."

"Yes, it is."

She whipped around. His smile had vanished.

"Julian," she said, her voice unsteady, "you're the one who asked me over here to snoop around in his business. You're the one who suspected something was wrong."

"I suspected I missed something and I was right," Julian said. "Why do we have to dwell on it?"

"It's suspicious as hell."

"It was, and then I heard his explanation, and now it isn't. But because you're insistent on finding something wrong with him, his reasons aren't good enough."

This is it. Our first fight, Natalie said. It hurt her heart and her hands were trembling so that she clenched them into fists, but she couldn't stay silent.

"I don't understand why you're so eager to protect him. Sixty-five thousand dollars times three checks, just gone—"

"I'm *eager to protect him* because he's my friend. That's what you do for friends; you trust them. He has *never* given me cause to doubt him, not in six years, yet it took you all of six minutes to decide he's no good. What has he ever done to merit such disdain?" Julian narrowed his eyes. "Is it because he's gay?"

Natalie reeled. "*What?* How can you...? My best friend is...I'm not even going to dignify that with a response."

"Then what is it? You've disliked him from the start. Why?"

"I don't…I don't know why. Something about him…"

"He rubs you the wrong way?"

"*Yes.*"

Julian shook his head. "Sorry, that's not good enough."

"Not good enough," Natalie repeated. "No, I suppose he'll have to rob you at gun point before you'll realize he's stealing your money. Maybe *that* will be good enough for you."

She could see the anger rise in him as if he were transparent: a red flood that burned and brought acid to his tongue when he spoke to her. "I can see it was a huge mistake asking for your help. One I won't make again."

"Don't you dare try to turn this around on me, as if I—"

"In all the years I've known him," Julian said, trampling over her words, "David has said and done things for me that I appreciate; that I am thankful for; that make me glad to call him a friend. The fact that these things have happened outside your awareness does not make them any less true."

"Then why, Julian, didn't you just *ask him first*?"

He said nothing for a long moment. Natalie crossed her arms over her chest in bitter triumph, but instead of conceding honestly he said, "You're right. I should have. I should have known better than to trust your biased judgment."

Natalie stared at him. "That's crazy." She stormed out of the bedroom. He followed after.

"Yes, it's crazy to remain loyal to a friend…"

"Loyal?" She grabbed her purse and sweater. "Blind and gullible is more like it."

For a split second she thought he would lose control and the temper David had told her about would break free. His eyes widened and she could see his jugular pulsing. But instead of exploding, he spoke in a tight, contemptuous tone that froze her blood. "I think it's time that you leave."

Tears threatened but she held them back. "I was already going," she said, and slammed the door behind her.

***

Julian watched her go, and the split second after she shut the door he wanted to call her back, to beg forgiveness. The red-hot flame of his temper had raced through him and then burnt out the instant she left, leaving him cold and riddled with shame. He slumped into the sofa, his head in his hands.

"Cogerme."

He glanced at the phone but recoiled at the thought of hearing her voice filled with pain or hatred, and knowing that he had put it there. Or she might not answer it at all. Fear that he'd ruined everything after the way he'd spoken to her wracked him hard.

Because she'd been right. I don't know why I didn't ask David first. Just a vague disquiet I've had where he's concerned. He tried to think how long he'd been feeling things were different with David. *Has it been a year?* Julian had been so wrapped up in Natalie he wasn't sure. But what he'd told her had also been true; David had been his only true friend for six years. The notion that he would betray Julian didn't seem possible. David's devotion had always been...*intense.*

Julian heaved a sigh. It didn't matter. He'd nearly ruined everything with both of them. David would come around, but Natalie? The anguished look on her face when he'd told her to leave was like a kick to the gut.

Why would I say that to her?

He went to his desk in the library and pulled out a pen and paper, hoping as he wrote, that the unfathomable mystery of it would unravel for him as he tried to explain it to her. But he found his words veering away from the ugly, and flowed toward his devotion to her, which held no mystery, only love.

When the letter was finished, he mailed it straightaway and then sat in to wait, feeling as if his life was on hold until she replied. *So be it,* he thought. *It's nothing less than I deserve.*

CHAPTER TWENTY-SEVEN

In the aftermath of her argument with Julian, Natalie felt Liberty's absence acutely. Marshall had vanished into the chaotic world of tax season and wasn't likely to emerge for another few weeks. She longed to call Liberty and spill it all; she suspected mutual commiseration over the pig-headedness of men would smooth over their own disagreement. Moreover, she missed her friend, wanted to hear her voice, wanted to curl up on her couch and drink cheap wine and watch one of those old kung-fu movies Liberty was such a fan of.

But it would be too unfair to call Liberty for her own selfish purposes. So she said nothing, called no one, and went to school and work, feeling as though she had a lead weight hanging around her neck.

And then she received Julian's letter.

It came to the café, and she found the gesture fitting. Two pages written on fine paper and with the pen she had given him, of that she was sure. She recognized immediately the candid, elegant prose of Rafael Melendez Mendón. She was stunned to find herself the object of such artistry. It was 'I love you' stretched out over two pages. The words were more than words: they left imprints and imagery in her mind, and put emotions in her heart—the exact feelings he wanted her to feel and understand. She felt saturated. She absorbed the words into her heart where they glowed.

And at the end:

Forgive me, my love, so that I may breathe again.
Your Julian

It was a slow night. Sunday night, and usually her night off, but she'd taken a shift to avoid sitting alone in her place, brooding. But the café was empty and she'd been doing nothing but brood anyway. Natalie wiped the tears from her eyes, picked up her cell phone.

"I'm sorry," were the first words out of his mouth.

"That's cheating, you know," she said.

"What is?"

"Writing to me."

"I know. But I screwed up and I don't have anything else. Can I send a car? I want to see you here. I want to *un*-tell you to leave. I…I can't believe I said that."

"It's okay," Natalie said. "I sort of called you crazy."

"I was. To hurt you…"

"Julian?"

"Yes?"

"I'll come over."

She heard him heave a tremulous sigh. "Thank you."

***

It was late when she arrived, after her shift. Julian looked chagrined as he kissed her cheek and walked her in. She stopped and took his hands. "Hey," she said. "It's all right."

He smiled faintly. "Come on. Let's sit. Would you like anything? Something to drink?"

"No, thank you."

He nodded warily and sat with her on the couch. The city's lights glimmered in front of them.

"I have to tell you how sorry I am for how I spoke to you the other day," he began. "In person, face to face, and not hiding behind my writing. That's cowardly and I apologize."

"Julian, we had an argument. It's no big deal."

"But it is. It's not just the words I spoke, but the tone. The disdain and contempt. It's awful, and I don't know where it comes from. Residual anger, I suppose, from my father's absence. That's the most obvious diagnosis, isn't it?" He sighed and looked out over the city. "No matter the source, my temper is horrible and you shouldn't have to witness it, let alone be its target."

Natalie heard David's ugly words resound in her head. *He threw a vase…* She didn't want to ask but she had to, even though some part of her was sure David was lying. "Has it ever been really bad?"

"It's never good."

"No, I mean has it ever become…more than just words?"

Julian's head snapped around and the expression of genuine horror on his face told her everything she needed to know. *Goddamn you, David. And me, for feeding such awful notions.*

"Oh Natalie, no," he breathed. "*Que Dios me ayude*, no. Never. I swear on my mother's soul, I would never…"

"No, don't." Natalie waved her hands. "I believe you."

"But I put that fear in you. I did. I'm so sorry."

She wanted to scream, *You didn't! David did.* But that would mean telling him they'd talked about him behind his back. Shame burned her cheeks. "I'm not afraid of you, Julian. Put it out of your head. Please."

The earnestness in her voice mollified him somewhat, but she could see he was still wracked by guilt. "Even so. I shouldn't have talked to you as I did. I shouldn't talk to anyone like that."

"Everyone says things they regret when they're angry, Julian," she said. "I did. It's what happens. It doesn't make you a bad person."

He shook his head miserably. "My mother was so kind. She never had a harsh word for anyone, not even my father. So it must come from him, mustn't it? I don't know what to do."

"Go to Rijeka," Natalie said. "Find your father's spirit there. Make peace with him."

He looked at her a moment; she could see the idea turning behind his eyes. "Will you come with me?"

"Of course, Julian. Of course, I will."

This seemed to bolster him but the lines and edges of worry kept his face from softening. Natalie fingered the pendant he'd given her, the one she wore always. An image flashed in her mind, bringing a blush to her skin and a thrill skimming down her back.

"I trust you," she told him. "You know that, right? That I don't fear your temper or your harsh words? That I love you more than I've ever loved anyone in my life?"

He smiled, touched and perplexed, both. "I do. Thank you. And I love you—"

Natalie hushed him with soft fingers over his lips. "Let me show you. My trust. My love. Let me…" She rose from the couch and started for Julian's bedroom. She threw a coy, "Stay there," over her shoulder, marveling at her own flirtation.

In his room, Natalie stripped naked—but for the Victorian pendant—and put on a silky robe he'd bought for her to wear when she stayed over.

At the bathroom mirror, she tucked the necklace out of sight, and fluffed her hair so that it settled prettily around her shoulders. Her cheeks were flushed and she took a deep breath. She stopped at the bedside and found a condom in the nightstand drawer. *I can't believe I'm doing this,* she thought, slipping the packet into the robe's pocket.

Julian was standing at the windows, staring into the city lights, and turned to watch her approach, his eyes widening as he took her in, naked beneath the robe.

"I have a request," Natalie said huskily, and her heart began to pound.

"Anything."

"Close the blinds."

Julian pushed a button on some remote. Silently, the blinds came down, but the pot lights in the ceiling and those in the kitchen provided more than enough illumination. "The lights?" he asked, his voice thick.

"Leave them." She moved to stand before him and pushed him down onto the couch while she remained standing. She bent, kissed him softly, the pendant swinging between them. She straightened, nudged his legs apart with hers. He watched her, his mouth slightly ajar, as she rested one knee on the couch between his thighs and lifted his shirt over his head.

Natalie drank him in, the beauty of him. She rested her fingers on his shoulders and let them trail down the muscles, down over his biceps and then back up, over the slope of muscle between his neck and shoulders. Down, she grazed the soft, hairless skin of chest, down farther to his abdomen. The hard lines were made harder as his body flinched under her teasing touch.

She straightened, stood before him, her pulse thundering. They'd made love in the daylight but his body had been over hers, covering hers. Now the lights seemed so bright...

But desire defeated her hesitancy.

Slowly, she undid the robe and let it fall to the floor, so that she was naked before him. But for the pendant. It lay between her small breasts; the cold metal gave her a shiver. Or perhaps it was what she was about to do.

"Natalie..." he groaned, reaching for her.

She shook her head and knelt on the carpet, between his knees. She ran her hands up his thighs, her gaze never leaving his, until she reached the waistband of his pants. She undid the zipper and button with surprisingly steady fingers, and slipped them off, then his boxers.

She stroked him, feeling the hard and softness of him. She found the condom in the discarded robe and rolled it over him, also with hands more deft than she had thought. Then, before she could talk herself out of it, she settled herself on his lap, slid down on top of him.

"Ah god, Natalie."

"Do you...like it?"

He could only nod. His desire bolstered her and she began to move.

Slowly at first, self-consciously, her movements unsure; the lights seemed so bright. Her nakedness filled his eyes. He glanced to where they were joined, his expression rapt and almost pained with desire, and Natalie felt a flush suffuse her skin. But her own need was consuming her like an inferno; she set a fervent rhythm, rising and falling on him, pressure building inside her with every movement. She clung to his neck as she rode him harder and harder. He bucked beneath her, gripping her hips, thrusting up as she came down. They'd been passionate before, uninhibited, but this was something else altogether.

Natalie felt some cold part of her break free and let go. She gave herself up to him completely, to the sensations building deep within her, to the pure, unbridled, unthinking need for him. And through it all, their love wound around and through the carnal desire; a perfection of emotion and sensation, married and bound, with no beginning or end. No she or him. Just them. *Just us,* she thought and then threw her head back as the release came, throbbing and pulsing through her and through him, together.

She sank down on him, melted against him, smiling to herself with satisfaction.

"Oh my god, Natalie..."

She held his head to her chest and stroked his sleek black hair. And then, like a little sigh, "Rafael..."

***

They retreated to his bed where she tucked her back against his chest, and he wrapped his arms around her. She hadn't slept well in the three days since their argument and now sleep tried to claim her quickly.

"I want to sleep now. Talk to me as I fall asleep, Rafael. Talk to me in Spanish."

She felt him nod and then he spoke, his voice a gentle rumble against her ears, lulling her with the beauty of his voice, his language. She recognized a few words; he was speaking simply, slowly, and inexplicably his heart had begun to pound against her back.

"*Te amo con todo mi corazón. Te quiero para siempre. Te quiero hasta el día que me muera. Te amo,* Natalie."

Te amo. She sighed heavily; sleep was dragging her down. "I love you, too."

"*Cásate conmigo.*" His voice was hardly more than a whisper. "*Por favor ser mi esposa, Natalie. Por favor…*"

Por favor. She knew that, of course. And *esposa*…It sounded familiar. A word similar to its English counterpart. *Mi esposa…* Some voice in her mind, distant and faint, screamed at her to wake up and listen. *Yes! Yes!* it cried.

"Yes," Natalie murmured, and then she slipped under completely.

CHAPTER TWENTY-EIGHT

David Thompson was having a shitty week. First, Julian had decided to keep that insipid Natalie in his life after all. He'd had three days of bliss watching Julian shuffle around the apartment in misery, waiting for her to reply to some letter he'd sent her. David thought no one mourned as beautifully.

These were the times David cherished, when Julian's heart was bruised and he was susceptible to ministrations of comfort. David was certain that a little more pain, and then a little more of his own shoulder to cry on, and Julian would discover that the one constant in his life, the one person who never hurt but always helped, was David.

But when he came into the apartment on Monday morning, Julian was nowhere to be found and the cloying scent of Natalie's perfume was all over his bed sheets.

David cursed and locked himself in his office. The charity donation statements were almost done. He'd spent his entire weekend making them from scratch: copying the logos and making false headers from three different charities he thought Julian would approve of. Then he'd had to create false declarations of donations with painstaking care for authenticity. Julian wouldn't look too closely but Natalie would. She would know too, that no one handed over huge amounts of cash, not even for charity. He'd have to somehow work it out that only Julian would see the donation statements and put an end to the mess. *But how can you keep taking the money now to pay Cliff? They'll be watching you, Julian and Natalie both.* And despite all, he still had to deposit the newest dividend check—the one Julian had intercepted—in order to make the April payment.

When he got in trouble as a child, his mother used to warn him he was treading on thin ice. *I have to get out of this mess with Cliff. I have to.*

A little after ten o'clock he heard the security console beep and then someone rummaging in the kitchen; Julian coming in from his morning jog, David guessed. Natalie had class during the day. Julian was alone. His heart thudding dully, David gathered up the false statements and headed out.

The tinny sound of Len Gordon's voice over the speakerphone stopped him. He peeked around the corner to watch Julian make some breakfast and talk to his editor. He looked invigorated from his run, and content, at ease with the world. David's hands grew cold and the papers rustled like fall leaves as they slipped out of his hands.

"That is fantastic news, Julian. I can't tell you how happy I am to hear it."

Julian smiled wryly. "I'll bet you are."

"Oh, come on now. You know I only want what's best for you."

"Yes, Len, I know. You've been great."

"What made you change your mind? After all this time?"

David leaned in, his heart in his throat.

"There are several reasons. But foremost, it would make my girlfriend happy to have the writing appreciated by someone other than her." Julian smiled to himself. "Just don't tell her I said that."

"Your girlfriend is my hero and you *can* tell her I said that. Now, what do you envision?"

Julian sliced bell peppers as he spoke, casually and completely unaware that he was destroying David with every successive word.

"I don't want a lot of press," he said, "but I suppose that would be unavoidable to a certain extent."

"Completely unavoidable."

"Then here's what I want: I want to get it all done at one time. No more than one press statement, or whatever you need, to go along with the book's release and promotion."

There was a gurgling sound on the other end. David imagined Len sitting in his posh office in a Manhattan sky rise, choking on his lunch at his good fortune.

"Are you saying you're willing to promote the book?"

"If I have to." Julian cracked two eggs into a skillet. "I'd like to have its publicity coincide with the so-called 'big reveal' and then I'm done. One book tour, one round of interviews, and nothing else."

There was silence on the other end and then, almost tearfully, "You'll do a book tour?"

"*One* book tour," Julian said. "No more. Not for any other book. It's a one-time deal. If I have to suffer the curiosity, I'd rather just do it all at once and then go about my life, honestly and openly, but not in the public eye. I can't imagine there'd be much of a fuss about me anyway, so don't get it into your head to create one."

"Of course not," Len said.

Of course not, David sneered. *Not Len Gordon...the man who implores Julian to give up his secret at every available opportunity. Not Mr. Discretion...*

"And not yet," Julian said. "Our deal is still on. The book isn't finished. I haven't even begun transcribing it into the computer. When it's done, we'll go from there."

"You're the boss," Len said but David could hear his ear-to-ear smile.

Julian must have too. "Nothing crazy, Len. I mean it."

"It is what it is, Julian."

"I'm not a movie star." Julian neatly folded his omelet and slid it onto a plate.

"In the literary world you are."

"Toni Morrison is a star," Julian said. "Gabriel García Márquez was a star, *Dios tenga en su Gloria.*" He crossed himself. "Stephen King, J.K. Rowling..."

"Yeah, yeah, yeah. Your humility is giving me a headache," Len chuckled. "So what's the ETA on the book? One month? Two?"

"I'm not sure," Julian said. "Maybe a month before I can send you anything, at least."

Len's sigh sounded like a small hiss. "You torture me, Julian. You really do."

"Cry it out on the yacht *Coronation* bought you."

The two men laughed. David felt as though it was at his expense. They said their good-byes and Julian sat down to eat his omelet and read the newspaper—the newspaper David had thoughtfully left on his desk that morning. Because he cared.

Like an actor doing a second take, he snuck back down the hall, opened and closed his office door loudly, and came into the living room.

"Good morning," Julian beamed but it faded as David approached. "Are you feeling all right? You look a little gray."

"It's nothing," David muttered. "Or maybe something," he said, thinking of what he needed to do. "Maybe I should go home so you don't get sick too."

"Go home so you can get better. Don't worry about me," Julian said. He wasn't afraid of illness, never had been. *He never gets sick. Ever.* David's blood curdled at the unfairness of it all.

"Here are the charity donation statements you asked for," he said dully, holding out the papers. "I found three months' worth, but I can get more if you want to see them."

A pained look flitted over Julian's face. He hardly glanced at the papers, let alone made a move to take them. "Go home, David. Get some rest. If there's anything you need, please call me."

Magnanimous this morning, aren't we? David sneered. Julian could afford to be. He was successful, wealthy, loved and in love, and about to become famous to those who cared about such literary things. But a shard of fear cut through David's self-pity when he thought of what would happen to Julian should he reveal himself. *The danger...* He instantly felt terrible for mocking him.

"Yes, maybe I'll do that. I'll go home and rest." He hoped the sweat that had broken out on his forehead appeared symptomatic.

"Thank you, David," Julian said, "for all your hard work. And for forgiving me for not going to you directly over this whole thing. You're a better friend to me than I have been to you."

David muttered something noncommittal, and moved as quickly as he thought plausible for someone coming down with the flu. Outside, he revved his Audi and tore down the streets. He felt like vomiting. The irony made him want to cry.

David slowed his car down long before arriving at Orbit, the dread taking the urgency out of him. He rolled into the small parking lot behind the club, mindful of the glittering puddles of shattered glass that menaced his tires every time.

Cliff's third-in-command, Jesse—his cousin or nephew or some such—answered his knock at the back door.

David had always thought Jesse should have been a cop or firefighter, someone in uniform. A blond, good-looking man in his mid-twenties; he had the appearance and charisma of someone competent and sharp, who watched the world through weary-beyond-his-years blue eyes, as if there were too much to fix and not enough time to fix it all.

"What do you want?" Jesse asked. "Is it delivery day already?"

"No," David said, drawing himself up. "Is Cliff here? I need to speak with him."

Jesse peered over David's shoulder, nodded once, and opened the door. "Make it quick. I don't think it's a good idea for you to be seen hanging around here."

"I agree." David followed Jesse along the dimly lit hallway, their footsteps clapping on cheap linoleum. "If you three would leave me and Rafael alone, you wouldn't have to see me here ever again."

Jesse didn't say anything.

The hallway was short and dingy, with scuffed white-walled paneling and fluorescent lighting that cast a greenish tinge to everything. Three doors opened on tiny offices and a storage space on one side. On the left, there was one door and that led, after a longer corridor, to the public restrooms and then the club. At the end of this hallway was Cliff's office. The door was closed. Before Jesse could knock, David took his arm.

"Help me, Jesse," he pleaded. "You've always seemed like a good guy. Help me convince Cliff to end this. It's getting bad. I'm scared."

"Let go of my arm."

"Please. This is getting dangerous and you know it."

Jesse seemed to hesitate.

"It can't go on forever," David prodded. "You know that. You're the only one who knows that, I think."

The other man looked up at him and pity flashed behind his eyes. But then he said, "It's not my decision to make. Talk to Cliff." He knocked on the door while David sagged.

From inside: "What?"

Jesse opened the door. "David Thompson's here to see you."

Cliff glanced up from the pile of papers on his cluttered, detritus-strewn desk, his expression sharp. "The fuck, Jesse? You bring him in here?"

"He said he needed to talk."

Cliff swore again and tilted back in his chair, making it creak under his girth. He looked David over with ugly blue eyes—pig's eyes, folded in flesh—and laced meaty fingers behind his head of straw-colored blond hair.

David straightened to his full height and said, "It's over, Cliff. No more."

Cliff raised his bushy blond eyebrows. "Is that so?" He nodded at Jesse. "Shut the door. And stay."

Jesse obeyed.

"What's got your panties in a twist now, Dave?"

"Ju—Rafael Mendón is going to go public. You can't blackmail him anymore. It's over," he repeated, hoping the simple voicing of those words would make them true.

"Is that a fact?"

"You can't blackmail someone for a secret they're no longer keeping."

"That is true." Cliff held out his hands. "I guess that means I'm now blackmailing you."

"What?" David screeched. "What...what do you mean?"

"You said it yourself. You can't blackmail a person for a secret they're not keeping. I couldn't give two shits what the writer does. So he blows his cover?" Cliff shrugged. "Big deal. But it's *you* who has the secret now, Dave. You've been stealing from Mendón for almost a year. Two hundred grand. That's a big, expensive secret, Dave, and if you want to make sure Mendón doesn't find out about it, you'll keep making your deposits here. To me."

David swallowed hard. "No. I won't do it. I can't."

Cliff settled back into his chair. "Oh, I think you can find a way." He nodded at Jesse, indicating that this meeting was over.

"I'll go to the cops. I will, Cliff, I swear it."

He expected threats or refusals. He didn't expect laughter. Cliff leaned back farther in his chair until he was in danger of falling out of it. Tears of mirth streamed from the corners of his eyes to become lost in the flabby folds of his cheeks.

"Aww," he huffed, "isn't that adorable? Is that just fucking *precious*?"

David's cheeks burned. "You think I'm bluffing? Watch me, Cliff. This ends now."

He turned and opened the door. It jerked to a stop and slammed shut again—Jesse's hand splayed flat on the door, his arm barred David's way.

"Jesse—"

With speed that belied his huge size, Cliff was out of his chair and slamming David against the wall, one meaty hand wrapped around his neck. "You don't talk to Jesse, you talk to me."

Pain radiated up David's skull and he gasped frantically for breath, clawing at the hands that held him. "I...I..."

"You think I'm stupid?" Cliff snarled. "You must think I'm stupid to barge in here like this and make demands you have no business making."

There was no correct answer to that question and David couldn't answer anyway; he struggled to gaps the smallest breaths. Cliff held him for what felt like another eternity, and then let go. David slid to the ground, gasping.

Cliff moved back to lean against the front of his desk. "I'm going to clarify a few things for you, Dave, so that you'll know better next time you to try to fuck with me." He counted off on his thick fingers. "First of all, you're not going to the police. Not now. Not ever. You'd be incriminating yourself as an accessory and you'll go to jail. That's a fact. Secondly, you're not going to go to the police because if any one of us—Jesse, Garrett or myself—get nabbed, your writer friend dies. You get me? You think I don't have other guys? Guys who, with a word from me, wouldn't put a bullet through his eye? It'd be pretty easy to do, once he reveals himself and all. Real easy."

David shook his head, whimpering. "No, no, no."

"Yes, yes, yes." Cliff chuckled. "If I get pinched, Mendón is *dead.* Are you picking up what I'm putting down, Dave?"

David nodded miserably.

"And thirdly, because you come in here, causing all this trouble...next month I want thirty thousand dollars."

"Cliff...I can't! It's too much. And you don't understand," David cried. "He's selling the stock. He won't get the checks and then I can't—"

"Again, not my problem. I don't care what you do or what it takes, but I want my thirty thousand dollars on the first of every month or your boyfriend's going to wind up with a hole in his head, you read? Now, get out."

***

Jesse watched David shuffle out of the office like a sick old man. After he was gone, Cliff's fierce expression and clenched fists relaxed. He chuckled and resumed his seat behind his desk.

Jesse shuffled his feet. "You haven't told anyone else about our deal, have you?"

"Of course not," Cliff sniffed. He knocked a cigarette out of the battered pack on his desk and lit it. "Dave doesn't need to know that. How else am I going to keep him in line?" He snorted a laugh. "Right now, I got him thinking we're the fucking mob."

Jesse jammed his hands in his pockets. "Why don't you cut the guy some slack? He looks like he's on the edge already. All nervy and twitchy. I don't like it."

"No, but you like the money, don't you, Jess?" Cliff was smiling through a haze of blue smoke. "You didn't seem all that concerned about poor Dave's mental health when I cut you your share last month."

Jesse shrugged. "Just think it's getting a little out of hand is all." He glanced at Cliff from the corner of his eye. "You really going to off this writer guy?"

"It'll never come to that."

"How do you know? Thirty grand?" Jesse blew air out of his cheeks. "What if Mendón catches him taking it?"

"Then the party's over, fun while it lasted, no harm, no foul. Dave wouldn't tattle on us after the fact. He wouldn't want to put Mendón 'in danger.' You saw him, right? The fag's obviously in love with the guy."

Jesse opened his mouth to say more but Cliff was getting that look in his eye—the one he usually got right before he called in his 'little' brother Garrett to crack some skulls.

"All right, you're the boss," Jesse said, holding up his hands. He turned to go.

"How's Marietta feeling? Better?"

Jesse stopped, his back to Cliff. "Yeah, better. Thanks."

"That extra money is helping to pay down some of those medical bills, yes?"

"Yeah, Cliff. It is."

"Yeah, I thought so. Your cut of thirty grand would help even more, I'm guessing."

"It would, boss. Thanks." Jesse went out and held the door as it closed. Sometimes it slammed shut if one wasn't careful and that pissed Cliff off.

He made sure it didn't.

CHAPTER TWENTY-NINE

The sun was warm on Julian's face; his immense windows were streaming with sunlight. Dust motes danced, and in his hand the velvet box turned over and over. He smiled. All of the pieces in his life were coming together, converging on one point in the not-too-distant future. He couldn't see it clearly yet; it was a starburst on a vast horizon. The new book, the end of his anonymity, and Natalie...His hand holding the box squeezed.

It was so easy, it was almost frightening. He had only to do his work and love her and the rest would fall into place. He could hear her laughter, taste her on his lips, and he marveled that she was his.

Julian opened the box. The sunlight was caught and refracted in a thousand tiny prisms that seemed to have no end to their depth. His pulse quickened and he snapped the box shut again, turned it over and over again. He rested his chin on the other, his fingers concealing the pensive smile.

I already asked and she said yes.

It didn't count, of course. A whim. His love for her had prompted the words to pour out, and she'd been half asleep and unaware, not comprehending. But she'd said yes, and it had thrilled his heart, and solidified the certainty he'd had almost since the first night they'd spoken: that he wanted to spend the rest of his life with her. He'd bought the ring half-wondering why he hadn't bought it sooner, and cherished the hope she'd say yes when he asked again, properly.

The front door beeped and then opened, pulling Julian from his thoughts. David came in, carrying some small parcels and two coffees, the white cups branded with the familiar green mermaid.

"Morning, Julian," David said, and gave a quick glance around. "Natalie here?"

Julian could hear him strain to sound casual. "No, David. She's in class."

"Okay. I just didn't want to intrude."

"You're not. You never are." Julian felt warm all over. "I think you've surmised by now that I plan on going public. Everything will change when the new book is published, but please don't fear you'll be lost in the shuffle. I want you to remain a part of my life, as employee and friend. I mean that."

A flicker of a smile came and went on David's face. "It's just going to take some time to get used to, I suppose. When, uh…when do you think the book will be finished? A couple months?"

"I thought so," Julian said. He extricated himself from the sunbeam with a stretch and went to his desk in the library. He flipped open the first page of the first of five composition books. "But now I'm thinking it might be sooner." He bit his lip, reading over the first lines. "At the risk of sounding arrogant, I think this is my best work yet."

"Sooner?" David asked. "As in…weeks?"

Julian shut the book. "I think so. I don't believe it's going to take me as long to polish it up as I had thought. It sort of…flooded out of me in a rush and I don't believe there's too much I want to change."

"That's nice," David said and busied himself with something behind the kitchen counter.

Julian smiled. David had never cared for the particulars of his writing beyond handling the income it generated. He hadn't an artist's heart. Not like Natalie. Natalie who loved her numbers, who could order the world with their exactness and yet see infinities between them. His hand found the box he had stuffed into his pocket.

"It's all Natalie's doing. She was my muse, in a manner of speaking. Just being in her presence made it so easy to connect to the part of me that produces all this." He waved his hand at the stack of books and then took out the black velvet box. He opened it, held it up even though David was too far away to see much more than the glitter of diamonds.

David stopped whatever he was doing. His face was colorless, his mouth hung open like a door torn half off its hinges.

"I know it's another adjustment," Julian said, "but I'm showing this to you first. I want you to understand that your inclusion in the new life that is about to begin is not a fluke or lip service."

David seemed to recover himself. He traversed the space between the kitchen and living room, carrying the two coffees. He handed one to Julian and peered into the box.

"It's a beaut."

"Do you think she will like it?"

"I don't think she'll be able to help herself. Look at those rocks!" David chuckled and took a sip of his coffee. "Mmm, that's good stuff."

"It's not too much?" Julian inspected the ring again. "She has such delicate hands…"

"She'll love it." And then Julian found himself engulfed in David's embrace. "Congratulations."

Julian was careful not to show his discomfort. He had never minded David's physically exuberant manner before, not even after David had confessed he was attracted to him a year earlier. But now David's embraces hummed with a strange tension, and Julian had the notion that his friend would just as soon strike him as he would hug him. He recalled the night of David's confession, and a pang of guilt dimmed his joy. *Is it still hard on him? To see me with someone else?* He started to ask but David retreated to his office with a broad, parting smile.

Julian retired the ring to his pocket. He had only the faintest idea about how he would propose to Natalie and it wasn't in San Francisco. There was a lot planning left to do but that would come later. His book waited.

He sat at his desk in the library and started up his laptop to begin the work of transcribing the hand-written work into the electronic, editing it as he went. He had toyed with the notion of doing this at the café but he needed to focus. It was well and good to have the buzz of the city around him—and Natalie's intoxicating presence—as he put his story down for the first time, but now he needed silence and to look at it with a critical eye. He drank the coffee David had bought—a vanilla-flavored latte—and set to work.

The digital clock on his desk showed eleven-thirty when Julian's stomach churned uncomfortably and drew him out of his story. He took several deep breaths but the nausea came fast and quick. He hadn't even time to run for the bathroom, but scrambled for the wastebasket under his desk. He got it just in time. A second, violent surge immediately followed the first, and dizziness assailed him. Blood rushed to his face with pressure as his stomach clenched to empty itself. He gasped for air and then swallowed—a mistake as his stomach wouldn't tolerate even his own saliva.

Julian fell to the floor and rolled his weak, jelly-like limbs into a ball to wait until the nausea passed. For ten minutes he lay still, willing his body to right itself and settle from the vicious episode. When he thought it was safe to move, he stumbled to the sofa and hauled himself onto it. Unthinking, he swallowed again—the acrid flavor of soured vanilla. With shocking immediacy, he vomited again but there was nothing left in him, only air and bile and saliva that dribbled off his lip. His heart galloped in his chest and his hands shook as if electric current ran through them.

"David," he called when he could. "Help me."

***

David laid a cold compress on Julian's forehead and dabbed his mouth with a washcloth. "The flu is still going around," he said. "That must be it. You have all the symptoms."

Julian nodded weakly. He lay on his bed, one arm flung over his face. Earlier, David had watched the effects of the ipecac syrup take hold from the cover of the hallway. Julian had called for him, and David rushed in; the valiant hero who could stand the sight and smell of vomit—anything for his beloved.

He helped Julian to his bedroom, helped him change into an undershirt and pajama pants, his eyes lingering over Julian's body when he wasn't looking. He set him up with ginger ale and soda crackers, and another dose of ipecac just when Julian started to improve. Good friend that he was, David held the wastebasket and wiped Julian's mouth with great care when it was over.

Julian slept and in the early afternoon, felt strong enough to try to eat again. The diuretic David laced his soup with had him stumbling to the bathroom, and then more vomiting with another dose of ipecac-laced ginger ale. By early evening, Julian's skin was a ghastly ashen color with bright flushes of red on his cheeks and neck. He couldn't get out of bed by himself and so David held off on the diuretics. No sense in getting too messy.

Around seven o'clock, his cell phone on the nightstand rang. "It's probably Natalie," Julian croaked. "Tell her…"

"I'll handle it." David answered the phone with a curt, "Yes?"

"Uh, David?"

"Hello, Natalie."

"Hi. Is Julian there?"

"He is, but he has taken ill with the flu. He can't speak to you right now." Julian was watching him. He flashed a smile that didn't translate over the phone line. "If he's up to it, he'll call you in the morning."

"Wait, David. He's sick? Is it very bad?"

"It's the flu," he said, barely keeping the irritation out of his voice. "The usual symptoms."

"I'd like to speak to him."

Julian struggled to sit up. "I can talk to her…"

David waved his hand as if to say, "It's no trouble at all." To Natalie he said, "I think it's best that he rest. We'll see how he's doing tomorrow."

Julian sank back into the pillows.

"Good night, Natalie. Thank you for calling. I'll be sure to pass on your well-wishes."

"Yes, tell him—"

David hung up. "We'll try her again tomorrow." He patted Julian's hand and took the tray of crackers—uneaten—and the cup of ginger ale toward the kitchen.

"David," Julian said, his voice was sleepy-sounding and pathetically weak. "Could you bring me some water, please? I'm so thirsty."

"Of course."

"And David?"

"Yes?"

"Thank you for being here."

David met his eyes. "I will always be here for you, Julian. Always."

In the kitchen he exulted. Would that this was his life permanently: complete mastery over that which he desired and complete dependence on him from same. Here was control. Here was total absence of panic and fear and helplessness. Natalie was locked out and Julian was at his mercy, unable to do anything but allow David to minister to him as he wished: to touch his skin, to change his clothes, to brush the hair from his eyes. It was a slice of perfection he wished he could stretch out indefinitely, but a few days would suffice for now. When Julian emerged on the other side of this illness, he'd take it easy, work slower—if at all—and, most importantly, he'd have a new appreciation for David who had cared for him when he needed him most.

David whistled as he poured Julian a tall glass of water. Three drops of ipecac diluted instantly and vanished. He carried it into the bedroom, and held Julian's head as the poor man drank gratefully. And when Julian vomited again, heaving and coughing with an intensity that was almost frightening to behold, David knew Julian was grateful to him for holding the wastebasket.

CHAPTER THIRTY

Natalie called Julian twice the following morning and both times received no answer. She was dressed and ready for class, but instead of walking down to 19th Ave for the bus to the university, she called a cab. She asked the driver to wait out front as she dashed into a local market and emerged with a bouquet of sunflowers, some steaming chicken soup from the kettles, and some ginger ale. She found it romantic, in an odd way, to imagine sitting with him, reading to him from the book she'd grabbed off her shelf—the *Collected Stories of Katherine Anne Porter*—or snuggling with him to watch an old movie.

But a twinge of something ugly tingled along her nerves to think that David had been taking care of Julian and might still be there when she arrived, unannounced. If David was still there, she'd insist he leave no matter what he—or Julian—might have to say about it.

Angelo was on duty that day as the doorman; he tipped his hat to her with familiarity, and Hank the security guard ushered her to the elevator, as her arms were laden. At Julian's door, she didn't bother to knock but keyed in the security code he had given her several days ago. Until now, she'd never had cause to use it. Until now, she had never been so glad to have it.

She opened the door to find David pacing the living room, his hand clapped over his mouth in panic. His clothes were rumpled and looked slept-in and she knew he'd been here all night. The apartment stank of sour foulness. Natalie's stomach twisted, not for the stench, but from fear.

"What is going on?"

David let out a little shriek and then practically sagged in relief. "It's…he's…"

"Where is he?" Natalie said, but she was already setting down her parcels on the coffee table and heading toward the bedroom.

"Oh my god, Julian…"

He lay horizontally across the middle of the bed, on his left side but awkwardly. His left arm was splayed out behind him, his face was blank, his blue eyes staring at nothing while his mouth worked, speaking unintelligible Spanish. His sides heaved rapidly with gasping breaths, his lips were cracked and his eyes sunken so that Natalie thought he couldn't possibly be the same man she had seen two days ago. A ghastly half-smile stretched his lips at the sight of her.

"Oh, ahí estás. He traído… las flores, al igual…que usted pidió."

Natalie rushed to him. "Julian!" His forehead was burning to the touch and dry as paper. Panic galloped through her, making her tremble. She rolled him over with effort so that he was on his back.

"Llegué tarde hoy… pero te prometo que… no volverá a suceder."

David's shadow filled the doorway. "What's he saying? I only speak a little. I think he's babbling…"

"What happened here?" Natalie screeched. "Why is he like this?" She raced into the bathroom and returned with a wet washcloth as David paced and stammered.

"He has the flu. I mean, that's what I thought. But he won't stop vomiting. And I haven't given him any…I haven't given him anything to eat or drink."

Julian's eyes looked through Natalie in a way that made her own stomach clench. She felt his pulse and cried out in alarm. Its irregular, weak flutter was terrifying.

"Oh my god, call an ambulance! Why haven't you called an ambulance?" she shrieked.

"An ambulance? He really needs…?"

"Yeah, David, he really does!" Natalie reached for the phone by the bedside and tapped 9-1-1 with shaking hands. "I need an ambulance, please." She gave her name and Julian's address. "Oh please, hurry."

She hung up and took Julian's hand in hers.

"Agua…"

She whirled on David. "You know what *that* means, don't you? When was the last time he had water? What is going on here, David?"

"Why are you so pissed at me? How should I know?" David shot back. His voice quavered. "He's sick. I was taking care of him."

"Yeah, you were taking care of him," Natalie muttered sourly. She hurried to the bathroom and returned with a small glass of water. Her hands shaking, she held it for Julian to drink.

Most of it spilled over his chin but she managed some into his mouth. It came back up immediately.

Natalie backed away slowly. "This isn't the flu." She wrung her trembling hands, paralyzed by fear and helplessness. "This is something else. Oh god…"

"I don't know what to do for him," David said and for once Natalie agreed.

The ambulance arrived in ten minutes though it felt like ten years. The EMTs were quick and efficient, exuding a cool competence that calmed Natalie. The words "severe dehydration" passed between them, and in moments they were wheeling him out of the apartment. Only one person was allowed to ride to the hospital with them. Natalie precluded David from even attempting to try with a dagger glare.

"Right, you should go," he said, as if it were his idea. "I'll meet you there."

"Is he going to be all right?" Natalie asked one of the EMTs who rode in back with her. He fiddled with plastic bags of clear liquid and adjusted the air mask they had put over Julian's slack mouth.

"Best to hear from a doctor, ma'am," he said with practiced ease.

Natalie bit her lip. "I heard you say he was dehydrated? Is that very bad?"

"Can be," the EMT said. He was young and good-looking, the kind of guy she imagined some women wouldn't mind breaking an ankle for. He flashed a brilliant smile that meant nothing to her. "He's stable now, we got fluids in him. Try not to worry."

She took Julian's limp hand in hers and clutched it protectively. *As if that were possible.*

***

At San Francisco General, Julian was extracted from Natalie's grip and a polite but insistent nurse ushered her into a waiting area while he was wheeled away. As he vanished from sight, the strength left her. She sank into a stiff brown chair, put her head in her hands, and cried behind a curtain of her own hair.

David blew into the waiting room a few minutes later, arms flapping, hair flying.

"Where is he?"

"In with the doctors," Natalie said dully. She sniffed.

"Good. Any news yet?"

"No."

"Okay. Right." He sat a few chairs away, leg jumping, and rifled through magazines or skimmed over pamphlets about how to better manage diabetes, and which kind of cholesterol was good and which was bad. He glanced up to see her staring at him.

"What?"

"What happened, David?"

"I told you. He had the flu. It got worse. I'm not a doctor, Natalie."

"Why didn't you call one? What were you waiting for?"

"I panicked!" David screeched, drawing a disapproving glare from the nurse behind the glass. "What do you think happened?" he hissed. "I asked him if he felt like he needed to go to a hospital but he said no."

"Really? You speak Spanish all of a sudden? It wasn't incoherent rambling after all?"

"No, no, before. Before he started talking like that. Last night he wasn't this bad."

"That's when you should've gotten him some help."

"He didn't want help!" David cried. "You know how he is! He's stubborn…and intimidating. He said he wanted to sleep and so I let him. Get off my back, Natalie. I'm scared shitless too."

Natalie didn't want to back off. If she did, the fear would swoop in and destroy her. Better to hold on to the anger and direct it at David instead of being untethered, drowning in grief. *Not again! I can't do this again.*

When she realized her parents were gone she remembered searching for something; somewhere for her to go or do or think that wasn't that awful pain, as if her soul had been trying to leap out of her body like a jumper from a burning building. And now a doctor was going to round the corner and she'd have to do it all over again. Only this time, there wasn't another migration north, another city, another do-over. She didn't have it in her. Her hands clenched until her nails cut her palms.

"I hate you," she seethed at David and instantly regretted it. *God, what an ugly thing to say…*

His eyes widened in genuine hurt. Then his open, clownish face took on a sharp, incisive look she had never seen before.

"You think you're the only one who cares about him?" He snorted. "You're so selfish. You don't even know how lucky you are."

"I know *exactly* how lucky I am," Natalie said, "and if you've ruined it…"

"And what about what you've ruined for me?"

Natalie sat back in her chair.

David's scorn was potent. "Oh, hadn't occurred to you, had it? That maybe there was an entire other dynamic going on that you know nothing about?"

"He doesn't…I mean, he likes *women.*"

"Do you honestly think it's all about sex? A man like Julian? He thinks on different levels. He sees *people* and not just *gender.* I've always had hope." David's eyes filled with tears and Natalie found her heart softening against her will. He wiped his eyes and took a breath. "But you're here now and it is what it is. I'm just the employee again, except you *hate me* and will tell Julian to get rid of me and so I can't even have his friendship."

"David—"

"And now I'm supposed to sit here, while Julian is *fighting for his life*, and worry about what *I've* ruined for *you.*" He snorted. "Yeah, that's fair. That's all kinds of fair."

Natalie swallowed, her fingers plucking the ratty hospital upholstery. "You're right," she said. "I'm sorry. I never looked at it from your perspective. I apologize."

David wiped his nose with his sleeve. "Apology accepted."

They sat in a tense silence, the worry for Julian hovering over them like a dense, black thundercloud and they waited to know if it would break open and sweep them up into a terrible storm or blow over.

Finally, a doctor—a blonde woman of middle years—approached. Her face was kind but passive, Natalie couldn't read it. *Please…oh, please…* Her breath was locked in her chest with her pounding heart.

"I'm Dr. Cannon. Are you here for Mr. Kovač?"

"Yes," Natalie and David said in unison.

The doctor smiled. "He's going to be fine."

Natalie closed her eyes as a deep and forceful relief swept over her. "What was wrong with him?"

"Severe dehydration, likely brought about by the flu. The excessive vomiting and diarrhea can trigger it, and muscle cramps make it difficult to take in fluids later. But the saline drip is already stabilizing him. Fortunately, he is showing no signs of kidney failure or cerebral edema—swelling of the brain, to be more plain—though I have to say he's fortunate you brought him in when you did or I might not have been able to give you such an optimistic prognosis. He'll have to stay the night, of course, while we run some tests."

"What kind of tests?" David asked at the same time Natalie said, "Can I see him?"

The doctor smiled at her. "Of course. Room 114, curtain D."

Natalie hurried to the hallway, hoping her lack of inclusion would make David take the hint. Apparently it did, as he remained behind, and she forgot all about him as she entered the small room where ER patients were held before transferring upstairs.

Julian looked wan under the sheets. A tube fed oxygen into his nose. Another dripped saline solution into his veins. His eyes were closed, his head tilted to the side. Natalie approached, torn between letting him rest and forcing him to wake up and make him speak coherently; his earlier delirium had been so frightening.

She sat beside him and took his hand—the one not punctured and laden with needles and tubes—and kissed his fingers. He opened his eyes and smiled drowsily at her.

"Hi."

"Hi, love."

He glanced around, his brow furrowing—all of his movements were slow and tired. "Hospital?"

"Yes." *Kidney failure, brain swelling...* She plastered on a bright smile. "You're going to be just fine."

"What's wrong with me?"

"Nothing serious," she said. "You were just dehydrated. From the flu." But it didn't sound right. It didn't sound like *enough*. Not coming from the kindly doctor and certainly not from David.

Julian nodded and drifted off again. Natalie curled up beside him on the bed, one arm over him, like a shield, and watched over him as he slept. *Something isn't right about this,* she thought, listening to the *beep beep* of the machine that monitored Julian's pulse.

Not right at all.

CHAPTER THIRTY-ONE

David left the hospital without speaking a word to anyone for fear he'd burst into tears. He saved that for the privacy of his car. He tore out of the parking lot and pulled over onto 22nd Street. There, he leaned his head on the steering wheel and sobbed for a good fifteen minutes.

I almost killed him.

Yes, agreed another voice, *and the hospital is going to run some tests. When they do they'll come to the same conclusion.*

David was thankful he'd had the foresight to fill out Julian's hospital admissions paperwork incorrectly but it didn't matter. The guilt and pain of Julian's suffering overshadowed everything.

"I didn't mean to hurt him so badly." He raised his head and wiped his tear-streaked face in the crook of his arm. "It was an accident. I just wanted him home safe with me." He heaved a tremulous breath. "I'll tell Julian everything. He won't care about the money. He didn't even notice it was gone. He'll care that I've been suffering, putting myself in danger, trying to protect him. We'll figure out a plan to get out from under Cliff. We will. Together."

***

Julian was released the next day but much to David's irritation, Natalie stuck to him like a burr. She was always over, taking care of him, spending the night, taking time off from work and school. Julian said fondly that she was nursing him back to health.

She's not nursing him, David thought, *she's standing guard. From me. She knows.*

His confession to Julian was prepared and ready, but giving it in front of Natalie was not in the plans. Finally, four agonizing days later, he couldn't stay away. The hospital's test results would catch up to him any minute. David needed Julian alone, to tell him everything before he heard it elsewhere and got the wrong idea.

David took a steadying breath and keyed open the door.

She was here.

He smelled her perfume again, stronger now, wavering in the air like the stink of rotting flowers. Muffled noises—laughter, and the pop of a champagne cork, unmistakable—came from Julian's bedroom. They hadn't heard him come in. The little beep of the security console had been drowned in their celebratory noises. But what celebration? David moved slowly, hardly daring to breathe, towards the bedroom.

The door was cracked open just wide enough for him to peer in, beckoning him to come and see. He couldn't resist. The blinds had been drawn and the room was cast in a warm, yellow glow from one lamp by the bedside. In the dimness, two figures knelt on the bed, facing one another, naked and laughing and grappling lustily.

Natalie had a champagne glass in her hand—David couldn't see a bottle from his vantage but he just knew it was Dom Perignon or something equally precious that she was carelessly sloshing on Julian's bedspread. Julian didn't seem to care, but laughed as he kissed her.

David's breath hitched. He forgot about his confession and the old familiar, guilty thrill raced through him.

The pall of sickness was gone from Julian already. He was there, naked and hale, his lean body warm and brown in the dim lights, with shadows playing over his skin, delving into the sharp lines of his muscles. It had been a long time since David had had something to take home to his own bed. It was the one advantage to Julian having a woman around: images burned into his memory to be altered later. Mental Photoshop he called it.

David prepared for the lust that tightened his groin and made it throb with a dull ache. Instead it was his heart that ached as he watched the pair of them, oblivious to his presence, become lost in each other.

Natalie took a sip of the champagne, and bent her head to kiss Julian. It poured into his mouth and in the ignited fervor of their kiss, a trickle of it escaped. One shimmering trail leaked from the corner of Julian's beautiful mouth and began a slow journey to his chin. David watched, transfixed, as this phenomenon that went unheeded by Natalie.

The unfairness of it all was like a kick to his stomach.

Julian was turned on—duped, David thought—by Natalie's kiss, and he flung her onto her back. She squealed with laughter; the champagne flew from her hand to stain the bed sheets, and then Julian covered her body with his. He drove into her with a fury and David was afforded an unobstructed view of Julian's thrusting form, his ass clenching and unclenching, while Natalie was buried, practically unseen beneath him but for her legs wrapped around his waist. At any other time it would have been the perfect scenario; hardly any Mental Photoshop needed.

But David stepped away from the door like a sleepwalker. He closed his eyes against stinging tears, and gripped the back of a chair in the living room to keep from sinking to his knees.

It should be me…

David's breath came in ragged gasps and he opened his eyes. The apartment was a blur through his tears and he struggled to breathe. *I'm drowning*, he thought and whirled around, searching for the door. He made his way over and stumbled from the apartment. In the hallway, he caught his breath and the agony twisted in his gut, simmered in the hot acid and boiled into a rage. Julian loved *her*.

The thought careened around his mind, popping and bubbling until his face burned. He realized his blindness. He had blamed Cliff, blamed *himself* for the awful predicament when all the while it was Natalie's fault. She'd seduced Julian and convinced him to reveal himself. He'd said so himself. Hadn't he told Len it was Natalie who'd convinced him to go public? She didn't love him. She wanted his money and she fucked him without appreciating who he was, and left David standing on the sidelines, watching her squander little moments of pure beauty in favor of her own satisfaction.

His confession forgotten, its reasons burnt to ash by his fury, David strode with a purpose toward the elevator. His earlier confusion and fear seemed silly. It was all so simple now.

***

Natalie was pleased her champagne kiss had fired Julian up as it had. He attacked her, pinned her to the bed and let his passion have free rein. And she accepted him fully, eagerly, clutching him as he rode her with animal lust, all remnants of his frightening illness having vanished.

His face was buried in her neck, the harsh, hot gasps of his breath sounded loud and she added her own until they were in harmony, a perfect rhythm and unison that extended far deeper than the motions of their bodies. And in the short space between their shared breaths, she heard it. A tinny little *beep*. Her eyes flew open in time to see the security console flash red and then back to orange.

David...

The ecstasy that had been building in her subsided with shocking immediacy. She gasped at the ugly, hollow feeling that remained, even as Julian shuddered with pleasure. She held him tightly. Over his shoulder she noticed that the bedroom door was ajar. Not a lot but enough.

After a few moments spent catching his breath, Julian retrieved her fallen glass and filled it with the champagne—a celebration of the news that she would graduate with honors this June. He brushed the hair from her eyes and bent to kiss her, but stopped, frowning. She'd tried to keep the ugly feeling in her gut from showing on her face, but he must have seen a shadow of it.

"Everything all right?"

She nearly told him she suspected David had spied on them but the gray days of their argument came back to her. *You have no proof. David might have realized what was happening and fled out of discretion. He didn't spy on us.*

Except that he did. She knew it as surely as she knew her own name.

She smiled. "Everything's fine.

CHAPTER THIRTY-TWO

The rain fell steadily into the late afternoon. It tapped on Natalie's apartment windows, streaking them with crystalline rivulets. She packed a few more items of clothing in her bag, and her laptop. She had plans to spend the weekend with Julian, and work on her accounting coursework while he edited and transcribed his book. He had thought it a nice idea to spend time together and didn't see it for what it really was: protection. When she was around, David stayed away, and that's all that mattered to her.

Her cell phone rang just as she was zipping her bag. Her heart ached to see the number.

"Liberty…"

"Hi, Nat. How's tricks?"

"Oh, Liberty, I'm so sorry—"

"No, forget it. I'm the asshole. Marshall told me everything. I should've believed you."

"It's okay. I shouldn't have said what I said. About you and Marshall."

"Maybe not. Or maybe it was totally spot on. Anyway, I only have a minute before my client shows up and just wanted to make plans to hang out, catch up, and hear all about your famous millionaire boyfriend. As one does."

"I'd like to talk about *you*. It's been far, far too long. I miss you."

"I miss you, too. Are you free Wednesday?"

"That's perfect."

"Okay, Nat. Well…uh, talk to you later."

"Bye."

Natalie ended the call and sighed. Things weren't one hundred percent between them, but she felt as if a huge weight had lifted. She hadn't realized how big of a hole Liberty's absence had made in her life until she was back. *Woman cannot survive on man alone,* she thought and grinned.

She took up her bag when her front door buzzed. She went to the wall-mounted console. "Who is it?"

"It's David Thompson. I need to talk to you. Let me up."

Natalie felt her chest tighten. She fought to keep the irritation out of her tone. "Actually, I'm kind of busy."

"It's urgent. I need to talk to you. It's about Julian."

Of course it was about Julian; they had nothing else to talk about. But Natalie heard the panicky edge to his voice and a cold pang of fear settled in her gut.

"What is it? Is he okay? Is he sick again?"

"Just let me up, for chrissakes. I'm soaked."

Natalie hit the button to unlock the gate below, and left the door ajar for him, her thoughts awash in worry, so that when David burst through her front door, she let out a little shriek.

"Jesus, David, you scared me." She closed the door behind him as paced her tiny living area. "What's happened? What's wrong?"

David was flapping around her small space like a caged bird. He wore a long trench coat, its shoulders and back streaked dark with rainwater. His hair was plastered to his face and his glasses were fogged. He ran his hand over his mouth again and again as he paced.

"Okay, Natalie, listen. This is serious. This is no joke. No, no joke at all."

Natalie inched toward her door. "What? You're starting to frighten me. Just...calm down and..."

He whirled on her. "I've been doing a lot of thinking and this is the bottom line: you have to leave Julian alone. You can't see him anymore. You just can't."

"Okay, that's enough." She turned to the door and opened it. "I think you'd better leave."

"I mean it, Natalie." David pushed past her and slammed the door shut, making her wince and her heart jump into her throat. "You don't understand what's happening. You should have just stayed out of *our* business."

"I don't know what's happened to you, David, if you're on drugs or what, but this is ridiculous," she said, her voice sounding steadier than she felt. "Now, please leave or I'll have to call the police."

David shook his head vigorously. "No, no, you won't be doing that at all." He tore at his hair in a sudden flash of fury. "You stupid bitch, why? Why did you have to show up? We were doing just fine without you!"

Without another word, Natalie moved toward her cell phone on the coffee table. From the corner of her eyes she saw a flap of coat and then a dark shape gripped in David's hand. Time slowed down for an instant, reality became bent and twisted as she understood, before she turned to face him, that David had pulled a gun out of his pocket and was now training it on her.

She uttered a little shriek and dropped to her knees beside the couch, huddled against it, one arm thrown over her head. "No, no, no, please, no…" Mind-numbing fear paralyzed her senses and she fought for breath. *This isn't happening. How can this be happening?* "P-Please," Natalie whimpered from under her arm. "Put the g-gun away…please."

David behaved as though he hadn't heard her. "You have to stop seeing him. You have to disappear out of his life. Do you get me?"

Natalie screamed as he brandished the gun over her, then prodded her in the shoulder with it.

"Say it! Say you'll leave Julian alone!" he thundered, and with equal and alarming suddenness, he backed off and resumed pacing. "You don't even *know* the problems you've caused, do you? No clue at all."

Natalie peeked from behind her arm, gulping air to try to calm her racing heart. "David, please. I can't…I can't talk to you with the gun out. I can't." She began to cry, hands shaking and teeth chattering. "Please put it away…and I—we'll talk. Please."

David ceased his pacing and after a moment of deliberation, returned the gun to his pocket. "But I'm leaving my hand on it. If you try anything…"

Natalie bobbed her head, sobbing with relief. "I won't. I swear it. Thank you. Thank you."

"All right, get up," David barked. "Get on the couch and listen because I'm not going to tell you this twice."

Natalie crept slowly, her arms and legs so stiff with fear they could hardly bend, and moved from the side of the couch to the front and sat on one end. She hugged a pillow protectively to her. David moved his pacing so that he was in front of her, one hand shoved deep in his pocket that drooped with the weight of the gun.

"Here's the deal. You aren't going to see Julian anymore. Do you understand me? No more. Not ever again."

"Why?"

"To keep him safe!" David roared and Natalie cowered behind her pillow. "Don't you realize the danger you've put him in? All this talk of him naming himself? It's all because of you! Before you, we were doing *just fine*. But now, everything's all messed up and it's all your fault."

Natalie thought of the dividend check and the missing money. "The money…It's about that money, isn't it?"

"That's none of your business. It was *my* business, but you just had to stick your nose up in it, didn't you? I was doing my job. I was keeping Julian safe, but now…"

"What do you mean? What have you done, David?"

"I didn't mean to. I was drunk and I said some things I shouldn't have. Some things I swore I would never say."

"What are you talking about?"

"All I have is Julian." The man looked as though he were about to cry. "And after five years, I couldn't…I couldn't take it any more. A year ago I asked him if he felt the same…and he said no…" Tears spilled from beneath his glasses. "He said no, so I just started driving. I found a bar and I got drunk and I had no one to talk to but the bartender. And you're supposed to be able to tell a bartender anything and it's safe. Like confession. So I told the bartender how much I…how much I *appreciate* Julian and what he's done for me. And I kept talking and drinking and talking and drinking, and then I told him who Julian was. It just slipped out! But the bartender wasn't supposed to know about Rafael Mendón, and he sure as hell wasn't supposed to have *read* him! He wasn't supposed to know he was reclusive; he wasn't supposed to *care*. But he did. Goddammit, he did."

He broke down. He stood, bent and sobbing in the middle of Natalie's apartment, his tears mingling with the rainwater dripping from under his hairline.

Natalie set aside her pillow and held out her hands—still trembling. "David, it's all right. I'm sure it's not so bad as you think…"

David whirled on her, the gun in his hand free from his pocket. The terror gripped Natalie all over again, and she cowered against the couch.

"This is why you're so damned stupid! You don't know! Those men? The bartender and his cousins or brothers or whoever they are? They are *dangerous*. And the only way to keep them off Julian is to pay them. But I don't have any money. I have to give them Julian's money. For his protection. I can't let anything happen to Julian. And dammit, if I had just kept my stupid mouth *shut!* I tried. I tried another way to keep him safe, but no, no…You had to butt in again."

"What do you mean, you tried 'another way'?"

"I just wanted him home. Safe. So I could take care of him. That's how it's supposed to be."

Natalie's skin suddenly felt cold all over, another layer of fear settling over the first. "David…did you *poison* Julian? Oh my god…"

"No. So? I was trying to help him."

"He could've died."

"He could die now!"

David shrieked so loud, Natalie prayed one of her neighbors would hear and call for help. A noise complaint. Anything. But David took control of himself and wiped his face in the crook of his gun-toting arm.

"So that's the deal," he said in a calmer voice. It was as though sharing his terrible secret had been eating him alive and now that it was out, he could breathe a little easier. "Cliff and his guys won't hurt Julian if I keep paying them every month. But if I don't—" he gave her a look that chilled her blood—"they'll kill him."

Natalie felt the bile rise to her throat. "David, you have to go to the police. You have to."

"You're so full of yourself, aren't you?" David said. "I saw that about you right off. You don't think I haven't thought of that a thousand times since this whole nightmare began? You don't think I would have done that if I had thought it would save Julian?"

"David…"

"It won't. I don't know how many friends Cliff has or how deep this thing goes. So Cliff gets arrested and then what? He gets pissed off, that's what. What happens to Julian then? What kind of revenge do you think they might take?"

Natalie had no answer. She reeled as this strange, horrifying reality settled into her bones like a deathly chill. "Damn you."

"Oh, shut up. Don't take that holier-than-thou tone with me. This is all your fault. Things were going along *just fine* until you showed up."

"Were they?" Natalie spat back. "Things were fine and dandy as you've been stealing from Julian to keep a bunch of blackmailing criminals from killing him?"

David raised the gun as though he meant to strike her with it. She cried out and cowered again.

"I said shut up," he said. He lowered his hand and said in a dirty voice, "You wouldn't know any of this if you hadn't wormed your way into his life. You just want him for his money and now that you've convinced him to reveal himself, you'll soak up his fame too."

"That's not true," Natalie said through her tears. "I love—"

"Don't say it!" David thundered. He rubbed his eyes with one hand; the rollercoaster of emotion was clearly exhausting him. "This is what you're going to do: You're going to tell Julian you're breaking up with him. You're going to leave him and never see him again. He'll retreat into anonymity where he belongs, and he'll be safe."

"It won't work, David. He's still going to reveal himself. It has nothing to do with me."

"You are such a *liar*," David whined. "You *told* him to reveal himself. You told him…"

"I did *not*," Natalie said, wiping her tears. "I told him I'd support him either way. The decision is his. He—"

"He's happy with you," David said, as though the words tasted sour in his mouth. "Or thinks he is. Breaking up with him will crush him enough that he won't have the energy to finish his book or deal with the press. And by the time he gets over you, I'll have convinced him to stay where he is, that he's better off. Where's your phone? Your cell phone?"

Natalie raised her tear-streaked face. "What? *Now*? Over the phone? With you here? How on earth am I supposed to do that? What can I tell him that he'll believe? I saw him yesterday. David, I'm supposed to see him *tonight.*"

"That's not my problem." He spotted her iPhone on the coffee table and thrust it into her hand. "I don't care what you tell him but you had better make it believable and you had better do it now."

She tilted her chin, defiant. "And what if I tell Julian the truth? He can go to the police himself, get protection, leave the city if he needs to. I—"

Natalie's words ended in a choked gurgle of terror as David laid the muzzle of the gun to her temple. "If you try to take him away from me, I'll kill you."

Natalie whimpered, sobs caught in her chest. She imagined his finger would slip—he was so nervous—and then she'd know nothing. She'd just cease to be. Every moment was possibly her last. She fought the urge to vomit.

"O-okay," she whispered. "Please. I'll do what you say. I'll do it. Just don't hurt me…and don't hurt him. Please…"

"Don't make me hurt him." David withdrew the gun. Natalie sagged against the pillow. "I don't *want* to hurt him. This whole thing is to protect him. That's why you have to break up with him believably. He has to think you're serious." He waved his gun at the phone in her hand. "Do it. I want to hear this."

"I-I don't know what to say."

"You know," David said, his voice low and dangerous, "I was just going to come in here and…and end you. Make it look like a robbery gone bad. But I decided to give you a chance. Besides, Julian would think you died loving him and then where would I be? He'd *mourn* you, when he should *hate* you. So you call him now and you tell him you never want to see him again. Right…now."

A thousand thoughts swarmed in Natalie's mind like bees, stinging, buzzing; a chaos from which she could not possibly organize some coherent rationale with which to break Julian's heart. Then her frantic gaze alit on the muzzle of the gun trained on her. The cold sliver of fear that slid down her back was oddly calming.

"The heart wants what it wants," she murmured, "but the mind is afraid…"

"Call." David wagged the gun at her. "*Now.*"

Natalie, feeling like a passenger in her own body, watched her fingers find Julian's name in her phone and press it. She put the phone to her ear. Beside her, David settled himself to listen, his gun steady on her.

"Hey," Julian answered brightly. "I was beginning to wonder what happened to you. Weren't you supposed to come over tonight, or is that just my wishful thinking?"

Natalie froze. He sounded so natural. So unaware. As if he were on the other side of some alternate reality, one in which life was normal and free of gun-wielding maniacs, while she was on the other side, in a realm of terror and madness. She wanted to dissipate into a million pieces; disappear into the phone and reappear where Julian was, safe and happy.

"No, you're right," she told him, "I was supposed to come over."

"Natalie, what is it?" The smile had left his voice. "You sound terrible. Please don't tell me you're sick now, too."

Natalie pressed her lips together. David made a 'let's go' motion with the gun. "Actually, I am a little under the weather. I have to cancel tonight."

"I'll come over. Can I bring you some soup or—?"

"No," Natalie said. The concern in Julian's voice was making it nearly impossible for her to continue. "No, you can't come over. In fact…" She swallowed hard. "I don't want you to come over. Not tonight, not tomorrow, not ever again."

He laughed shortly, incredulous. "What?"

"This is not a joke."

A pause. "Okay."

She closed her eyes and spoke. The words formed a split second before falling from her lips. "I've been doing some thinking lately. Back to the night when you told me who you were. I told you that your books were more than just wonderful writing. I told you that they are my refuge."

"Yes." Each word dropped in her ear, heavy with dread. "And?"

"And so then you come into my life. You become the love of my real world, *and* you are Rafael Mendón, the love of my sanctuary. To know that you are the creator of so much of my happiness…it's too much. I can't put that much of my life into one man's hands."

"Natalie…" His voice trembled. "What are you saying to me?"

David nudged her with the gun to keep talking.

"You can't be separate from yourself," she said, her own voice vibrating like a broken guitar string. "I can't have just Julian. But I can have just Mendón. I can read the books and keep that joy to myself. I'm sorry, but I'm just not strong enough to lose both of you."

"Natalie." Julian was breathing heavily now. "What is happening? What the hell is happening? I don't understand. I don't...*Over the phone? You're doing this to me OVER THE PHONE?*"

"The heart wants what it wants," she whispered, and glanced at the gun in David's hand, "but the mind is afraid."

"No. *No!*" Julian raged. "This is bullshit. This is...insanity. I will not be torn out of your life like this. I need to hear this from you. I need to *see* you say it."

Panic lanced through Natalie. "What? No, don't..."

"You can't do this, Natalie! I *will not* let you! Not like this!"

"Julian, no!"

The call ended and Natalie stared at the phone in her hand, her heart thundering, her mind numb. *Maybe David didn't hear. He'll leave and Julian will come and I'll explain. We'll run. We'll be safe.*

David snatched the phone out of her hand and dropped it into his coat pocket. "He's coming over, isn't he?"

She said nothing.

"*Isn't he?*" The gun pushed against her temple and she bit back a scream.

"Yes!"

"Okay, okay." David withdrew. "That's fine. We can do this. I'm going to stay out of sight—"

"I won't let him in," Natalie cried. "I won't—"

"You *will*. You tell him whatever it takes to end it forever. If I hear one word I don't like..." He heaved a breath and held up the gun. "Him. You. Me. But him first, so you can see what you made me do. Understand?"

"You goddamn bastard," she whispered. "Go to hell."

CHAPTER THIRTY-THREE

It took Julian twenty-five minutes to show up at Natalie's place. She felt every minute tick by with agonizing slowness and yet it seemed like it took no time at all. She spent it crafting more arguments to get him to leave fast. *Or else David will kill him. He'll kill us all.*

The buzzer buzzed and Natalie jumped.

"Let him in," David said, slipping into her bedroom alcove and pulling the curtain. "And remember what I said. I'll be listening."

Natalie let Julian up with a shaking hand. He burst through the door a moment later, and she screeched, backing herself up against the curtain behind which David lurked.

"Where is he?" Julian demanded, storming into her living space. He dumped his messenger bag on the floor by the couch.

Natalie's heart plummeted and blood turned to ice in veins. "Wh-who?"

"Your friend. Marshall. Or what's her name...Liberty. They were here, weren't they? Giving you bad advice? Telling you to get rid of me? They had to have been, since I cannot fathom what could have changed between *yesterday* and tonight."

He spun around, his gaze searching, and Natalie was sure he'd go to her bedroom alcove and find David there, crouched like a villain in a bad movie.

"No," Natalie said quickly. "It's not them. I-I told you why—"

He whirled on her, his blue eyes blazing. "You *told* me the most inexplicable, atrocious bunch of *bullshit!*"

"It's not bullshit!" she countered, even as her heart screamed the opposite. "It's the truth and you need to get out. Now. I don't want to see you again."

"Why?" Julian's face was a mask of fury. "Why now? What happened? I need to see the words come out of your mouth. *Tell me!*"

Natalie recoiled, her numbed mind scrabbling for the reasons she'd come up with waiting for him to arrive. "Y-You're planning on revealing yourself. That means press, publicity, travel. You'll be gone for long stretches and you'll meet many new people...Other women! Women who are more interesting and…and more exotic than I am. You'll be tempted to live it up and I can't handle losing you like that, piece by piece."

"Live it up?" Julian spat. "You think the moment you're out of sight, I'll cheat on you? For what? To make up for *lost time*? That's what you think of me?"

No! I know you never would. "I don't know."

"You don't know," he repeated, mocking. "But you're quite certain of my inability to be faithful to you. That you've seen written in the stars."

"I don't…I'm not saying that would happen, I'm saying it's possible that things could go wrong between us and—"

"This!" Julian cried. "This is something going wrong between us!"

"I'm sorry," she heard herself say, and the words sounded so small and weak. "But you need to leave now."

Julian struggled to calm himself and took a step toward her. His voice was softer now, pleading. "No, Natalie. I don't…Something's not right. This isn't like you. Please. Tell me the truth. Why are you wrecking us?"

The only thing preventing her from breaking down was the fact that David was not ten feet away, waiting for it to happen.

"I told you," she said. "If I stay with you, I am putting my heart and soul into your hands. I can't. I have to have my refuge, something that just belongs to me. To keep me safe."

"Safe," Julian said, tears outstanding in his eyes. "You want to be safe. But let me tell you something, no one is safe. You think that you're the only one putting your heart and soul into another's hands? You think I haven't risked *everything* for you?"

Natalie, with a wail of anguish in her throat she couldn't unleash, felt that no matter the danger, no matter that this was 'pretend', she was making a terrible, terrible mistake.

"Please don't hate me," she whimpered. "Please."

His stony expression crumbled as he really looked at her. "What is happening, Natalie? You're saying these horrible words, but your eyes…Your eyes are *screaming* something different." He took a step closer, she took a step back. "You don't seem sad or even angry…you're *terrified*. Why?"

A sudden, vague suspicion crossed his face, and he turned to glance around her apartment. His gaze landed on the bedroom alcove, around the corner from the living area, hidden from view. "Is there—?"

"Yes!" Natalie burst out before Julian could move or say another word. "I am terrified. Of you. That's why I did it over the phone. I didn't want to suffer that terrible temper of yours. I was afraid…" She swallowed hard, the words stuck in her throat like knives. *Do it. Or he'll find David and David will kill him.* "I was afraid you'd hit me."

Julian staggered backwards, his suspicion forgotten. His face paled and she watched his heart shatter right before her eyes. "We…we talked about… I would never…"

"I'm not taking any chances." Natalie squared her shoulders. "Now go."

His eyes widened at the cold, callous tone of her voice.

"I can see I was horribly mistaken about you," he choked. "I was a fool, blinded by a poor imitation of love, for how could you have ever loved me? Me, who is inconstant and…and *violent.*"

He shuddered and staggered to his bag.

Natalie felt tears scorch her eyes, and she clutched herself to keep from flying at him, holding him, screaming that it was all a lie.

"I am not the man you accuse me of being, and I'm not going to be. I will not live in that ugly, suspicious perception."

He pulled out the five composition books. His latest novel. Slowly, with trembling hands, he laid the books on her coffee table.

"You don't want me," he said brokenly. "You want him. So take it." He turned away. "It was already yours."

He shouldered his bag and walked out, closing the door carefully behind him.

The strength went out of her, and Natalie fell to her knees. In the second before David emerged from her bedroom, she swept the composition books under her coffee table where they scattered amid some accounting texts and loose papers. There was a chance he didn't hear Julian give them to her. Natalie didn't even know what prompted her to hide them in the first place. A sudden, strange instinct. And then the tears came. She knelt, hugging herself and sobbing, rocking back and forth, as David locked her front door and stood before her.

"That was better than I could have hoped," he said with grudging approval. "It's over, but I remind you: don't think to call the cops. I'll be staying real close to him. Real close. Living with him. We'll be living together," he said again, obviously liking the sound of it. "If I catch even a whiff that something's up, that you warned him or are up to something, I'll just…I'll end it all. We'll die together. He and I."

Natalie said nothing, stared at the ground.

"Cliff and his cronies aren't going to let it go, either. Let me handle it. You're out now. You're free. Go about your business. Forget it ever happened. Forget all about him."

Natalie stood up as if drawn on puppet strings. She faced David, raised her hand and slapped him across the face. Hard. So hard that her own hand stung with the force of it.

Rage boiled in his eyes as her handprint bloomed hot and red on his cheek. He raised the gun as if he'd strike her with it, but laughed instead.

"Okay." He adjusted his glasses that she'd knocked askew. "You can have that. I won, after all. I *won.*"

He left, shutting the door with a bang, and Natalie let out the wail of anguish she'd been holding in. He was gone. The gun was gone.

Julian is gone.

She staggered back to the coffee table and pulled out the stack of books. She clutched them to her, cradled them, sobbing, and waited until her racing heart and roiling stomach calmed down. It took a very long time.

CHAPTER THIRTY-FOUR

David hadn't wanted to wait too long after leaving Natalie's place to get to Julian. The fear that she'd call the police anyway was as sharp and hot as the slap on his face. *No. She knows he'll die if that happens. That I would end him...*But would he? He recoiled from the thought. He wasn't a murderer, of course not. But more and more the gun in his hand seemed less a weapon and more of an escape. A respite from the pain of watching that which he loved most in the world give his love to another. And perhaps stronger than that, the gun promised an end to the maddening chorus of whispers in his mind that constantly reminded him of his failures, of his loneliness, of the immense pressure that pushed down on him like an unseen hand.

No, I can handle it, he told himself. *Natalie is stupid, but not stupid enough to risk Julian. I'll just have to be vigilant.*

The hours just after the break-up were crucial, and he wanted to ensure Julian's train of thought started heading in the right direction. Julian would need a calm, steady hand to lead him away from these crazy notions of coming out of seclusion and back into the security and safety of anonymity.

But first he had to wait until the damned imprint of Natalie's hand faded from his cheek. David sat in his car in the parking garage under Julian's building. He checked his reflection in the rear-view, cursing the humiliation of it.

Fifteen minutes later, the mark on his cheek had faded into a blotch of redness. It would have to do. He raced up to the penthouse to find Julian standing ramrod straight, staring at the night skyline with bloodshot eyes, his arms crossed over his chest, his face expressionless.

"Oh, hey," David said. "I...hope I'm not disturbing you. Just...uh, left something in the office."

Julian didn't reply; didn't acknowledge his presence.

"Is...everything okay?

"No, David, it's not."

"What's wrong?" David approached and stood beside him. "Are you all right?"

"Natalie and I..." He clenched his teeth. "We've broken up."

"Oh gosh, Julian. I'm so sorry. That's a real shame." He laughed shortly and said, "Well, sure sounds like you could use a drink—"

Julian rounded on him with a sudden speed made all the more startling for his stillness before. "Why aren't you surprised?" he demanded, his voice hoarse and thick with old tears. "Why aren't you asking what happened? Did you have something to do with her leaving me?"

David stammered and stuttered, tripping over the coffee table in retreat.

"What? No...Of course not! Who am I to Natalie? She hates me. What could I possibly say that she would listen to?"

Julian considered this and then abruptly turned away, the haunted expression returning. "Someone said something to her. I just can't believe that she would do this when...when we were so happy."

"What happened? I mean, what reason did she give?"

"She wants the writing instead of me. And..." he added, hardly audible, "she's...afraid of me." His jaw worked for a moment. "She's afraid I'm violent."

David opened his eyes wide, aghast. "What? But that's crazy! You're the sweetest, kindest, most thoughtful—"

"My temper is bad," Julian said, without hearing. "I told her that I struggled with it, with being hurtful and cutting with words. But I never...I don't know how it got into her head that it's worse than it is."

Yes, I wonder... David stood beside Julian and laid his hand on his shoulder. "What are you going to do?"

Julian's eyes flickered to David's hand and back. His tone was dangerously casual. "I'm not sure, David. What do you recommend I do?"

David turned his caress into a hard pat and then withdrew. "I recommend you do what any man would do in this situation, and that is get good and drunk."

He watched as some of the tension eased out of Julian, his eyes lost their suspicious glint and all that remained was pain. He sank down on the couch and laid his head in his hands.   ·

"It doesn't make sense. None of it. It's not her. Something's happened..."

David sat down on the couch's arm, resisting the urge to touch Julian again. Julian's sweater was fine, black cashmere, fitted to his beautiful physique. David loved him in black...

"Sounds like typical, fickle female behavior to me," he said, and then regretted it. *As if I would know.* But Julian seemed not to have heard.

"What if she was…mistaken? Listening to bad advice from her friends…?"

David frowned. "Mistaken? Julian, she broke your heart. She accused you of abuse! Abuse that never happened! You can't reconcile with her."

"I can't?" Julian asked from inside his hands.

"Why would you?"

Julian raised his head. He was defeated. The fire of his anger had gone out, and the formidable man was gone. "Because I love her."

"Sometimes that's not enough. Or maybe, in this case, it's too much."

"What do you mean?"

David kept his gaze straight ahead, speaking in a casual tone, as if his observations were just coming to him off the top of his head and not crafted out of Natalie's own words.

"Maybe it was all too much for her. Her favorite author is Mendón. She falls for you. You're Mendón. And then there's talk of you coming out of seclusion…" David shrugged. "It was probably overwhelming to the poor girl. She was used to such a simple life."

"If that's true, then perhaps she just needs time…"

"No," David said, "I think, maybe, she *belongs* to her simple life. She belongs in it and wants to keep it. Things were moving very fast for a while there, and even I was worried for you. I mean, the ring? Marriage?"

He watched those words strike Julian a one-two punch.

"You seemed to forget the reasons why you keep Mendón private, how dangerous it could be for you." He slung his arm around Julian's shoulders and squeezed in a half hug. "I hate to see you get hurt."

Julian glanced up. "What danger? You think the world cares whether I'm some…writer?"

"You're not just *some writer.* You're a genius. Young and talented. Brought up in poverty by a single mother. Overcame incredible odds. Yours is a remarkable story, and the world would go crazy to hear it. They wouldn't leave you alone." He saw his words were having no effect on Julian—appealing to his ego never worked. David swallowed and tried a different tack. "Your mother was a wise woman. I'm just thinking about what she would have wanted."

The icy stare that met this comment could have frozen a desert. Julian slid off the couch and returned to his cross-armed post, staring out of the windows at the magnificent cityscape lit with a million lights. "It's late," he said tonelessly. "Go home, David."

David tripped off the couch, his feet tangling clumsily. "Well, I came over because I have a bit of work to do in the office here…"

"Fine."

David eased a sigh. "Okay, good. Maybe later you'll be up for a drink or two."

Julian said nothing.

"I hope you know I'm here for you should you need me."

No reply.

He didn't want to leave but Julian's wintry silence was pushing him toward his office. "Okay, good night, Julian."

Julian didn't move or respond. David was inclined to feel hurt over Julian's cold shoulder until he remembered his victory that day. He'd won. Natalie was gone and he had Julian all to himself again. All the man needed was time to realize who had always been there for him and who had smashed his heart to pieces. *I would never do that to him. Ever.*

On his way past the kitchen, he saw Julian's cell phone on the counter. David snatched it without breaking his stride. In his office, he flung himself on the couch. The gun-wielding unpleasantness with Natalie had left him more drained than he realized. He patted his pocket where the weapon hung heavy next to Natalie's cell phone. Julian's cell phone joined it. Another precaution. Not enough, not by a long shot but it would have to do for now. His eyes immediately began to close. The worst was over but he still had a long way to go to keep Julian safe.

***

Julian watched the night's shadows thicken until the twinkling panorama of city lights was his apartment's only illumination. The awful conversation with Natalie scrolled through his thoughts, like a passage from a book that he was unable to rewrite into something that didn't make his heart ache or his stomach writhe. He sat on the couch, bending knees that creaked from stiffness and stared at nothing.

David's words filtered into his mind. Danger. There was danger in coming out of his self-imposed isolation. His mother's warnings about low men and dishonest women joined David's words. He thought of Natalie. He had revealed himself to her and she had discarded him, taking what she thought was the best part of him. Is that what his mother had meant? Was that the price that she feared he would pay again and again?

"She was right after all," he muttered darkly, and anger lanced through him...and then faded. To lose Natalie...to never talk to her, or hear her laugh; to never touch her or kiss her or make love to her again...Pain gripped his heart in a vise and seeped into his gut, twisting his insides until he thought he'd be sick.

David's advice to get drunk sounded better and better. The pain needed dulling. But not with David. He guessed his assistant was still in his office. Or maybe he'd gone home. It didn't matter. It was astonishing how quickly nothing really mattered.

Julian went to the liquor cabinet off the kitchen and grabbed the first bottle—some expensive French brandy—and swigged it straight. He coughed after it went down, and took another. It wasn't working; the pain felt bottomless. He took the brandy back to the couch and slumped down.

Something wasn't right. Natalie wouldn't end it without warning. Just like that? He felt as if she'd taken a shotgun and blasted him in the chest. He drank deeply from the bottle, again and then again, until his stomach began to protest.

"The heart wants what it wants." His words were already starting to slur. *I have to see her again. I can't let it end like this. I can't...*

He stood up and fell back down. He peered blearily at his watch and deciphered that it was near midnight. Too late to return to her place, drunk and desperate. *I don't want to scare her.*

"But I already have."

He flung his arm over his eyes, and lay back on the couch. That was the real reason. She was afraid of him and so there was no going back. How could he? He could promise he'd never hurt her; could tell her he wasn't capable, that his soul recoiled from the very idea. But it was too late. The seed was there, planted by him even as he'd sought to expose his flaws to her honestly. Any time they argued, it would be there, lurking, and he knew that neither one of them could live like that.

"What happened?" he moaned. "We were happy. So happy…"

The bottle fell out of his hand and the dark liquid poured out, like blood from a deep wound.

CHAPTER THIRTY-FIVE

Panic raced through Natalie in currents that left her weak and shaking. She called Liberty on her landline, her hands trembling so badly she dropped the phone twice. "Come over and bring Marshall. Please. It's serious. I need help."

"Of course, I'll tell him to pick me up right now," Liberty said. "But Jesus, you sound terrible. Are you okay?"

"Just…hurry."

They arrived together and she burst into tears at the sight of them.

"Oh honey, it can't be that bad," Marshall began but Liberty elbowed him quiet. She studied Natalie's face that was pale and blotchy, her eyes alight with fear.

"No, this is serious. What is it, Nat?"

Natalie sat on the couch and told them about David's visit. They listened raptly, Marshall next to her and Liberty perched on the ratty chair. Their faces morphed from disbelief to concern to outrage. When she'd told them David pulled out a gun Marshall jumped in his seat and Liberty hiccupped, "Holy shit!"

"I'm sorry to have told you all this," Natalie said miserably when she was finished. "I'm sorry to get you involved but I'm too scared to be alone."

Marshall glowered. "Where is David now?"

"He's sticking close to Julian." Tears filled Natalie's eyes again. "He's there, at Julian's house. And Julian doesn't even know. I don't know what to do."

"Call the police," Liberty said automatically. "Right now."

"No! God, no! David will hear them coming. He'll…he'll k-kill Julian. And the blackmailers…If David gets arrested, they'll come after Julian too. He told me. He told me how it would happen."

Marshall made a negating motion at Liberty when she started to protest. "Now let's think this through," he said. "Who are these so-called blackmailers? How do you even know they're as big a threat as David says?"

"I-I don't."

"So maybe they're bluffing. Maybe they saw this sniveling little rat and decided to take advantage of him. You say he's got the hots for Julian?"

"Yes."

"And he probably blabbed that to the bartender as well. Or maybe the bartender read between the lines. I'll bet they're a two-bit operation playing off David's fear for Julian."

Natalie nodded. "Maybe. But how can we gamble with Julian's life like that? David said they'd hurt him if the money stopped."

"I call bullshit on that one," Liberty put in. "Marshall's right. Once David's in jail, there's no benefit to offing anyone but adding murder charges to their rap sheet. That threat's only useful to keep David in line."

"Okay," Natalie said slowly.

"Okay, so we call the cops," Liberty said.

"No!" Natalie cried. "David's with Julian now. All it will take is for him to hear one siren. Or a knock at the door. You think the police will storm the apartment and catch him unaware? Maybe bust through the windows like in some movie? With no proof but my word?"

"Honey, you can't do nothing."

"I don't *want* to do nothing but I can't do the one thing I know will get Julian killed. I won't. We just have to get Julian away from David. That's it. That can't be too hard, can it?"

"Not at all," Marshall said. "I'll to go down to Julian's building and hang out until the weasel leaves."

"Then what?"

"Yeah, then what?" Liberty demanded.

"Then I follow him, maybe distract him with my over-abundance of charm and wit, and you call the cops. Easy-peasy."

"No, Marshall. I can't let you," Natalie said while Liberty shook her head in agreement. "I can't just sit here while every one I love is out risking everything for me. No—"

"You did the hardest part," Marshall said. "You suffered David's scary insanity and you broke up with Julian to keep him safe." Anger flashed in his hazel eyes. "David put a gun to your head, honey. And that pisses me off. A lot. The way I see it, he's got some payback coming."

"Oh Jesus, now is not the time to get all butch on us," Liberty snapped. "He's got the gun, like you said. All I see happening is that he hears sirens and that's it. No more Marshall. Uh uh. No way. *Call the police.*"

"All I see happening is that David hears sirens and that's it," Natalie told her, her voice choked with tears. "No more Julian."

Liberty leaned back in the old chair, meeting Natalie's eye for a moment before looking away.

Marshall cleared his throat. "Look, David's clearly got a few screws loose. There's no possible way his little plan can hold together. We get him alone, get him arrested, and let the cops deal with the blackmailers. Okay?"

"Okay," Natalie said. "But what if it's not enough?"

"What do you mean?"

"Even when he's safe, Julian will still hate me. The things I said to him," Natalie whispered. "I-I told him…I feared him."

Liberty frowned. "Who? David?"

"Julian," Natalie said. "To break up with him. I told him I thought he'd…And he was so hurt. Liberty, I betrayed him. He told me personal fears, about his father, and I just *used* that to wreck him. I wrecked *us,* just like he said."

Marshall gave her a squeeze. "Honey, it wasn't real. We'll sort this all out and he'll know the truth. He'll understand."

"What if he doesn't? I had to say the worst thing. To get him out before David…"

Her words trailed as her gaze found the stack of composition books under her coffee table. She extracted herself from Marshall and gathered them on to her lap. "Everything I said to him was a lie," she murmured, running her fingers along the cover of the first book. "That I feared him…and that I needed this. These books…my refuge. I chose Mendón instead of Julian."

Liberty and Marshall exchanged concerned glances, but they faded out of her awareness as she opened the first page. Julian's tiny, precise script filled the paper in black ink. Her heart ached to read the first sentences, like greeting an old friend for the first time in years. A new Mendón book; familiar and yet tantalizing new…but the beautiful words dwindled to pen scratches on paper in her eyes.

She shut the book and looked up at her friends, smiling through tears. "There's no truth in that at all." She set the stack of books on the coffee table. "I don't want the writing. I want Julian. I can't…I can't keep hiding in made-up worlds where nothing bad happens that I can't turn the page on. I have to…live."

Liberty reached over and took her hand. "Uh, okay honey. I think you need to rest now. You sound a little burnt out."

Natalie nodded and stretched out on the couch. The adrenaline that had been surging through her veins had run its course. She couldn't keep her eyes open. "Will you stay with me? I was so scared. In the movies, someone points a gun and they just put their hands up. But it's so much worse than that. So much…"

She closed her eyes and someone covered her with a blanket, someone stroked her hair. She felt sleep dragging her down and half-feared she'd have terrible nightmares of David's gun but there was nothing but blackness.

CHAPTER THIRTY-SIX

David's hands trembled so violently, he dropped his cell phone twice. The third time he managed to take the picture of the dividend check from EllisIntel, and *whoosh, i*t was gone, spirited into the separate checking account. *But I can't do this anymore. I can't.* Now Cliff wanted thirty every month, and Julian wanted him to sell the stock. The two opposing forces that were crushing the life out of him. He'd have to find another $30,000 from somewhere else, and if it came from the regular expenses or royalties, Julian would notice. Maybe not right away; his break up with Natalie would consume him, but for how long?

He clutched his desk as the pressure built into a full-blown panic attack. His breath came in short, panting gusts and his pulse raced until he thought his heart would explode. His thoughts raced just as fast; he imagined them careening around his brain, bouncing off the walls of his skull.

Yes, what about Natalie? She'd seemed cowed, but what if she wasn't? What if she called the police after all? I can't be everywhere all the time. If she's stupid enough to betray me, Julian will have to die.

His hand found the gun in his pocket and it somehow brought him a small modicum of calm, but one born of a deep, deep melancholy. His racing thoughts felt suddenly submerged in thick, grave-cold gelatin, and grisly visions swam up at him from the murk.

Julian would have to die. David would have to watch his gorgeous head break apart, reducing the mind that concocted beautiful words to a mess that a man with plastic-gloved hands would scrape up later. The reduction of something perfect and sublime to something insignificant and mundane...the power of it made David giddy but saddened him too. He would have to take his turn. He couldn't live without Julian and the world wouldn't let him live for snuffing out such a light.

His own death would not be such a monumental thing. It would be quiet and small, but he would know peace. His mind would be silent. At last, the chattering voices that hinted at danger in everything and everyone would also be reduced to smatters on the wall.

Maybe better to do it now before the forces ranged against him tightened their hold, and the maddening itch in the back of his mind grew unbearable. Maybe better to shock them all with his audacity. And what better punishment for Natalie—the cause of all this madness in the first place—than to destroy Julian for her a second time?

As if in a dream, the apartment folded and he stood before Julian's bedroom without having taken a single step. A slant of morning sunlight spilled over Julian's sleeping form. His face was turned away, his body still but for the gentle rise and fall of his chest. In a heart's beat, David stood over him, and touched his fingers to his warm skin. Julian's head turned, his eyes opened, he smiled sleepily. David smiled back, through tears, and raised his other hand. Julian's eyes widened as the barrel of the gun met his temple.

The shot was loud, there was so much blood…so much…

David jerked violently like a sleeper rudely awakened. He was in the kitchen, at the sink. *How did I get here?* His hand was in his pocket, his finger around the trigger. The safety was off.

"Dear God," he said, and swallowed over a throat that had gone dry, and clicked the safety back into place. The phantom gunshot had silenced the maddening chorus of whispered warnings. Now they began again. *Right on cue,* he sighed, hanging his head.

Julian shuffled out of his bedroom, giving David a start. He looked like shit. There was no better way to describe it. His curls had run amok and shadows ringed his eyes. It was clear that despite all time he spent in bed, he wasn't doing much sleeping. *He won't come out of seclusion now. Surely not*, David thought, pleased. *And he isn't in any shape to do any work on the book…*

The book.

And just like that, a plan bloomed in David's mind to save them both.

Julian's dull gaze flickered to David. "What are you doing here?"

"I came to see how you were doing. And I have a favor to ask."

"Sure."

"My apartment complex is being fumigated for termites and I was going to shack up with my parents. But now my mother is sick, so I was wondering if you wouldn't mind me crashing here for a few days?"

"Fine." Julian sank onto the couch and proceeded to stare dumbly at the view surrounding them.

David heaved a breath and watched Julian's silent misery. David longed to smooth his hair and kiss his lips and tell him that everything would be all right. But he didn't know that himself. *Unless my plan works.* He couldn't allow himself to hope.

***

It was after noon when David pulled into Orbit's parking lot with a fat envelope of hundred dollar bills in his hand. He tore out of the car, his dress shoes slipping on the gravel, and raced to the back entrance. He had to hurry. Every moment spent away from Julian was dangerous.

Jesse admitted him from the back and led him down that hallway. Garrett, Cliff's beefy blond brother was leaving Cliff's office just as David approached.

"Hold up, Garrett. Stay. Both of you stay. Dave didn't behave himself so well last time," Cliff said from behind his desk. Smoke encircled his head. "You have something for me?"

He was enjoying this too much, David thought. A two-bit mafia boss in a ratty chair and cheap fluorescent lighting.

"I have it," David said, and his hand reached to the inner pocket of his sport coat. He tossed Cliff the envelope. "But I can't do thirty grand every month. I just can't."

Cliff flipped through the envelope then set it aside, satisfied, and heaved a sigh. "Dave, Dave, Dave. Not again. Didn't we go through this before?"

"Yes, but Cliff..."

"No buts, Dave. I got too much shit to do to listen to your whining. Same time next month." He jerked his chin at Jesse and Garrett. "Get him out of here."

A swell of anger washed over David, drowning his fear. "No."

Cliff looked up from his paperwork and blinked. "No?"

"Come on, David, let's go," Jesse said in a weary voice. He tugged at his arm but David pulled free.

"It has to stop. And I think I know how. I have an idea. One that will work for all of us."

"Is that so?"

"Yes."

Cliff narrowed his piggy eyes. "You have one minute."

"What if…" David swallowed. "What if you had one big score? One final score that set you up for life and you wouldn't have to worry about money ever again?"

"Well, that would be hunky-fucking-dory, now wouldn't it? You got some magic beans to sell me, Dave?"

Garrett sniggered like a bull. Jesse did not.

David closed his eyes. Once spoken, there'd be no going back. The plan was a good one, though, and David thought it would work. It *had* to work. The ordeal would be over and he and Julian would be free of Natalie and Cliff both.

"Julian's latest book…Rafael Melendez Mendón's book, I mean. He wrote another one. No one has seen it yet; it's rough and hand-written. He says it's his best one yet."

"And?"

"I can get it."

"Yeah? So?"

David blinked. "Then you…you'll have it. I'll give it to you."

"The fuck am I going to do with a book?"

"Sell it," David said, confused, "on the…uh, black market."

Cliff stared at him a moment more, and then burst out laughing.

David's ears grew hot. "It'll be worth millions! You'll be set for life!"

"Dave, you crack me up. But you're also one stupid motherfucker, you know that?" Cliff leaned over his desk. "First off, how the hell we going to authenticate something like that? We'll use the tried and true 'Because Dave Thompson said so' method? Secondly, that shit has to be fenced. Only I happen to be fresh out of fences at the moment, so that book would be about as useful to me as a pile of dog turd."

David felt his sliver of hope melt away. "But…"

"But…that's not to say your plan doesn't have its merits. No sir." Cliff laced his fingers over his protruding belly. "In fact I think it has potential."

David looked up. "It does?"

"This is what we're going to do: you're going to give us this book and we're going to ransom it *back* to Mendón for our millions."

"What? No," David said. "He might not pay. And even if he did, I'd have to tell him...No, he can't know what we've been doing. Please, Cliff."

"This is a bad idea," Jesse put in. "We're getting in too deep."

Cliff ignored him. "Relax, Dave. Mendón doesn't have to know shit. Tell him the place was robbed and the book was stolen."

David wiped his nose, thinking. "He won't know I was involved."

"Right-o."

"Then I tell him that the robbers have contacted me because they recognize what they have."

Jesse snorted. "You think he'll believe that? That a bunch of crooks out looking to steal the TV and grandma's pearls *also* know who Mendón is? Ridiculous."

David squared his jaw. "Cliff did."

Cliff bellowed more laughter. "That's right. Us seedy bottom-feeders know good literature when we see it, don't we Dave?"

David wasn't listening, his thoughts ran ahead a mile a minute. "Then I tell Julian that the robbers want one million dollars for the book's safe return. I help negotiate the exchange, you get your money, and you leave us alone forever."

"Whoa, whoa, whoa, snowflake," Cliff said. "Let's not get ahead of ourselves. *One* million dollars? What do you take me for?"

"Two, then."

"Three," said Garrett from his post in the corner. "One million for each of us. Unless Jesse's too chickenshit, in which case, I'll take his share."

David shook his head. "He won't pay that much, Cliff."

"Jesus, Dave, do I have to think of everything? If he won't pay it, you will. With his money. You have access, right? Tell him you couldn't bear the thought of his precious book in our dirty little mitts and you impulsively—and out of *love*—" he sneered, "took it upon yourself to rescue his book."

David thought this over. It could work. Julian would be mad but not for long, not when David's intentions were so benevolent.

He looked at Cliff. "And then that's it? You won't bother us again?"

"Scouts' honor."

What do you know of honor? David thought, but he was more relieved than anything. "Okay, just give me a few days to plan it out. Make it look real. Okay? Deal?" He held out his hand for Cliff to shake, but the big man stared at it as if David had offered him a rotting fish.

"Get the fuck out of here, Dave. I'm tired of looking at your goddamn face. Come back in a few days with the book or I'll see you next month with... *forty* grand." He leaned back and laced his hands behind his head. "You know. For my troubles."

CHAPTER THIRTY-SEVEN

Julian woke up the next morning the same as he had the day before, and the day before that—three days since that awful night at Natalie's place: with a pain in his heart that slugged him like a mallet. The clock on the side table showed that it was after noon. Always an early riser, this new habit felt alien to him. But then his entire world was different now. His pillows beckoned him to retreat into sleep and he almost succumbed. But the conversation with Natalie replayed in his mind, like a terrible song stuck on repeat. Only this time, at the end, he recalled a different conversation.

Go to Rijeka. Make your peace.
Will you come with me?
Of course I will.

Julian squeezed his eyes shut for he could remember the way she'd held him and how soft her hair was against his cheek. He thought he would have given anything to hold her again.

"I could go," he said aloud, countering his thoughts. "I could go and when I come back I could tell her…" He didn't know what would happen in his father's homeland. But he'd have tried. He'd have done something that might change everything.

Julian threw off his blankets and took a much-needed shower. The headache of a mild hangover thudded dully between his eyes but washed away under the hot water. Yes, this was something he could *do*. Something he could show her and maybe, just maybe it would be enough.

After the shower, he dressed in a pair of jeans, t-shirt, and a blue sweater that Natalie loved because she said it was the exact color of his eyes. The mallet slugged him again, and he laid his hand on his chest. *Keep going. Just keep going.*

He packed enough for two weeks, hoping whatever it was he needed to do there wouldn't take so long, and trundled the small luggage bag into the kitchen. He searched around for his cell phone to call the car service. He hadn't seen his phone, he realized, in several days. He turned to the wall phone and then realized he had no idea how to get to Croatia. It would surely take more than two flights, lots of connections…

David could help him. He'd planned all his travel to Uruguay when Julian had been researching *Coronation* and had done a fantastic job. He thought to call David but remembered he was staying right here. Something about his mother being ill and his own apartment was being fumigated for…rats? No, termites.

Julian went to the office and heard nothing from inside. It was late for David to still be sleeping, but Julian didn't want to barge in and startle him. He opened the door quietly to find it empty and a mess. Two bottles of Jack Daniels, a liter of Pepsi, and a cocktail glass half-filled with both sat on the coffee table beside the couch. The air smelled of sweetly tinged alcohol, and the remnants of fast food meals were strewn about. David's sport coat hung over the end of the couch like a flaccid tongue.

Julian frowned at the mess then remembered David had told him once that he had always needed to be careful about his alcohol intake; Julian wondered what prompted this binge.

Everything's all turned around, he thought, leaving the office. He had almost closed the door when he saw his cell phone on the floor near the couch. *Odd. I must have dropped it.* He took it and left, closing the door behind him.

In the kitchen, he turned the phone on and looked for missed calls from Natalie, messages that said she'd had a change of heart and wanted to talk. There were none. There was nothing, as a matter of fact. His call history had been erased. That was odd too.

He used his cell phone to go online and scrolled through a list of airlines that would take him to Croatia. Lufthansa had a flight from SFO to Zagreb with one layover in Frankfurt. And it left in three and a half hours.

Julian hesitated. He felt unprepared, rushed, unwilling to venture into his father's territory, afraid of what he'd find or that he'd find nothing. Then he thought of living the rest of his life without Natalie and called the airline.

*** ***

David raced back to Julian's place, panic streaking through him and making his hands tremble. He'd stepped out to replenish his liquor supplies that had dwindled faster than was safe. But lately a mild buzz was the only thing that kept his nerves from feeling like they'd explode at any moment.

In the parking lot of the convenience store he discovered Julian's cell phone wasn't in his coat; it must have fallen out. *He could be calling Natalie right now…* That problem joined the other, constant worry that gnawed on his nerves. *How on earth am I going to stage a break-in when Julian's here all the time?*

The plan to steal the latest book was a good one, if only he could leap frog over the actual doing of it and get right to the part where he and Julian lived happily ever after. He snorted a laugh. Nothing was ever that easy for him. Nothing.

At the front door, David heard the sounds of Julian moving about the kitchen. His chest constricted and his ulcer flared in a perfect harmony of dread. He opened the door and tried not to run inside.

"Oh, hello. Good to see you up and about," he said, injecting false cheer into his tone. Julian was not only up, he was showered, dressed, and tucking his cell phone into his back pocket. *Oh my god, he knows he knows he knows...*

"Who were you talking to?" David asked, forcing his voice into a normal range.

"The car service. I'm going to the airport," Julian answered, and David watched him stuff his passport into his leather shoulder bag.

"Oh. Where...uh, where are you going?"

"Croatia," Julian said, and checked his watch. "If I make the flight." He looked at David with concern. "And how are you, David? You don't look well, to tell you the truth."

David ran a hand through his greasy hair and hugged the little brown bag of whiskey against him more tightly. "Uh, yeah. Worried about my mother is all. You know how that is. But uh...why Croatia? I mean, right now? For how long?"

"Two weeks, I think. Maybe more. I'm not sure yet. This situation with Natalie has me in turmoil. I...I have to get away. To think some things through."

David nodded. Was this good or bad? Certainly good that he wouldn't have to monitor Julian's whereabouts at all times, but all it would take was one phone call to Natalie and David would be destroyed.

"I think that's a good idea," he said. "Check out for awhile. Get some rest and uh...not think about...stuff here."

Stuff? David mentally kicked himself. But Julian seemed not to have heard. He moved to stand before the windows, arms crossed, like some majestic lord surveying his domain. David went to stand beside him.

"I mean, I'm sure a vacation is just what you need right now."

"It's not a vacation," Julian said. "I used to think I'd go for myself. But it's apparent to me that the idea of Natalie and myself are tightly bound. So I'll go for her too in the hopes that when I get back…" He stared straight ahead, his voice hard. "Maybe we can start again."

David's thoughts raced. *At long last, a break.* He didn't like all this talk about starting over with Natalie but he'd deal with that later. With Julian gone, he could design a beautiful robbery in which a few minor treasures and Julian's book could be spirited away. No mess, no fuss…He glanced at the library desk where the stack of notebooks had sat for the last few weeks.

No book.

Oh dear god, now what?

Julian had his leather shoulder bag with him. Was it there? Was he going to work on it while in Croatia? David swallowed hard.

"So will this be a working vacation or are you going to leave the new book alone until you get back? Maybe give it a breather…?"

"I don't have the book."

"Oh?" David forced his voice to sound as casual at as possible. "Where is it?"

"Gone."

"What does that mean…exactly?*"

"I gave it to her."

"You…you gave it to who? To Natalie?" David felt like the earth was spinning out from under him. *When?* And then he knew when. The other night. *And I was* right *there.* And she didn't tell him. Hid it from him…A red haze descended over his eyes.

"Yes, I gave it to her," Julian said tiredly. He turned from the window. "And there's not going to be another one. Not for a long time, anyway, if ever."

David mustered every bit of will to keep from bursting into tears. "But…but why?"

"Because it belongs to her. It always has," Julian said, his eyes heavy. His cell phone buzzed a text. "The car service is here."

"O-okay," David said faintly. "I…I'll walk you down."

In the elevator, David felt anger burn away his tears. *That bitch. That meddling, conniving bitch!* At the curb, his smile was wide and stiff as he opened the door to the sedan.

Julian lay his hand on his shoulder before climbing in. "Take care of yourself, David. I don't like to see you struggle with old demons."

My demons, David thought, his cheeks aching to hold the smile as Julian climbed into the car. *What about your demon, Julian? The one who has you so thoroughly duped, you can't let go of her, even after she stomps on your heart?*

David watched the sedan pull away, a tumult of emotions stirring his gut. Now it was inevitable. He couldn't live the rest of his life worried about Natalie Hewitt. Julian wasn't going to let her go so he had to *make* him let her go; like prying a child's fingers off a dangerous toy he shouldn't have.

He asked Angelo, the day doorman, to hail him a cab while he took his cell phone out of his coat where it had been sharing the pocket with his gun. He punched Cliff's number. The odious man answered and for once, David wasn't afraid at all.

He told Cliff where Mendón's latest book was and when Cliff started swearing at him that kidnapping some woman was not part of the deal, the calm surety of David's own voice shocked him into silence.

"She's a liability, now and into the future," David said. "But I can't get in her place; she won't let me near her. Send Garrett for her."

"And just how is Garrett supposed to do that without making a scene?"

David told Cliff exactly what Garrett should say. "She'll trust that, believe me. And I'll...I'll take care of her myself when I get there."

"Mighty tough talk, Dave," Cliff said as a cab rolled up to the curb in front of David. "You sure you got the balls for this?"

"You want your three million dollars or not?"

Cliff laughed nervously. "Yeah. Yeah, I do."

An ugly sneer curled David's lip. "Then go get her."

CHAPTER THIRTY-EIGHT

For the second day in a row, Liberty and Marshall sat on a bench outside Julian's condo complex, trying to look inconspicuous. Marshall succeeded, dressed in casual finery, but Liberty struggled. She'd put on jeans for this excursion instead of one of her usual vinyl skirts and torn tights, and shifted uncomfortably on the bench for the millionth time. *Levi Strauss was an asshole.*

Marshall faced the entrance while Liberty sat with her back to it. She peeked over her shoulder and then gripped Marshall's hand as two men walked out of the sky rise to a waiting sedan at the curb.

"*Finally,*" Marshall said. "I've missed a shit-ton of work playing I Spy…"

"The dark one's got to be Julian," Liberty said. "The oily-looking prick in the rumpled suit must be David."

"They're not leaving together."

They both looked around as Julian took off in the sedan, leaving David on the curb. He spoke to the doorman and the doorman stepped off to hail a cab. David made a phone call and by the time he was done, a taxi idled at the curb. He climbed in.

"This is perfect. I'm going to follow the weasel. You call Natalie."

Liberty gripped Marshall's arm in a vise. "Be careful, I mean it."

"If you don't let go, I'm going to miss my chance to say, 'Follow that taxi!'" He pecked her cheek. "I'll be careful, I promise."

He slipped out of her grip and whistled shrilly between his teeth. Liberty peeked over her shoulder. Another yellow and black slipped up to the curb and Marshall got in it just as David's cab left the drive. She watched, gnawing her lower lip, as Marshall's cab flipped an illegal U and followed David's taxi. She rolled her eyes. *He probably showed the driver a c-note.*

After both cars were gone, Liberty trotted up to the doorman. The forest of towers that rose around her thwarted the sun's warmth and she shivered inside her ratty old-man golf sweater. *Or maybe I'm just scared shitless.*

The doorman smiled at her. She smiled back. His nametag said Angelo and he was young—perhaps early thirties at most—

and had rather nice brown eyes that were the exact warm shade as his skin.

"Hi, Angelo."

"Hello, ma'am."

"Have a light?"

"Of course, ma'am."

"You can stop calling me 'ma'am' if you don't mind. It adds ten years to my age every time you do it."

"Yes, ma'am." He flicked a lighter and she cupped its flame around her cigarette, protecting it from the wind that had picked up. She rocked back on the heels of her ankle boots and affected what she hoped was a casual air.

"You must get cold standing out here."

"That's why they give us the coat and gloves, ma'am."

"That's the *least* they can do, right?" She chuckled nervously. "So listen, I came here to visit my very good friend, Julian Kovanch, and it looks like I just missed him. Any idea where he went?"

The doorman smiled. "Yes, ma'am." He watched her, amused, then said, "Mr. *Kovač* went to the airport. After that...?" He held up his white-gloved hands.

"The airport? You're sure?"

"Yes, ma'am."

"But you don't know where he went? Or for how long?"

"Even if I did, ma'am, I'm not at liberty to say."

"I am! My name is Liberty." She chucked him on the arm. "Ha, sorry, bad joke. But seriously, my name is Liberty."

"Is it?" Angelo asked. "I like it. I like your whole vibe, if you don't mind me saying."

"Oh, sure, why not? What's a little flirting in the middle of a life and death situation?" Liberty laughed dryly. "So anyway, do you happen to know where that guy, David, went? Not the airport too, right?"

Angelo grinned. "I don't think so."

"Thank you," Liberty said. "You've been a big help. I'd tip you if I had any money whatsoever."

"What about dinner?" he called as she skipped down the stairs.

"I don't have any of that either."

Around the corner, Liberty whipped out her cell phone to call Natalie. The phone rang and went to the machine. "Oh, you've got to be kidding me." She dutifully waited for the beep. "Nat, it's Lib. The coast is clear, you can call Julian. But why aren't you picking up? I'm on my way."

She hung up and kept trying as she hurried to the nearest Muni station. There was no answer on Natalie's end. Underground, Liberty's reception was spotty. She managed one more call that went to Natalie's machine, and then her phone lost all service.

"You have *got* to be kidding me."

She shouldered her way to the door, intending to get off at the next stop, get aboveground, and try again. When the Muni train broke down, trapping her under the city, she gave the doors a hard kick.

"You have got to be fucking kidding me!"

***

The car service was efficient; Julian made it to SFO with plenty of time, even for an international flight. He sat in one of the sleek leather chairs in the Lufthansa business class lounge, his foot tapping and his fingers drumming the armrests. Someone had brought him a glass of champagne and it sat untouched on a table beside him. *She should be coming with me.*

He took up his cell phone, put it down, picked it up again. The stewards were milling about the desk at the gate; they'd start boarding at any minute. He ran his thumb over Natalie's name on his contact list. *And tell her what?* He hadn't a clue. Only that it didn't feel right to leave and yet he didn't know what he could do to get her back if he stayed.

"*Cogerme,*" he swore and then jumped as his phone rang. His heart hammered in his chest but it wasn't Natalie. The number was unfamiliar. "Hello?"

"Julian Kovač?"

"Yes?"

"Mr. Kovač, I'm so glad to have you on the line. Relieved, actually. This is Dr. Cannon from SF General. I was your treating physician two weeks ago when you were admitted for severe dehydration. I've been attempting to contact you for several days now."

"What about?"

The gate opened and a put-together woman with a blonde chignon and crisp uniform was looking over a passenger manifest.

"Firstly to apologize, Mr. Kovač. We strive to provide the most professional level of care but our lab staff was temporarily reduced—by the flu, coincidentally enough—and the results of your blood work were delayed. Additionally, it would seem that your admission forms were incorrect, making it very difficult to contact you. But we now have the lab results..."

Julian felt a vague disquiet unravel in his gut. "And?"

"Well, Mr. Kovač, given your symptoms and what your friend, Mr. Thompson, had told us about your illness's progression, you were treated and released as a flu patient when, in fact, you were not."

"I was not."

"We found no evidence of any flu strain. We did find, however, a marked increase in emetine levels in your blood work."

The blonde with the chignon put an intercom to her mouth and in a clipped German accent requested the first and business class passengers to please begin boarding.

Julian stood up and trundled his bag toward the gate to stand in a short line behind a man in a herringbone suit. "What does that mean?"

"High levels of emetine, as well as an abnormal EKG— which you had— can point to ipecac toxicity. Are you familiar with ipecac syrup?"

"It induces vomiting, doesn't it?"

The herringbone gave him a pinched glance over his shoulder.

"Yes. It triggers severe vomiting, much like what you had experienced. We see this in bulimic patients who take it to purge, and we administer it ourselves to drug overdose victims or those who have swallowed poisonous material. But you are neither a bulimic nor a drug addict—so far as the rest of your blood work indicated—and the severe nature of your dehydration is consistent with an intense consumption of ipecac syrup—and diuretics as well—over the course of twenty-four hours."

Julian froze at the front of the line. The woman asked for his boarding pass.

"And since you were quickly too incapacitated to ingest the syrup on your own for that long…Well, frankly I got a little nervous and thought I'd check on you personally."

"Your boarding pass, sir?" The blonde woman held out her hand. Julian stared at the woman and she pursed her lips in faint disapproval.

Over the phone, Dr. Cannon cleared her throat. "Mr. Kovač, do you understand what I am telling you?"

"Yes, doctor. Thank you. Thank you very much." Julian hung up. *David…what have you done?*

"Sir, I must insist on your boarding pass."

Julian snapped to like a man waking suddenly from a doze. "What? No…Sorry." He stepped out of the line. Heart hammering, he found Natalie's cell number on his contacts and pushed it. It went immediately to voicemail, which meant hers was out of battery life or turned off. He called the café. The girl who answered said Natalie called in sick. He called her home phone. No answer but for the answering machine. He hung up, called again. No answer. Julian started to walk through the terminal, calling, getting her machine, hanging up.

He walked faster and faster. The fifth time her machine picked up, Julian tossed the phone in his bag and ran.

***

Natalie stepped out of her shower and hurriedly dried off and dressed. But instead of going out, she paced her small living area, fighting the urge to run out the door. The waiting was terrible. Liberty and Marshall were bravely staking out Julian's complex and here she sat doing nothing. Three days of nothing. She'd called in sick to work and going to school was out of the question. Impossible to sit in class and pretend everything was perfectly normal while Julian was living with a madman. But Liberty and Marshall had so far reported no sign of either him or David. The terrible fear that David had snapped and killed Julian took hold in her mind and would not let go. *What can I do? If David sees me…*

The intercom buzzed, making her jump. She peeked out of her window that overlooked the street in front of Niko's. A huge white Cadillac Escalade was parked on the street, adjacent to Niko's. She went to the intercom at her door.

"Yes?"

"Yeah, this is Carl. From the service."

"What service?"

"Is this a Miss...Natalie Hewitt?"

"Yes."

"I've been instructed by a Mr. Julian Kovač to pick you up."

Natalie's heart leapt to her throat. "Julian sent you?"

"Yes, ma'am."

She sagged against the wall with relief. "Why didn't he call me to tell me?"

"I can't answer that, ma'am. I have my instructions. I'm to take you somewhere safe. He also said to tell you that he knows all about David, and..." Carl cleared his throat. "And that he loves you...uh, ma'am."

She touched her hand to her lips. *Wouldn't he call himself?* She hadn't left her place in three days for precisely that reason. She glanced at her old answering machine and saw that the red light was blinking. A call had come in while she was in the shower. Hope surged again. "Hold on, please."

She played the first message and rejoiced to hear Liberty tell her the coast was clear, that Julian was safe from David. *Everything's going to be okay,* she thought. She went back to the intercom. "Carl?"

He sighed uncomfortably. "Ma'am, this is really none of my business, but he also said that he'll write a hundred books for you or never write again. Whatever you want."

Natalie almost laughed. *I just want you, love.* "I'll be right down."

She gathered the stack of composition books and shoved them into a bag, intending to give them back to Julian. *Give them back and take him in my arms instead,* she thought and raced down the stairs. She opened the gate and then fell back as a huge shape filled the doorway.

"Surprise!" said the hulking blond man in front of her. "Pretty good, right? *Ma'am?*"

He bellowed laughter and then stopped. Recognition dawned between them at the exact instant. Garrett. One of the men who harassed her months ago, whom Julian had thwarted with boiling milk. Natalie backed away, her feet scraping on the cement stairs. Terror lanced down her spine, turning her limbs to jelly.

"You..." she breathed.

He grinned luridly. "Well, ain't that something. Looks like we're going to have our date after all."

Natalie whimpered as his meaty fist connected with her temple. Pain radiated over her cheek and head; her eye felt like it was going to explode. His fist came again. She reeled and he caught her before she fell, her head lolling against his shoulder. Her vision blurred, stained red. He hefted her with one hand and peered into her bag.

"This it?" He snickered. "I'll just carry this for you, *ma'am*, shall I?"

He slung his arm around her waist and half-walked, half-carried her to the Escalade, parked just past the windows of Niko's Café. Upstairs, she heard her phone ring, the sound growing fainter and fainter…

CHAPTER THIRTY-NINE

Cliff looked ready to explode. His pudgy face was beet red and a vein pulsed under his widow's peak. "What the hell do you mean, he's *out of town?*"

David squared his shoulders and met Cliff's unyielding gaze. Behind him, he could practically feel Jesse's anxiety, almost as tightly wound as his own.

"He's gone to Croatia. Won't be back for several weeks."

"Several *weeks?*" Cliff's eyes bugged out of his skull, and then a thought crossed his eyes, and he leveled a finger at David, his voice low and deadly. "Are you fucking with me? Because if you are, Dave…"

"Of course not, Cliff, listen," David said. "It's perfect. It's more plausible that his place would get robbed while he's away. You'll have to wait until he gets back to make the ransom demand, but isn't three million dollars worth it?"

"No, it's not. This whole thing is fucked," Jesse said from behind. "Cliff—"

Cliff held up a hand for silence and rubbed his fingers over the bridge of his nose. He stared at David for a moment and then laid his hands on the desk. "Dave, I have Garrett over at that Natalie girl's place right now, to bring her here. Just what the hell are we supposed to do with her?"

Jesse stormed forward before David could answer. "Garrett's where? To bring…who? What the hell is going on, Cliff? Kidnapping? You want to add that to the rap sheet? Along with extortion and embezzlement and…who knows what else?" He ran a hand through his longish blond hair. "No way, man. No way."

"Jesse, I need you to shut the fuck up right now."

"Cliff, this is crazy—"

"She won't be here long," David said, silencing them both. His mouth went dry. "I told you, I'll take care of it. I promise."

Cliff seemed reluctantly mollified but Jesse stared at him, incredulous. "You're going to off some chick, David? Really?" He turned to Cliff. "This is what it's come down to? *Murder?*"

David started to retort but Cliff rose to his feet. "Are we going to have a problem here Jesse? Because all I'm hearing out of your mouth is that we're going to have a problem."

Jesse stared between them for a second, and David thought Jesse might make a break for it. He looked like he wanted to run. *I don't blame him. I want to run too.*

"No, Cliff," Jesse said. "No problem. I just...I think we all need to be very careful here, right? Let's not get carried away. Okay, David?"

"I agree," Cliff said, sitting back down. "Garrett's not back yet, Dave. Go get yourself a drink at the bar. You look like you need it. It'll calm your nerves. Tell Kyle it's on me."

"Yeah sure. Liquid courage," David muttered. As he walked past Jesse, he could see the man screaming at him with his eyes to not do whatever it was he thought he had to do.

David smiled wanly. *It's too late, Jesse. There is no other way.*

He made his way from the back offices, through Club Orbit's dance floor—still mostly empty due to the early hour—past the pool tables, and took a seat at the bar. He ordered a gin and tonic—nothing too strong; he'd need all his faculties tonight—but strong enough to blunt the edges of the fear and revulsion of it all. He sipped his drink that tasted watered down and tried very hard to get his rampaging thoughts under control.

"Bad day?"

"You could say that," David muttered.

"I've been there."

David looked up. Kyle, the bartender, was at the other end, stocking beer bottles. David swung his head the other way. A young man, large of frame and dressed in casual yet elegant clothes sat a few stools down. He had ginger hair and a warm smile. David returned it with a wan smile of his own.

"No offense, but I don't think you've had a day as bad as this."

The man shrugged his broad shoulders. "Try me."

David studied him. A come-on? Or friendly conversation? He couldn't tell. "No, you don't want to hear my problems."

The man shrugged again. "Suit yourself. Although they say that talking about a thing takes the sting out." He chuckled. "Of course, so does this." He held up his cocktail glass and took a swig.

David cracked a smile. "Yeah, it does. Just...tough day at work."

"I hear that. What do you do?"

"I'm an...assistant to a...I'm a personal assistant. A wealth manager. You?"

"Real estate," the man replied dourly. "I know, right? In this economy? Why do you think I wandered into this sleazy joint?"

David laughed despite himself.

"I'm Evan Harris."

"David Thompson."

Evan offered his hand and engulfed David's in a strong, warm grip. His expression was open, suggestive, interested, and David was suddenly aware of how unwashed and unkempt he was. He leaned back, smoothing his greasy hair and cursing inwardly at his continuing terrible luck. Any other night and he would have been better dressed, showered, and open to the advances of a handsome stranger.

Evan reached into his pocket and studied his cell phone. "Sorry, I've got to take this." He pulled out a fat billfold and laid a twenty on the table. "Yours is on me, David Thompson. The least I could do. For your bad day and all."

He got up and wended his way to the front doors. David jumped off his stool and followed him.

"Wait! Evan, wait!"

Evan strode outside the club and around the corner to an alley. David trotted after.

"Evan..."

The ginger-haired man flinched and dropped his cell into his pocket as David caught up to him. Evan was even better looking in the club's neon signs and the streetlights. He wasn't as beautiful as Julian, but tall and built and wholly masculine.

"Listen, tonight is a shitty night," David said. "Really. But maybe tomorrow we could...?"

A flash of surprise crossed Evan's face but then he smiled, a smile with a sharp edge to it that David found wholly enticing. It had been ages since his presence had garnered anything but sour or suspicious looks. "Tomorrow? Hmm. I don't think I have anything going on. What about dinner at my place? If that's too weird..." He laughed in a self-deprecating way that David found extremely charming. "God, listen to me. Is it *very* obvious I've been out of the game for a while, or just *extremely* obvious?"

David laughed. "You're doing fine."

"Am I?" The sudden hungry purr in Evan's voice took David by surprise. "I can do better."

David found himself backed against the cement wall, Evan's body pressed to his, his mouth crushing his lips. *Is this really happening?* But it had been so long since anyone had touched him. *So nice...*

Just as he relaxed into the kiss, Evan's body jerked and a deep, nauseating ache burst in David's groin. Evan kneed him again, then delivered a punishing left hook that sent David sprawling to the trash-and-cigarette-butt-strewn ground. His head spun, and his crotch glowed with pain. He tried to scramble away on his elbows and knees and then Evan's knee on his back pinned him to the ground.

"My name's Marshall, asshole." Hands pawed around the pockets of David's coat. "I'm a friend of Natalie's. I was about to call the cops but I'm glad to have this opportunity to beat your ass first for what you've done to her."

"No," David moaned. The injustice of it all...the *humiliation.* A white-hot thread of rage burned through his blood, giving him strength.

"Where's the gun, David?" Marshall leaned over to pat around David's left pocket. "Ah, here we are." He slipped his hand in the pocket and David threw his elbow back. He connected with Marshall's eye and the bigger man cursed. David felt the pressure ease up enough that he could crawl out from under him.

He was on his knees when Marshall's strong hand gripped his collar and yanked him backward awkwardly. David yelped as some ligament in his knee stretched and then tore with a searing burn. Marshall, kneeling behind, snaked an arm around his neck and began to squeeze while both of them tore at David's left pocket for the gun.

Marshall was quick but David could feel where the gun lay heavy in his pocket and got to it first. He didn't pull it out; Marshall was too strong and would easily wrest it from him. David pressed down, keeping his arm rigid while Marshall tried to pry it from his fingers. His knee screamed, his vision began to fill with starbursts. He bit down on Marshall's wrist mercilessly and then reared back again. Cartilage crunched and gave. Marshall reeled and David slithered free.

Marshall fumbled blindly, tried to grab hold of him but it was too late. David leveled the gun.

"You stupid, stupid man."

Marshall held up his hands. Blood poured from his nose, maroon in the dusky light. "Now, wait…"

"All I wanted," David said, breathing hard, tears choking his throat, "…all I've *ever* wanted was to be with Julian. Why is that so hard for everyone to understand?"

"It doesn't work that way, David," Marshall said. "Now, put the gun down and we'll talk about it—"

"Will we, Marshall? Will we talk? You didn't seem so eager to *talk* when you were slamming your fist into my face. In fact, I seem to recall you saying you were *glad*." David sniffled. "I don't want to do this. But I don't have a choice. Natalie did this to you, Marshall. This is all her fault. I hope you know that."

"David, wait…Don't…"

David's hand trembled badly and the gun felt like it weighed a hundred pounds. *No! I'm not this!* But what choice did he have? *None.* He cocked the hammer.

Marshall squared his shoulders. "Julian can't love a murderer."

David jerked his shoulders in a shrug, tears falling. "Who's going to tell him?"

He pulled the trigger.

***

Julian careened his rental car—a Mercedes SLK350—from SFO back into the city, all the while cursing David's name and muttering colorful threats under his breath. Easier to do that than to consider what might have happened—or be happening—to Natalie.

Things were falling into place. He couldn't see the entire picture yet but he saw enough. *The missing money. It has to do with the missing money. Natalie knew David was up to no good. She knew it and I let him off.* The thought of what that mistake might have cost him—or Natalie—was too terrible to contemplate.

His curses grew louder and more imaginative as he hit every red light along 19th Ave. He arrived at Niko's Café a little after six o'clock, double-parked the rental, and raced to the wrought iron gate. He buzzed her intercom several times. No answer.

Work. She's at work. She feels better and is at work. Or school. You're flipping out over nothing.

But Natalie didn't have night classes and the person at the counter was Niko.

"Julian, my boy," Niko said. "I hope you're here to tell me how my Natalia is doing? She calls in sick three days ago and I hear nothing since. Not like her."

Julian opened his mouth but nothing came out. *Three days...*

Niko's face went pale. "Oh no. It is bad? Oh dear, oh dear." He fished a key out of his pocket and pressed it into Julian's hand. "I own this building. You check on her, yeah?"

"Yeah."

Julian's pulse pounded in his ears as he tore up the stairs to her apartment, and turned the key in the door. "Natalie!" Her place was small; it took ten seconds to determine she wasn't there. It wasn't ransacked, either, though Julian didn't know why he expected it would be. *Because something is terribly, terribly wrong.*

Back downstairs, he told Niko that Natalie was likely at school and that he'd go look for her there.

"Julian?"

He spun around at the sound of a woman's voice. Not Natalie; a black-haired woman in a baggy green sweater rushed in the door, her kohl-lined eyes wide with fear.

Julian took the young woman by the arm and steered her out of Niko's earshot. "You're Liberty, right? Tell me what happened. Where's Natalie? She's been missing for three days?"

Liberty furrowed her brows. "No. She's been holed up in her place, afraid to leave in case you called. But now she won't answer her phone."

"She's not there now, I checked," Julian said. "Just what the hell is going on?"

Liberty wrangled her phone from the oversized sweater pocket as a text came in. "Marshall. He's followed David to a place called Club Orbit. In the Tenderloin." She looked up at Julian. "You know it?"

"No," Julian replied. "I don't know a goddamned thing."

"I'll fill you in on the way."

Julian stopped at the counter. "Niko, if Natalie comes back, tell her to call me. Or you can call me if you hear anything." He scribbled his number on a napkin and slid it over to the man. "And if you think you should…"

Niko nodded solemnly. "I know, young man. I call 9-1-1."

CHAPTER FORTY

The drive was a rumble of an engine beneath her; a nauseating, dizzied excursion Natalie experienced from the back seat of the Escalade. Blood from her split eyebrow dripped onto the leather seats. Night fell outside the windows and Garrett was an ugly, hulking shape in the front seat, laughing loudly and singing badly to the radio. Natalie's awareness came and went. Pain was her only constant; an ache in her head kept time with her pulse.

Finally, she felt the tires beneath her crunch gravel and then he was there, clutching her wrist and yanking her from the car. His breath was sour beer and smoke. "Nice and quiet now, thatta girl."

She registered a parking lot behind a dingy white building. A door and sign, *Club Orbit parking only. Violators will be towed at owner's expense.* Then she was inside. Linoleum, buzzing fluorescents, the distant thump of house music. Then a storage room that was two walls of cement and two walls of chain-link fence. Garrett dumped her inside among the toilet seat covers and boxes of cleaning supplies.

He loomed over her, a giant in the dim lights. His eyes were stupid, his leer obscene. If someone cut him open, Natalie thought, maggots would spill out.

He adjusted the bulge in his jeans. "You ready for me, sweetheart? I'm going to break you in half."

Natalie scrambled backward on her hands and heels, knocking over a wall of individually wrapped toilet paper rolls. "No," she breathed. "No! *No! NO!*"

Garrett kicked a roll out of his way, huffing a low laugh. He knelt down in front of her, reached for her, and then a shape crashed into him, grabbed him, wrestled him on to his back.

"Are you out of your mind?" A blond man straddled Garrett. "No way, man! *No way!*"

"Jesse! Garrett! What the hell?"

Natalie's panicked gaze swiveled to another man—a fatter, older version of Garrett—standing outside the cage of the storage room. "That's her, eh?" he said, and ran his hand over his mouth as if he didn't quite know what to make of her. He turned to the men, his gaze hardening. "You two. Get up. This isn't Romper Room. We got shit to talk about. Where the hell *is* David?"

"Still at the bar."

"Get him."

Garrett nodded and turned to go, then suddenly swiveled and buried his fist in Jesse's midsection. The air whooshed from the blond man and he crumpled to his hands and knees. Natalie watched, horrified, as Jesse made a strangling sound and then coughed. Blood splattered the cement floor.

"Jesus, Garrett!" Cliff cried. "What that hell was that for?"

"He knows what for," Garrett said. He hauled Jesse out of the storage room and dumped him on the floor outside. "I'm not done with you," he told Natalie, locking the chain link door. "Not by a long shot."

A phone rang in a back room somewhere. Cliff gave Jesse a hesitant look then went down the hall in the opposite direction as Garrett. Natalie watched him walk away with her bag—Julian's book inside—on his arm.

"I'm sorry," Jesse said, wincing. "My daughter is sick. I needed the money. But I never thought Cliff…" He shook his head. "I'm sorry."

"What's going to happen to me?" Natalie whispered.

He looked at her and the answer was there in every pained line of his face.

"David?"

"Yeah."

"Help me," she pleaded. "Please."

"I can't. Garrett…I think he busted something in my gut. I can hardly move."

"Do you have a phone? We can call for help." Her gaze darted around frantically. "In my purse. A keychain. It has a thing… a panic button…"

Jesse shook his head and coughed. Blood splattered the front of his shirt.

Natalie recoiled, panic and fear racing through her. She searched around the small enclosure for something, anything. In front of her was a box. *Bleach cleansing spray, 24 count.* A sudden, fiery rage swept through her and she dove at it. Two fingernails ripped in half as she tore the cardboard open but she hardly felt the pain. She hauled out a spray bottle of bleach disinfectant and scooted back to her spot, glaring a challenge at Jesse.

"Don't do it," he said tiredly. "It's just going to make it harder on you."

A door opened down the hall and Cliff reappeared.

"Ah Christ, look at you, Jesse." He shook his head. "You gonna fall in line or what? I checked over the book. Looks legit, for our purposes anyway. Three million dollars. Feeling a little more *positive* about what we're doing here? Because I think Marietta might just make a full recovery if you can pay the docs that kind of money. Right?"

"Not this way, Cliff," Jesse said. "Not like this…"

"Goddammit, I don't have time for your—"

Cliff didn't finish his sentence. A door opened at the end of the hallway. House music poured in and then became muffled again. Running footsteps sounded hollowly, and then Garrett and David Thompson were there. David's hand shook as if he had palsy.

Garrett chortled. "He's fucked."

"What happened, Dave?"

David's eyes were wide and staring, his gaze roving all around the hallway. His coat was torn and dirty. "I killed him."

"Who?"

He found Natalie, eyes round and disbelieving. "Marshall. I killed Marshall."

CHAPTER FORTY-ONE

Liberty told Julian everything she knew as he sped the rented Mercedes over the streets of San Francisco. As she spoke, Julian's silence grew stonier; his hands clenched the steering wheel and jerked the stick as he shifted. Liberty clutched her cell phone in her lap in a vise as her own panic tried to swamp her. She battled it by talking.

When she was finished, she felt calmer, though not by much. Julian said nothing, stared straight ahead, and did what the rental's GPS told him to do to take them to Club Orbit. Liberty glanced at him sideways. Extremely handsome with an artistic intelligence about him; masculine yet emotional. It was no surprise that Natalie had fallen for him.

"So you're a writer, then?"

"Yes."

"A real important one, right?"

He glanced at her briefly before returning his eyes to the road. "You're trying to decide if I'm worth the trouble. If I'm worth the risks the three of you have taken on my behalf."

"Something like that."

"I'm not. If anything has happened to Natalie…" he waved his hand, "…it's all shit. How's that for literary? If anything's happened to her I'll never write another word."

"Yeah, okay. I mean, I'm sitting here all calm-like but that bastard is with Marshall right now—"

"You should have called the police immediately," Julian stated, his voice like ice. "For Natalie. Gotten her somewhere safe."

"You think I didn't say that, like, a million times? But she was too scared. She had a gun pointed *at her head*. That's all she could think about—David doing the same to you." She glanced out the window, remembering what Natalie had told her and Marshall that first awful night. "She loves your books, you know? I mean, obsessed. They helped her get through all that shit with her parents even when we couldn't. *I* couldn't. She never talked about it but I never asked. I wouldn't have known what to say. So she used your books instead. To escape."

He said nothing but she saw the muscles in his jaw clench.

"But now, it's different. She's different. I know David forced her to say some shit she didn't mean, so don't believe it. She loves you. I've never heard anyone talk about someone the way she talked about you. She loves you. More than anything, really. More than the books. Okay?"

"Okay," he said, barely audible, and he took a hard right the GPS told him to take, tires screeching.

"And where the hell is Marshall?" Liberty demanded of her phone. "He's supposed to call me after he's got the cops on David."

"What's happening up there? Is that the club?"

An ugly, cinder block-looking slab of a club was rife with people milling out front, many clustering around a side corner. The wail of sirens could just be heard emerging from the distance.

"Oh my god, Marshall." Liberty's heart plummeted to her knees. "Let me out! Let me out!"

Julian brought the car to an abrupt halt on the street parallel to Orbit, and they both raced across, into the crowd.

"Let me through, dammit." Liberty pushed through the bystanders and let out a little whimper when she overheard one say, "Some dude got capped."

She rounded the corner to a dirty alley and found Marshall sitting against the wall, his chin resting on his blood-splattered collar. She shoved her way past more people and knelt beside him.

"Marshall! *Marshall!*" Liberty turned his chin to her and bit back a scream. A gash of torn and burnt flesh streaked from his temple, along his scalp, just above his ear. His cheek and shirt were painted red but the blood flow had slowed.

Marshall raised his head. "Little shit shot me. He actually did it."

"I thought you were dead!" Liberty screeched. "Dammit, don't ever do that to me again or I'll freaking kill you!"

"I'm okay, honey, really." He looked up at Julian. "You must be him. Hey, I'm a big fan." He chuckled and then winced.

"Where did he go?" Julian demanded.

"Just missed him. Back inside the club."

The wail of sirens was loud now, and the night colored with red and orange flashing lights. Liberty held Marshall's hand, calmer now that it seemed his hideous wound looked worse than it was. *But holy fuck, one half-inch to the right...* She shuddered to think about it.

"It's okay," she told herself and then him. "You're going to be okay, you big dummy. The cops are going to handle this now."

"Our author didn't get the memo," Marshall said tiredly.

Liberty twisted around. Julian was gone.

***

Marshall is dead. My sweet, smart, hilarious Marshall...

Natalie's beleaguered mind tried, all at once, to imagine a world without Marshall Grant in it. Like trying to swallow a gigantic pill, to force it to go down and then move on. Impossible.

Men were shouting, chain link rattled, but it all came from far away. Then David was in the cage with her.

"They don't know it was me!" he shouted over his shoulder to the other men, knocking aside boxes to get at her. "If I leave now, it's nothing more than a drive-by or street fight. But you." He stood over Natalie, seething. "It can't be easy, can it? Nothing is easy with you. I was just going to end you, but no. Now there's a connection. Now you have to *disappear* too. Get up, Natalie. *Get up!*"

"You killed Marshall?" she cried. "Why? *Why?*"

"I said, get up!"

David lunged at her. Natalie screamed and raised the spray bottle of bleach, pulling the nozzle again and again. The bleach caught David full in the face, in his open mouth and in his eyes, fogging his glasses. The storage unit smelled like an indoor pool. Natalie began to cough as the vapor found her too, but she shoved David aside and got to her feet.

Half-blind, she ran with her arms outstretched, feeling for the door of the storage unit. She found Garrett instead. The big man loomed over her, grinning obscenely, his dull eyes filled with an ugly promise.

"*You goddamn bitch!*" David screamed from behind.

Natalie yelped as he took a fistful of her hair and yanked her back. The muzzle of his gun on her temple was still warm. *Marshall...* The strength in her legs slipped away and she would have fallen had it not been for David's painful grip on her hair.

"The cops are here!" Cliff hissed. "They're outside my goddamn club. Get her out of here. Now!"

"What do you think I'm trying to do?" David whined. His eyes were so bloodshot from the bleach there were no whites left.

Tears coursed down his cheeks, and his nose leaked. "But I need your car. Gimme your keys."

"My what?"

"I can't do it here! She has to vanish. I'll take her to Land's End."

Natalie quailed. *This isn't happening. This is some sort of nightmare I just have to wake up…*

David stomped his foot. "I came here in a goddamn cab!"

Cliff jumped. "Dammit all, give him your keys, Garrett."

"My Escalade? No way!"

"This is bad," Jesse said mournfully from the floor. Blood stained his chin and the front of his shirt. His face was a ghastly ashen color. "All of it. So bad."

"You shut up," Cliff bellowed. To Garrett, "You can buy another goddamn Cadillac! A whole fleet! But we gotta get him out of here now!"

Garrett spat a curse and handed David the keys. He sneered at Natalie. "Too bad, baby. We coulda had some fun."

David dragged her out, into the night, into that hated white SUV. He forced her into the front seat and kept the gun on her as he made his way to the driver side, limping hard on his right leg.

"Put on your seatbelt and keep your hands in your lap," he ordered. "If you try anything, I'll kill you."

"Like you did Marshall?" A moan escaped Natalie and she clapped her hands to her mouth as the horror of it hit her in the chest like a lead weight. Then the words poured out of her in a hysterical stream. "Did you kill Julian too? Why don't you just kill me now? Kill us all. And kill yourself, you rotten bastard—"

"You shut up!" He started the car and drove it out of the parking lot slowly so as not to draw attention, and avoided streets that would take him to the front of the club where sirens blared. "I *would* kill you. Right now. Then dump you where no one would find you. But the way my luck runs, I'd get pulled over with your stupid body bleeding and dead in the front seat, and then where would I be?" He tried to maneuver a turn with only his right hand while his left held the gun close to his body, trained on her. "No, no, I did *not* come all this way to lose my chance with Julian now. You'll get what's coming to you soon enough," he said, "And when it happens, no one's going to know about it but me and the Pacific."

Natalie turned away, watching the city she loved go by in the dark. David turned frequently; white street signs loomed and then passed. Hyde, Turk, Arguello. It was a quiet Sunday. Light traffic ahead and no blare of sirens behind. She leaned her head against the window as the truth sunk in: no one was coming to get her.

CHAPTER FORTY-TWO

The first police cars were pulling up to the front of Orbit as Julian strode into the club, head down, fists clenched at his sides. The bouncer wasn't at his post at the door; probably with the rest of the crowd, gawking at Marshall. Julian went in.

House music blared and a few oblivious club-goers still undulated on the dance floor. Julian went past the pool tables. Without breaking his stride, he snatched a cue from the hands of the nearest guy and kept going, ignoring the obscene shouts that chased him. On the other side of the dance floor was a door marked Private. Julian went straight for it, clutching the pool cue in one hand, shoving aside dancers with the other.

He didn't see any security cameras but that didn't mean they weren't there. He pressed the cue against his leg and rapped on the door, keeping his head turned away from the little peephole.

From inside, "Yeah? That you, Kyle?"

Julian pitched his voice low. "We gotta situation out here, boss."

"No shit. Get in here."

The lock turned and the door started to open. Julian slammed his shoulder against it, sending a portly man staggering back. They locked eyes for a split-second and Julian saw the guilty fear dance in and out of the man's eyes. A red haze of rage descended over Julian until he felt saturated.

"Where is she?" he growled and then slammed the cue into the man's knee without waiting for an answer.

The man cried out and went down, clutching his leg and writhing.

Julian raised the cue, like a golfer teeing off, and whacked the man's shoulder. "Where is she?"

"Ah! Christ, Garrett, help! This lunatic is going to kill me!"

"I got this, Cliff."

Julian looked up to see the man who harassed Natalie at the café all those months ago inexplicably striding down the hallway toward him. Julian pointed the cue at him. "You," he seethed.

He met Garrett in the middle of the hallway. The big man swung a meaty fist. Julian ducked easily and answered by swinging the cue at Garrett's head like a baseball bat. It connected square; Julian felt the blow reverberate up to his elbow. Garrett's head whiplashed to the side and he stumbled back. A slow, ugly smile spread over his lips.

"Well, if it isn't the Milkman," he said, and spat a wad of bloodied saliva onto the floor. "Let's go."

His huge fist came like a wrecking ball. Julian dodged and swung the cue but Garrett caught it with his other hand and spun like a shot-putter. Julian struck the wall hard, ricocheted off, and the two men grappled as the stick rolled on the floor at their feet.

In close quarters, it was harder for Julian to dodge Garrett's fists. Pain exploded across his cheek and eye, but he answered with a solid right that flattened Garrett's nose. The big man grunted, gripped Julian by the front of his black hoodie and sent him flying down the hallway, toward a blond man who sat slumped against a storage room. Julian hit hard—the air knocked from his chest and his head rapped the linoleum.

Garrett picked up the pool cue and snapped it in half over his knee. "I'm going to fuck you up, Milkman." He brandished the two pieces, both splintered at the ends, and sauntered toward him.

"Get him out of here, Garrett!" Cliff cried. He limped down the hallway toward them. "The cops are *here*. Get him out, get him out!"

Garrett ignored him and swung at Julian with both splintered halves of the cue. Julian ducked and drove his shoulder into Garrett's midsection. It was like trying to shove a mountain. The blows rained down on his back and head, and Julian was forced to let go. He staggered back and saw stars as the butt of the cue struck him across his temple. He reeled and went down again.

"Okay, okay, he's beat, now get him out," Cliff said. Someone was pounding on the club door. "Ah, Christ, I gotta deal with cops and I'm all fucked up. And Jesse. What are we going to do with him? No, no, it's over. Garrett, we gotta go. We gotta go, *now*."

Garrett watched Julian struggle to his feet, a slow, stupid smile spreading over his face. "Not yet, Cliff. Won't take but a second. You got this coming, Milkman. You got it coming a long time."

The pounding on the club door was louder now. "Police! Open up!"

"Garrett!" Cliff cried from the back exit. Julian was dimly aware the man had Natalie's bag on his arm. Cliff waited half a second, spat a curse and ran out.

Garrett seemed not to have heard either him or the police. He banged the two broken cue pieces together. "You ready, Milkman?"

Julian took a rigid stance, searching frantically for a weapon. His eye caught the bright red of a fire extinguisher on the yellowed wall and then Garrett attacked. Julian dodged right, toward the extinguisher, and took both blows of the broken cue to the meat of his shoulder. He grunted and tore at the canister. Garrett swung the cue across his midsection, stealing his air and bending him in half. The follow-through was an upward blow that struck Julian under the chin. He staggered backward and fell onto the linoleum.

"You're done, bitch." Garrett charged.

Julian watched, his arms coming up to block though he knew he stood no chance. This guy was going to kill him and he'd never find Natalie, never tell her he was sorry or that he loved her more than his own life. He'd gladly give it for her now except that David had her somewhere and Julian's death simply meant her own.

The blond man, Jesse—who had appeared all but dead himself—grunted and there was a flurry of motion as he entangled his legs with Garrett's. The big man went down. Hard. The splintered ends of the cue went under him.

Julian scrambled backward on his hands and heels, like a crab, and got to his feet. He watched with horrible fascination as Garrett sat up, the thinner half of the pool cue jutting from his gut. Garrett stared at it for a moment, curious, then yanked it free and tossed it aside.

"*Dios mio*, man, go down." Julian yanked the fire extinguisher off the wall and swung it at Garrett's head. It made hollow *clanging* sound as it struck, and Garrett dropped bonelessly to the ground.

Julian stood over him, breathing heavily, bleeding profusely from his chin and temple. He tossed the extinguisher aside, disgusted.

"Land's End," Jesse wheezed. "David's taken her to Land's End."

248

Julian stared at the man for a second, realizing he'd already given up hope. "Land's End," he murmured. Down the hall, the club door was shaking on its hinges. He needed the police but he couldn't afford to be slowed by them either. "Tell them," he said.

Jesse nodded. "I will."

Julian tore down the hallway to the back door of the club, half-expecting a squad of police to be waiting to stop him, to arrest him or detain him, but so far the parking lot was empty. He pulled up the hood of his black sweatshirt to conceal his bloodied face and forced himself to walk, hands jammed into his pockets, head down. He'd parked the rental car on the other side of the street in a red zone but no one had noticed. An ambulance pulled away from Orbit —with Marshall and Liberty in it, Julian thought—and more squad cars rolled in. Police officers questioned bystanders. No one paid Julian any mind.

He slipped into the rental and punched 'Land's End' into the GPS. He spat a curse as it offered several options—three or four lookout places to park or hike.

Julian prayed as he tore the car down the darkened street. *Mama, if you're watching over us, guide me to her. Before it's too late.* He felt no answer to his plea and desperately chose Eagle Point because—his stomach roiling with terror at the thought—it was close to a high cliff with rugged shoreline below. *Anything. I'll do anything. Let it be the right place. Let me reach her in time.*

The Mercedes was fast. It took everything Julian had not to floor it, and when he hit the long straightaway of Geary Street, he did.

CHAPTER FORTY-THREE

Natalie took the stairs slowly, both for fear of the final destination, and for the more banal reason: it was a dark, moonless night, and she didn't want to turn an ankle. *As if it matters,* she thought dully. The stairs that zigzagged up and down the seaside park of Land's End were notoriously steep. She'd hoped to hike them someday with Julian, to take in the breathtaking view of the Bay, walk the labyrinth of small stones at Eagle Point, and watch the waves crash on Mile Rock Beach below. She'd have liked to do a lot of things with Julian, she thought; fill the years together. But that was not to be.

"Where is he?" she asked over her shoulder. David limped behind her, the gun a dark shadow in his hand. "Do you think he has any idea what you're doing right now? That you killed—" her breath hitched "—you killed a man and you're going to kill again? Do you think, wherever he is, he can even imagine it?"

"Shut up."

"I don't think he could fathom it," Natalie said, her voice sounding strange in her own ears, too calm for what was about to happen. "Julian's too full of love to imagine that someone close to him would be capable of ending a life. Never mind two. You think he won't know it when he sees you? That he won't read it in your eyes?"

"I said, shut up."

"I think he will," Natalie said. The ocean crashing against the shores of Mile Rock Beach was louder now. They were almost there. "I think it will be the first thing he sees when he looks at you. Whatever you think might happen between you and him died when…when Marshall did. It died with Marshall."

"He'll never know," David said. He sounded numb. "It'll be weeks before he gets back. By then, I'll have gotten used to…what I did."

"Where is he, David?"

"It doesn't matter."

"Then tell me."

"Croatia."

Natalie stopped. "Croatia."

"That's what I said." David nudged her with the gun. "Move."

Rijeka, she thought, and the tears came now, blurring what little vision she had in the deepening dark. *To make amends. To make peace.*

She stopped and clutched the railing, sobs wracking her, her legs threatening to collapse. "Don't do this, David. Please. I can't...I don't want to die. Don't take me away from him..."

David made a strangled, tear-choked noise. "Now you know what I've been feeling. Now you know *exactly* what it's been like for me, watching the two of you..." He sniffed, wiped his eyes, and pushed the gun into her arm. "Keep going. We're almost done."

The stairs ended and the labyrinth sat at the edge of the cliff. Its stony pattern was hardly visible in the meager light of a night that seemed so black and dark. Natalie could just make out the ankle-high rocks that curled and turned and coiled toward a center. She'd hoped there would be people walking it and taking in the view of the Golden Gate Bridge, but it was late on a cold Sunday night. There was no one.

"Okay," David said. "This is it."

Natalie hugged herself in her thin gray sweater, her dress swirling around her knees in the frigid wind. Below, white-capped waves crashed and gnawed on the rocky shore.

"Get...uh, get on your knees," David said. The gun in his hand trembled.

"David, don't," Natalie said. "You won't be okay in a week or two. I promise you. Julian will know because it will be there, written in your eyes. If you do this...he'll see it."

"Shut up."

"I know because I've...I've seen it."

"You've seen what?"

She looked up at him and even in the darkness she could see the terror behind his glasses. The desperation.

"My parents. I watched them die and it doesn't leave. Not after two weeks, not after two years, or three or four..." Natalie clutched her sweater, staring, as the terrible memory crawled out of its grave, whole and unbroken, all at once.

"The screams came first. Screams and screeching tires. I turned around and saw my mother...my beautiful mother. She turned too. She saw the car coming and reached her hand out to my father. He sprang on his heels as if to push her out of the way

251

but it was too late. That drunk man barreled his big ugly green car into them…that huge, heavy machine they had no chance of withstanding, and they broke and bent like straws against it and under it and I saw the life knocked out them…I *saw* them alive one second and then dead the next. I saw it."

The pain of that horrible day flared and then settled to a dull ache, like an open wound finally sewn shut. She sighed and let it go, feeling as if a shadow had been lifted from her, a heavy burden set down.

But too late. I'm too late. "Don't do this, David," Natalie said. "You know how bad it is…you saw Marshall…"

He shook his head. "No, I turned and ran. I ran before…" He heaved his own breath, steeling himself. "It's too late," he said, echoing her words. "Too late for me if I turn back now. That makes it too late for you. Let's get this over with."

Natalie felt the tiny spark of hope burn out. She dropped to her knees beside the curls of stone, shaking until she thought she'd break apart. David took a step closer. Then another. Natalie waited for calm, for a sense of peace to fall over her but it didn't. Instead, anger mingled with fear, and her hand curled around one of the labyrinth's rocks beside her.

"I'm sorry," David said, raising his arm. "I know you don't believe me, but I truly am. I didn't want this to happen. I…"

Natalie clutched the rock, tensed and ready. It probably wouldn't work. He'd probably kill her anyway but at least she'd die fighting. And then a voice came out of the dark, a slender figure in black raced toward them, like a fleet shadow or ghost.

"David! Wait!"

David gasped. "Julian?"

Natalie sucked in a breath but didn't dare look at him. She kept her head bowed as fear and hope clashed within her, both giving her strength. She clutched the rock at her knee more tightly and waited.

***

She was still alive. Even before he'd finished tearing down the endless stairs, Julian saw the two dark figures at the cliff's edge; Natalie kneeling at David's feet and David's arm, rising.

"David! Wait!" Julian raced across the labyrinth, to the center, keeping his eyes trained on David; if he even looked at

Natalie he'd falter and the tiny flicker of a plan he'd formed would die. And so would she.

"Julian?" David breathed. "How…how are you here?"

"I couldn't stay away," Julian said. "I couldn't get on the plane and leave you. Not without first telling you…" He paused to catch his breath, to quickly find the words, any words, to save Natalie.

"Tell me what?" David asked, his eyes saturated with hope and love that despite everything, Julian almost felt sorry for him…Almost. The gun in his hand was pointed at Natalie. It took everything Julian had to inject his voice with longing and regret and not race forward and tear David's throat out.

"For six years, I was searching for something, never realizing it was right in front of me the entire time." Julian took a step forward until there were ten feet between him and David. "But you don't have to do this." He waved his hand in Natalie's direction. "You don't have to prove anything to me. I know the depth of your devotion. Let me prove mine. Let her live so that I can choose, David." He took another step closer. "You will be so much happier, so much more *certain,* to know that I could have had her but I chose you instead."

There was a silence but for the relentless wind. Julian held his breath until his pulse crashed in his ears like the waves below. He could practically feel David's yearning, like a tidal pull.

David sniffled, tears flowing freely now. "I want so badly to believe you," he said, "but I think you're lying." He cocked the hammer back on the gun aimed at Natalie's head.

"*No!*" Julian screamed and then fell back, choking with relief as David didn't shoot but swiveled the gun back toward him.

"Pretty words," David sobbed. "Smart words, but see? Lies. All lies. She still has a hold on you, despite all. You, her, me. Like I promised her. So she could see what she did. How she ruined everything."

Julian knew he was going to get hit but he might still be able to save Natalie. His eyes met hers for a split second, the shortest goodbye…but before he could spring forward, Natalie gave a little cry. She surged up, driving into David, and slammed a jagged rock into his knee. His scream joined the wind as his leg bent at a sickening angle, and he fell hard to the ground.

The gun's report was loud and Julian actually felt the wind of the bullet streak past his cheek as he dove forward, and then he and David were tumbling, wrestling, rolling toward the cliff's edge.

"I'm sorry! I'm sorry!" David cried, even as he tried to turn his gun on Julian.

"Why?" Julian slammed David's hand against the ground, and the gun tumbled away. "Why did you do this to her? Why?" He struck him once across the face, sending David's glasses flying, and then his hands went around his throat and began to squeeze. David scratched and struggled, his face bulging, his eyes, bloodshot and streaming. They met Julian's, wordlessly pleading for mercy, and cloudy with pain and longing.

A rush of raw grief rose in Julian's throat. "Damn you, David, you were my friend…"

His grip loosened. David hurled a handful of dirt into Julian's eyes and slammed his elbow into his already bloodied chin. Blinded and reeling, he felt David roll out from under him and then heard a startled cry. They were too close the cliff. Julian shot forward, onto his stomach, blindly groping. His hand caught David's wrist and then he thought his arm would be torn from its socket as David swung over the side and started to slide down the rocky incline.

"David, no!" Julian gritted his teeth, his shoulder screaming. David's wrist was already slipping through his fingers.

"I can't, Julian," David cried. "I can't just be your friend. I tried…For six years, I tried."

"We'll get you help," Julian said. He slid toward the cliff's edge. He scrabbled his feet against the loose rock. He heard a small grunt from behind him and Natalie's hands around his leg, pulling. His slide toward the edge slowed but David's hand was slipping.

"David," Julian said through gritted teeth. "Hold on…Climb up."

"No," David said. The water churned and thrashed below, like a hungry shark. "You have to let go, Julian, because I can't. I can't let go…"

Julian held on with every bit of strength left to him, and still David's hand slipped through his. The intense pull on his shoulder vanished; Julian felt the emptiness in his palm and heard the roar of the waves. Slowly, he got to his hands and knees and peered over. He saw nothing but frothy water and jagged rock. *I'm sorry, David. I'm so sorry...*

Soft hands gripped him and pulled him firmly away from the edge. Natalie.

She knelt beside him, the wind battering her, swirling her hair. He saw blood—black in the night—staining her cheek from a cut above her eye. He raised a shaking hand to her face, touching her lightly. He felt warmth and softness, and a strangled sob escaped him.

"Natalie..."

"I can't believe you're here," she said, her hands pressing lightly on his chest, as if to prove he was solid. "I thought I'd never see you again."

He wrapped his arms around her, held her fiercely. "I did this to you. I should have listened. I should have believed you. You never trusted him. Never."

She shook her head. "You couldn't have known how bad it really was. He was your friend. But oh god, Julian..." She shuddered against him. "He killed Marshall. He killed him and..."

Julian's chest tightened. "What? No, Marshall's not dead."

"He's...he's not?" Natalie looked up at him. "Are you sure? No, he told me...David told me he killed him."

Julian cupped her cheeks in his hands, his eyes boring into hers. "Look at me. David hurt Marshall, but he's okay. He's at the hospital with Liberty and he's going to be okay."

Natalie sagged against him, and he did nothing but hold her for a long time.

CHAPTER FORTY-FOUR

The officer wrapped a blanket around Natalie. She moved out of Julian's embrace long enough to pull the itchy wool around her, and then rested her head on his shoulder again. Another officer offered Julian a blanket as well, but he declined. They sat on a bench near the parking lot, at the top of the trail. A dozen officers milled about, talking in low voices, the area lit by the beams of their squad cars. An ambulance added its spinning lights to the night that slowly became day. Behind her, down below, more officers were at the labyrinth, taking pictures, and waiting for the medical examiner to come and retrieve David's body from the surf.

"We have to get some preliminary information," said Officer Valdez, "while the EMTs have a look at you."

Officer Valdez had a kind face and a warm smile. He'd been the first to find them, the first to call Niko and tell him that everyone was all right, the first to explain how Jesse Tate had told another police unit at Club Orbit to send help here.

"Full name as it appears on your birth certificate?" Valdez asked Julian as an EMT dabbed his chin with gauze and adhered a butterfly bandage to the split skin.

"Julian Rafael Melendez Mendón Kovač."

There's the big reveal, Natalie thought. *A police report instead of a press release.*

Officer Valdez's pen hovered over his notepad. "Uh, would you mind spelling all that?"

***

At the hospital, Natalie's bruised head was looked at and they administered a rudimentary test for concussion that she passed. Julian received six stitches under his chin and eight more at his brow, and then they were finally allowed to see Marshall.

His head was wrapped in gauze and he was groggy from the pain medication but he smiled to see Natalie and Julian come in. Liberty sat coiled in a chair beside his bed, gnawing on the cuff of her ratty sweater.

Natalie hugged Marshall carefully, tears raining on his hospital gown, and then she and Liberty flew at one another, hugging and crying.

"Holy shit," was all Liberty could say at first, over and over again.

Julian stood over Marshall's bed, seeming at a loss for words.

"Don't do that. It was nothing," Marshall told him, his words slurred from pain meds. "An elaborate ploy to get into your next book."

They stayed until a nurse kicked them out so that Marshall could rest. It was after five a.m., she reminded them. Liberty wasn't about to be budged, so she held Natalie close to say goodbye. "Tell me what happened. But not today or tomorrow. Someday."

"I will. I love you, Lib."

"Love you, Nat." Liberty wiped her eyes, and then turned to Julian. "Get over here." They embraced and Julian kissed Liberty's cheek and whispered, "Thank you" in her ear. She waved him off and returned to her post on the chair.

Julian and Marshall clasped hands. Julian's face looked pained as he took in Marshall's white bandages again.

"Don't you fret," Marshall said, his words bumping into one another. "I'd do it again in a heartbeat…for her." He winked blearily at Natalie. "And she for me and you for her and one for all, and we're just the four fucking Musketeers up in here."

"Right," Liberty said, rolling her eyes, "and D'Artagnan's had too much Percocet tonight."

Natalie leaned over and kissed Marshall's cheek. There was so much she wanted to tell him but all that came out was "I love you."

"Love you. I love everyone," he said, drifting to sleep. "Love everyone."

***

Detective Swanson, a sharp-looking woman in charge of sorting out the case, permitted Natalie and Julian to go home and rest until later that afternoon. "It's going to be a long day of making statements," she warned them, "so be prepared to do a lot of talking."

"I can't stay here," Natalie told Julian when they stepped into her place. The memories of David with his gun to her head haunted her little studio. "I don't think I can stay here ever again. And David's office at your condo…" She shivered and Julian nodded grimly.

"I'll call Detective Swanson and let her know we're going to a hotel."

Natalie packed a small bag of clothes. Julian was just getting off the phone when she came out.

"The detective says that they think Jesse is going to be okay. He had surgery for a ruptured spleen and it was a touchy night, but he's alive."

"We have to make sure they know how he helped us," Natalie said. "If it weren't for him, Garrett would have..." She shivered again.

"Did he touch you?" Julian asked, his eyes dark.

"No."

"Swanson says he's alive too. I thought I might have killed him. If he touched you, I will. I'll kill him."

"Then I'd lose you all over again." She took his hand. "He didn't touch me, I promise." She didn't yet know all that had happened in the time before Julian found her at Land's End aside from what she'd heard him tell the police at the scene, and then she had been in a trance of relief, she'd hardly heard. "What about your book?" she asked, to pull his thoughts from Garrett.

"They found it. With that older guy...Cliff. I'm glad," he said. "For your sake."

"I'm glad too," she said. "But not for me. I'm glad that beauty still exists in the world."

"I feel that way about you. I thought I had lost you..."

He shook his head, his eyes heavy. Now that it was all over, he was filling the quiet spaces with regret for what he missed about David. He turned away to stare out of her window.

"Last year," he said quietly, "when he told me he had feelings for me, I was torn. I couldn't imagine working closely with someone I cared about but who didn't care for me in return. I wondered if it would be better if I let him go. For his sake. But I couldn't do it. He was my only true friend and had been for five years. He assured me it was okay, that *he* was okay. But obviously he wasn't. He needed help and I didn't see it, and it cost him everything." He looked at Natalie, his eyes cloudy with regret. "And you and Marshall nearly paid the same price. I don't know that I can forgive myself for what happened to you—"

"Julian, don't," Natalie said, moving into his arms. "It's over. It's okay. *I'm* going to be okay. I'm not going to let any of this

258

haunt me. There will be dark moments…emotions I can't predict. But I'm going to face them head on. No more hiding." She smiled faintly. "It's what my parents would want for me, I think."

The pain came as it always did when she thought of them, but it was a dull ache instead of a sharp stab. It would never disappear altogether, but she knew it would get easier with time. Natalie went to the bookshelf and took up the photo of her and her parents at the ski resort.

"Julian, this is my father, Curtis," she told him. "See that tired smile? He took his family for a nice vacation, intending for everyone to have a good time, and instead is met with complaints at every turn. He was so patient. And kind."

Julian smiled faintly. "I can see it in his eyes."

"This is my mother, Tammy. She hated to fail at anything, and had never been skiing. After falling on her rump more times that she could count, she wanted to call it a day."

"She's beautiful."

"She was," Natalie agreed. "And this is me. I'm not smiling because I was thirteen years old and tethered to my parents for two straight weeks. But I told them I loved them, every day, since I could talk. Including the day they died."

"I'm proud of you," Julian said. "You're so brave. To face this…and David."

"I had to, for you," Natalie said. "And for them. And for me."

"It's good to meet them."

She smiled at the picture and tucked it into her bag. "I know they would have loved you."

***

They took a cab to the Handlery Hotel on Union Square, and once alone in the elegant suite, Julian drew the blinds closed against the morning sunlight. He started to turn down the bed so that they might get some much-needed sleep. But Natalie shook her head.

"I want to take a shower," she said. "Will you help me?"

"Of course."

She ran the hot water and got undressed. He followed, stood behind her and ran his fingers through her hair, rinsing the memory of David's yanking grip. He soaped her back and shoulders, and the bruises on her wrist where Garrett had grabbed her.

She turned to face him. "My turn."

His back was dark with bruises, and the two lancing purple streaks on his left shoulder looked terrible. As the soap ran off, she ran her hands over these, and traced her fingers along the dark splotch on his abdomen. He'd fought hard with Garrett, she knew. It was a miracle he wasn't hurt worse. Much worse.

They said nothing, but she could feel the ugliness and terror of the night slipping away, leaving exhilaration in its stead. These sensations, the hot water, Julian's hands where they touched her, and his warm skin under her own…Even the fading pain on her brow. She relished it all, reveled in it, felt it try to burst out of her. She wanted to laugh or cry or both. *No, I want more…*

She turned to Julian and he was there, his mouth on hers, his body pressed against her, wet and warm. *Yes,* she thought. Yes to all of it, to life, to the good and the ugly, the pain and the love. But especially yes to him, to this moment that almost never happened.

The kiss was hard and deep under the water that fell like warm rain. Natalie's eyes fluttered open, and she saw the white of the bandages on his temple. "Your stitches can't get wet," she breathed.

"I don't care."

"I do." She reached behind her to shut off the water. "Take me to bed."

He carried her to the bed and they were joined effortlessly, one movement of many that fused them completely. He lay over her and the water streamed out of the dark curls of his hair, down his cheeks, like tears. She broke their kiss to look at him, to take him in. His eyes captured her in prisms of blue and her breath caught, unable to look away. *Let me stay here forever…*

He nodded, as if he could hear her thoughts. "I'll never let you go."

She gave herself up to him, sharing her vitality with him and taking his into her until she felt saturated with love and the sheer joy of being alive. The pleasure built and then peaked for them at the same time, an affirmation, a reward. A laugh burst from her and her heart soared to see his brilliant smile, for she knew then that everything was going to be okay.

When the searing pleasure subsided into a warm glow, they remained as they were, unmoving but for their mouths that whispered and smiled and kissed until the need awoke again. They celebrated a second time then slept dreamlessly, haunted by nothing.

EPILOGUE

"I'm free." *Eduardo stared across the wide vistas outside the city walls. "You'll come with me?"*
"I've never been past the gate," Sara said. "I'm afraid."
"So am I." He took her hand. "But now I feel invincible."
"Me too." She laughed. "How can we feel both at the same time?"
Eduardo smiled. "That's love."

—*The Origin of Silence*, Rafael Melendez Mendón

Natalie sat at the pool's edge, on the rooftop terrace of the Gritti Palace. She trailed her fingers in the water and basked in the glorious Italian sun. Her cell phone buzzed and she smiled to see Liberty's number.

"It's got to be seven a.m. in California!"

"Actually, it's six a.m.," Liberty said with a yawn, "but waking up at ass o'clock is just one of the many sacrifices I make for my friends."

"Such a martyr. Saint! I meant to say saint."

Liberty snorted. "So how's tricks? Let me guess: you've spent most of your tour of Europe with your nose in that new book of his, right? Whazzit called again?"

"The Origin of Silence."

"Right. Be honest. You've read it ten times by now, right?

Natalie smiled to herself. "Nope. Only once." She'd only needed to read it once, and felt as if she could have recited it word for word. *It's the story of us.*

"I just might believe you," Liberty said, laughing. "How was Croatia? Where did you go again? Reykjavik?"

"That's Iceland. We went to *Rijeka* for about eight days."

"You say potato…How was it?"

"It was absolutely stunning. Just beautiful, and Julian was so happy to be there."

Happy wasn't the right word. Julian had found it challenging and painful at first, then ultimately exhilarating to be there, to learn that his father had been more than the inconstant ghost who'd haunted him for so long. But she didn't tell Liberty that.

"He reconnected with family he never knew he had. Filled in a lot of blanks. It was amazing."

"Happy to hear it," Liberty said. "And then you're in Italy for what…a few more days? Then Paris?" She heaved a sigh. "Such is life for the nouveau riche."

"We'll be back in San Francisco at the end of the month. Hopefully the house will be done by then."

"That Victorian mega mansion? Don't hold your breath."

"It's not *that* huge."

"It has to be," Liberty said, "to hold all your books. I swear, between you and Julian, don't be surprised if the city library comes knocking to borrow a few."

Natalie laughed. "It won't be *all* books. It's old and beautiful and perfect. You'll see." She smiled to herself. "Anyway, how is Marshall?"

"Aggravating, as usual. He's all hot and heavy with Carter. *In love* with Carter, he says. *Carter*. They both have last names for first names. It's so cute I could puke."

"I'm so happy for him." Natalie's smile slipped. "But how *is* he? I feel like I can't go too long without seeing him. I start to get nervous."

"He's fine, honey," Liberty said. "Really."

"Okay. And what about you? How are things with Angelo?"

Liberty sighed. "Slow. Things are so uncharacteristically *non*-dysfunctional for a change, I'm petrified I'll screw it up. Plus, my agent would kill me if I lost focus. See how I worked that into the conversation? My agent. I'm still quite stunned over that development."

"You shouldn't be. You're long overdue for the recognition."

"Yeah, yeah, yeah," Liberty said, though Natalie could hear how the compliment touched her. "Will you be back in time for the last leg? *My agent* says we wrap up in S.F. early in August."

"Wouldn't miss it," Natalie said. "I start work that week at Solar Initiatives too, so—"

"So you'd be in double trouble for not being in town, mostly from me."

Natalie grinned. "Right."

"All right, hon, I'd better let you get back to your glamorous Italian palace life. Plus, *my agent* doesn't want me talking too long and tiring out my voice."

"Oh stop," Natalie laughed. "Hey, give Marshall a big kiss and one for you too."

"Will do. Love you, Nat."

"Love you, Lib."

Natalie hung up and thought about turning the phone off entirely. The view of the city from the top of the Gritti was stunning. To her right, the Grand Canal was a blue swath between sandstone homes and shops that still looked like they belong to another time.

Julian appeared a little less than an hour later. "After six of these interviews, you'd think I'd develop a tolerance." He sat down on a lounge chair beside her. "So. Ready for dinner?"

"Dinner?" Natalie laughed. "It's not even five o'clock. And don't forget my gondola ride. You've been putting that off for days."

"So much to do, so little time," he said with a grin. "Come on, let's eat. I can only talk about myself for so long before I start to feel like a bear in a trap, ready to gnaw my own leg off to escape."

"That's a lovely visual." He stood and she took his hand. "Okay, food then boat."

He kissed her sweetly. "We'll see."

***

The sun was just beginning to set, casting glowing embers over the mouth of the Grand Canal as they set off from the Gritti. They ate dinner, and then strolled the canal, past shops full of handmade carnival masks and blown glass jewelry. Julian offered to buy her one gorgeous Murano pendant in rose-colored glass but Natalie laid her fingers over the micro mosaic willow tree she wore around her neck always.

"This is the only jewelry I need."

"Is it?" he asked, a strange smile gracing his lips.

"Yes." She kissed that smile. She never tired of kissing him, nor he of her. *We're a constant menace of PDA,* she thought and giggled. "We have just two days left in Venice," she reminded him as they left the shop. "Two. And who knows how busy we might get…"

"Are you trying to tell me you want a gondola ride? Right now?"

"Right now. Before I burst."

"We can't have bursting. Okay, let's see if we can find something close."

They walked a few blocks off San Marco in search of a *servizio* that would take them along the quiet back canals of Venice as well as the Grand. They found a gondolier in black pants and black and white striped shirt, leaning against his gondola and smoking a cigarette. Julian negotiated with him for a minute and then said, "Okay, we're set."

Natalie clapped her hands with joy as their gondolier—Luca—handed her in. Julian sat beside her and they pushed off.

Luca took them through the quiet, narrow canals, using the pole to push off the old sandstone homes. He said nothing, but called out around corners and called *Ao! Heh heh*! as he maneuvered them around other gondolas.

Natalie watched, enchanted, her hand clutched in Julian's, as the sun sank, setting the stone homes to glowing. The wrought iron flower boxes burst with color above them, and then their canal spilled onto the Grand where the water was a swath of blue velvet in the dying sunlight.

The Canal was busy with other gondolas, some holding as many as seven people, most carrying fewer than four. They all pushed upward, floating closer together while their gondoliers called and whistled to one another. Lanterns glowed.

"It's so beautiful," Natalie commented to Julian.

"Mmm," he replied, a small, pensive smile on his face.

"Are you not enjoying it?" Natalie asked. "You're not bored are you?"

"Bored?" Julian laughed though she noticed a slight twinge of nerves in his voice. "Watching this unfold through your eyes is nothing short of miraculous. But we could use some music, don't you think?"

"I suppose…"

Julian gestured at someone and an accordion began to play. A violin joined it, and then a man began to sing—a gorgeous tenor in a gondola near the prow of their own. The gondolas carrying the musicians converged on theirs to form a small flotilla that held their boat still on the water that glowed in the setting sun.

"Julian." She clutched his hand tighter. "What have you done?"

The music surrounded them, a song of love as old as the city, and then Luca turned around and held out his hand to Natalie. Her heart pounding madly in her chest, she took it and let herself be pulled to her feet. "What…?"

Luca turned her around, steadied her, and there was Julian on one knee, a small box in his hand.

"Natalie Hewitt," he began, his voice thick and his astounding blue eyes shining, "there's something I've been meaning to ask you."

She clapped her hands to her mouth, dimly aware of other passengers in other gondolas watching intently, elbowing one another and pointing.

"I love you, Natalie, so much that I…" Julian's breath hitched and his words were tremulous. "I can't express it, not in a hundred books or a thousand poems." He opened the black velvet box to reveal an antique diamond ring that glittered in the setting sun. "But I can offer you a ring, this symbol of infinity—my infinite, boundless love for you—and ask you to marry me. Will you?"

"Yes," she said in a tiny voice, and then half-laughed, half-sobbed at the audience straining to hear. "Yes. Yes, of course! Oh, my beautiful love, yes."

The people in the gondolas burst into cheers and applause, as did those watching from a bridge above them. The musicians and singers started up a lively song, vibrant and celebratory.

Natalie heard none of it, saw none of it. Only him. She sat beside him and let him slip the ring over her finger. His kiss tasted of his salt tears, and her own, and then she pulled away and held his face in her hands.

"You already asked me, didn't you?" Natalie said, a beautiful, hazy memory tugging at the corners of her mind. "I remember…"

"Yes," Julian whispered. "I already asked."

"And I said yes," Natalie said. "I said yes to you, even in my dreams."

End

266

Thank you for reading, and I'd love if you could take a moment to tell me what you thought. Any and all feedback is greatly appreciated!
http://amzn.to/1D5LHPn

For new releases and information please like my Facebook page:
http://bitly.com/1yrzVvI

And follow me on Twitter at:
@EmmaS_writes

Here's a sneak peek of

UNBREAKABLE
City Lights Book II: Los Angeles

Available now!
http://bitly.com/1Gq05AY

Alex

"Help us! Help him!" I screamed again, and could have wept with relief as officers started my way. "You're going to be okay," I told Cory. "You're going to be *just fine*."

Cory's response was to slump against me heavily, his head lolling to the side. His breath had quieted to the barest whisper.

"No! Cory, wake up!"

No response. His eyes were open halfway, glazed with pain, and his mouth worked silently as he struggled weakly to draw breath.

Then I found myself in a sea of legs as S.W.A.T. and medical personnel surrounded us. They took Cory from my clutching arms and bent over him, working frantically. An officer knelt beside me and asked me questions but I hardly heard him. I just watched, horror twisting my heart, as an EMT opened Cory's shirt and jabbed something into his chest. Blood spurted and Cory gasped, jolting upright, and then sinking back down, his breath deeper now.

"Alex…"

I shoved my way through and took his hand in my bloody ones, trying not to stare at the instrument—that looked like a pen casing—jutting from his right pectoral.

"I'm here. I'm right here."

He smiled faintly and then winced in a soundless scream as they lifted him onto to a gurney. They raised the head so that he was partially upright, while another EMT bent him forward to staunch the wound in his back. Then we were moving. I jogged alongside into the morning sunshine for the first time in four days, and then into an ambulance.

It seemed the blood would never stop flowing. Blood from behind Cory, blood leaking around the tube in his chest. They put an oxygen mask over his mouth and that became stained red as he coughed.

I clutched his hand tightly, so tightly. "Please don't go," I whispered. "Please stay with me. Cory, please. Stay…"

He wheezed for breath. It sounded so labored and thick with blood. His dull gaze landed on our entwined hands and his lips curved up ever so slightly, a weak version of his crooked grin.

He held on.

Weakly, struggling, in agony, he held on, drawing upon the great reservoirs of love and bravery I knew he possessed. He held on for his little girl. For his father.

And I liked to think that maybe, if only a little, he held on because I refused to let him go.

Made in the USA
Lexington, KY
24 February 2019